HER-BAK

"CHICK-PEA"

THE LIVING FACE OF ANCIENT EGYPT

HER-BAK
"CHICK-PEA"
THE LIVING FACE OF ANCIENT EGYPT

ISHA Schwaller de Lubicz

HODDER AND STOUGHTON

FIRST PRINTED IN ENGLISH . . 1954
SECOND IMPRESSION 1964

Responsible for the translation from the French:

CHARLES EDGAR SPRAGUE

Illustrations by:

LUCIE LAMY

PRINTED IN GREAT BRITAIN FOR
HODDER AND STOUGHTON LTD., ST. PAUL'S HOUSE,
WARWICK LANE, LONDON, E.C.4 BY
LOWE AND BRYDONE (PRINTERS) LTD., LONDON

AUTHOR'S PREFACE

The first edition of POIS CHICHE and HER-BAK—privately printed in a limited number of copies in Cairo—was destroyed when the Imprimerie Schindler was burnt out during the riots of 25th January, 1952.

For this translation we have rearranged the material, adding illustrations and information which will help to facilitate understanding of the subjects treated.

This new arrangement is in the form of two separate volumes:

1 HER-BAK, 'Chick Pea', The Living Face of Ancient Egypt—This book describes Chick-Pea's initial education: through the lessons of nature and the master craftsmen, and later through the teachings of the Outer Temple.

2 HER-BAK, the Disciple of Egyptian Wisdom—which comprises the training of the disciple Her-Bak in the Inner Temple, and contains important authentic expositions of the essential teaching given there. This volume ends with a series of commentaries on the philosophy of the subjects treated, explaining Egyptian symbolism in a way more readily accessible to modern mentality.

I would like to express my gratitude to the devoted translator of HER-BAK, Charles Edgar Sprague, whose difficult task was rendered even more complicated by the necessity of adapting himself to the Egyptian way of thought, and to Ethel Talbot Scheffauer, whose poetic feeling and sympathetic interpretations were of valuable assistance in the translation.

I also wish to thank the illustrator of this book, Lucie Lamy, whose scrupulously accurate drawings have been taken from the mural decorations of the tombs. Their sources are given in the List of Illustrations.

Finally I wish to pay affectionate homage to our late collaborator, Alexandre Varille, erstwhile member of the French Archæological Institute in Cairo, Scientific Expert in the Service of Egyptian Antiquities, and corresponding member of the Académie des Sciences, Belles-Lettres et Arts in Lyons. With unerring critical sense, based on deep Egyptological erudition, he untiringly verified the accuracy of my assertions about the teaching given in the Egyptian Temple. His ideas will always live on in this renascence of our work.

ISHA Schwaller de Lubicz

CONTENTS

Part One

CHICK-PEA

Part Two

THE APPRENTICE

Part Three

HER-BAK
THE PERISTYLE OF THE TEMPLE

LIST OF ILLUSTRATIONS

INTRODUCTION

THE purpose and meaning of this book is contained in the twofold name 'Chick-Pea—Her-Bak'.

Ancient Egypt presents two faces: one 'living', filled with charm and humour; the other hieratic, containing a lesson in every feature. He who wants to know and understand her must not separate these two faces.

Whatever it be—the facts of daily life as depicted in the tombs of private individuals, the sporting feats of a Pharaoh, or certain mythological accounts studded with ribald details—in every instance these concrete images serve to teach abstract principles hidden within, which in turn reveal universal laws.

In this an important part is played by personal names. That the symbolic value of names has been used as an element in initiation is attested in countless inscriptions. Even the names of things bear witness to the constant solicitude to establish a relation between the thing and its essential quality or its function: thus the name of gold—*neb* or *nub*—also denotes the lord or master, because it expresses the quality of balance, which is characteristic of the noblest of all metals as well as of human mastership; or the word *men*, the expression for permanence and stability, gives a name also to monuments (*menu*), to bases or foundations, to the thigh (*men.t*), and to the port, where ships come to rest.

The name was held to be a definition of the essential nature of the individual and the plan of his development. That is why one person could receive several names according to the stages of his evolution.

It is thus that the name of Her-Bak expresses his nature and his aim: *bak* (or *bik*) is the name of the falcon, the symbolic bird of *Horus*. *Horus* is the principle of purposeful super-evolution, to which mankind ought to aspire.

Her is the name of *Horus*, and also means 'face', and, moreover, 'on, upon', so that the expression *her-bak*—playing in the typical Egyptian manner on the relation between the two words—means at the same time 'falcon-face' and 'face of *Horus*'.

But in addition *her-bak* serves as name for the chick-pea, because this pea carries the pattern of a falcon-face, with the characteristic eye of the bird of *Horus*.

'Chick-Pea' (French: *Pois Chiche*) is therefore the translation of the concrete symbol for *her-bak*, and has been chosen as name for the boy who seeks his way until that day when the deeper sense of Her-Bak, 'face of *Horus*', will become his light and his name.

The story of Chick-Pea—Her-Bak shows in the life of an individual the path of progress which might be called 'the ascent of the Temple', if by 'Temple' is understood the whole structure of Egyptian Wisdom, with its metaphysical system, its practical applications, and its methods of work.

The Egyptian inscriptions express in various forms the idea that the Temple is the projection of Heaven upon Earth, that is upon the world limited by the horizon; the horizon being the line joining Heaven to this world, whether this world be understood as our Earth, or the area contained within the walls of a temple, or our own body.

The true living temple of Egyptian Wisdom is *Man*, who embodies the cosmic principles and functions, the *Neters*. And temples are 'houses' in which the symbols of these *Neters* can be seen in order to teach man to recognise within himself the elements of the great world whose image and epitome he is.

But the Temple of the Sages is the Teaching itself, or rather the life-giving atmosphere in which real communion takes place between those who seek and those who know. Seen from this angle, the whole of Egypt is 'the Temple', and its entire history the history of man, of the living symbol of all cosmic functions. The crowns and the sceptres of the King represent the powers acquired through the development of consciousness by which he becomes the King of Nature and of all inferior creatures.

The part played by the Egyptian temple was that of selecting and forming individuals capable of aspiring to this ideal type and of receiving the legacy of the ancient Wisdom. It is possible to recognise successive stages in the formation of the developed individual. The three principal stages are the subject-matter of 'Chick-Pea' and 'Her-Bak'.

The preliminary stage was the awakening of the latent consciousness by cultivating the power of observation, the recognition of values and the sense of *responsibility*. It could be summed up in these words: experience life, look and discriminate. It is the simplicity of the child in the school of Nature.

The second and the third stages were the progressive initiation into the knowledge of the *causal laws*, graduated according to the possibilities of the student.

This programme of 'successive stages' was symbolised in the sequence of the dynasties:

(1) By the progressive development of the texts from the concise and enigmatic inscriptions of the Pyramids up to the prolixity of the Ptolemies.

(2) A corresponding progress in the participation of the functionaries, and ultimately of the people also in the prerogatives of the Pharaohs with regard to religious and funeral rites.

The story of Chick-Pea refers to the accomplishment of the first phase. It has been reconstructed from the abundant records contained in the mural decorations of private tombs, and by many stories and popular tales. Chick-Pea is an attempt to evoke the atmosphere of *his* environ-

ment, the character of *his* earth, the language and point of view of *his* surroundings, the influences and circumstances which can help or hinder this
preliminary education.

Her-Bak introduces us to the second phase, with a glimpse of the
theological and hieroglyphic symbolism, and leads up in the third phase
to the supreme question of the various destinies of man.[1]

Chick-Pea and the characters of his story represent certain elect beings,
who draw from within themselves the force of discrimination by which
they act like the seed in the centre of the mass of fruit. The mass is neither
worse nor better than other 'masses', but the Wisdom of the seed determines the quality of the fruit.

The education of Chick-Pea, though *seemingly* elementary, is as important as the teaching given to Her-Bak, for it portrays the conditions which
are indispensable for understanding the ancient Wisdom.

These are:

The uncovering of the 'inner ear', which the Egyptians regarded as the
first requirement.

Simplicity of heart and mind (the factor opposed to the complexity of
modern thought), and finally the spirit of synthesis, opposed to our
analytical mentality.

Thanks to the acquisition of these capacities, Chick-Pea becomes Her-
Bak, and can draw near to the wisdom of the masters.

Her-Bak is the *student* still free to choose the material and the quality
of the teaching he is to receive. He will later become[2] the *disciple*, the
maker by his own choice of his own destiny. He develops in the company
of other disciples, each of whom is the embodiment of some aspect of
human Seeking.

As for the reality of the Master presented in Her-Bak, *this Master is
Egypt*; that is to say, the ancient Wisdom, whose formidable task having
been accomplished has left its testimony in the language of architecture,
sculpture, and hieroglyph.

Nevertheless, the understanding of this symbolism calls for a mental
outlook so different from our modern way of thinking that it requires a
considerable effort of adaptation. The science revealed by the Egyptian
monuments is something different from a collection of ideas. It is a knowledge of the causal laws by which Nature reveals symbolical forms and
expressions; these give a living concrete meaning to abstractions which
could not otherwise be expressed.

This is why the teaching of the ancient masters cannot be transmitted
by theoretical formulas. It would not even be sufficient to gain access to
the 'keys' if we did not adapt our way of thinking to their spirit of synthesis and our way of seeing to their simplicity (that is to say, we have to
free ourselves from the distortion wrought by prejudice, ready-made
theories, and other restrictions of our mental processes).

[1] See *Her-Bak Disciple.*   [2] In *Her-Bak Disciple.*

The purpose of Chick-Pea and Her-Bak has therefore been to create a mental *atmosphere* which could correspond to the Egyptian background. The reader is invited to go with him as a partner in his search, entering into his doubts, his set-backs and his discoveries. Then the gates of the Egyptian temple will open before him one by one until, having gained the necessary equipment, the travelling companion can in his turn embark upon the pilgrimage.

All footnotes are by the author, unless explicitly marked "Translator's Note" or "T.N."

1. "LOOK AT YOUR IMAGE"

(Granite falcon, Temple of Edfu, Ptolemaic Period)

Statue of the symbol of *Horus*, the large falcon crowned with the red and white double crown. A monolith of grey granite, chosen and cut so that a vein of red granite forms the beak of the falcon.

This statue stands near the door of the hypostyle hall of the great temple of Edfu, which was consecrated to *Horus*, and in particular to his "labours" or conquests.

The symbol is that of Her-Bak's name: *her* = Horus, and also the face; *bak* = falcon. Her-Bak therefore means falcon-face, and thus "face of *Horus*".

(page 6)

2. "THE SUMMIT DOMINATED THE VALLEY OF THE DEAD"

"The Summit" is the culminating point of the Theban mountain-chain, on the western bank of the Nile. Its pyramidal shape is so pronounced that one might think it was deliberately cut in this way so that its symbol might crown the "Mountain of the West", the necropolis of the kings of the XVIIIth, XIXth and XXth dynasties.

"The Summit" was supposed to be inhabited by the *Neter* of Silence, the snake *Mersegert*, which sometimes was also called "The Western Summit". At the base of this mountain, on the edge of the Valley of Kings, canyons cleft the rock, and the folds served as shelters for the pilgrims on the way to the Summit.

(page 154)

3. "EACH COLUMN WAS A BOOK . . ."

(Columns at Medinet Habu, Funereal Temple of Rameses III)

Colonnade of the terrace behind which lies the hypostyle hall of the great temple of Medinet Habu (in Thebes).

Each column in a hall or gallery has a particular meaning according to its place (its Number) and orientation. This orientation is usually defined by some sign, say, a lightly engraved vertical line. The inscription must be read with the column's situation in mind.

The hypostyle hall of the great temple of *Amun* in Karnak—where the "Visit" in the story of Her-Bak (Chapter XXXVII) takes place—contains 134 columns. Those of the central nave measure 24 metres (approx. 75 feet) in height with their capitals; the 122 columns of the side-aisles have a height of 13 metres (approx. 40 feet), and a circumference of 8·40 metres (approx. 26 feet).

(page 226)

"LOOK AT YOUR IMAGE"
(Granite falcon, Temple of Edfu, Ptolemaic Period)
(page 6)

"THE SUMMIT DOMINATED THE VALLEY OF THE DEAD"

page 154

"EACH COLUMN WAS A BOOK . . ."
(Columns at Medinet Habu, Funereal Temple of Rameses III)
(page 226)

PART ONE
CHICK=PEA

THE FIRST DAY

' Is this the right way, O my donkey? . . . You are lost? So am I. This country is new to us both: sand everywhere, as much sand as fields! And this long wall that goes on and on, without end. . . ."

The sky was so bright that its whiteness was blinding! On the eastern horizon, a line of arid hill-tops marked the edge of the desert stretch. The stony sand came right up to the living earth, and abruptly gave way to the cultivated fields, which reached as far as the irrigation ditches.

The huge boles of the date-trees swayed their palm-crowns, whose dark tufts seemed to fan the brown earth houses seeking the shade at their feet.

The yellow dust of the desert verged upon the gold of the corn and the deep green of the newly sown fields.[1]

There is no middle term in this land of contrasts: it is either drought or flood; either barren sand or exuberantly fertile mud. It is ruled by two rival powers: the Sun and the River, whose common spouse must be made pregnant or destroyed, the one or the other, without concession, compromise or excuse.

Without excuse. . . . O, Egypt, O land of the *Neters*.[2]

On the other side of the path which ran along the cultivated fields a high wall cut off the view, much to the anger of a curious child day-dreaming on his donkey:

"It's a mountain, this wall! What can it enclose? It is *so* high! It must be meant to hide something . . . something immense! Whoever saw any-thing built so high! It would no doubt take a long time to ride around it, as long as it has taken us to get to the new fields. . . .

"The new demesne entrusted to my father is finer than the old one, but it is farther away from the market! Hi, comrade! On your way again. Hi, hi, liven up a bit!

"My father is a great farmer. . . . I won't be a farmer. My father has told me: 'You'll be a scribe!' What do you think of that, comrade? Have you ever carried a scribe on your back?

"My life, there's a bit of shade! Whoa! Stop here. I've travelled long enough without seeing anything; salt and doum-nuts are no soft cushions

---

[1] The earth uncovered by the fall of the Nile is so rich that it can bear two suc-cessive crops.

[2] The *Neters*, usually translated 'gods', actually expresses the functional principles of Nature.

for my behind! Stop, I say, stop! I want to know what there is behind this wall!"

At the foot of a sycamore the donkey quietly stood still under the lowest branch. Nimble as a monkey, the boy caught hold, and little by little clambered up to the top of the tree. But the height of the wall still defied the eye of curiosity.

The Sun stood high, it burned down on the little uncovered head. With a sigh the boy clambered down again, and called for the donkey to give him his back.

"Ho there, you! Give your back and look after your master. And do try to stand still a moment!"

But the dangling legs sought in vain for support.

"Oh the scamp; couldn't he wait for me! . . ."

Downcast, the child went in search of the beast. His naked feet went pit-a-pat on the hoof-prints following the narrow track which skirted the wall. He uttered a sudden cry of joy; in the wall there was a gate.

The naughty ass was forgotten. Without heeding that he was in full view of the guard hut near by, he sought for an obliging gap in the boards. . . . He climbed on the large buffer-stone, clasping the gate-handles with his fingers.

"Hi, you rascal! Come down on your feet, or I'll throw you down on your head. . . ."

The observer jumped down from his dangerous post and turned around to face the angry watchman; then he saw the donkey, tied up near the hut, without his load, shamefaced like a trapped fox.

In his anger he was oblivious of the inequality between himself and his opponent. "You have stolen my provisions: the bread, the nuts, the basket of salt! You give me back my loaves, or the beer you make with them shall swell your belly like a dead dog's!"

The watchman advanced threateningly towards the defiant urchin: "And where are you from, you tramp, born yesterday. You son of your ass!"

"No, not born yesterday—yesterday I tied my loin-cloth:[1] mind you treat me now as a man. I've grown up now! The Nomarch[2] thinks a lot of my father; soon I shall be a scribe, and then I'll have you kiss the ground at my feet on a wet day."

"And you are going to kiss the sky with your backside!"

The large black paw seized the loin-cloth 'tied yesterday', turned the future scribe bottom upwards and, with an adroit somersault, back on his feet.

The victim gnashed his teeth and struggled; but the torn loin-cloth remained in the watchman's hand.

[1] At puberty, a boy received a loin-cloth called *dayu*. This act was expressed by the formula: "to tie one's loin-cloth".

[2] Nomarch: ruler of a 'nome', a province (T.N.).

"You son of an ape, give back my *dayu*! Give it back, I say."

Like a wild cat, the naked boy threw himself at the arm which brandished the precious rag, he scratched, bit, was shaken off, fell to the ground, jumped up again, bounced, pranced, mad with rage. . . . Then suddenly ran off towards his donkey, who was munching the thatch of the hut. In a jar water was cooling; with full hands the boy took salt out of the basket and threw it into the clear water.

The furious watchman dropped the loin-cloth and pursued the culprit, who, while in full run, tried to find his *dayu*. . . . Alas, nothing of it remained; the last shred was disappearing between the teeth of a goat.

Big sobs shook the distracted youth—his new *dayu*: the proud conquest of his young manhood! He screamed; he howled like a wolf at the moon, while the watchman, jeering, gloated over his revenge.

"Will you shut up, you accursed jackal?[1] If you go on like this you will only stir up the afrits[2] of the Red Desert! Shut your beak, you *ngeg*,[3] you mad chattering bird!"

The truncheon rose again . . . but a powerful grip stayed the threatening arm:

"Who blasphemes the names of the sacred animals is himself ripe for the jackal! What has this child done to you?"

Beneath the haughty gaze the brute cringed, daunted, and came to lick the master's feet, trembling.

"What has this child done to you?"

"May your Grace know that this louse tried to force his way in through the gate. This louse has thrown salt into my drinking water. . . ."

The boy shouted: "I, this louse! I have thrown into your water the salt you had stolen from me! This louse! You have stolen its loaves! This louse! You have torn its *dayu*! . . . He has taken my loin-cloth; now I can't go back to my father!"

The Master, amused, looked on in silence. The boy, ashamed, snivelled and sucked up his tears: "Only yesterday have I tied my loin-cloth. . . ."

"Already?"

"What will my father say? This morning I rose proud as a man . . . and now I am naked . . . naked."

"And *before* yesterday? Were you not naked?"

The boy, taken aback, hesitated. "I . . . I didn't know it then."

On the grave face was a broad smile: the big hand took the little hand. A few steps and the gasping child saw the gateway of mystery flung open before his eyes.

Dumbfounded, trotting behind the immense Man, he regretfully passed all too quickly through porches, courtyards, and passages between

---

[1] The jackal is the symbolic animal of the *Neter Anubis*.
[2] Evil spirits.
[3] *ngeg* (chatter) is the epithet given to several mythical birds.

high walls. Suddenly a cry of stupefaction escaped him; on either side of a column two colossal figures confronted them: gigantic and over-whelming, they reduced to minute proportions the stature of the man no less than that of the child. Chick-Pea scarcely dared to raise his voice:

"Are they gods?"

"No."

"Kings?"

"Yes."

"Are you their servant?"

"Yes."

"Then why are you so small?"

The man, from his height, measured with his eyes the little thing that interrogated him. Chick-Pea grew bolder:

"You don't say anything; don't you know the answer?"

"No."

"Do you know their names?"

There was no answer.

"At least you know your own name?"

"And you? Do you know yours?"

"Yes. Mine is 'Chick-Pea'."

"Perhaps one day you will understand that this is a proud name."

"Why?"

The man led the child before a golden falcon crowned with a high *pshent*.

"Look at your image."

"My image?"

"Chick-Pea, Her-Bak,[1] Falcon-face, little *Horus* in embryo. Behold and remember."

"He is too tall for me," sighed the boy ". . . or I am too small! Is he a god?"

"If you wish. His eyes are yours, his ears are yours, his nose is yours, only your mouth has a cleverer tongue. The day that you give birth to his heart in your heart, he will be god in you."

"No one has ever spoken to me like you. Is it true what you are telling me?"

"So far as I know it, yes."

The little finger pointed towards the golden *Horu*

"Tell me the god's name."

"It is your own."

"Chick-Pea?"

"If you wish; since his face is engraved upon that pea. Nature's images never lie."

---

[1] Chick-Pea, Her-Bak, a play on words, on the name of the chick-pea which carries the design of a falcon's face, the bird of *Horus*. Her-Bak means 'Falcon-face'. (See *Introduction*.)

"I've seen living birds which looked like him, but they didn't shine like he does, nor did they wear bonnets on their heads! Are they gods, too?"

"What is a god, Chick-Pea?"

"I've never thought of that! It is sure to be 'one' who knows all that men don't know, and everything else, too." He waved his arm round the horizon.

The Master's eye scrutinised the boy's face. "Tell me, when you are asleep, do you know when the Sun rises?"

"No; of course not."

"And if your eyes were bandaged, would you know when it sets?"

"No. I couldn't know that."

"But those birds know it, and they are never wrong; they know when the sun is due to rise, when it is highest, and when it is about to set. They are cleverer than you."

"Do they know other things?"

"Learn how to ask them."

"Will they answer? Do you believe they will?"

"If you observe well, your own heart will answer."

"How must one ask them?"

"Be silent and watch."

"No one has ever told me such things."

"Today is the first day. . . ."

The large chest heaved a deep sigh. 'Today is the first day.' Fortunate he who can utter this word at such an age.

"But you are forgetting yourself, Chick-Pea: you notice no longer that you are naked?"

"I don't think of it now; it doesn't matter. Tell me, will you keep me with you? I'll make beer for you, like my mother; I know how to make it from bread."

The man smiled sadly. "No, it cannot be done. You must learn many things . . . first."

"I'll learn with you. I'll be a scribe and learn how to read."

"That would be a great pity. First you must decipher another book. What does your father do?"

"He is a farmer. The great Lord has just changed our demesne. But I won't be a farmer!"

"And why not?"

"It's a stupid job: working the earth the whole day long!"

"The Earth is your nurse, my little friend. The trees, the flowers, and the seeds that quicken—if you know how to watch them—will teach you more than any scribe can ever know, with all his 'counting by thousands' and his intelligence which claims to understand everything."

"I don't think my father is learned at all."

"That is because he has not yet found his 'first day'."

The murmured reply was lost to the child who, comparing his small

size with that of the colossus, had climbed on to the pedestal in order to
see better.

But a priest was passing. . . . Whack, whack! A couple of powerful
slaps descended upon the observer's behind.

"Will you get down, you impure one, profaning the divine pedestal
with your sacrilegious feet!"

The boy turned in consternation, thinking he had angered his big
friend; but he, with a severe mien, imposed silence on the priest, who
kissed the ground before him.

"If the heart is pure, so are the feet," he said in an icy tone. "Go now,
and bring a fresh loin-cloth for my new disciple."

"Your disciple? . . . Your Grace can of course not be mistaken, but
does the 'disciple' know how to read already?"

The Master led the boy close to a wall.

"What is this sign, little one?"

"It's an eye."

"And this here?"

"A foot."

"Tell me what they mean to you."

"The eye is looking at me, and the foot . . . is set down. Oh, it wants to
walk."

The priest said triumphantly: "Your Grace will note that he knows
nothing."

"And you, tell him what you know."

Moving his lips disdainfully, the priest held forth: "This divine character which is the image of an eye, is read *ar*; it is a horizontal sign. The
other is read *b*; it is the sign of the foot; vertical, relative as to height,
taking the form of a foot although it is a leg, and suggesting the leg
although it is a foot. Among other canonical interpretations . . ."

"That will do for today; but if *Râ* could wipe out from my cycle fifty
of its circuits, I know well enough which of the two kinds of knowledge
I should choose!"

"May I hope to hear it from your lips, oh Master of Wisdom?"

"Certainly: it would not be your knowledge."

"Nevertheless, oh Prophet, the sacred characters of *Thot* and *Seshat* . . ."

". . . have been inscribed in the palms, in the beak of the ibis, in the caw
of the raven, long before they were ever written upon our walls! But
your learned brain does not know these things! Go and come back: my
friend is waiting for his *dayu*!"

Timidly, Chick-Pea seized the edge of his robe: "You have said 'my
friend'. . . . Will you keep me with you?"

"No, little man; another master is waiting to awaken your heart."

"Where is he waiting for me?"

"In your garden, in your barley field . . ."

"But I have never met him before!"

"You did not know how to look for him. He likes children's questions; ask the seed how it opens, count the palm shoots, learn to tell the time with the birds; ask the north wind whence it draws its vivifying breath, and the south wind whence it gleans its fire."

"But who will answer?"

"He whose name you bear."

THE FAMILY

No doubt the donkey would find the way home; and the boy, his eyes full of the mountain of marvels, let himself be carried along by his dreams.

Above all other things hovered the great golden falcon. . . . There was gold in the reeds, gold in the canals, gold in the waving ears of corn. Gold was even in the distant palm-trees. A fairy-like glory gilded his new farm today and turned it into an enchanted oasis.

The sharp trilling of a buzzard awakened him; instinctively he looked up to measure the height of the Sun. . . .

With short little steps the ass picked his way along the edge of a ditch. A couple of crows scratched the ground, seeking their pittance of food. Chick-Pea observed them with compassion: "Today they're not afraid of me!" He stopped the donkey, took a loaf from the basket and, crumb after crumb, joyfully threw it to them. "Whoever saw such foolish crows—they won't touch the bread! These birds are stupid. But might one not say that they have the same opinion of me? Who, then, is the idiot? Chick-Pea, you still have a lot to learn!" The crows disdainfully turned aside from the bread to prefer some dung. Fussy sparrows jumped at the offering with hurried pecks. The news spread . . . some wagtails came up, a flight of starlings settled. The ass, seizing his chance, browsed on the corn.

One loaf was not enough. "This is a day of rejoicing. Chick-Pea comes into his own, and all his vassals are celebrating in his honour. . . . I did not know they were so pretty!" One loaf . . . two loaves . . . three loaves . . . the basket was emptying and the hungry flock kept asking for more.

A laughing voice improvised a song. "Here he is, here he is, O brother mine! Chick-Pea has come! The crocodile hasn't eaten him; the Nile hasn't swallowed him; the watchman hasn't beaten him!"

"What's that?" The rider pricked up his ears at this ill-timed chanting; his eye looked for the impertinent intruder. Slender and naked, the little girl appeared among the corn. She gave a cry of surprise and ran towards the house, shrieking with laughter. "Chick-Pea is feeding the sparrows! Chick-Pea is letting the ass eat the corn."

The birds, foreseeing the end of the feast, quarrelled over the scraps. But the generous hand, having distributed its largesse, dismissed them with a sweeping gesture. "Enough for today: I will come back!" Not a glance at the basket that now was almost empty, not a thought for the ravaged corn. A dream was in his eyes and sun in his heart.

The gorged ass started up heavily, but the little feet spurred him. Two thin legs beat like wings and whipped up his flanks to a heightened rhythm.

"Gallop, old friend: it's time to go home."

Gaping on the threshold, his mother watched the triumphal entry. The little girl chattered, the woman silently assessed the contents of the basket, worked out the loss, and tried in vain to understand. . . . Suddenly she noticed the new loin-cloth: "You have a different *dayu*! What has happened?"

Crouched in a cool corner of the earth house, his head in his hands, his elbows on his knees, Chick-Pea for a long time refused to answer the questions put by his mother and the neighbouring women who had crowded in.

"I have done no harm. I will tell everything to my father, but only to him! He is the only one who will understand! He will be surprised at my beautiful adventure; he cultivates the earth, so he must know many things. . . ."

A tall figure appeared on the threshold.

"Father!" With a leap the boy was on his feet, but his thin voice was lost in the medley of tale-telling: the scattered bread . . . the late return . . . the *dayu*. Accusations, yappings; each of the goodwives harping on one of the details.

The boy planted himself in front of his father, pushing the gathering aside with his arms. "Turn all these gossips out! My story is not for women. I will tell you everything."

An imperative gesture emptied the room. "Now speak."

"Well, then, I want to be a farmer."

"Are you mad? Since when are you your own master? . . ."

"You are not pleased? You could teach me what you know: how the seeds open, and when the birds go to sleep. . . ."

"And to tell me this you have driven away the neighbours? What nonsense have you been up to? What are you trying to hide from me? By whom have you been beaten this time?"

"What? Have they told you . . . ?"

"Don't stammer. Answer me."

The boy tried to assert himself; he closed his eyes in order to hold on to his dream.

He spoke, but he spoke into the void: there was no echo. The father listened, with frowning eyebrows and an obstinate, distrustful look. Chick-Pea tried to move him.

"You, father, do you know the great walls with the pictures? Have you seen the pointed stones which shine like the Sun . . . the large . . ." He broke off: an impulse of modesty closed his lips at the thought of the golden falcon. He described what had happened. The father shook his head.

"Nice work you've done there! Now that priest will be after us, and there'll be trouble with the scribes!"

"Are the scribes bad?"

"Theirs is an intelligent profession; they count in thousands, and all our welfare depends on them! If my son were a scribe, I should be held in fear by everyone, and my tomb would be honoured too."

A grey cloud darkened the room. "O, my father, cannot my brother be a scribe if I work on the farm? I will be your pupil, and you shall teach me all that you know about the plants and the birds . . ."

His father did not open his mouth to answer. Standing in the doorway, his long, thin, bent body seemed to shut out the light. His closed fists tightened nervously, undecided, like those of a wrestler before a threat he cannot understand. In his hollow eyes lurked fear, the force of habit, the opposition to anything new.

"Oh, what a senseless child; is this the son of my loins? Who has encouraged him to dispute my decisions? Who is the intruder that interferes in my house? Is there not trouble enough with the rats, the khamsin[1], and the scribes? Must I also bear with the caprice of my son and the follies of a priest?"

The man's voice was full of rancour; his hard look precluded all appeal. Chick-Pea saw his father with new eyes. This was no longer 'the protector': it was the head of the family who could determine his fate and bind him to his service; and this service was *the earth*, the earth which had curved his back, dried out his hands and his heart. "Since when, Chick-Pea? Always! And I, am I not bound as he is, for always?"

This 'always' terrified him: was it not the very opposite of the joy he had known for a short moment? A great distress pervaded him. He rose

[1] South or south-west wind, dry and burning, which blows over Egypt and carries the desert sand.

and went to the stable; crouched against his ass, he gave free rein to his dream and his sorrow.

"Chick-Pea, are you asleep?"

From too much crying the boy had become drowsy and had fallen asleep.

The little girl gently shook her brother: "Are you crying, Chick-Pea?"

"I've finished crying, I'm going away!"

"I did not want all this bother to happen, Chick-Pea, I didn't want you to cry; look, you haven't even had your meal; I have kept some bread for you."

"The house is too sad."

"No, it's your eyes that are sad. . . . Come! I'll show you the frog garden; you haven't seen it yet—come along!"

She dragged him by force through the corn.

"Leave me, Mut-Sherit, I want to go . . . far away from the farm, far away from my father, somewhere where men are free!"

"Where would that be?"

"I don't know. . . . I'll search until I find it."

"Oh, Chick-Pea, behind the farm you'll find the old farm, and then other farms."

"All right; then I'll go into the desert."

"The afrits will strangle you!"

"The afrits? . . ." At the thought of the evil spirits Chick-Pea's courage gave way; the little girl took advantage of this.

"Come along, you have not yet seen the new garden, nor the pavilion for our Lord and Master's leisure! It is not his house, for they say his house is large and beautiful, in another garden, far away; you would have to take your donkey to get there!"

Chick-Pea said nothing; when he reached the gate of the enclosure, he sat down on the stone at the gate-post, mute and savage and waiting for he knew not what.

For a new little heart, the day had been heavy indeed! Why was the evening so different from the morning? . . . A strange music throbbed in the air and enveloped him. The voice of the wind was never so sweet . . . no bird had so full a song! "It is the blind man's harp," murmured the little girl.

> *Why laugh, why weep?*
> *Why journey on the stream?*
> *Why seek happiness*
> *Beyond one's horizon?*
> *Desert, mountain and plain,*
> *Is the light they share not one?*

> *Master of the evening and morning,*
> *Servant and king of the Two-Lands,*
> *O, thou who determineth*
> *For each place its horizon,*
> *Whoever seeks thee within himself*
> *Finds his own kingdom*
> *Free from all slavery!*[1]

The sulky little face had softened. "Let me go, Mut-Sherit." Timidly, Chick-Pea went through the gate and looked for the singer. Under the acacia, near the large pool, the blind man still ran his fingers over the strings. "Come nearer, child."

At the knees of the blind man Chick-Pea crouched down, ecstatic with delight. "But you can't see me! . . ."

"I have felt you coming! Why are you sad, little one?"

"But . . . I've said nothing!"

"No. But I know how to listen. If the light in my eyes has gone out, it enters my heart through my eyes."

The blind man gently touched and felt the little face with his fingers. "So young, and already so disenchanted!"

"People are wicked."

"Look at the birds. . . . The Sun touches the horizon, does it not?"

[1] For French text of this song, see page 293.

"That's right. How do you know?"

"The leader of the buzzards calls them; it is his second signal; when he calls for the third time, the king of the sky will be asleep."

"Then it is true? . . . The birds know it?"

"Learn to listen, and joy will return to your heart. Have you seen the lovely blue lotus-flowers?"

"Oh, what a pity! They're faded."

"No. They go to sleep in the evening and their young buds go under the water for the night. They, too, know the time: in the morning they unfold and at noon they throw out their seeds."

"Then my great friend spoke the truth!"

Wonder-struck, the boy told his story; the beautiful adventure came alive once more . . . and the blind man smiled.

"Remember this day, little one, remember it: the dawn of this morning will stay with you all your life, never allow the wickedness of men to darken it. Shadow gives the light its splendour. . . . Look: the last buzzard has gone to rest and the darkness rises from the ground. The hyena and the jackal will soon go forth and follow their vile calling; but are they wicked?"

"No, for they must eat!"

"And by eating they are doing some service. . . . The falcon drinks the blood of the birds: is he wicked? You do not dare to answer; let it not worry you, little one! Nature is neither good nor beautiful: she obeys! Râ alone is great, for his light illuminates and touches everything—filth as well as beauty—and nothing defiles it; that is what your heart ought to do, my child!"

On the knees of the old man, the happy little head rested, and the song of the harpist lulled him to sleep:

> *I sing of your rest,*
> *I sing of your love,*
> *Beloved Earth, O loving Earth,*
> *Beloved of the Sun,*
> *Ta-urit, O Kemit, O Apet!*[1]
> *Prodigious womb . . .*
> *Accepting all seed,*
> *O motherly one!*
> *There is none you refuse;*
> *To you all are alike:*
> *Cobra, vulture, or dove;*

---

[1] *Kemit*, black earth, is the Egyptian name of Egypt; one of its other names is *Ta-meri*, beloved earth, or, more verbally, earth-'loving'; *Ta-urit* and *Apet* are names of the goddess of fertility. See *Her-Bak Disciple* Index: *Apet*.

Sweetness and venom fraternise
Your breasts suckle as twins
The enemy brothers
Beloved earth, loving earth,
I sing of your love.[1]

[1] For French text of this song, see page 293.

FLAX

THE south-west wind was heavy with sand it had picked up in passing over the burning desert; it made the slightest task a burden. A man carrying a sheaf of flax would drag himself painfully, like a sledge laden with stones. . . .

Long was the procession of boys who carried the flax to the threshing-floor, and the leader of the team was in a hurry.

"Hey! You, the boy in front, Fatty! Anyone would think you were a lot of asses coming back from the gold-mines!"

"And let the boy in front tell you that our tongues are as dry as that of a blacksmith!"

Short and stocky, Fatty was well named; his lifted arm steadied the sheaf on his head. He looked like a heavy pot of earthenware, with his arm for handle.

Chick-Pea was trotting along behind him, trying to understand the Why of things. "In the old farm it was much prettier; they used to cut the flax when the flowers were blue. Do you know why, Fatty?"

"Because you get finer thread from it."

"Then, why hasn't this flax got its blue flowers?"

"Because they have withered away, they're dead."

"I'm not a fool! Why do they reap it after the flower is gone?"

"Because it's gone to seed."

"Fatty, why do they reap it when it's gone to seed?"

The leading boy turned round, showing a sweating face as large as a full moon.

"To feed the seeds to asses like you: if there were no seed, what would there be to sow? . . . Really, Chick-Pea, you feed on questions instead of onions!"

The procession came to a stop, waiting for the leader to move on.

"Hey, are you going to grow roots there? Get along there, run, hurry!"

Fine-Speaker took his chance to pass in front. He was tall and thin, with a knowing eye and scornful mouth. With a shrill voice he started singing:

"I tell the whole lot of you: you are slackers all! Who can act while he speaks. It is I! Who knows when to act. It is I!"

"Listen, Chick-Pea, your brother is a smart one!"

"Fine-Speaker is always good at talking. . . ."

Under the crushing weight of the growing heat, they reached the threshing-floor at last.

"Here we are, comrades; down with the loads!"

They seized the sheaves and beat them against a great jar; the seeds sprang out and covered the threshing-floor with a thick layer. . . . All round the bundles of stalks were piling up, like a little protecting wall.

"What a harvest! There surely will be seed grain enough and in plenty!"

Imprudence! Oh, you rash ones! Beware of saying something good is bound to happen. . . . The Sun shot rays of alarm: a copper-red light made the Amenti glow; the trees stood out in malachite green against the leaden eastern sky. An oppressive silence hung over everything. Hastily birds flew past, low, almost touching the threshing-floor. And in the distance: the yellow storm . . . one could already feel its hot breath, and everything that lived huddled down and was silent. . . .

It was coming nearer. It had crossed the river, whipping the water up to foam . . . it flattened the grass and reeds and tore branches from carob-trees; raging whirlwinds sucked seeds and scorpions from the palm-groves. . . . The dishevelled palm-trees bent down, sprang back and lashed the face of the wind; immense trunks curved their backs under the menace: short, vertiginous swaying, then the sharp smarting crack as their pillars were broken. . . .

After the palm-grove, the fields!

"Look out! The wrath of the desert is upon us!"

The deep roar grew. Yellow darkness covered everything. . . . The fiery sand was now storming over them, blazing its way into their eyes, parching their lips and tongues . . . choking their lungs!

The team leader lost his head and ran off to get instructions from someone above him. What were the boys to do without their leader? Like rats they each made for a hole. . . .

Chick-Pea, appalled, saw the bundles already flying through the air, the seeds scattered, the harvest lost. He shrieked into the wind:

"Listen, you band of eunuchs! Double fish ration for everyone who does what I say. My father will give it—I promise it on my life!"

"Is it true?" The runaways returned. Some of them liked to eat perch, one was tempted by the thought of gudgeon, others followed. . . . Head down, eyes half-closed, they braved the sand and the wind. Chick-Pea gave orders: they obeyed. The seeds were hurriedly swept into one big heap and the sheaves thrown over them like a carpet.

"Quick! Quick! Down on the sheaves! All lie down and hold together!"

Just in time! The cyclone was upon them. The boys stretched face downwards on the sheaves, with their heads buried underneath their arms, held on and waited. The sand whipped their backs and ears, lashing and burning the skin, grinding between the teeth.

The cyclone passed; the hurricane swept through the trees and fields; all that could fly with the wind was carried aloft and away, as if a huge broom had cleaned out the threshing-floor. . . .

The cyclone had passed. Nothing but a mist of sand remained, stagnant, opaque, and blinding; all leaves looked the colour of earth.

Dazed, badly knocked about, the boys remained motionless, half unconscious.

Then Sita arrived with the scribes to make a record of the catastrophe.

"I have done nothing wrong, our Master will judge! Never has there been such a cyclone since the beginning of time!... O brothers, what is this? This heap, is it a pile of slain ones, struck down by the god in his fury?"

Fatty, hearing these words, shook off his coating of sand under the eyes of the astonished men, coughing and spitting he showed the harvest safe and sound:

"Look here, oh Sita! It is your son who gives you all this flax! Look what Chick-Pea has done!"

Chick-Pea came out in turn; he was yellow and his eyes were white, he looked like a fish made of sand.

"Get up, boys! Father, I could have done nothing without them.... And, father, I have promised them a double ration of fish."

The father listened speechless; with his stick he lifted the bundles of stalks and calculated the value of the crop....

"This certainly is an achievement! But I somehow cannot make sense of it! Go, Fatty, fetch the donkey men to take the seed away. Today the donkeys shall carry the bundles to the ditch."

Chick-Pea dismissed his team with a gesture.

"Follow him! And let these boys have some beer, too!"

"By my life," said Sita, "is that my son? He has become more than a match for his father."

JEALOUSY

WHEN Sita came home, Fine-Speaker, his eldest son, was sitting near the entrance, black envy in his soul and the tortuous grin of a hyena on his face. Sita asked him:

"Do you know how Chick-Pea has saved the crops?"

"How could I not know it?" Fine-Speaker replied. "The labourers have sung his story all along the way; even the dogs know it! And the neighbours speak no more of you, but of Chick-Pea. . . . Before another day is over, it will come to the ears of the Master: Chick-Pea will get all praise, and you will henceforth count for nothing before the Lord Menkh!"

The father answered: "No one will revile my name, but they will say as I do: 'Let us praise the father who begot him!'."

Fine-Speaker rose, he poured out a tankard of beer, offering it to his father with a sigh.

"My father, the great farmer Sita, is surely worn out with fatigue, that he thus forgets the insolence of my younger brother! O my father, the good he has done today will change into evil tomorrow; if you turn a blind face to what you can see, your labourers will laugh behind your back and you will lose the favour of your Master!"

"What evil, then, has he done?" asked the father.

Fine-Speaker replied: "Is it not enough that he is wayward as a cat: going his way, alone, without giving any heed to the hand which fed him, without listening to the commands of him who begot him?"

"Don't be disheartened because of your brother's ways; tell me frankly what you want of me."

"O my father," said Fine-Speaker, "am I not your eldest son? Have I not precedence over him? It was your duty to bequeathe me your tenancy, and to him you offered a chance to become a scribe; now this unworthy son refuses and tries to take my place."

"O my son," replied Sita, "your anger makes you unjust: Chick-Pea is not trying to take your place. He is but a child and as yet knows nothing of life; if I give him an order, he will have to obey."

Fine-Speaker replied: "My beloved father averts his eyes from the obvious! He gives his heart to the ungrateful son and suffers him to rob his father of the support of his old age. Listen to my words: I will not allow my brother to rule over me! O my father, let me become one of the scribe-accountants of the demesne. Have I not been educated in school? Have I not the favour of Akhi, the son of the chief accountant, who went to school with me? Am I not quick-witted and well-spoken? I

shall quickly become a scribe-inspector and you will be a prosperous man. And since Chick-Pea 'bathes his heart' in the toil of the fields, let him drag the plough that his oxen may have a lighter burden! Let him carry his donkey's fardel! Let him be a father to his calves! Let him hatch the eggs of his geese! Let him feed the motherless duckling! I shall always be near to survey the work and to protect your interest: taxes shall not crush you; I will see that all accounts are rendered in your favour. . . ."

Sita the Farmer pondered long over what had been said to him. Knowing well this son who was to continue his name and being well aware of the hardness of his heart, he did not dare to oppose him, but meditated upon how far he should go in granting his desires.

Then he perceived the scribe-intendant of the demesne, who was approaching him with joyful greetings:

"Oh Sita, honest servant, who has his master's praise, good health to you! I bring you news which will cause rejoicing in all faithful vassals, whose model you are. The third day from now will be a day of honour for the noble Lord Menkh, our excellent Master. For the Pharaoh, L.H.S.,[1] has presented him with a statue accompanied by great benefactions; and our Master calls upon all officials and servants concerned to be present at the reading of the Deed of Gift. Attend, therefore, to hear the testimony of these high favours and to render him homage."

Sita replied: "Assuredly I greatly rejoice in this, for Menkh is a just

[1] L.H.S. is the abbreviation for Life, Health, and Strength, the standard rendering of the formula *ankh-udja-seneb*, which often follows Pharaoh's name.

master to his servants. He is praiseworthy among the most praiseworthy; his mouth destroys the lie and gives birth to truth, and in him the oppressed find their support. I shall therefore do as you say. But you, O learned scribe, relieve me from worry in an affair which troubles me at present: my eldest son, here, is desirous of becoming scribe-accountant in the service of the demesne. What is your counsel on this point? Can he be trained in this art and take over the office I desire for him? Will he be accepted among the sons of people whose standing is higher than mine? And will he, some day, have charge over his younger brother to whom I shall pass on the land entrusted to me?"

Weighing his words, the scribe answered: "Assuredly, O Sita, shall I help you if I find an opportunity to act on behalf of a servant who is worthy in his master's eyes. I shall willingly lend you all the weight of my influence, knowing that in doing so I shall not oblige a thankless one; he who knows how to fatten succulent geese would not fail to give a firstling to those with a delicate palate. Fine-Speaker, my son, you will certainly become my pupil!"

And the scribe rose and left; but Sita and his son walked with him a part of the road, and the high official took pleasure in telling them in detail of the preparations for the ceremony and of the merry-making that would accompany it.

And after this, when father and son came home, they found Chick-Pea, his mother and his sister, who had just arrived. Sita told him what the scribe had said, and Fine-Speaker described with relish the festivity that had been announced.

Full of wonder, Chick-Pea shouted: "O my father, never have I seen anything of this kind; allow me to be at your side when you render your homage to the Master."

But Fine-Speaker interposed: "You, Chick-Pea, should first of all learn to know your place. I alone shall accompany my father, for I am the *heir*, and I shall learn the art of scribe and shall be accountant of this demesne. And I shall have charge over your work, and you will behave towards me as it becomes a younger brother. Go and wait upon us, and fetch us 'bread-beer'!"[1]

Chick-Pea kept his mouth shut and did not answer. He fetched two loaves from the large earthenware jar and set one of them before his father; but his sister Mut-Sherit caught hold of the other and laid it before her brother, saying:

"Are there no women left in this house?"

And Chick-Pea smiled and muttered:

"One day my mother spoke to me thus: are there no gods more powerful than men. . . ."

And, having eaten, he fell asleep.

[1] 'Bread-beer' was a customary formula meaning daily nourishment in solid and liquid form.

V

SCARECROW

THE barley by the riverside had already taken on a golden sheen: the harvest would be abundant; people rejoiced. No doubt the master would order that a large share be left to the gleaners.

As the harvest-time drew near each farmer posted his team to keep watch on the crops. At long intervals a reed hedge protected a family against the wind; that was the straw hut, the field dwelling for the 'Perit' season. The stars of the sky were its ceiling; in it there was no idle mouth, for the old had stayed at home. The woman had come to look after her man, the girl to look after the goat, the goat to give its milk, and the donkey to serve to carry the burdens.

They watched and waited. Meanwhile they prepared sickles, nets, and the bindings.

As the day declined, they fetched fresh water and filled the large jars. Then they took bread and onions from the pots.

The heat had been heavy upon them; the night was serene and their sleep sound.

The dog guarded the gate near the jar: his office was to bark. "And should I not bark when the neighbours' dog is barking. . . ." Thus felt every dog, in each straw hut—dogs large and small, black and yellow, all the dogs that dreamt beneath the moon. . . . "And what is this? . . . A rat! Why have they tied me up? Ah, I'll bark, bark, bark."

. . . But the day was so heavy and the night was so sweet. Nothing disturbed the sleepers.

The Sun had risen. The Sun stood high. And again the Sun descended towards the mountain, having given the corn a little of its gold.

Among the ears stood a pillar; its stones were cemented with mud; it rose above the barley, it reached the height of a man's head. High steps led to its summit, from which one could survey the field. The platform on top was narrow, very narrow.

Sitting on the pillar the tireless watcher brandished a long fibre whip.

"Hi—hi—hi—you impudent sparrows! You lousy, shelterless lot! . . . Hi—hi—you chatterboxes, grumblers, and drivellers! You gluttons, bringing up twice what you eat, without ever stopping! . . . Hi—hi— you thieves! Don't you ever listen to your belly? Still guzzling when it is full!

"Hi—hi—pshch—pshch—you gang of insatiable ones! . . . The neighbour's barley is better than mine: go away, go away, eat flies, eat worms, but leave my grain alone! Hi—hi! . . .

"Shall I have no peace? Only women can yell a whole day long without tiring. Oh, what a cloud of pilferers, there, under my very nose: must they be as greedy as all that? Greed? Really, Chick-Pea, don't you think yours is a silly job? Does one still hanker after bread when one is no longer hungry? No! These sparrows are no longer hungry: just greedy for corn, as the cat lusts after the mouse even when it has eaten! True enough, and yet: if the mouse held no temptation for the cat, how could one remain in the house? My dog trembles for greed after quails. Fatty always dreams of fish; for his fish ration he would work like ten men. And Fine-Speaker? If he did not burn with the lust of holding others under his sway, he would sleep the whole day long and the night as well. And my father? I don't really know what there is that might tempt my father . . . he is never glad: is his heart perhaps empty of all desires? My own heart grows bigger every day: now it's no longer a jar, but a bottomless basin! Not a flood could fill it: I desire everything and most of all what I don't even know! Chick-Pea—this is bad: your heart is too heavy for your belly!"

The Sun, too, had become too heavy for the watcher. He was dozing and his head lay heavy on his knees. Suddenly a clod of earth struck him on the shoulder and crumbled into dust.

"Hi, you there, watcher on the pillar: does one sleep on a ladder? Who are you? What's your name?"

"My name? Chick-Pea!"

"Chick-Pea what? The gardener? The gooseherd? The harvester? Your trade of yesterday is never that of tomorrow. What is your duty today?"

"I am the 'chief-scarecrow'. See those pillars? Five are under me: one north, one west, one east, and two south. My staff keep their eyes on me: if I am alert, so are they; if I sleep, so do they, and the sparrows have a good time. No sinecure, this job!"

"No job is a sinecure, O Chick-Pea! Even the gooseherd must keep his geese on the run so that they digest their food while his own belly is empty. Is he really the master of his geese? The harvester is ruined by rats, the gardener by locusts. . . . Why not leave all this, and learn my trade: the scribe is better off!"

"There is something in what you say, O Khui, but the scribe never learns how the birds build their nests, nor what the wind brings us, nor the thousand things which neither calamus reed nor palette can tell me."

The scribe rebuked him: "O child without reason, the science you speak of does not fill your jars. But the scribe is never poor. He checks, he keeps accounts, he is of those who receive and not of those who have to give; he is feared and respected by everyone!"

Chick-Pea climbed down from his pillar; he walked at Khui's side and said:

"I shall think over your wise words, O far-sighted scribe; but now I want to test your power: grant me a favour. Our good master Menkh has called upon my father as well as the other farm managers of the demesne to attend at the donation ceremony. Khui, make it possible for me to be there as well!"

"Do you realise what you are asking for, Chick-Pea? This is no little thing, for the Chief of the Cadastral Surveys hates chatterboxes. He has ordered his guards to admit no one to the house except scribes, officials, and invited servants."

"Thèn, wisest of scribes, I will be your helper, your faithful assistant."

"My assistant, Chick-Pea? And how, tell me, could you assist me?"

"How? Can I not count up to ten on my fingers?"

"Indeed, Chick-Pea, yours is a wondrous art. And could you perhaps count on your toes as well? Add two for your nostrils, subtract one for your mouth: how much remains?"

Chick-Pea, knocked flat by so much knowledge, reflected, then he said: "O Khui, do me the favour I ask you. A friend has given me a piece of red ochre, it will be the best your calamus reed has ever tasted. Never will such fine red titles be seen in a record."

Khui, the clever scribe, had to laugh.

"Truly, Chick-Pea, none is more cunning than you. But your offer is acceptable. Be it as you wish: you may hold my palette and sit at my feet as a watchful servant near his master."

VI

DESIRE

"Your lips are silent, O Chick-Pea. What is the matter with you?"

"The question that fills my heart does not dare to pass my lips."

The harper smiled; his fingers caressed the head the boy inclined towards him.

"When a word is conceived in the heart, it is already recorded in heaven. Say all that is in your thought."

"Know this, O Mesdjer: you are more than a father to me; your blind eyes see clearer than mine. My head is filled with what I see every day, it is crammed like the ferryboat on a market-day; my heart leaps with desire towards one thing . . . and then towards something else . . . it does not know what it wants, nor what it does not want!"

"Your speech is flowery like a scribe's discourse. Is that Chick-Pea who is speaking? Speak without circumlocution. Open your mouth. What question torments you?"

"This: I want to know what has power to fill you with yearning?"

The blind man pondered silently over the boy's question.

He drew the foot he had crossed over his knee nearer to himself; then he muttered:

"What a strange, strange question! I? I take every day what the hours bring me. . . ."

"There, you see, you have not answered my question. I have observed my ass: he is willing to run for a handful of barley; I have observed my sister: she told a lie for a trinket; and I have seen our neighbour: when he covets, he steals!"

"You speak truly, O Chick-Pea! The strength of desire tells the vulture where to expect a corpse: on the battlefield he fastens his eyes upon the losing party; so strong is his greed that it makes him foresee the future."

"I am frightened to think of it: greed makes beings wicked."

"Yes, but greed gives them also daring and energy; he who does not know this, knows nothing of human nature."

"And you? Are you without desire?"

"I have a boundless thirst for light—for the Sun."

"Were you, then, unhappy when you lost them both?"

"On the contrary, my desire for light became so violent that it taught me to search for the Sun in my heart; then I knew the true meaning of light. If a flower does not desire light, it closes itself and receives it not; the tauter the bow the more implacable its arrow. If your belly had no desire for the bread you eat, it would not produce what is needed to transform it into your flesh. . . ."

"But I am still little; I am not grown up; who knows what I shall covet?"

"When you go to market, you make use of your ass: or is he your master?"

"O Mesdjer, I fear my ass would make many a silly blunder under my orders. . . ."

"There is a time for the sprouting of the seed; another for the harvesting; the first essential is to sow. Be glad that you are still little; you observe all living things with a fresh heart; learn now how they transform themselves; that's what you must do! Do you know why your father sprinkles the flax with water when it is laid out in the pit?"

"He hasn't told me. Surely it is to clean it?"

"Don't you know that in order to make it pure all that can rot in it must rot? That in order to make a *durable* thread one has first to *destroy* what otherwise might later be corrupted. Of course, one must save the fibres at the right moment, and afterwards one trusts the Sun to burn away what is impure."

"And then it becomes white?"

"Not yet; first it is broken and long threads are drawn; and these threads are watered again so that they rot a little more. In this way everything in them that is corruptible is consumed; and of the purified flax are made those fine linen tissues."

"But how can it become so fine after having been spoiled?"

"Nothing has been spoiled in it that was pure; but nothing can be reborn without having undergone the test of having everything corruptible destroyed."

"That is very hard for me to understand."

"O Chick-Pea, it is even harder for a man made arrogant with learning! The flax will several times return to bloom before my words will have matured in your heart; but every season has its mystery and holds its lesson! Have you looked at the flax before the seed bolls grew?"

"My father's flax had blue flowers."

"It is a spring plant. Blue loves the youth of morning and Sun; sometimes the flax has other shades, but its natural colour is the bluish grey of the moon."

"But, Mesdjer, the moon is not grey, she is white!"

"As white as silver; and yet her light is blue. Do you know what the moon is called when she is full?"

"They say she is called *meh*. . . . Oh! That is almost the same as the name of the flax: *meha*!"

"Precisely! And this word gives you also the name of the north: *meh*, whence the cold wind comes. Know then, that the flax becomes very fine only if it is exposed to the north wind!"

"How do you know all these things?"

"When I still had my eyes, I looked; later I uttered the *names* which our wise men gave to everything on Earth: *thus did I sometimes divine what had been in their minds.*"

"When you speak to me, my heart leaps like a young goat! In order to know all that you know, it would, I think, even try to learn to master its own ass. Is it greed that is the heart's ass?"

"First learn to know this ass, O you impetuous rider! The road is long . . . you will have a few storms to encounter!"

VII

DONATION

"O my donkey, this is not a day for idling rooted to your place! Go on! And hurry, for I must arrive before the others! Don't stick to the road, let's cross the field, we do not want to run into Fine-Speaker and my father. . . .

"Hey, my friend, have I managed well? True, I shall not wear a scribe's robe, but I shall hold his palette. I shall see the Lord Menkh in his glory, his magnificent house on which I have never yet set eyes.

"Oh, you glutton, you may graze on our way back; look at all those people overtaking us; gee-up, gallop, gallop along!"

The crowd gathered and thickened around the mansion. Chick-Pea found Khui; scribes and officials arranged themselves in order of precedence.

People arrived and went to their seats. Chick-Pea gazed, dazzled by the decorations of the hall and the mural paintings. Who had ever seen such brilliant colours, such lofty columns? And those lotus-flowers, was one not tempted to try to pick them?

And now joyful cheers resounded as the royal scribe approached, the messenger of Pharaoh, L.H.S. All backs were bowed, like corn-ears under the wind, and each one, as he rose again, showed a radiant face, for the hero of the day was the Lord of the demesne, Menkh, the Great Master of Craftsmen. How majestic he looked seated on his dais, among his sons, his friends, and his stewards.

The royal scribe, the Majordomo Sebek-Nekht, stood erect, holding in his hand the Royal decree. In a loud voice he recited what His Majesty had decreed in the royal palace L.H.S., to wit:

"In the year XXX, 3rd summer month, second day, His Majesty has ordered that, as mark of his favour towards a friend, a granite statue be granted to the noble Master Craftsman of the Royal Workshops, Menkh, in recognition of his praiseworthy conduct. This statue is destined for His Majesty's temple, where it will be erected beside a colossal statue of the King. To this endowment is added the grant of a plot of land of 50 arurs[1], so as to enable Menkh to establish a service of offerings which must be paid daily."

Menkh's heart was highly gratified on hearing these words, for it was no little thing that was happening to him as a reward for his devotion to the realm and the Pharaoh.

[1] *arur*: Egyptian square measure = 2,756·25 square metres or 3,295·25 square yards.

He slowly rose and spoke the following words, as if he were addressing the King himself:

"The God, your Father, acts according to his decisions. As long as the Heavens last, his deed will last, stable in Eternity. I am my Master's grateful servant and shall act in accordance with all his wishes."

Having spoken thus, the Noble Lord resumed his seat. He beckoned his secretary to approach, who, unfurling a papyrus, commenced the reading of a deed which Menkh wished to make known to those present.

"Listen to the text of a wakf[1] stipulating my funereal endowment, to ensure perpetuity, when I shall 'have caused the wood of the sarcophagus to prosper'[2] and rejoined my burial vault in the necropolis.

"I establish the endowment by this deed, concerning my estates, my bondsmen, and my herd, for the benefit of the statue of my Master who is in his temple. Specification: 25 + 15 + 10 arurs = 50 arurs which His Majesty has conferred upon me; such was my loyalty in his service.

"When, then, the God shall be satisfied with good things and the statue

[1] Endowment, the revenues for which are drawn from an inalienable estate.
[2] This expression is used for the state of a deceased person awaiting his resurrection.

shall have received its provision, then offerings shall be brought to the servant-here-present, by the hand of the priest whose duty it is, according to the daily routine:

List of Items

Loaves at the rate of 30	5 loaves
Loaves at the rate of 40	7 loaves
Total	12 loaves
Beer at the rate of 30	2 jars
Wine	2 jars
Turtle-doves	2 of these
Vegetables	6 bundles

"And I say:

"Listen all you temple priests and prophets who are yet to come: His Majesty has given to me as well as to you, bread-beer, meats, vegetables, and all good things to nourish you in the temple. Do not act from excessive covetousness towards my goods, for I had no thought of increasing them while I was on Earth.

"I have not sought incessantly to accumulate since I have endowed this wakf, being a man of integrity, whose god knew that he would try to increase in perfection, a contriver of profitable things for the servants on his demesne. I have driven no one from his task. I have never fraudulently taken the property of anyone else. Acts of dishonesty I hate above all.

"And here, in conclusion, I have this to say: May God punish any Royal Master of Craftsmen who shall be my successor, and any priest of the temple, if they would profit from my goods! May he not leave them in peace to enjoy their office. May he deliver them to the fire of the King on his day of wrath. May the uræus on his forehead spew flames on the crowns of their heads, destroy their flesh and devour their body. They shall become 'as Apopis on the morning of the New Year's Day'.[1] They shall not receive the honours due to virtuous people. They shall not be able to swallow the offerings of the dead. No libations shall be poured for them. Their wives shall be violated before their eyes. Their offices shall be taken from them and given to men who will be their enemies. Their KAS[2] shall be separated from them. Their dwellings shall collapse and fall to the ground.

"But if, on the other hand, they see to it that this wakf be properly executed, may they receive all possible good. They shall attain the age of retirement and pass on their offices to their children after an old age full of years of happiness!"

Loud snoring was heard. . . . Fortunately for the sleeper, it was drowned

[1] Legend of the snake Apopis, which is battered and bruised on the first morning of the year.
[2] The spiritual body of man. See *Her-Bak Disciple*, Index: KA.

in the cheers which congratulated the Master who had been so highly honoured.

Chick-Pea woke up, roused by bursts of laughter from his neighbours; the red ochre on his palette had left a mark on his forehead and the tip of his nose. . . .

"Oh, Chick-Pea," said Khui, "now you have done your first writing!"

After the notables had put their seals to the document, Menkh called his special secretary and spoke loudly:

"Let it be inscribed, and let everyone know what I have decided.

"I grant, to mark the occasion of this felicitous day, a double ration of beer to my good servants, and let ten sheep be killed, and meat distributed to all.

"Kakem, my faithful servant, shall receive a couple of oxen from my stables, in reward for the excellent work he has incessantly done for me.

"Unfer shall receive ten sacks of barley, to nourish his fourteen children.

"To Sita, I grant as personal property, to be passed from son to son and heir to heir, a little field which belongs to me, situated at the riverside, and adjacent to the demesne of Sabu."

Loud cheers rose in thankfulness for the generosity of the master of the demesne. The servants thus favoured approached to kiss the ground before him.

It was then that Sita and his son Fine-Speaker saw Chick-Pea standing among the scribes . . . and so violent was their surprise that they did not know any more where they were! But Chick-Pea rejoined them when they left the hall, and said:

"This is a lucky day for you, O my father! As for me, I have decided to work on the land with you. But the scribes have told me that Thot[1] has marked his seal on my face. . . . Hence it shall happen . . . as he may decide."

---

[1] *Thot*, the *Neter* of sciences and the hieroglyphs.

THE FIELD

THERE were many donkeys to do the work in the field, but there was none like the house donkey: he ate and slept near his masters; he was Chick-Pea's ass, he was the ass on which one rode to market, who knew the way, the hours and the habits; he was the *carrier*, the powerful one, briefly: THE donkey.

He was handsome: grey, with a brown cross on his back. He alone had the right to crop and to dung this field until flood time, this field which was Sita's pride. And indeed, the pasture was worthy of the ass! After the high waters, when the ground emerged, the grass would be dense and malachite green; and again when the donkey had grazed and dunged it, both donkey and meadow would be quickened and invigorated, and the barley would grow there finer than in any other field!

That is why today the ass was on his property and Chick-Pea was with his ass.

And Chick-Pea was happy; the Nile flowed past the meadow, and river and banks were a magic world. Barques with great white sails were gliding upstream; one heavily filled with earthen pots and jars; another packed with farmhands and carrying also a cow and her calf. A long barge glided down from the South, laden with a mountain of straw and grain.

The shimmering water cast reflections blue as lapis lazuli; on the banks the cucumber and pumpkin plants already bore green fruits. Two plovers told each other their adventures.

To the south the meadow adjoined Sabu's. The neighbour's son guarded his field in the shelter of a straw hut; whereas Chick-Pea had chosen near the bank a fine corner filled with the shadow cast by a large sycamore and a group of acacias. His figure blended into the tree-trunk, and his simplicity into animal instinct.

The fertile field was the favourite meeting-ground of flocks of birds, according to the season, according to the hour and the degree of softness of the ground. Swallows flew over it, skimming the ground when the humid heat beat down the midges. The family of hoopoes chose it for their domicile; near the stream the mother taught her chicks to strike the ground with their beaks in order to make the small earthworm come out; the little hoopoes tapped and tapped, hit too far and hit too near and at last, annoyed, tried to share in the worm which mother had found.

Around the donkey grazing near a ditch a council of little white herons —with haughty beaks and short tails—were stamping the softened ground.

One of them, more daring than the others, followed the donkey step by step, waiting for the propitious moment; the donkey pulled out a tuft of grass: the bird dashed forward, unearthing a worm under his nose. A jerk of the ass's head chased him away as if he were a fly: already he was far to the rear. But hardly had the donkey lowered his nose, when again the bird was almost between his teeth! And so this comedy continued, between the patient ass and the greedy, timid and profiteering heron.

A couple of crows fought off some buzzards who tried to take their pasture. And Chick-Pea recalled numerous legends about the marriage of the crows, and their fidelity, even when widowed.

What a stir in the neighbour's grain field! A company of swerving swallows made peace with clouds of sparrows in order to speed up the pilfering before night fell.

But suddenly there was silence, they flushed and scattered in headlong flight, a sharp trill had sounded: the falcon's battle-cry. And there he was . . . the slender, tapering crescent of his wings outlined against the blue sky; he soared in a straight line, leaning on the void, with successive dashes without any·wheeling; his glance was not dazzled by the Sun! He soared so high that the threatened bird felt reassured . . . and then, in a perpendicular drop, the falcon swooped on his prey, seized it in his claws, plucked it in full flight and pierced its heart to drink its blood.

Chick-Pea was worried, torn between admiration and disgust. He turned his glance towards the peaceful river; there a kingfisher lay in wait for a fish, hovering over the prey in trembling suspense; suddenly he dropped like a stone, plunged in his beak and snapped home. . . .

Always killing to live, always killing to eat; was there no world where one could live without killing? . . .

The light declined and the day birds assembled their tribes; the gliding buzzards soared higher to snatch the last rays of their master. A deafening uproar burst out in the mimosas: the sparrows sought their roosting-place and changed their minds every moment; they quarrelled, pursued each other, they envied each other, they chirruped, they chattered, they hopped about, they flitted from branch to branch . . . and the creaking tree, shaken by the beating of all those wings, waited trembling for the end of the cataclysm.

What silence! The sparrows had gone to sleep: when they shut their beaks the earth was mute! Then—Wav! Wav! the rallying cry of the little white herons called the stragglers. They formed up in large triangles and glided smoothly with flapping wings towards their resting-place. Then the fighting began between the different occupiers, and the black attacked the white ones, the croaking fury of ravens tried to chase away the newcomers. The two whirling groups seemed like merciless wrestlers. . . . But the evening hour, as always, imposed silence and peace.

The heat had declined with the sun. Chick-Pea came and sat down near the riverside, which a lapping of waves agitated in shining scales.

He saw the Atur[1] gliding noiselessly, he that comes from so far away, from the unknown, and goes so far away, towards the unknown. . . .

"So far, so far away—and what does one find there so far away? The two ends of the world? . . . What are the two ends of the world? This flood that streams down incessantly does not seem to turn round: does it never come back again? Then it is never the same water again! And all this water, where does it come from?—Mesdjer has said: from the two abysses of the sky. My mother said: from the two abysses of the Earth; which is the truth?

"How fresh and cool it is, that north wind! It awakens life, it makes you light and gay! One could let oneself be carried away by that water, so swiftly does it glide, it flees from the land of the hot wind, and rushes to meet the wind that is fresh and cool. This is a broad road, this fine river, a broad highway with two banks, and these two banks are not alike: the other one is hotter than this one. Is that because of the mountain or of the burning sand? Fortunately, there are palms and cultivated fields!

"My father has told the truth; it is the Nile which gives us the Black Earth; without it, the 'Red Earth'[2] would kill both plants and animals."

The hour of the second dusk had come, the magical hour of Egypt. While the bat already triumphed in the night, the horizon lit up for the second time; the whole eastern sky lay in darkness, the Zenith was of sombre blue, the mountain stood out as a black silhouette; but the rising night irradiated all with a flow of green and rosy gold, which once more set ablaze the horizon of the western sky. The river, losing its reflections, shimmered like an opal. Was this a mirage of darkness enfolding the light . . . or a rebirth of colour?

And now into this riot of colour silently glided a ghostly fleet. Coming from the dark south, the shapes revealed themselves as they approached the coloured water and took form in fantastic shadows; the boy held his breath for wonder. . . .

Splendid was the largest vessel under the breadth of its sail and the out-spread fan of its ropes! From the stern to the prow which was haughtily lifted, the sweep of its hull arched it like a fine cup.

The sixty oarsmen were ready to make good the flagging of the breeze. The sail was lowered, and all the oars struck the water rhythmically; it was truly beautiful. On each plank stood fifteen sailors handling the long oars. The boatswain gave them the rhythm; the helmsman kept to the poop-deck, with a rope he steered the huge, bladed stern-oar used as a rudder.

[1] Atur means the River, that is, in Egypt, the Nile. At the period of inundation it takes the name of Hapi.   [2] The desert.

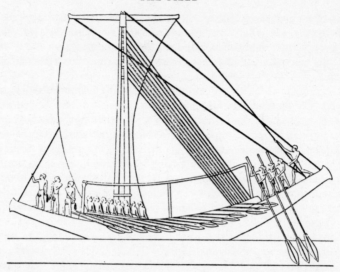

The following barque was less luxurious but quite as big; large crates confined the captive animals. Servants and sailors called to each other on the two escort feluccas, and Chick-Pea could distinguish the words of their shanties. The flotilla approached and the details became clearer. What a pity that there was so little time to watch this rare wonder!

But suddenly a strange manœuvre changed the course of the leading vessel: the helmsman grew excited . . . the pilot, standing on top the cabin, shouted orders: "*Sta ur!* Face to the East! . . . Look out: we are almost aground! This is not the river; these are shallow waters. Look out! . . ." The ship approached the bank, the helmsman handled his boat-hook . . . a shock made the ship vibrate. "Aground!" The Nile ebbs, and the sandbanks shift constantly.

Standing near the planking, the master of the ship listened to the captain's report. Oh what luck! An order was given, and the whole flotilla gathered around the boat of wonders; the mooring-stakes were lowered, and the hammers and the ropes, and each barque was secured for the night.

The boy danced with joy and prepared for his camping too. He could not let this godsend slip. Hoping to catch the sailors' eye he looked for brushwood and prepared a fire. He ran to the straw hut to borrow a light from the neighbour's: fire and water were the two things no one would ever refuse. The neighbour took his drill-bow, the kindling wood spun and caught fire. Chick-Pea ran carrying his firebrand and lit his fire. And lo, from the large vessel a gangway was lowered. A sailor came down and climbed up the bank; Chick-Pea shouted: "Welcome!" The sailor said: "Our crew is safe and our huntsmen, too. Boy, can you get us some dry wood and milk?"

"Be in peace, traveller, you shall have what you wish! Allow me only to spend a few hours on your ship."

Chick-Pea galloped his ass: "Hop, companion, today we have to hurry! . . ." He returned even quicker, loaded with dry wood bundles and milk vessels.

On board the large cargo vessel he was received with open arms. The sailors and huntsmen sitting around the fire on which the fish were grilled, invited the boy to share their food. And while they were eating, Chick-Pea eagerly watched the rough faces which must have known so many adventures.

Never had explorers a more enthusiastic audience! Questions and answers criss-crossed:

"You have seen the end of the Nile?"

"Towards the south, no one has seen it, except perhaps the serpent which drinks its water and which is battered and bruised every New Year morning."

"Is it a real serpent?"

"I know only what people say."

"And the Nile always remains as broad as here?"

"Sometimes the mountains squeeze in its two sides; sometimes it seems to invade the whole valley. In Elephantina, the rocks give it a back as round as that of a herd of hippopotami."

"That must be dangerous to navigate!"

"Of course, and the ship won't take the risk: the water cascades over the rocks! So we stepped on the backs of the crocodiles."

"Don't listen to that liar! There is a channel dug in order to get around that cataract."

"And beyond the canal?"

"There we went on until we reached the landing place which leads to the hunting grounds."

"And you have always travelled on the Nile?"

"No, I have also crossed the sea."

"What is that: the sea?"

"It is the 'great green lake'; there is water there, much, much water! It's like a Nile so vast that you can never see the two banks! For a whole month you may sail on it without seeing any land. On the Nile the waves are as high as gudgeons; but on the sea the waves are as large as houses!"

"Then the gudgeons in the sea are as big as the waves?"

"Ay," said a sailor, "I have seen some as large as the ship, but those are not called gudgeons."

"What is there on the other side of the sea?"

"It's the land of Punt, the country of resins, incense and perfumes."

Another sailor said:

"I have travelled the other sea, that of the north, into which the Nile disappears; we have landed on an island where one can find wonderful fruit!"

"Then there are many seas? Where is the end of the world?"

"I do not know. You must ask the scribes. But it is said that the centre of the world is on our Earth, there down in the north, near the 'White Wall' of Memphis."

"Are there other Niles?"

"In Egypt there is one only and it is a *Neter*, for it allows us to live and is alone capable of conquering the desert!"

Chick-Pea did not reply; under the moonlight the silhouettes of the barques stood out on the silvery river.

From the master's ship rose a beautiful song and the men listened in dreamy silence:

"We greet thee, Hapi, our stream,
Issued from our Earth,
Giver of all gifts.

We greet thee, O renewer,
Bearer of all essence; power of each sap;
Goal of all yearning of the Earth's produce!

O shining one, issued from the gulfs of the darkness!
O magician who leads towards the light
All living seeds which thou hast brought us!

Guide of the seeds, nourisher of grains,
Multiplier of granaries,
Provider of breasts and udders!

Fertile male, thou begettest thyself,
And thou burgeonest like a woman;
Young and old, ageless, immortal.

River of life, no living being but must know thee ;
Dew of heaven, thou fertilisest the deserts.
O King and Law of that which thou quickenest!

The movement of thy flow reigns, in the Two-lands,
The 'becoming' and destiny of all seeds,
Thy harmonious course gladdens the banks.
Thy confusion creates confusion; thy wrath frightens and provokes Typhoon;

The throwing up of the flow kneads the arid ground into fertile clay;
Through thee is Sobek, the crocodile, fertilised.

The earth flooded with light brings forth verdure;
Every creature of the earth is clothed by the full measure of thy gifts.
Through thee, the barque floats over the shallows.

Thou separatest and assemblest;
Thou bindest together the two irreconcilable banks;
Thou bringest and quickenest the black earth.

Thy growing is the sign of all rejoicing;
The earth quivers in its very marrow,
And even its arid bones are moved. . . .

For thou quenchest the thirst of the most thirsty,
And the most naked is laden with thy gifts;
But he whose thirst is satisfied ignores thee.

Thou governest the festivals of all Neters,
And all the sacrifices of their first fruits,
And the measure of all their offerings.

O thou, who canst not be outnumbered!
O mysterious one who springest unendingly from the abyss
Without ever exhausting thyself!

No man knows thy secret caverns;
No writing has ever revealed thy name,
But every fruit of the earth bears thy signature!

By thee is it nourished and transformed:
And lo:

It achieves its perfect accomplishment."[1]

[1] For French text of this song, see pages 294–5.

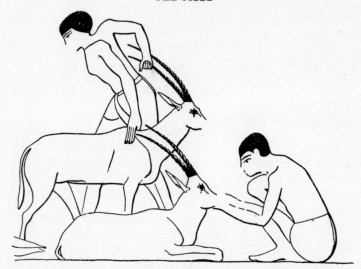

The voice became silent; a roar was heard, and barking replied.

Chick-Pea rose to visit the animals; a huntsman followed him hurriedly: "Don't go alone, boy, at night the wild beasts are dangerous."

They visited the greyhounds and the captives which were shut in solid cages; gazelles, an ibex, the fine oryxes with long slender horns, and the showpiece of the exhibition: three leopards destined as an offering to the Lord High Seneschal.[1]

"We have also brought a monkey, but he is chained to the cabin of the master."

And in the depth of the night, rocked by the northern breeze which sang in the ropes, the huntsmen told of their adventures.

[1] See footnote, Chapter XVIII, 'Judgment,' page 95.

FISHERMAN

"WHAT if I became a fisherman? . . ."

Since his visit to the ships, Chick-Pea knew a novel feeling: the yearning for travel, for setting out towards the 'unknown', towards the 'far away' beyond his horizon. . . . And lo, as he created and modelled his dream, he began to perceive the notions of distance and time; they were related to each other by means of transport; and the only means of transport he knew was his ass!

The more he thought it over, the more he realised the difference between the dream and the means. "What do you say to it, comrade?

Would you be willing to go and look for adventure? Where to? Straight ahead! What are we going to see? The banks of the Nile and the fields; you will still be able to crop grass and barley, but harvest will soon be over. . . . Besides, we must not remain in the fields during the night: wolves and wild cats are roaming about. But that does not matter. We can travel higher up, on the edge of the valley, you won't find green fodder there; still, there will be thistles and tamarisks: no food for me, those! Doubtless there will be hares, but hunting them—no, I don't like that trade. What then shall I do? Go through the desert? Horned vipers and hyenas are no better than wolves. . . . I did not think it would be so difficult to live by oneself. Hey, friend, I don't think that journey would last long, we would not get very far, we two, would we? By ship it would be easier and quicker, but there it is: I have no ship!

"And if I were to learn a fisherman's trade? I could become a sailor on the Nile; and later I might also sail on the Great Green Lake. . . ."

Fantastic visions arose: the sand became a billowing sea; giant fishes swam about in it; the mountain was a monstrous wave, the boats on the Nile sailed on a meadow-green sea, with cargoes of unknown animals, mountains of fruit and precious stones. And to make this dream come true, what a simple starting point, and how easy of access: to become a fisherman!

Chick-Pea jumped up eagerly. He went to his friend Fatty and explained his plan to him. Squatting on the ground, clasping his knees, Fatty let him talk, and weighed each argument as a boy who knew the weight of his body and of his usual loads.

"It is not easy to change your way of life, Chick-Pea! You know what you have, but you do not know what you are going to get! Could you really leave your mother and your father?"

"Is she really my mother? Am I not a stranger both to her and to my father? Look here, Fatty, I can't remain a farmer always: the peasant is bound to his land: I don't like to be attached!"

"The dog does not like to be chained either; still, hunger drives him back to the house."

"The birds of passage find their food all over the world."

"You're dreaming, Chick-Pea—birds have *wings* to fly from land to land!"

"Don't you think that the wish to fly can make wings grow?"

"Your mind's wandering, my friend! Anyone who wants to leave the place which gives him a living, to risk the unknown, must be mad."

"The swallows leave Egypt."

"But they return."

"The sailors leave their country."

"But they return!"

"What then is this force which attaches people and animals to their earth? Is there not everywhere sand, fields, a river, a mountain?"

"No. No other earth is theirs; the earth of the stable in which I sleep is mine; when I wake up, I walk on my ground! Our earth is mud, true, but it is *our earth*; and who leaves it will always return to it."

Chick-Pea listened to this in his heart; then he said: "I shall return to the place which will teach me what I want to know."

"Hey, you who are trying to attain that which can't be attained, rather than grasp after the sky you should search under your feet: your country can teach you the trade which suits you.

"But if you want to work without bread-beer, then stay alone; if you want to eat other people's bread without tiring your limbs, you'd better become a scribe! Best off is the servant of a good master; to be sure, he has no wings, but his belly is always filled!"

"Fatty, do all boys of my country speak like you?"

"Yes, by my life! You are the only fool among them."

"Well then, my friend, I want to become a sailor."

"You forget that you are bound to this demesne."

"What does that matter: I can begin by becoming the fisherman of the demesne."

Fatty looked at Chick-Pea and laughed; then he shrugged his shoulders and rose.

"Hey, get up! You bold heart, thirsty for adventures, be it then as you wish! Let's go and see Pipu's father: we'll talk it over with him."

The fisherman's house was not far from the bank. In a little yard, lines were drawn over posts: fishes opened out flat hung upon them to dry. In a low room a box contained dried fish. The mother rose to welcome the two friends and showed them the way to the bank.

"You will find Pipu there with her father, he has just come back from fishing."

On the steep bank by the moored boat two men were busy counting the fish before a squatting scribe.

In the middle of the boat the little girl Pipu sat beside the fisherman among all the live or gutted fish. Her hands, arms, legs, dripped with blood and slimy water; her hair and her face, from which she chased the flies with her wet arm, were spotted with fish-scales and slime. Fatty gripped the two arms of Chick-Pea and helped him to jump into the boat.

"O Remy, great fisherman, I bring you a boy who wants to learn your trade."

A pungent smell half-choked the boy, a smell of fish blending with the acrid stench of the sun-baked guts. The fisherman was busy filleting an enormous 'batensoda'.[1] Appraising the new apprentice with a glance, he smiled and gave him his knife.

"Welcome! There is plenty of work to be done. Sit down and let us see how smart you are."

Chick-Pea tried to overlook the knife; he remained standing among the gasping victims which squirmed under his feet.

"Great is your skill, O Remy! There is a fine variety of fish in your boat."

"True," replied the fisherman, "as the fisherman, so is his catch! But what are you waiting for? Take the knife and show how keen you are. Gut those perches and clean them, and be quick about it, if you want my praise!"

[1] The Egyptian fishermen called this catfish 'Schal baten soda' which means 'Schal with the black belly'.

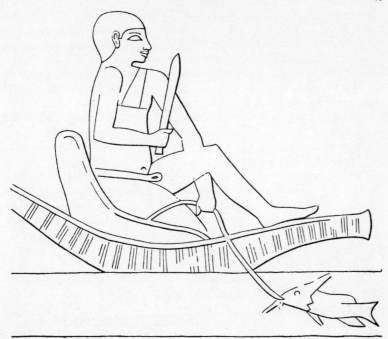

Fatty, seeing Chick-Pea's confusion and his disgust, pushed him sharply and sat him down among the messy entrails; he pressed the broad knife into his hand and gave him a large living fish: "All right, fisherman, down to work!"

Chick-Pea, all stiff, tried to struggle against the horror which sickened him; his hand grasped the knife mechanically. Fatty seized it; with a short pull he forced him to split the fish which still wriggled in his fingers; merciless, Fatty forced the cramped hand to empty the entrails, to pull out the bones; then he handed the fish to Remy.

The fisherman looked at the scene with a twinkle in his eye.

"Well, mate, when do you want to start here?"

Chick-Pea rose, stammered a few words and staggered out of the boat.

When they were far enough away, Chick-Pea went down again to the river and washed.

Fatty washed too, laughing, then pulled him along and raced him through the barley-fields.

When they were tired, they stopped near a ditch; but Fatty failed to distract his playmate. Chick-Pea remained silent and obstinately kept his eyes on the sky where white flakes were condensing, whose origin he sought in vain.

What was that strange cloud advancing from the south like a large wavy triangle? . . . The cloud darkened a corner of the sky, and now the forms of birds became visible, white, with black points. Fatty observed the flight and the colours: "The storks!" They approached, and slowly sweeping around they circled overhead, while a detachment remained behind like a rear-guard. Another cloud appeared in the west, a third in the south-west. They followed each other, arranged themselves, circled and circled in one place, awaiting one could not tell what order before they made a decision. And soon further formations became visible in the south-east and yet others from the south.

Chick-Pea untiringly observed this exodus. Two long hours passed. Fatty admired them expertly.

The vast expanse of birds seemed to cover the sky and to seek a resting-place. Some storks detached themselves and came down, scouting, while the main body went on circling in the blue air, slowly, without showing any signs of fatigue. And here at last the final cloud! And now, after some hesitation, a deluge of birds swooped down on the chosen ground, forming themselves into groups.

"They are tired," said Chick-Pea.

"Yes, they will rest themselves this day and this night; but they will post sentries around their camp, who will stay awake."

"Are they going to leave tomorrow?"

"They will decide according to the wind. The south wind will carry them to their goal; as soon as it comes, they will shake their wings, circle and fly off. They will circle first, they will make several wide circuits, very, very slowly, and then each stork finds its own place in the travel-order; they form the triangle, which stretches out like an immense swallow-tail and then comes the real departure . . . northward."

Chick-Pea looked in turn towards the three directions of the sky from whence the migrating birds had come.

"So this is the gathering before the great journey! But tell me, Fatty, do you understand how the storks can communicate across space to meet here on the same day? . . . They obey some leaders, since they move to-gether; but how can they transmit orders at such great distance, right, left, or ahead. I could not speak from here to Mut-Sherit; why can I not do what the bird can?"

"Oh, you, you want to understand what no one can understand. I know what one has to know: when the lentils are ripe, I hurry to prepare my net, for the quails will come soon, and while they feast one can catch whole mountains of them."

"And those quails, where do they come from?"

"I don't know; but however far off they are, they know when the len-tils are due, and so I know when the quails are due! There is a useful science for you, a science that will fill the belly."

Chick-Pea remained confused, confronted with this practical oppor-tunism, but some constant worry haunted him.

"There, you see, Fatty, there are things which can force an animal to leave the place where it lives!"

Fatty burst into laughter.

"Oh, I knew, I was sure, you would not dream of profiting by the lesson! You feed on questions, not on quails."

Chick-Pea left his friend hurriedly, for Fatty had spoken the truth: questions choked his heart, and the harper alone could perhaps answer them.

A long time he spoke to Mesdjer; telling him his dream, his failure as apprentice, the story of the storks. Mesdjer followed with amusement the thread which held the thoughts together:

"Your feeling is right, little man; there is some force which drives the bird to this or that place. Sometimes it is the instinct of self-preservation, the need for a particular climate or food. But it is obvious that birds also feel attracted by certain flavours or smells.

"Each animal has its own passions—like human beings; and all passions have as aim to add, for some time, fullness and savour to life."

"But not all animals want the same thing, do they?"

"No. Each animal and each plant has its own nature and particular properties which give the colour and form according to which the appeal of life expresses itself in their various instincts: the greed for food, for hunting, or for love. The stronger that greed, the more intense is their life."

"Still, oh Mesdjer, if my ass eats too much, he becomes heavy and dull!"

"*That is because he has filled his emptiness: he has quenched his desire.* The simple animal does not worry about this and seeks only to gratify its desire. The strongest animal is that which tries to live a tenfold life, rather than to satisfy its needs. Thus the cat finds more pleasure in the hunting game than in the fact of eating the mouse."

"Oh, Mesdjer! One might almost say that the mouse itself cannot keep away from playing with the cat. . . ."

"Yes, Chick-Pea, risk is a stimulant, sought after by many animals. Each animal, each plant, according to its own nature, plays a game that exalts or weakens the life forces which cause their sympathies or antipathies. An animal does not reason; it experiences directly. That is its superiority over the intermediate age of our Mankind—that phase in which man—deceived by the incomplete testimony of his senses and his reason—has allowed the instinctive consciousness to atrophy without as yet having learnt to use his intuitive faculties which are 'the wisdom of the heart'."

"Is then the animal a model for man?"

"Every animal is the summing-up of a character which is perfection of its kind, because it does not dissimulate what we call the defects; it is wh⌐

it seems to be. If you observe each species, you will find there some aspect of the passions which are the driving force of our own life."

"Oh, Mesdjer, the animal does not think as men do; can it then experience our desires, our sorrows, our jealousy?"

"All the urges of the passions express vital natural impulses, and it is the animal in us which gives rise to them. The wise man is conscious of them, he knows how to give them their true name and to make use of them as you direct your donkey. But the wise man is rare, and egoism finds a thousand reasons for giving those impulses legitimate motives and flattering names. The human passions are life-impulses which have been perverted . . . and so skilfully perverted that it is very difficult to discover, beneath their complications, the almost divine power which is their source. . . . Hence I do not say all this for 'serious' people, but for the child Chick-Pea, who would know how to observe, without criticism or judgment, the impulses of passion within the animals . . . and how to find their equivalents in himself. Has Chick-Pea understood?"

Chick-Pea, at that moment, had allowed himself to be fascinated by the wiles of the bee-eater birds who caught bumble-bees in full flight, knocked them dead against the trunk of a palm-tree and greedily swallowed them in one mouthful. His reply was a question:

"Are then the animals forced to obey the lust to eat one another?"

"They are forced to obey the demands of hunger. Their instinctive nature makes them look for the food that suits their organism. You yourself sometimes feed on meat and fish. . . . But man perverts this vital impulse by overshooting its mark: necessity gives an excuse for gluttony, and for the hunter an opportunity to exert his cruelty."

"When a man and a cat kill birds to eat them, is the man more guilty than the cat?"

"Man or beast, whoever kills becomes thereby subject to the law of Osiris,[1] which is a merciless pendulum and always acts reciprocally. Kill and eat if you want, but know what you are doing; seek no excuse and accept the consequences: that is the only way for man to attain little by little to higher consciousness."

"Who will give me the courage?"

"Disgust with your impotence, desire to break the chains of this animality."

[1] *Osiris*, *Neter* of Nature and principle of perpetual return to existence. See Pl. VI; cf. *Her-Bak Disciple*, Index: *Osiris*.

HARVEST

THE leader of the team raised his voice, so that all harvesters could hear him:

"Hey, comrades, listen! Hurry up! Today is the day of the barley, the festival of the barley! And you, musician, how dreary you sound! Are you playing us lullabies, you lazybones?"

This last day the harvesters were tired and their progress slow. One behind the other, two elbows apart, they cut the barley at knee level, seizing the ears with the left hand and cutting them deftly with the right. The binders followed on their heels, bundling the ears and tying them into sheaves.

Chick-Pea found the sickle heavy; it burned in his hand, but he did not allow his weariness to show. He had told his father: "I shall work like a man!" and in return for this promise he had obtained the sickle.

But now, hearing the voice of the overseer, he ran after the musician and began to sing, finding the words in his memory and beating the rhythm with his arm:

Mow, my sickle, mow the whole field.

The long-haired barley you have cut down,
The tall ears of corn you have brought low,
Reap, my comrades, and sing with me.

Mow, my sickle, mow the whole field.

A skilful craftsman has carved your hard wood,
Curved like the crescent of the young moon,
And inlaid in it the silex teeth.

Mow, my sickle, mow the whole field.

You are handsome to look at, O new sickle,
And you make your way, cutting the ears,
As the boat makes headway, cleaving the water.

Mow, my sickle, mow the whole field.

The corn is powerful: its grain is my food.
But stronger my sickle, stronger by far,
Before it flees the spirit of barley.

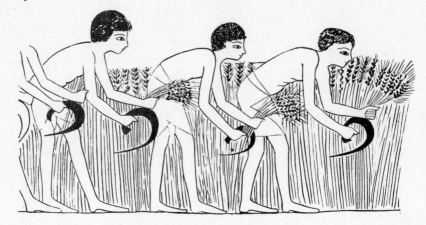

Mow, my sickle, mow the whole field.

Let the Neter Nepri[1] *be preserved*
From ear to ear, the sickle pursues him
To the last shelter, the final sheaf.

Mow, my sickle, mow the whole field.

Reapers, let's spare the sacred sheaf!
Let us plait the barley! Neter *of the* neper.[2]
We save you from the winnower's hand.

Mow, my sickle, mow the whole field.

We will keep you in the 'twofold granary';
There revive our grain and recall the spirit
Who has flown away in the winnowing wind.

Mow, my sickle, mow the whole field.

Perfect will be the next year's harvest,
Rich in ears and fertile in seed;
Sheaf of the ending, Oh protect Nepri!

Mow, my sickle, mow the whole field.[3]

"That was beautiful," said one of the harvesters, "it's sure to turn out like that, as you have said."

[1] *Nepri:* the *Neter* of corn.
[2] The *Neter* of the *neper* is the 'spirit of the corn', which is pursued until the last sheaf which, therefore, is kept religiously as protector of the granaries.
[3] For French text of this song, see pages 295–6.

"Look out, here are the donkeys! Make ready to have the harvest carried away."

In a pit-a-pat trot the donkeys entered the field. . . .

"Hey! Comrades, fill those large sacks . . . full, up to the brim! More! Press it down, put your stick against it! Tighter! Tighter! . . . You there, press it down with your knees! Yes, that's right! . . . And load your donkeys quickly! And you there: hold your ass, this big load is for him. See that it is well balanced!"

So rich is the harvest: they are short of donkeys to carry it off!

"Then fill the yoke-nets as well! . . . Hurry up, fellows, fall in with the donkeys. . . . My life, that's a handsome procession!"

Pit-a-pat and pit-a-pat, pit-a-pat and pit-a-pat, the donkeys leave the

field; pit-a-pat and pit-a-pat. . . . "What a mulish beast!" Pit-a-pat and pit-a-pat, the she-ass follows her foal; pit-a-pat and pit-a-pat, the foal is falling back, pit-a-pat and pit-a-pat, "I am big; I am trotting by myself!" pit-a-pat and pit-a-pat, "Hmm, grass! And a stone!" Galloping, galloping, "Where is mummy, where is mummy?" Pit-a-pat and pit-a-pat; they're arriving at the threshing-floor, pit-a-pat and pit-a-pat. . . .

"Whoa! Unload! Put it on the floor! Hurry up, we must finish by sunset! Take the barley by armfuls, build up the stacks! Pile it up! Pile it up!"

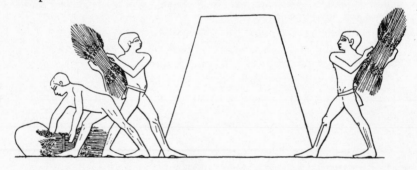

Never before had Chick-Pea worked so hard in the fields!
Never before had he slept so soundly!

The lowing of a calf awakened him. "Hey, you, 'Under-the-Finger', stop singing! Today you will go and eat straw in the fields!"
Sita himself surveyed the departure of the flocks; he was pleased with the number of cattle and their handsome looks; the cattle-herds took pains

to drive them in good order. "Hey, you little calf there, will you follow your mother! . . . And you, mother, go ahead, your calf is no longer thirsty."

On the road, while the flocks passed by the stacks which had been piled up the night before, Chick-Pea said to his father: "These are fine stacks, but there would be more of it if we had cut the stalks at ground level."

"What you say makes little sense," his father replied. "If we did as you suggest, what would the flocks have to eat for the next few days?"

"Oh well! Are there no other pastures, so we need not waste our straw reserves?"

Having spoken thus, Chick-Pea felt very satisfied with his clever piece of advice; but his father looked at him and laughed:

"Truly this big wiseacre does not know the first thing! How could the earth nourish the seeds if the cattle did not help with their dung?"

Confused, Chick-Pea cast down his eyes, but then he suddenly wondered why the same could not be done with the flax, and he asked: "But if the flax stalks are pulled out, the cattle will not be able to pasture on the field."

"You're right," Sita replied, "that's why I shall sow grass there, which suits the sheep. Their dung is cooler. Any other dung would burn the linseed."

"But, father, didn't you tell me that our river was the food of the earth?"

"Surely, it is its food, and the verdure is rich when it has flowed by, but for the seeds the earth needs a warm fire."

Chick-Pea remained perplexed; then he asked: "What fire is there in dung?"

Sita was speechless; nor did he know what to answer. For some time he walked in silence; then he murmured:

"What shall I do if this son who works on my land, furrows his thought before he furrows my fields. The bird will soon have pilfered the grain and ruin will be on my house."

Chick-Pea became sad in his heart over these words; then he thought it over and grasped his father's hand:

"Have you not also said: 'You must know the first things'? And from whom shall I learn the first things if not from my father?"

And for the second time the father said to himself: "Am *I* really his master?"

From this day onward, Sita began to instruct his younger son in everything he knew about agriculture. He told him how the fields were measured at the beginning of the harvest. He showed him the process of treading out the ears on the thrashing-floor first by the oxen and later by the donkeys which trotted around in dense ranks.

He set him to practise cleaning the corn. Chick-Pea separated the chaff with the fire-fan; he thrashed the grain; it gave him much pleasure to pour it out from high up with the two scoops, so that the wind could blow away the chaff, then he helped the women to pass the grain through the sieve. He looked on as the straw was trodden out by the cattle; he helped the workmen to pile up the straw with forks to make solid stacks of it; and he himself planted in the centre of the stack the large papyrus umbel which consolidated it.

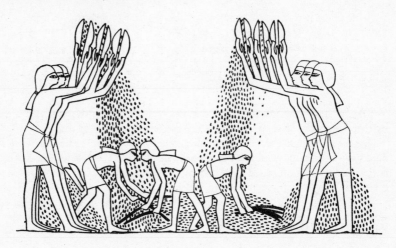

And while he worked, he observed the scribes who checked the stacks, the scribes who measured the corn with a bushel, the scribes who surveyed the garnering, the scribes who knew how to count by thousands and ten thousands of millions and how to multiply them with all the grains of the harvest! For all the registers and all offices must bear witness to the gathered amounts, so as to legitimise the taxes and tithes.

THE GODS

AFTER the harvest work was done, there came a happy day for all labourers, for the Master of the demesne spoke thus:

"Let there be given bread-beer and other good things in abundance to all, for this has been a good harvest! And let there be offerings made to *Rennutet*,[1] in accordance with custom."

And it was done as the Master had commanded.

Chick-Pea and his friend Fatty followed together the people who wandered towards the shrine of *Rennutet*. Chick-Pea was too small: he could not see anything through the crowd. Fatty said:

"You have been living in far away fields, and have never beheld anything like this. Climb on my shoulders and watch to your heart's content."

Chick-Pea did so and feasted his eyes on the novel spectacle.

A platform was cut into the rock, and on it an image of *Rennutet* in the shape of a woman with a snake's head; she was seated on a throne and held on her knees the little *Nepri*, the *Neter* of the grain, whom she suckled. A priest presented a small flat sheaf of plaited barley-ears; another priest offered two quails; some priests carried high bouquets of flowers, skilfully mounted in the shape of superimposed horns.

Sistra and cymbals sounded in rhythm. Frankincense spread fragrant smoke. After the ritual gestures had been accomplished, the faithful approached in turn, bringing wisps of cereals, birds, and white loaves in order to obtain the protection of the goddess for their granaries and seeds. Having laid down their offerings they withdrew and joined the spectators who were watching dances and games.

Fatty grew tired of serving as a grandstand: "Hey, you, climb down! Those sacrifices are always the same thing; come, let's have some fun and eat with the others."

Squares and roads were crowded with rejoicing people; beer and all the sweetmeats the Lord Menkh offered them were distributed everywhere.

Groups thronged around jugglers and acrobats; two men danced face to face, skilfully spinning their sticks; a monkey turned somersaults and played pranks with the audience.

Chick-Pea had never before seen such a festival. He succumbed to the easy-going gaiety and excitement of freed instincts; he danced with the dancers and laughed with those who laughed. While Fatty stuffed him-

---

[1] *Rennutet* is the goddess of harvest. Concerning her metaphysical principle and her important functions, see *Her-Bak Disciple*, Index: *Rennutet*.

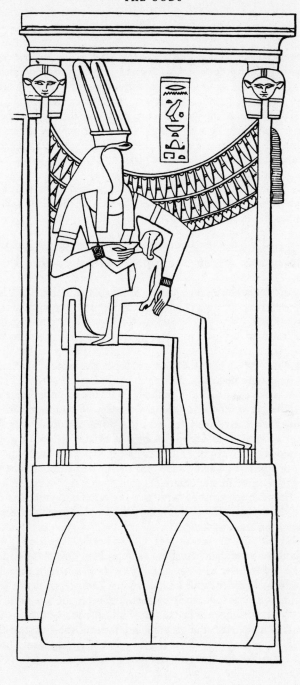

self with meat and cakes, Chick-Pea sat with the wine-bibbers and listened to the songs of the guitarists and storytellers.

On the way back, Chick-Pea walked in silence, dazzled by these new merrymakings. Fatty, swollen with food like a bladder-fish, dragged him as if in tow. A stone niche at the fringe of a field sheltered an enormous snake of granite. Chick-Pea went near, and looked at the remnants of food, at the plaited corn-ears and flower bunches. . . . Offerings, carousings, dances, songs, whirled around in a saraband in twirls of smoke: where was he? . . . He looked for his friend, but Fatty had already yielded himself to the whirl!

"Get up, Fatty! Come along. Let's go home!"

A snore was the answer. . . . And then Chick-Pea in turn was engulfed by that saraband, and sliding down at the foot of the niche fell heavily asleep, under the eyes of *Rennutet*.

Next morning, when the earth grew light, Chick-Pea's first glance rose to the stone image looming, impassively, over the withered sacrificial flowers.

"Here, *Rennutet* the snake; there, *Rennutet* the nurse. . . . Is this a whim of the priests or a story for little children? I like stories, but these images are dumb."

Chick-Pea hurried home to question his father. He met him near the stables:

"Who is this *Rennutet*, father? And what is the idea of making those offerings to a stone snake?"

"Since it is the custom," Sita replied, "why try to understand it?"

"But, father, if you don't understand it, why do you make offerings?"

And Sita answered: "Why should I not do as the others do? It is unwise to go against the orders given by the priests. I don't know much about these matters, but your mother's father was a lay priest attached to a temple. She might be able to tell you more. But a tiller of the soil has no need to know of these matters."

Chick-Pea was not satisfied with this answer. Following Sita's advice he went to his mother, Hemit, his heart full of amazement that she should never have told him anything.

He found her busy preparing beer. Chick-Pea held his tongue until she had finished her work, and set about helping her. This was nothing new to him: he knew how to make the barley swell through the night, to crush it, and to knead it with leaven. Hemit had prepared the dough at daybreak; now it was sufficiently swollen, the moment had come to bake it. Chick-Pea helped his mother to put it into the red-hot earthen vessel; he covered it again with the glowing lid and put the pot into the prepared sand. Then he watched for the moment when the vessel had to be taken out again, for the dough must remain raw inside.

When the fierce heat had sealed the crust he took the bread out without burning his fingers, and brought it to his mother. But Hemit was already working at something else: she was pounding loaves, which had been baked earlier, with a syrup-like juice and filtering them through the trellis of a basket. And when this preparation was finished she poured all this juice into a jar.

Suddenly Chick-Pea shouted: "That is not the kind of work you do every day. . . ."[1]

"I am making sweet beer with date juice, since today it is still the festival of *Rennutet*." With these words she took a few drops from the jar and sprinkled the floor.

"What are you doing, mother?"

"Libations for *Heqit*," she replied. "May *Rennutet* protect our granaries and make our house prosper." She squatted down and Chick-Pea sat down in front of her.

"You, Chick-Pea, you live like a monkey, ignorant of these matters. It is useful to know the gestures by which one can make the *Neters* favourable."

The boy moved nearer to his mother. A sudden warmth bathed his limbs like a sunbeam. . . . Was not this moment as if a dream took shape, as if an unknown world was unveiling itself?

Why had he not sought this before?

His eyes lit up, his heart opened. "Mother," he said, "tell me what you know about the *Neters*."

Hemit glanced at her son with surprise. "The *Neter*," she answered, "is the god who protects something. *Rennutet* is the Mistress of the harvests and the granaries; that is why we offer her the firstlings of the harvest and the fruits of the season."

"Are they those little brooms they make of barley-ears," cried Chick-Pea. "They are not so pretty as the plaited crescent they make of the last sheaf! Do you know other *Neters*? You've named *Heqit*: who is she?"

"*Heqit* is the *Neter* of the beer; *Khnum* is the *Neter* of marriage, just as *Thot* is the *Neter* of the scribes, and *Seshat* the *Neter* of writing."

"But what is the *Neter*? Tell me more."

"The *Neters* have statues which are carried in procession among the people on festival days; sometimes they utter oracles. They have priests, who are powerful. They are rich with gold, silver, and precious stones of all kinds."

"And you, mother, do you understand what a *Neter* is?"

"Have I not told you what I have been told? What more need you know?"

"If the *Neters* are powerful, why do they need statues?"

---

[1] For ordinary beer, the broken loaves were soaked in water, and then the preparation was fermented, brewed, and filtered.

Hemit looked at her son with stupefaction. . . . "That," she replied, "must be so that they can receive offerings. If I put a bowl of milk near my door, then the cobra will be well-disposed towards us. The priests say: 'Fear the gods and bring them presents, then they will not be unfavourable towards you.'"

And the boy, speaking to his own heart, muttered: "Are the gods perhaps as wicked as men? . . ."

He realised that he would get no further answer. Sadly he left his mother, for he felt a stranger in his house. For a long time he wandered about in the fields. And lo, when he came to the garden, he heard some chords of a harp and ran to look for the blind man.

The harper listened silently to his account of the festival, the father's words, and the mother's explanations. He gravely shook his head: "What is the matter, little man, what is the matter? A doubt has entered your heart; it is contracted by bitterness. Let not fear invade you: for fear is opposed to light."

"O Mesdjer, my mother has spoken to me only of the *fear* of the *Neters.*"

"I know, my child. That is how priests have power over men. But how many men are seeking the truth? How many are governed by love of equity, without fear of punishment?"

"Who then metes out the punishment? The priests or the *Neters?*"

"The *Neter* is *Nature's* law; the priests interpret it as they understand it; but has a man power to modify the Law? . . . Child, you are too young to judge; follow the voice of your heart: it will lead you towards greater truth!"

"O Mesdjer, tell me more! They say that the *Neter* descends into his statue; but where is that *Neter* when he is not inside his image?"

"What you call image, they call in the temple '*the form of the Neter*'. But now tell me: if the Sun did not warm the earth, could the palm-tree grow? Could the dates ripen?"

"No. It is the hot summer that reddens them."

"Right. But if you expose to the burning Sun the barleycorn which is to germinate or the egg which is to be hatched, what happens then? Will the barley sprout? Will the egg bring forth a chick?"

"No. They will die. The Sun will have burnt them to death."

"And yet, the creating Sun, the vivifying Sun, and this destroying Sun, are they not always one and the same Sun?"

"Yes, there is only one Sun!"

"There is certainly only one for us. But the Sages gave him different names according to his forms: when he begets the world, he is *Khepra* in

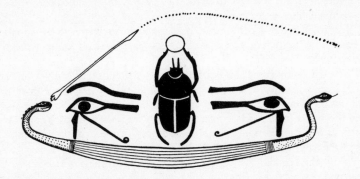

the shape of a scarabæus; as vivifying king he is *Râ*, but they put the shape of a viper beside him, whose venom can be fatal; and at the end of the day he is tired, like an old man, and his name becomes *Tum*. Do you understand the forms of the *Neter*?"

"Yes, Mesdjer, all that you tell me there, is alive. Why then do the priests make statues which are dead?"

"I'll tell you: if they had not carved *Rennutet* in the stone, would you have tried to know her?"

Chick-Pea listened to this with attention, then he took the blind man's hand between his own: "Well then, tell me what you know about *Rennutet*?"

The blind man answered: "That which makes the grains grow on top of the ear, that which nourishes the dates up there in the palm-tree, that is the secret of *Rennutet*. But you do not yet even know the secret of the one who gives birth: how can you understand the secret of the one who nourishes?"

Chick-Pea heaved a sigh which brought a smile to the harper's face; but the insatiable boy went on questioning:

"Is it long ago since people carved the first stone gods?"

"Listen to this: my father's father's father said to my father's father: 'No one remembers the name of the first man who carved the image of *Khnum*, the divine potter who modelled the egg of the universe. . . .' But a wiser man than I will later answer your questions, for the images of the gods have loftier purposes than to accumulate offerings.

"I will tell you the word which has been the treasure of my life: one day, when I still had my eyes, a Sage passed my way and said to me: 'If you want to know anything, ask Nature about it; the scarabæus will teach you the beginning of your history.'

"Well, I have followed this advice, and here is what I have learnt: *Khepra*, the sacred scarabæus,[1] has no female; to beget his progeny he fashions a ball made of cattle dung; in it his seed will gestate. And this ball he rolls from the east towards the west with his hind legs; thus he never turns his face away from the east.

"Just so does the World move, in an opposite direction to the apparent course of the stars; for one thing is the appearance and another the real movement.

"The scarabæus buries his ball for the exact duration of one Moon; and his progeny, hatched in the motherly ground, takes shape in the bosom of this dung. Then, without losing a day, he unearths the ball and throws it into the water, and when it opens in that water, then his progeny comes forth, as *Râ*, the morning, issues forth from *Nu* the primordial water of *Nut*,[2] the celestial *night*.

"Now this scarabæus beetle is black like the darkness which lies at the beginning of all things, and on his feet he has as many toes as the thirty days of the solar month."

"That's funny," Chick-Pea interrupted. "He counts the days on his toes . . . !"

"As you say it, thus it is true. Concerning his name, that means *becoming* and *transformation*."

Sitting on a tree-trunk with his finger in his mouth, the boy listened to the old man, and muttered: "Oh yes, I had seen it, but I did not know!"

And Mesdjer replied: "Know then, that you do not *know* yet!"

---

[1] See *Her-Bak Disciple*, Index: Scarabæus.

[2] *Nut* (French form *Nout*) is pronounced with a long *oo*, rhyming with route, loot (T.N.).

FLOOD

DESPONDENCY! Drought! Dearth!

Hapi has abandoned his earth. His sluggish, low waters uncover lagoons and sandy spits. Is it you, O *Hapi*, or is it perhaps the crocodile of *Seth* with its devouring breath, which contracts and withers all life on the thirsty earth? . . . Your spouse, beautiful and fertile in her swarthiness, has taken on the hue of the 'Evil One',[1] ruddy as he are the bald fields, ruddy are the scorched meadows, ruddy are the dusty trees whose leaves the south wind has withered.

Animals and men are dejected; they languish, waiting for you, O *Hapi*, as for their saviour. . . . They count how many days there may still be to wait: *Râ* will soon have reached the apex of his course. Prepare to awake, O *Hapi*! We are weary. . . . We are weary! Our tongue is dry in our mouth; our breath burns; our limbs fail us. Draw the north wind towards you in your caverns; may it rise and bring you back! Our strength ebbs away without you! We are weary! We are weary!

The great day draws near. The irrigation overseers supervise the cleaning out of channels and ditches by the riverside tenants.

"Have the stairways on the banks marked out again! Have the shovels and baskets ready!"

All able-bodied men descend in dense single files to the bottom of the channels, take up their load and reascend in order to unload the earth on the other side of the embankment.

"The toil is hard, the heat is great. We perish of drought! We are weary! We are weary!"

"Hurry now. It is *Hapi's* bed you are making ready, so hurry, for the hour is near."

The watchers at the Nilometer in Elephantina announce a slight rising of the level. The Nile is rising! The Nile is rising! Beasts and men shiver with greedy excitement. The cracked earth seems to widen its fissures even more, the better to suck in the divine waters. The Nile is rising. A fresh breeze from the north is its first foreboding. The Temple guardians announce to the chief scribes that the waters will arrive shortly. . . .

The Nile is rising! A greenish slime makes its low waters glutinous: that is the green Nile, the forerunner; it is the foul water of the early

---

[1] *Seth*, principal of burning, sterilising fire. For the rôle of this *Neter*, see *Her-Bak Disciple*, Index: *Seth*.

days![1] The Nile is rising . . . now the unhealthy verdure has gone. The
people rejoice, for the *Neter's* bounty has descended upon Egypt!

The Nile is rising! Isis has shed this divine tear which gives the flood
free course.

"She is coming, the water of the celestial life; she is coming, the water
of the terrestrial life. For you the sky is burning, for you the Earth is
shivering at the birth of the *Neter*! The two mountains open, the *Neter*
manifests himself, the *Neter* takes possession of his body."

The priests immolate black bulls and strew lotus flowers over the
waters.

The Nile is rising! It fills the channels and ditches, it soaks into the two
banks. . . . Men and animals revive; palms and leaves return to life.

The Nile is rising! The chief scribes pass on to the farmers the feverishly
awaited forecasts: "The floods will be very abundant; but with Amun's
protection no damage will be caused."

The Nile is rising! Now comes the red water; the blood-coloured Nile
rolls its heavy waves. The dates obey the signal: their weighty bunches
redden in the palm-trees.

The Nile is rising! His flood, swifter and swifter, rolls its heavy, slimy
waves; their whirling eddies around the landings of the banks are like
funnels of liquid mud.

The Nile is rising! . . . But all has been arranged so as to prevent the
flow from carrying off the black earth. Minute dykes made of mud re-
inforced with straw square the grounds off like a basket-trellis ready to be
filled with *Hapi's* gifts.

At the edges of fields, of the river and its channels, large reed-planta-
tions, millet-grass, or papyrus lift their high stalks and form a dense filter,
retaining the deposit of precious silt. Thus, little by little a demesne in-
creases, or a little island is built up.

The Nile is rising! . . . Its flood overflows and spreads over the banks;
the water soaks in. Ducks find as many puddles as they care to look for.
Rats walk on the high roads; scorpions and tarantulas emigrate towards
dry sandlands.

The Nile is rising! . . . Its waters invade the fields; the animals retreat before its advance. Hunted out from the straw-shelters, they retreat; the
small wild beasts pour back into the desert; the snakes draw nearer to man.

The Nile is rising! . . . Soon it will have submerged the valley. The sand
is its limit. Here and there, hillocks (*ia.t*)[2] emerge like long backbones
(*ia.t*), bristling with palm-trees, covered with houses and huts; here the
people are now dwelling, and here the animals take refuge.

The Nile is rising! . . . Innumerable birds fly downstream with it; the

---

[1] For four days the stench of the water is very great, and it lasts for about another
forty days. During this period the water is not drinkable and the fish are unfit for
human consumption.

[2] See *Her-Bak Disciple*, Index: *ia.t*.

cranes of Numidia dance for joy on the water-edge, for the reptiles and insects made homeless are food for them!

And still the Nile is rising . . . but now anguish appears on the faces of men. . . . Donkeys and cattle throng around the huts where the fodder reserves are piled up; water infiltrates into the houses; each village is now isolated; each hillock is a little island round which its inhabitants travel on rafts made of reed or papyrus.

Under the moonlight spreads a new world. The words 'our earth' have lost their meaning: a silver lake covers the valley, strewn with dark islands from which rise clusters of dark palms.

Greenish snakes slide down the slopes to drink from the water's edge; scorpions make merry in the pallid gleam. In the mudhouses and straw huts the heat has become humid and heavy; the sleep of the men is fraught with anxiety.

When they wake up their first thought is to measure the level. The islands are small . . . if the Nile rises any further, where shall they, compressed as they are, then take refuge to go on living?

"Oh, *Hapi!* Is it your will to destroy what you came to revive?" Men, women, children, everyone watches the water. . . .

And lo, at last the dawn brings them peace: *the Nile has stopped rising!*

"Hi, hi! Let us rejoice! The messengers from the temple have announced that the flood has found its level; half a day and the waters will begin to ebb!"

A long shout of joy swelled their breasts and everyone called blessings upon the One they had feared. The immense sheet of water received the homage of the human beings: with raised arms they shouted praise. They hailed *Hapi*, the 'benefactor', *Hapi*, who had deigned to refrain from becoming the 'destroyer'.

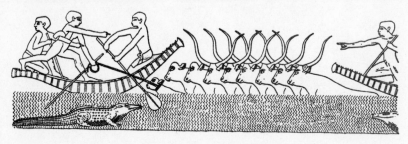

LIVESTOCK

THE time of 'slack' waters became a time of joy. The men repaired the
ploughs and checked the state of the granaries. The children, freed from
the oppressive fear, paddled on rafts towards fruitful fisheries. The immense lake was furrowed by frail skiffs and simple reed floats.

Chick-Pea was happy. He spent hours at the water-edge playing with
the ash-coloured Numidian cranes. Their fine tall legs with the black
feet were supple and skilled like dancers' legs. Their long beaks were
beautifully green, red, and black, like mottled stones. In the cool morning
and evening hours the cranes formed a circle or two opposed ranks and
danced, danced with the elegance of ballerinas! They jumped, capered,
turned about; they advanced, withdrew, saluted, stretched out, and leapt.

When the dance came to an end, Chick-Pea invented other movements.
The cranes observed him, imitated him and the game recommenced.

"Hullo, handsome dancer, you haven't seen *my* cranes yet!"

Turning about, Chick-Pea saw a raft coming towards the bank, skilfully handled by Fatty. "I've room for two: come along and have a look
at the birds I've caught with my net!"

What a pleasure it was to paddle on those waters as on an unknown sea.
The boys manœuvred noiselessly, they moved slowly and gently to keep
the craft balanced; they glided, turning and twisting amidst the little
islands, amidst ducks and waterfowl. They passed a house, almost sub-

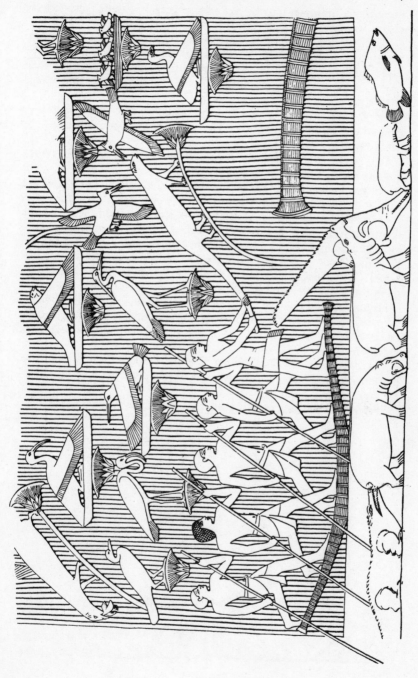

merged, and mimosas looking like tufts of grass . . . and a palm-tree: its crown was level with the water!

"Look right—let's avoid those animals!" Cows and oxen were swimming towards the dry land; the flood had caught them on the last little island it overran; from two canoes the cattle-herds were directing their beasts. In the leading boat a little calf was tied by a halter and wailed restlessly.

"Hey, look in front: look how that snake there is swimming! . . . And do you recognise my house? The landscape has changed a little! . . . Well, here we are. Draw the canoe in to land."

Fatty led his friend where some magnificent cranes received them without any signs of fear.

"Have a look at these, Chick-Pea! How do you like my catch? Haven't I got something fine into my net—just look, they're already tame."

Chick-Pea admired the birds. With a smile he acknowledged the courteous salute of a crane making its reverence, flapping its wings, jumping and dancing like a flirting courtesan. Other cranes came near and did the same. Their captivity did not seem to worry them. But Fatty intervened: "That's enough for today, you're going to tire them. I must fatten them for our Master, and it's dinner-time now. Let's get on with it!"

Having penned them in a corner, he started to cram them with some prepared meat-balls. Then he fed the geese and ducks; and when the beasts had had their fodder, Fatty chased them around to help their digestion.

Chick-Pea watched him without pleasure. Under a nearby palm-tree he noticed an old hunter who worked for the demesne, like his father. He sat down near him.

"Fatty is a smart boy," said the old man, "he breeds very fine livestock."

"Fatty doesn't breed his birds, he fattens them. That's a trade I don't hold with."

"Doesn't your father do the same?"

"My father crams geese for the Master and the sacrificial offerings. But it's cruel, and I never do it."

"Doesn't Nature do exactly the same? An ant will feed a plantlouse because it secretes a juice which the ant is greedy to get. Nature is never compassionate. An animal will eat another that is its natural prey, and will protect one that can be useful to it."

"That's selfish."

"It's the nature of a beast: each one obeys its instincts."

"And must man act like a beast?"

"Look at the boy over there, the one that fishes with a spoon-net. Have you never fished like that?"

"Of course I have. I've caught some gudgeon when the floods were over."

"And you have eaten your fish?"

"My sister cooked them and I ate them. They were good."

"And you have eaten again and again?"

"Yes, but I did not torture the fish."

"But you would also eat fish caught by your brother?"

"Yes."

"Well, then, don't be so conceited. You weren't so stupid last year, when you went hunting with me, to the wadis. We have had some fine days and fine nights together, and you weren't bored, were you? Admit it."

"That's true, I was happy. I saw so many curious beasts. But my pleasure was not in killing them—it was in observing their habits, their tricks. . . ."

"And would you have known those without hunting them?"

Chick-Pea remained pensive; the problem which Mesdjer had already touched upon[1] embarrassed him, and the hunter did not see it in the same light that he did. The boy sealed his heart, and allowed himself to be beguiled by the memories evoked.

As long as the moon shone, they relived the episodes of their adventures, the careful preparations to adapt themselves to the life-rhythm of the game, the study of its footprints and excrements; the pursuits, when eye and ear of man have to rival with those of the beast; the long hours of lying in wait, the moments of danger when the heart beats like a bell. . . .

But these narratives were told in low voices as if the memory were as shy as the hunted game. . . . And it is not meet to deviate from our path in order to listen to them at this hour. Perhaps there will be some other time for these 'wayside stories'.

[1] See Chapter IX, 'Fisherman'.

PROCESSION

"FATHER, when shall we get back to real work again?"
"After the procession festival."
"Mother, what are these new dresses for?"
"For the procession festival."
"And all those geese?"
"They are offerings for *Amun*, for the procession."
"The offerings are meant for the god, but who will eat the geese?"
"That's none of our business."
"Father, will you be going to the procession festival?"
"My Lord is dissatisfied if a man fails to show his zeal."
"And I? Can I see the procession?"
"For you, Chick-Pea, it is not necessary. The way is very long, and the ground is still soaking wet. But please yourself."
"And what *is* the procession all about?"

Such was the goal and such was the way; heavy for some and light for others; yearning towards the goal pricks the traveller like a harpoon and draws him onward. And the rhythm of song gives wings to the walkers' feet.

> *A tavern-tent will be set up,*
> *It will open towards the South.*
> *A tavern-tent will be set up,*
> *It will open towards the North,*
> *A tavern-tent will be set up,*

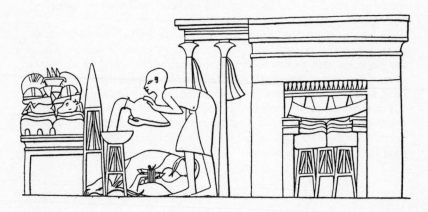

> *It will open towards the South.*
> *A tavern-tent will be set up . . .*

"Hey, Chick-Pea, are you deaf?"

> *It will open towards the North.*
> *A tavern-tent will be set up,*
> *It will open towards the South.*

"Chick-Pea, you're mad! To walk four hours without stopping!"

> *A tavern-tent will be set up,*
> *It will open towards the North.*
> *Drink, sailors of Pharaoh!*

"Oh, these lucky sailors! . . . Never shall I get to that tavern; my tongue is dry, my belly empty . . . and my feet drag in the mud! For my part, I'm going to stop here and eat my onions."

"You can eat your onions, Fatty, but I want to see the procession."

"You'll see it soon enough, your procession. If you don't see it on the way out, you'll see it on its way back; but stop now: I am as good as dead."

But Chick-Pea did not stop, he even started to run. He did not walk, he flew. He replied without turning his head: "Well, after all it was you who chose this long way!"

"But it is the shorter way! To see the boats one has to cut back towards the river between the two big temples."

"If you don't hurry, we'll be late; but whatever you do, *I* want to see the procession."

"Oh you head of a wild ass! . . ."

> *A tavern-tent will be set up,*
> *It will open towards the South.*
> *A tavern-tent will be set up,*
> *It will open towards the North.*
> *A tavern-tent will be set up . . .*

"Tell me, Fatty, does *Amun* travel towards the South?"

> *A tavern-tent will be set up . . .*

"The river sparkles towards the North"

> *Drink, sailors of Pharaoh!*

"Come along, I want to see the procession."

> *It will open towards the South . . .*

"I want to see the procession."

    A tavern-tent . . . a tavern-tent . . .

"I want to see the procession."

    A tavern-tent . . . [1]

The roars of joy of a delirious crowd roused the sleep-walkers out of their hallucinations.

Kneeling beside a jar, Fatty drank in draughts of the sweet beer. Chick-Pea had climbed upon a tree and became speechless with surprise: never before, even in dream, had he seen a fleet like this.

A wonderful galley glided past, as if framed by the flight of reflecting oars: the state barge of the King! Purple-stained carved wood glittering with precious ornaments, spread with brightly coloured matting. . . . The slender hull was gliding majestically, answering to the regular rhythm of the sixty oarsmen. All mouths opened to shout . . . and then remained silent, overawed. All eyes were fixed upon the King, L.H.S., Pharaoh himself, standing in the poop of his vessel.

"He is tireless, is Pharaoh, as he holds the steering-rudder, captain of his team of sixty men! And certainly, His Majesty's vigour is fine to behold, as he tows his Father *Amun* towards his Apet of the South. . . . For a powerful effort is needed to haul upstream the floating temple of the King of gods!"

Oh prodigy! Oh marvel blinding the eyes with its splendour, lifting all hearts with fervour! "*Amun! . . .* yah *Amun!*"

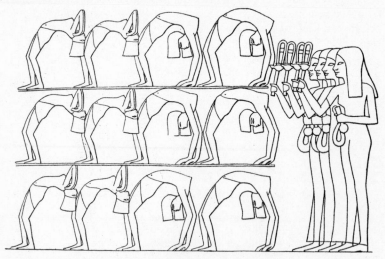

[1] For French text of this song, see page 296.

It was like an explosion of gold and silver! Everything was gold and
silver in Userhat;[1] every part of the hull shone with gold, *Amun's*
sanctuary was of gold, the masts of pine, wrought with gold, rose in
front of it, separated by two obelisks. On a high golden perch throned a
great crowned golden falcon. The heads of *Amun's* rams displayed on
prow and stern were of gold, crowned with the *atef* and the golden
uræus-snakes, and made *mu*,[2] the cloth of liquid silver, sparkle like a sunrise in the sky.

"Yah *Amun!* . . . Yah *Amun!*"

The straining oarsmen, proud of their office, grew ever more
excited under the religious chanting, the music, and the cries of the
crowd.

"*Amun!* . . . Yah *Amun!*"

Chick-Pea was dazzled. The escorts of the vessels marched past him on
the bank, under his very eyes. . . . A priest chanted a hymn of triumph;
soldiers marched proudly, armed with lances and halberds; plumed
horses richly harnessed pulled the two empty chariots of the Pharaoh;
negroes danced and played the tambourine. Beautiful girls played sistra
and menates. . . .

And then came the ensign-bearers, and the players of guitars and
castanets, which gave the procession its rhythm, while clapping priests
beat time for the steps.

The crowd was panting with enthusiasm: "Yah *Amun!* . . . Yah
Amun!" It was vibrating with the music, dancing with the dancers . . .
the people worshipped, prostrated themselves, shouted with joy. . . . And
when the last priest had passed, they lured the sailors to sing again, by

---

[1] *Userhat* is the name of *Amun's* ship.   [2] *mu*, water.

breaking with full voice into the song of hope for revelry, for the joy of
the unleashed people:

> *A tavern-tent will be set up*
> *It will open towards the South.*
> *A tavern-tent will be set up,*
> *It will open towards the North.*
> *Drink, sailors of Pharaoh,*
> *Sailors of Amun's beloved, the darling of gods!*

PROPHECY

THE procession of barques had vanished long ago; the spectators had scattered, some towards the temple, others to their homes.

Sitting on a knoll near the roadside, Chick-Pea was dreaming while his eye went out over the river, which was still far broader than its normal bed.

"So my disciple has seen his fill of the fine festival?"

The boy started at the sound of the voice; a hand was laid on his head, and his 'big friend' from the Temple stood by him, accompanied by a priest unknown to Chick-Pea.

Overwhelmed by emotion, the boy fell on his knees and his hands clasped the garment of the Sage, who sat down near him and smiled. "Have you grown dumb? I hardly recognise you."

"No, I am . . . I am so happy!"

The man scrutinised the boy's face: "Well, what do you make of all you have just seen?"

"I don't really know. It's like a dream. . . . But where do all these wonderful things come from, these gilded ships and those beautiful costumes? All those men who are perhaps Kings . . . or like gods . . . they walk and talk like men: I don't understand it. Where were they before? And where do they go when it's over? . . ."

The Sage looked smilingly at the priest; then he caressed the boy's forehead.

"You ask many questions at the same time! Yet, at the bottom of your heart only one question stirs you; ask that."

Chick-Pea held the bright glance; then after a moment he said: "Is all this real?"

The man nodded with satisfaction. "Right, you have told me what troubled you. Now I shall answer, listen well: concerning the King, one alone is for you *the King*.

"As to the personages and the wonders of the procession: all comes from the Temple and all returns to it. But you do not yet know what 'the Temple' is.

"As to your question 'is it real?' it is dear to my heart; but answer me first: since we parted, what have you learnt?"

"I have harvested, I have cut the last sheaf, and I know that the soul of the corn sleeps until the moment when it awakes in the earth. I have seen the flax rot, the flax which gives the fine white tissues.

"I have led the cattle into the fields to dung the ground; I know that the

Sun can mature the plants and that it can scorch them. I have seen the stork go away towards the north where it is cold!"

The priest impatiently interrupted the boy's little speech. "Master, allow me to refresh your memory: you are expected at the temple."

"The temple can wait. Go on, little man, what else have you learnt?"

"I have learnt that the plants and animals attract and repel one another, just like human beings. But what I do not know is why the storks travel away together, all at the same moment, without ever making a mistake! How can that be? And the cranes do the same thing at a different time, how do they do it? Who teaches them what they are to do?"

"Nature—the *Neters* whose images you have been shown today. We shall answer your other questions at a later time. Today I shall resolve the one question: 'Is it real?' Child, you are on the best and shortest road towards the knowledge of truth: Nature. Go on asking her, and do not allow the arguments of men to dishearten you. And when the *Neters* of the birds and plants shall have become your friends and shall have yielded up to you their secrets, *which they reveal only to children*, then you will be able to lift your eyes up to their images; but at that time *beware of forgetting as a grown man what they have taught you when you were a child.*"

He rose. Chick-Pea, saddened, wanted to hold him back.

"Be confident, boy, and continue! Have not the *Neters* led me to cross your path again?"

Chick-Pea looked after him, as he went away in the golden halo of the sunset, like one who sees, waking up, the image of a beloved dream blur and vanish. Still, on this evening he felt that the dream was taking physical shape; he felt the bond strengthening with one who was already more than a mere passing acquaintance, and of whom one might say that his 'presence' lingered although he was now distant.

On his way, the Sage answered the priest's astonished questions. "You do not understand what interest I can possibly take in the chatter of this boy? Oh Pashedu, you who are the head of the schools, you must learn to discern the gold nugget among the common pebbles!"

The master stopped at the water-edge and allowed the imperial purple of the moment to envelop and bathe him in silence. The sky, flooded with red gold, vibrated with light; and now this gold burst into impalpable dust, sun-dust, radiant dust; it flowed all over the mountain, and the mountain, conquered, lost itself in it; it transmuted even filth into light. The whole Earth was dissolved in this glory, and all shapes of the world resolved themselves in the universal matter: it was the blending into the Origin in which the farthest future is contained. . . . And the heart of the Sage perceived in it a nameless, imageless certainty: *the Certainty*.

"He will become great! . . . Oh Pashedu, consider mankind, how the phenomena of life and Nature are under the very eyes of them all; but they, in their puny selfishness, see only the few things of which they can make use. Very rare are those who seek the Cause for its own sake; very rare those who allow themselves to be moved by those phenomena of periodicity, attraction and repulsion which are the manifestations of the *Neters*. How many, do you think, are there of those who seek with their heart to divine the mystery which makes the waters rise to the sky and makes them descend again through Hapi to our Earth? . . . How many are those who, without arrogance, search for the power that moves and the law that is behind all this?"

"O Master, your words are just, but tell me this, what are your thoughts about this boy?"

The master contemplated in silence the Sun which descended upon the horizon, and said:

"For how many millennia has *Râ*, our master, been descending and re-descending into this mountain? How many times has he tinged with purple our marshes after the great floods? How many dead will he visit in the valley of Amenti? And how many of these has he raised up? Can these things be known to you, my friend? . . .

"If they cannot, then you must learn to distinguish the precious flower which sometimes floats on the marshland. . . . This child is such a rare being, whose unfolding has to be guided lovingly; his heart is generous and ignorant of greed; his curiosity is not idle, no vanity pollutes his quest; no fear inhibits him; that is why he will rise to the highest summits. Do not despise this prophecy; keep it in your heart, for he is blessed indeed who can help with this unfolding of an heir to Wisdom."

The priest was moved at hearing these words; he kissed the garment of the man who thus prophesied, for he knew that his words were not spoken idly. And he said: "Was it this, O Master, that the eye of your heart has been contemplating?"

And the inspired one answered: "No. For what I saw is beyond description. But I shall explain to you what you must know. From now on we must watch this child: his name is Chick-Pea, son of Sita, one of the chief farmers of Menkh; observe his life every day without letting him know of it, and report to me whatever may befall him."

And Pashedu replied: "Oh Master! By *Amun* and upon my life, I shall do for the child according to your will!"

THE GARDEN

"How beautiful is Menkh's garden! No good thing in the world but something of it is offered here: colours to rejoice the eye, bird songs to delight the ear, and perfumes for the nostrils. There is a large, a very large pool: what joy it would be to plunge into it among the frogs and in the middle of those lovely blue lotus flowers . . . if the Master were not there to see. But there he is, and the joy in my heart even grows. The Master is strong and well, his forehead touches the leaves of the vine-pergola under which he is seated.

"How good it is to feel the coolness when work is finished. The Sun, before going to rest, is pouring gold into the palm-trees. The birds, seeking a perch for the night, chirrup furiously, nimbly sparring for the possession of a branch.

"Why cannot I be the one who looks after this garden? He must be a good gardener, the trees are so well spaced out. I can count them on my fingers:

"One row of carob-trees: five carob-trees.

"One row of sycamores: five sycamores.

"Six doum-nut palm-trees, six date palm-trees, two fig-trees, and as many on the other side. And all of them will be heavy with fruit when their time comes!

"Wish I were my Master's monkey! He climbs up the trees and has only to stretch out his hand to taste of all these good things: now a fig, now a carob-pod.... Is the monkey luckier than Chick-Pea? Fatty would say 'Of course! He is a king: he can eat whatever he likes!' All his friends and all my comrades would think like that, all alike. If the neighbour left his nuts unguarded, there is not one of them that would not seize both hands full. In the quail season they cram their bellies so that they swell like water-skins. They are happy like the monkey. . . . And I, Chick-Pea, would I then be a monkey?

"There, I've got it: *I can leave the fig alone*, even though I should like to eat it; and that is what the monkey cannot do."

Chick-Pea might have gone on dreaming until nightfall . . . but the harp awakened him.

And behold, Menkh said to the blind man: "O Mesdjer, you are a master of your art, but I wish your song to be measured against that guitarist's: one song is not like another, one talent differs from another talent; I wish that you two should vie in virtuosity for the greater pleasure of my ears. Let then the musician be brought here."

And Menkh enjoyed the peace of this hour and took pleasure in playing with his pet monkey.

Such was the occasion chosen by destiny for introducing Chick-Pea to his Lord Menkh, the Master of Craftsmen.

Despite the pursuing watchmen, a furious scribe had penetrated into the garden; he was pale with rage; he peered searchingly into the shrubberies, as he walked up towards the Master, who showed an angry face. He threw himself at his feet. Menkh said:

"Am I not here to take my rest? Who has permitted you to disturb me?"

"O noble Master," answered the scribe, "the one I am in search of insults your justice!"

"What has he done?"

The scribe replied: "A man was being flogged because he had failed to pay the tithe. The criminal who is hiding in your garden rebelled against this act of justice and interfered: he snatched the stick and raised it against the arm which had stricken, and then fled to escape my wrath!"

"Do you know that man?" asked the Master.

"Chick-Pea," said the scribe, "that's his name."

"This is not actually my hour of justice; so let us settle this matter straightaway. Who is this Chick-Pea?"

A voice which tried hard to sound powerful said: "It is me."

Menkh looked at the youngster who was standing before him and remained dumbfounded: he found no fear in this face, no confusion in his

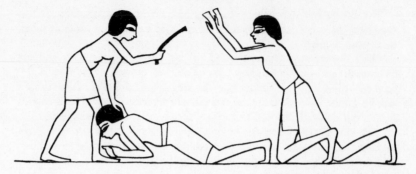

eyes. The scribe threw himself upon the boy with raised truncheon, shouting: "Who dares to remain standing so insolently upright? Kiss the ground before your Lord!"

Menkh raised his hand: "Leave him alone!"

Then Chick-Pea spoke and said: "O my Master, the man whom they were whipping could not pay the tithe, the storm had ravaged his harvest."

"What do you know about it?" asked Menkh. "Tell me all you know."

Now while the boy was explaining himself, the monkey had been hopping nearer and nearer; he skipped around the scribe and suddenly got hold of his truncheon and carried it off, hurrying away with long leaps to hide behind the sycamore. The scribe pursued him, and his fury knew no bounds! Thinking that no one could see him, he struck a mighty blow at the legs of the monkey, which hoisted itself up the tree with piercing shrieks.

His eyes half-closed, the Lord observed the scribe, the monkey, and the boy in silence.

And Chick-Pea grew worried; he kissed the Master's knee and implored him: "Listen, O wise Master, and have pity on that man who has lost his corn. Has then a scribe power to do injustice in your name? That scribe is a fox: do you want to soil your heart by lending him your ear? If you are a father to us, he is a ferocious crocodile. He can beat me for what I am telling you . . . but if you take up our defence, there will be loaves in the jars and great joy in our hearts."

The Master of Craftsmen listened and appraised the youth. He remained silent for a moment; then he spoke.

"Are you perhaps a tale-bearer? There are two things one must know: to weigh one's words well, and to sound the heart of one's listener. What is your answer to this, orator?"

Chick-Pea looked downwards and said: "I shan't say anything more than: 'I have spoken.'"

Menkh took the boy by the hand and stood him upright at his side; then he called to the scribe who was still standing at the foot of the sycamore: "You, stay where you are and make your report—and hurry!"

The scribe, well content, bowed and took a scroll from his belt and before reading it gave a complicated explanation. But while Menkh lent an attentive ear, his eyes followed the movements of the monkey, which, up in the tree, was searching for a strategic position on the branch hanging over the scribe. Menkh saw it and said: "O diligent scribe, give an account of that day with all details, read everything, and do not pause!"

Swelled with importance, the official unfurled the scroll and proceeded to read, when the monkey, quietly, like a dog-faced baboon on a water-clock, sprayed the reader with all that Nature had given him. . . . The scribe was asphyxiated and stopped reading; but the Master's voice was stern: "Who gave you permission to pause? Did I not tell you to hurry?"

Chick-Pea was choking with laughter under his grave mien. Oh, to be sure, life had beautiful moments! But how much easier it was to defend oneself when wronged than to keep silent in the moment of joy.

The reading was finished. Menkh looked at the man with the dripping shameful face; then he said: "You may go; I shall see justice done. As to the criminal, he may stay and introduce the singers."

The guitarist stepped forward and kissed the ground before his Lord. And Menkh said:

"Each of you is to sing of Love, whatever he conceives is the most beautiful. The guitarist will sing first and Mesdjer will follow, and each may answer the other as he pleases."[1]

The musician sat down opposite the blind man, took his guitar and began to sing:

> Let her come to the lotus-pond,
> My beautiful loved one,
> In her transparent shift
> Of fine linen.
> Let her bathe herself near me
> Among the flowers,
> So that I may behold her
> As her limbs emerge from the water.

The voice of the blind man answered across the chords of the harp:[2]

> I have heard this song before
> From other lips!
> It is true that love is the same,
> Always and everywhere.

[1] The guitarist is plagiarising an Egyptian love song which he has arbitrarily altered. For French text of this song, see pages 297–8.
[2] The harpist' answers are in text type.

H.B.—G

No, from the beginning of the Earth
No one has ever known
A love such as my love
For her beauty.

Poor little men on earth,
What a pity!

I shall sing my song
In spite of your presumptuous sarcasm!
I shall speak of the love of my beautiful lady
In spite of fools,
Of the envious, of the winds, of the lightning.
In spite of the gods!

Have pity on us, oh hurry,
Better to face the danger itself
Than the threat of it.

When I kiss her, her passion bursts into flame,
She intoxicates me!
And I am a happy man,
Having yet drunk neither beer nor sweet wine.

Excepting the sweet wine,
Another has said this before you.
Find something stronger.

When I see her, I come to life;
When she opens her eye my limbs grow younger,
Away from her my strength withers,
So that I no longer recognise my own body.

Hey! Handsome singer, if you must plagiarise,
Let the copy at least
Improve on the original.

No need is there for another's song,
And I will say my own words.
Never shall anyone have heard
Such a song of love:
When she bathes her beautiful body,
The colour of her limbs
Makes the lotus seem pale;
Nor does any fish disport itself with such grace
As her arm when it beats
Like the wing of a bird.

Oh! Choose for your loved one
Scale or feather . . .
Love is not so exacting!

Menkh roared with laughter, but the singer was by no means put out.

Who has not seen my beloved,
Knows not the moon in her splendour.
Her light burns my eyes
And the heat of her embrace
Is like glowing coals to my heart.

A burning moon, a blazing moon!
What an unexpected cataclysm!

May the account of her beauties
Never haunt you and tempt you
To steal her from me!
No torture too cruel
For your chastisement!
When she is far from me,
No breath is left in my nostrils,
Nor any remedy for my limbs' tremor.
And she, my beloved, does not want
Intoxication other than my ardour,
No other bond than my loving arms.

Menkh raised his hand towards the guitarist. "Your loving arms may now end their music. It is enough. Be without fear. We are not going to run the risk of being tortured.

"But I want to hear Mesdjer's song so as to calm our panic-stricken senses; you, take your well-earned rest."

A refreshing breeze shivered in the crowns of the trees; the night rose under the glowing sky. The arpeggios of the harpist preluded his song:

The young lover's love-song
Is fever of waiting and sighs,
Desire of embrace,
Possession's triumph:
Communion of bodies, he *and* she.

The love song of old age
Evokes memories and yearning,
Impotence and disenchantment.

But I sing of Love
Without lies or allurement,
Which knows in each season
Passion and Mastery,
Love, appeal and answer
All in itself;
The Love which does not split in twain.
O Nature, everywhere you divide!
Your love is conflict and death.

I sing of the other Love,
Which seeks neither him nor her,
Which gives without demanding
Any return.

Thus He owns within him
His Universe,
She no longer separates:
She is within Him; his Universe
Is filled with Her!

And like a Sun
That feeds on his own warmth,
Thus He radiates beyond the object,
And his own substance
Becomes light and passion.[1]

Menkh had been waiting until the last harmonies on the harp had died down. Then he challenged the guitarist: "Cannot you find any reply to this song?"

The man spat his contempt: "Maunderings of an old impotent!"

Menkh smiled: "That's what the scorpion said to the sacred scarabæus. Go, let them give you your beer; that is a suitable reward. And Mesdjer, you stay here with me."

---

[1] For French text of this song, see page 299

XVII

SEED-TIME

AFTER many days had passed, there was a big stir among the farmers of the demesne, and each one was busy checking the ploughs for the work of sowing. And Sita said to Chick-Pea:

"Make haste, and weigh the seed, for the waters are falling and the earth begins to reappear; tomorrow it will be as soft as we can wish, and we shall start sowing at dawn."

And Chick-Pea said: "What about getting the oxen-team ready?"

"That will surely not be necessary, for this mud is very soft, the trampling of the herd should be sufficient to drive the seed into the ground. But do not fret about that; when the ground dries, you will again have plenty of opportunity to try your strength at breaking the clods by plough or hoe. Then we shall see how much of a man you are!"

"But what about our field, father, your field, the one you have been given as reward—what will you do with that?"

"As soon as the waters have left it, we shall sow it, and make a fine pasture of it for our donkey: by grazing there he'll enrich the ground with his dung. After that I'll give the field back to the plough and give it the best seeds in our granary . . . and we'll have the finest barley-field in the Two-Lands!"

Chick-Pea liked this plan, for to him all these things were new; he turned a few somersaults in their honour and then went to carry out his father's orders.

And when the day came on which the banks of the river emerged from the water, Sita went out at dawn with Chick-Pea to have a look at his field. There he met his neighbour Sabu and Sabu's son, Penu, who were measuring what the water had left of their ground, and soon the two neighbours were in the midst of an argument, for the flood had removed the boundary marks and displaced the banks, thus altering the boundaries of the fields.

They argued for a long while without being able to settle the matter, and had already begun to raise their voices higher than was necessary, when Chick-Pea said: "I think I have seen a scribe whose office it is to measure the fields with a cord?"

At this Sita calmed his anger and said to Sabu: "All that you're saying makes no sense to me. Let us advise the Cadastral Survey that the inundation has shifted our boundary marks, and call upon them to re-establish them in all fairness."

The field-provost received orders to settle this matter in accordance with the Lord High Seneschal's[1] regulations. He summoned Chick-Pea's and Penu's fathers before him, so that he might hear their pleas before the Acts of Rights of Ownership were revised. Then the provost ordained that the land-surveyor in charge of the calculations concerning shiftings of boundary marks was to be called in the next day, to be accompanied by the appointed blind man, whose intuition was to decide in case of uncertainty. And lo, on the way back, Chick-Pea overheard Sabu secretly saying to his son: "Go tomorrow and tell the blind man that there will be a stone bottle of wine and a jar of sweet beer for him after he has given evidence."

But in his innocence Chick-Pea did not understand the import of the words and so he did not repeat them to his father.

Next morning the two neighbours met in the field, awaiting the arrival of the land-surveyor with the blind man. The land-surveyor laid out the coils of rope with the help of his assistants and began his research. This was long and tricky work, for the bank was badly displaced, and all traces of landmarks were obliterated; the scribes were busy taking notes of the arguments proffered by the contestants, but still they could not settle the conflict.

Penu seemed to take no interest in the whole affair, but he displayed a filial solicitude for the blind man who was sitting by himself, waiting for the moment when he would be called upon to give his evidence.

After lengthy calculations the Chief of the Office decided at last that they would have to leave the settlement of the boundaries to the blind

---

[1] See footnote, Chapter XVIII, 'Judgment', page 95.

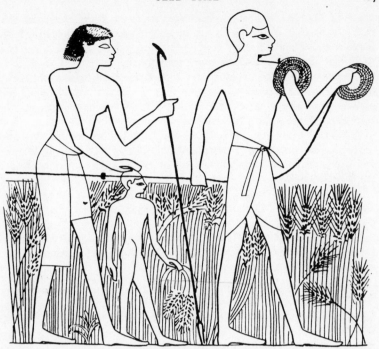

man's instinct. So Penu led the old man to the edge of the field and left him there alone to go silently to work.

And when his groping stick had come to a decision about the boundary between the two fields, Sabu and Penu protested that they were not satisfied with his decision, and Chick-Pea's father's face was dark, but he did not dare to object against the officials of his Master. So he returned home, saying to his son:

"Son, learn that it is no good complaining unless one can bring proof. Let us waste no time: tomorrow we shall sow the field; we shan't even wait for the Seneschal to put his seal to the verdict. Later we shall decide what course to take, according to the meadow's yield."

And it was done as Sita had said.

The grass grew fast in the fertile mud; the black ground was soon covered by fat pasture, as green as malachite. Now Sita examined his property again, and having compared it with his neighbour's, was satisfied that it had been considerably reduced to Sabu's profit. He gathered his children and said:

"The partition has been unfair, and our field has been very badly curtailed. But before I appeal to the Seneschal I want to produce clear evidence: now before the floods our ass grazed a tenth of the meadow in ten days; we shall see how long it will take him to crop it at its present size; that will be some evidence for my appeal. I shall have to go with Fine-Speaker to survey the cattle census, but you, Chick-Pea, will live in a straw hut and watch how the experiment goes."

After this speech, Sita went with Chick-Pea in the hot hour of the day to call on Sabu in his house, and told him of his plan. Sabu laughed and replied: "Oh Sita, what will the Seneschal say if you have an ass to give counter-evidence against his scribes?"

But Penu, who seemed to be dozing, slightly opened his eyes and drawled: "Let him do as he pleases, father. The scribes were not wrong; and I am sure the ass won't be able to graze the tenth part of that large meadow in ten days!"

"Well, Sita," said Sabu, "think well over what you are going to do!" And Sita replied: "My mind is made up; I am not going back on my decision."

"If such is your wish," said Penu's father, "to make yourself a laughing-stock for the Seneschal's tribunal, do so. But please tell Penu when you are starting, so that he can count the days as well, for our side."

Next dawn Chick-Pea went to the field, accompanied by his donkey which was carrying the reed matting for the straw hut, and started to build his shelter. When the Sun appeared on the horizon, he called Penu who was working in the other field and said: "Look, I'm letting the ass into the meadow now: this will be the first day."

Each of them was busy putting up his straw hut and, as they helped each other, the work was soon done. With Penu was a servant called Kiku, who kept an eye on the field while his master was absent.

Towards the middle of the day, Chick-Pea went to look how much the ass had eaten and he laughed: "Hey, comrade, at this rate the meadow won't give you so many days of pasture!" Then he felt drowsy, for the heat was too heavy. But his sleep was uneasy; he suddenly awoke, and saw Penu's servant Kiku giving the animal a brew to drink which looked something like carob-juice. He was surprised, but instinctively he kept his lips sealed and remained lying as if asleep. After an hour or so the ass began to bray and showed signs of such pain that Chick-Pea was tormented by great anxiety. He called Penu:

"Could you perhaps do something to cure my donkey? If you can't help me I shall have to see the animal physician: he is bound to know what is causing these pains."

Penu felt uneasy; he sent Kiku to fetch certain remedies, and then got busy looking after the poor beast. When the ass seemed somewhat calmer, Penu mocked Chick-Pea: "No doubt you have forced him to eat more than he is used to; henceforth he will be less voracious, don't you worry."

For the first time in his life Chick-Pea knew the meaning of suffering. Crouched in his straw hut, fists under his chin, he meditated in the clutch of unbearable horror . . . so then he had seen *Evil* in action . . . the hope of a little profit could turn a man into a criminal!

"Who hurts my ass, hurts me, since I love him. And it means robbing my father and the demesne . . . and all that for a scrap of ground! Penu was badly afraid we might find him out, but had no thought of repenting, and as if it were not enough, he lied and accused me! . . . Is there no shame in his heart?"

Chick-Pea made great efforts not to yield to his grief: he choked down a sob and bit his fists so as not to cry out loud in his distress:

"And I am too small and not clever enough to fight the man, not even Penu: I shouldn't have the courage to do the things he does! . . . Who will defend me against him?"

He had shed no tears and his wrath had calmed down; but great confusion remained where the veil had been torn: he knew now that man could be capable of doing infamous deeds in order to get what he coveted! Until now Chick-Pea had never known such wickedness.

He felt helpless and inclined to give up the struggle. But his father had gone away and had made him responsible in his absence. . . . What was he to do? He was unfamiliar with cunning: never would he succeed in foiling the wiles of that 'rat' Penu.[1]

Seen from this angle the situation looked somewhat less tragic than the day before (after all, a child cannot stand tragedy for long). He made a great effort to understand Penu. . . . And suddenly the idea of a game without malice occurred to him and prevailed upon him: for a very long time he thought his plan over and let it mature, weighing up its consequences and the great risks involved. "Obviously this Penu fellow didn't intend the ass to die, and now even less: he'd be afraid. . . . However, Chick-Pea, arm yourself with courage, and see it through! But now let's sleep."

When the dawn of the second day awakened him, Chick-Pea rose, alert and steeled with resolution. He took his donkey, called Penu and said: "I'm going to fetch some bundles of reeds to make a raft to while away some of these long days. I'll be back presently."

"Do as you please!" said Penu.

When Chick-Pea returned, he unloaded his ass and set him to graze in the meadow. But he soon saw him turn away from the grass with disgust. He ran over the field and found the reason for the repugnance: pig-excrements had been strewn all over the grass. Chick-Pea said nothing, but observed. By noon the ass had eaten no more than a few tufts of grass from the border of the meadow. His master, moved by pity, secretly gave him a handful of barley. But after his nap he found the donkey in a rage, kicking out with great vehemence, and in full flight from the

---

[1] *Penu* is the Egyptian word for 'rat'.

neighbouring meadow: the reason for his rage was a group of pigs. Chick-Pea called Penu:

"Your hogs must have come over into my meadow while you were having your nap. Send your servant to take their droppings away."

This was done, and filled the second day.

On the morning of the third day, rich dew had fallen and was glistening in the grass. Chick-Pea waited for it to dry before bringing his ass to the meadow. Once there, the beast grazed eagerly. . . . But suddenly he stopped and started braying, cutting capers towards the boundary between the fields. The object of his excitement was a she-ass, guarded by Penu. To be sure, on this day, the gallant animal did not think much about food.

The fourth day was a day of wrath, for this time the she-ass was accompanied by another male, and there arose such a tumult of jealousy that Chick-Pea had to tie up his donkey in his straw hut under the very eyes of his mocking neighbours. And that evening Penu came over to pay a call and said: "Your field is far greater than your father said: it would take much longer to crop it than he thought." And seeing Chick-Pea's stupid expression he laughed and added: "Of course, you could always help to graze it, and then there would be two of you."

And the fifth day came. The donkey started grazing with good appetite; but while Chick-Pea seemed to be asleep in the straw hut, Penu stealthily approached and gave the animal a stone bottle with some liquid which the beast drank avidly. Chick-Pea saw everything but concealed his apprehension under a snore. . . . But after an hour of uncertainty he was reassured: the donkey, intoxicated and weary after having gambolled about like a fool, had lain down and was fast asleep.

At the dawn of the sixth day, Chick-Pea caressed his ass with pity: "Poor friend! What new adventure will be yours today?" But what did it matter? Firmly resolved to keep to his instructions, he resumed his work in the shelter of his hut.

The adventure came in the shape of a pot of honey, which Kiku smeared all over the animal's skin, while Penu admired the raft Chick-Pea was making. Chick-Pea wanted to be faithful to his decision: to carry through his programme he had to remain blind and deaf . . . and he certainly suffered more than his donkey when he saw the greedy flies making its life a misery. And before the day was over he could resist his pity no longer, but went up to the ass and loudly complained: "O you clumsy dolt, I can see why you are angry; what kind of filth have you been rolling in?" And he took him to the water-edge and washed him.

This night Chick-Pea counted on his fingers to be sure to remember every trick of Penu's of the first six days. "Four days remain; what more can he think out? And what would my enemy do if he thought I was sick and without consciousness? He would not need to resort to quite so much wickedness. . . ."

So on the dawn of the seventh day, Chick-Pea groaned on his mat as one in great pain. Penu, not seeing him come out into the field, came over to visit him, and said: "Stay here and don't move; I'll bring you fresh water."

At evening, the sick boy seemed to have recovered and went to have a look at his field. "Why has so little grass been eaten?" He searched for the donkey and understood . . . the animal was trying desperately to rid himself of a coat of white paint which covered his nose and hooves. The boy could not help laughing. Today the idea was at least funny! He called Penu:

"Have a look at this! Where do you think can this fool have besmeared himself like this?"

Penu pointed at a pot lying in the grass: "So it was your ass who knocked my paint over."

And Chick-Pea replied in all seriousness: "Since my ass has done it, I'll replace your paint."

Penu regarded him with pity.

On the eighth morning, Chick-Pea showed himself very busy with his raft: his neighbour came running over to inquire after Chick-Pea's health, and so he asked him in a very friendly way whether he could count on his help to finish this task.

"Surely," said Penu, "I'll come as soon as I have fetched my provisions."

But Chick-Pea observed him as he returned. Hidden in the straw hut he saw him caress the animal while offering him yet another potion to drink. "Will he make him drunk again?" Chick-Pea wondered.

No, the donkey was not drunk, but so thoroughly purged that he had no further thought for food. And when at sunset he gave the poor beast some exercise, he comforted him, saying: "Take comfort, comrade, the end of the ordeal is near."

It was the dawn of a happy day which rose for the donkey on the ninth morning. His master, observing him secretly, was amazed to see him turn again and again to the boundary of the neighbour's field: looking more sharply he discovered that Penu was feeding him with melon peel. What ass could resist such a feast? Our ass certainly did not deprive himself, and made up in melons for the past eight days' fast.

Chick-Pea contemplated the meadow with anxiety. Next day, when his father would return, what could he tell him to explain why so little grass had been eaten? "Have you the courage, Chick-Pea, to see this game through?"

When light dawned again over the earth on the tenth morning, Chick-Pea felt a strong urge to remain near the donkey so he might feed at last without molestation. However, he returned to the straw hut and pretended to be heavily asleep.

Shortly afterwards the ass came sadly towards the straw hut, sneezing and coughing. Chick-Pea waited patiently until Penu had gone to the

village, then he examined the corner of the pasture where the animal had
been grazing. As he put his nose to the grass, an irritating smell made him,
too, sneeze and cough. But he laughed, well satisfied.

But as he rose from the grass he saw his father already on his way to
the field. Sita was calculating with surprise how small a surface had been
cropped, and grew very angry indeed. "Oh, this son whom I have brought
up! He has ruined the hopes I had set on this meadow! He has not kept
his eye on the pasture and given not a moment of thought to our interest!
Now our neighbour will claim that my field is even larger than it was
before the floods! Through your fault we shall be worsted in this dispute!"

Chick-Pea allowed his father's fury to calm down, before he spoke:

"May my father deign to listen to an account of what has been happening here. . . ."

He told his father every detail of what had happened in these ten days,
and added: "If I had not given Penu a free hand, as though I had been
blind, he might have injured—or even killed—our ass, and I should not
even have proof against him."

"Have you any positive proof against him?" asked the father.

"If you want that," said Chick-Pea, "you can go and smell that spot of
grass; then you will realise what tricks he has been up to."

Sita did so, and rose again quickly, trying to get rid of the fire that was
burning in his throat and nostrils. Without further hesitation he agreed
that the neighbour had acted with knavery, and he congratulated himself
on having this flagrant proof. He looked at his son without bitterness now
and gave him his orders:

"You, Chick-Pea, stay here. If you see that bandit Penu or his servant
Kiku, don't tell them that I have come back; I am going to fetch a scribe
to act as witness."

After a short while he returned with two judicial scribes. He asked them
to inhale a few handfuls of grass from the meadow, showed them the
white paint that had been spilled, and told them what tricks had been
played on each day; then he asked them to draw up a petition to the
tribunal of the Lord High Seneschal, appealing against the partition, and
claiming that a mistake had been made.

And when he arrived home with Chick-Pea, he gave the boy sweet
beer as on a holiday and said: "I will treat you as I would a friend, for
you have handled this affair far better than a mere faithful servant. But
you will no doubt have to face the tribunal, for I have made a complaint
against someone. Do you think you can keep your courage up until the
time comes?"

When the petition reached the Lord High Seneschal, he ordered an in-
quiry to be held. And the Field Inspector with his advisers presented his
report, and the two scribes gave evidence before the inquirers as to what
they had found.

The Seneschal, scenting a curious affair, made his inquiries about the plaintiffs directly from the Master of the Demesne, and Menkh, learning that the main hero was Chick-Pea, became strongly interested and advised the Seneschal to interrogate him personally.

When Chick-Pea was summoned to attend judgment next day he was overcome with terror. Forced to face the justice of men, he felt his courage fail, and he went to ask advice from the harpist.

"The Lord High Seneschal," Mesdjer replied, "is the representative of the Pharaoh, L.H.S., just as Pharaoh is the representative of the *Neter*. He is the Justice of the King; he is upright and does not allow the weak to be despoiled by the strong. Often he takes a walk through the streets before a court session, so as to hear the poor and simple folk speak; and he is stern with officials who transgress their rights and punishes them without mercy. If your case is righteous and you can give a truthful account of it, then you will have nothing to fear from the representative of Maât."

But the boy could not bring himself to make an accusation. Mesdjer said to him: "Did you not accept the responsibility for the experiment with the meadow? Well then, you must defend what has been entrusted to you."

And once more Chick-Pea found himself alone with his problem.

"Surely it was my duty to obey my father, for I belong to him as I belong to the demesne. Are there no men anywhere who do not belong to anybody?

"Why am I bound to the demesne?... True, I am fed by the demesne. Is there anything within me that is not fed by the demesne? My heart is not fed by the demesne: so my heart is free. My heart is fed by no one!"

But then he remembered the Sage, and this memory belied his words. "My heart belongs to him who feeds it," Chick-Pea whispered. "Why is he not with me to advise me today?

"Tomorrow I am going to accuse a playmate and a blind man!... Surely, if trickery makes men rich, Penu will commit other and more serious offences. And the blind man has betrayed the trust the Land Survey placed in him, but he is in a wretched position: if I prove the wrong he has done, he will lose his job. Maybe he has never betrayed his office before.... I shouldn't like to be in the Seneschal's shoes.

"And I, Chick-Pea, am to be the accuser!... Still, I cannot lie before Pharaoh's court. Poor Chick-Pea, what are you going to do?"

Throughout the whole day, squatting in his straw hut, he tried to recall every detail of the affair. He was trying to weigh up the exact value of a word and the effect of a gesture, as few men have done even in their maturity. But when the Sun sank towards the horizon, a sudden idea stirred him from his torpor: here was the answer to his problem and the deliverance from a nightmare! He jumped up and danced with joy in the golden reflections of the sunset, and then, without losing another thought over the matter, he ran to fetch the things he needed and came back to wait for the moment when Penu would fall asleep.

And then he busied himself with some mysterious work with only the moon for witness. And when he had finished, he fell asleep peacefully until the next dawn.

XVIII

JUDGMENT

AND the day of Judgment came.

The Lord of Equity arrived, the Lord High Seneschal,[1] Terror of Male-factors and Hope of the Oppressed, and sat enthroned, an image of immaculate Nobility, in the hall of 'the double Maât',[2] whose principle he embodied among men.

His seat was vaulted over by the baldachin, as the Earth by the Sky, as human law by Celestial Law. In his sceptre *Kherp* were gathered and harmonised the two laws whose concord creates harmony in the world of men. That is why he was sitting on an animal skin and with a skin beneath his feet, for the animal force is mastered by human consciousness of its own manhood, and thus the Seneschal was also called the 'Strong One'.

Many were the assessors and members of the Council; many the scribes sitting under his hand; many the ushers charged with keeping plaintiffs in order and dealing with unruly elements; their sticks were pliable, but might be used to good effect.

Chick-Pea trembled and danced from one foot to the other, waiting to be called. The lightnings of the skies, the Earth, and the 'Dwat' seemed less fearsome to him than the preliminaries of human justice. . . . Oh that he owned a hole, like a mouse, a nest, like a raven, a burrow, like a jackal, so as not to have to endure this ordeal.

"Silence!"

A hand was put on his shoulder and pushed him towards the place of hearing. With him were ushered in his father, Sabu, Penu, Kiku the servant, the blind man appointed by the Cadaster, and all the witnesses in the case. And then he recognised among the assessors Menkh, the Master of the Demesne, and suddenly, before Menkh, Chick-Pea felt that he bore responsibility, and a flame of courage flared up in his heart. . . .

Of the Seneschal he saw only the feet, for a firm fist had prostrated him, nose to the ground. As he rose again and straightened himself, he still had to lift his head upward to meet the eyes of the Seneschal, who was contemplating him with curiosity.

But while he had been kissing the ground, a personage had quietly entered whose presence surprised Menkh so much that he made a gesture

---

[1] The high dignitary mentioned in this chapter bears, in the original, the title 'Vizier'. In this translation, the title 'Lord High Seneschal' has been substituted for purely aesthetic considerations. (T.N.)

[2] Maât, whose name is equivalent to 'truth equity', is the *Neter* of Justice. See *Her-Bak Disciple*, Index: *Maât*.

of respectful beckoning: "He!" He could not be left among the common crowd. But the Sage put a finger to his lips and disappeared in the audience.

The Seneschal addressed Sita: "State your request and repeat the oath."

And Sita made declaration: "By the life of my Master, I will speak the truth. O wise Judge, after the boundary marks had been rectified, it seemed that the area of my field had diminished. So, lest I call upon Justice frivolously, I said to my son Chick-Pea: 'Let us see whether this field will give pasture to our ass for the same time as before the floods. If it does, the measure is just. But if he takes less time to eat all the grass, then I have been wronged, and if so, I shall dare to ask for a revision."

The Seneschal said: "Let your son speak for himself and let him repeat the oath."

Chick-Pea looked into the eyes of the Seneschal; then he said: "By my life, I shall give an account of what I have seen. But let me ask a favour of my Lord: allow me not to mention any name, and let the culprit be pardoned if he gives himself up."

The Seneschal passed a quick glance to Menkh, who was repressing a smile, then he said: "Why do you make this request?"

"Lord," replied Chick-Pea, "I must help my father to recover his property, but if the cheat admits his wickedness, then my ass and I are prepared to consider the whole affair as a joke."

The Seneschal was surprised. "Speak," he said, "omit nothing."

So Chick-Pea made his statement: "On the first day my ass was sick, very badly sick, for they had given him some brown herbal concoction to drink, which made him mad with pain. On the second day, he ate nothing, because of pig-droppings which had been strewn all over the field. On the third day my ass was tempted with a she-ass: what would you have done, O my Lord, if you had been in his place?"

In the audience all backs were bent with laughter. A truncheon threatened Chick-Pea, but the Seneschal raised his voice:

"Let him speak! Go on: what happened on the fourth day?"

Chick-Pea's success was worrying him; he stammered:

"On the fourth day . . . the fourth day . . . may my Lord forgive me, it was the same all over again . . . only this time they had brought a male ass along! It was even worse."

The laughter became a roar. The Seneschal raised his hand: "Go on; what did they do on the fifth day?"

"Oh! That day the ass drank, but he didn't eat a thing: he was intoxicated and slept it off. The sixth day was a great ordeal for both of us: they had smeared honey on his back, and the flies did not for a moment leave him in peace. I was simply mad with anger."

"And you were unable to say anything?"

"I thought they would resort to less harmful tricks if they thought they were dealing with a fool; so on the seventh day I pretended I was ill. In the evening again the donkey had eaten nothing, for all the time he had been worried with some white paint they had smeared over his nose and his hooves."

The Seneschal observed Penu, who was looking at Chick-Pea with the expression of one who is seeing an evil spirit. "And on the eighth day. . . ?"

"On the eighth day, O noble Lord, they purged him! . . . But the ninth day was a holiday for him. O Lord, if you have an ass, feed him melon peels and he won't look at any other food, so eager is he to feed on them. And that's what they gave him on the ninth day! And the tenth day brought us the needed evidence, for when my father arrived he could satisfy himself that they had strewn some terrible stuff over the grass which set throat and nostrils afire."

The Seneschal spoke to Chick-Pea: "And you are quite sure that this is what you have seen? Repeat the oath."

Chick-Pea affirmed: "All that I have said is true."

The Seneschal turned to Penu: "You were keeping an eye on that field together with your servant Kiku: which of you two has done that of which you are accused?"

"No one is accusing me," replied Penu, "and I have done nothing."

"The plaintiff has shown more generosity than you," said the Seneschal. "Tell me the truth."

H.B.—H

Penu shouted angrily: "If I am not telling the truth, let me be sent to Ethiopia!"

The Seneschal stopped him with a movement: "Moderate your voice, will you? If it was not you, it was your servant acting under your orders."

"On my life!" said Penu, "I gave no orders, I have done nothing."

The Seneschal turned to the assessors: "Make the servant speak."

Kiku was led forth between two sticks, he kissed the ground with trembling, then raised his hands and lamented:

"O you greatest among the great ones, richest among the rich ones, what importance can the word of a poor man have for you, a poor man who can do nothing by himself and has only one right, the right to obey."

"Obey then my word by speaking the truth," said the Seneschal. "Who gave the ass the poisonous brew?"

"How can I know it, if my Master does not? Is it not written: the servant shall have no eyes other than his master's?"

"Do not play with words, or the watchman may play with his stick. Answer without stammering: Did your master give you that order?"

"Which order, O great Seneschal? Is it not said: 'Your master will change his mind when the time of his bad temper will have passed.'"

"So you admit that he gave you that order."

"Have I said so? Is not the word I quoted on all schoolboys' lips?"

"And my word is that this liar be made to speak. Proceed."

Two sticks fell across Kiku's back. . . . He cried: "Stop it! I will speak. . . . O mighty of mighty ones, your justice is without deviation, but the arm which hits is blind: is a man then less than an ass? An ass has colics, and you have a man beaten . . . ouch! . . ." At a gesture the sticks had spoken again. "Stop it! Stop it! . . . I will tell you everything . . . the concoction . . . it is true . . . that donkey took it . . . but no one has mentioned the name of anyone who gave it to him. . . ."

"Then it was you who put the poison into it?"

"What poison, my Lord? . . . ouch! . . . ouch! . . . I will tell everything, but stop it! Can a dead man speak?"

"Speak up now, or there will be no more mercy for your back: and it will be you who will bear the punishment for your master's offence."

Terror-stricken, Kiku looked towards Penu, but Penu averted his face. Deep anger shot into Kiku's eyes and he cried: "If the master denies his obedient servant, does the servant remain his slave? My first master is justice, is that not true?"

"It is high time," replied the Seneschal, "that at last you should acknowledge this. Who put the poison into the brew?"

"O Lord, it was not the servant-here-present[1] . . . yet we were only two in the field."

[1] Respectful formula to replace the pronoun 'I' or 'me' when addressing a superior.

"Then it was your master Penu?"

". . . who did it? Alas, yes, my Lord. . . . But am I to remain under his vengeance?"

"First tell me what you know."

Kiku gave a detailed account of all Penu had ordered him to do, and the exact part each of them had taken in this business. Penu, hearing him speak, hardly knew any longer where he was standing. He wanted to shout 'liar', to deny everything, but the raised truncheons refreshed his memory. When he had confessed his guilt, the Seneschal turned towards the blind man and asked him to give his evidence concerning the fixation of the boundaries.

"All this we have heard casts considerable doubt upon the exactness of the new landmarks. Can you explain how it came about that you were mistaken?"

The blind man trembled so much that he had to be supported as he stood before the tribunal. He raised his hand to repeat the oath, but he could hardly bring the words over his lips. The Seneschal said loudly: "An honest man does not tremble before the judge: if you are lying, you know that you will be accursed by *Maât* and deposed from your office. Can you speak truly?"

Chick-Pea stepped forth and seized the blind man's hand: "O father without light, allow me to answer for you, for I have seen what was hidden from your eyes. Look back well into your memory whether you cannot read in it a little detail, and tell me whether it is not true that your stick, just when it thought it had found the right landmark, *hit upon a jar and a stone bottle which happened inadvertently to have been put on that spot?* . . . And is it not true that this jar and stone bottle dimmed the vision of your heart and led your judgment astray?"

Seized by terror, the blind man hesitated, but Chick-Pea went on: "Don't stammer; for if a lie is in my mouth, I shall be punished; but if my word is true, then neither you nor I ought to be punished, but the pots should be beaten, which troubled your heart."

A moment of surprise swayed the audience. The Lord High Seneschal questioned the blind man impassively: "Speak out: what is your answer?"

Prostrating himself the blind man declared: "*Maât* is my witness that the boy speaks the truth concerning the jar and the bottle."

The Seneschal scrutinised Chick-Pea's face: "If this could be proved, the blind man would be exonerated . . . but there is no evidence!"

Chick-Pea stepped from one foot on to the other with relief: "But there IS evidence, my Lord!" The voice of the judge declared with severity: "I do not believe it without seeing the evidence. Where is it?"

"O Lord, the jar and the stone bottle will be found . . ." He suddenly stopped. A quick glance passed between Menkh and the Seneschal: "Oh, I see . . . I see."

Chick-Pea, too, suddenly saw . . . that he had given away his ruse. The ground seemed to fall away beneath his feet . . . the jar and the stone bottle danced a mocking jig before his troubled eyes, entangling in his mind all the threads of the story.

In heavy silence all waited for the verdict of the great judge—who remained silent in turn. At last his powerful voice addressed the most eminent among the counsellors: "What judgment would you give in this case?"

"Since your Lordship asks for my opinion," replied the counsellor, "I should say that the person who put the jar and the stone bottle there should be whipped."

Chick-Pea was plunged into doubt and fear. A criminal . . . was he a criminal? Perhaps he was . . . he did not know any longer. The sudden onrush of a panther would be less dreadful than the great Seneschal's icy glance. "Let them banish me, let them jail me, but at least I want to know where my mistake lies!" He could not hold himself any longer, he broke down and blurted out: "Just Master, tell me . . . tell me . . . what should I have done."

Silence. Then the voice of the Lord High Seneschal rose anew: "I rule that he who has troubled the blind's man vision be whipped. Let Penu be kept in close arrest. You, Chick-Pea, rise. Are you not ashamed to tremble like a woman? If one has taken into one's hands the thread of a tangled skein, one must unravel it entirely, with a firm heart. If your conscience is clear, bring your request to completion: what is your claim?"

At these words, Sita began to speak: "I think my meadow has been curtailed in favour of my neighbour. I claim . . ."

But the Seneschal interrupted: "Let him be silent; the boy alone shall answer."

"O great Judge," said Chick-Pea, "how can I, who am stupid and ignorant, explain myself? I thought that man was capable of playing, like a cat, like a donkey. . . . But now I have learnt that when a man kicks or scratches, he means to hurt, not to play: but *must* one learn to play this kind of game? And what could I claim? I can count up to ten on my fingers: how can I measure my father's grounds? But you, great Judge, you know what we do not, or you would not be here today. Do not listen to Sabu, nor to Penu, not even to my father: they cannot calculate what the stream has distorted, but you who are learned, you can! You are just, and if you do it, my father will return into his own."

The Lord High Seneschal no longer tried to conceal his pleasure; he smiled at Chick-Pea and said: "My son, your words are full of reason. It shall be done according to your wish."

He commanded the geometers to be called for the following day, and then withdrew with Menkh, from whom he wished to learn more about this boy.

While they were still marvelling at his astonishing lucidity, the Sage was ushered in. He enquired of Menkh about Chick-Pea's family and said: "The earth has given him sufficient lessons; from now on he ought to study other subjects. Free this child from the servitude of his caste: he belongs to a different spiritual line!"

"He is a second son," replied Menkh. "The wrath of the eldest will be great, and his voice will rise against injustice."

"Tell him that the voice of the Temple has spoken, against whose decision there is no appeal."

Menkh bowed. "Master, you are He Who Knows and you shall be obeyed. But what will I do with the boy?"

"O Menkh, take him under your wing. You are the Master of Craftsmen, and under your care he will have opportunity to observe the transformation of matter. Let him go to a school as well; but I shall give instructions to the tutor, so that this wonderful candour be not meddled with. He is an exceptional case: it is the birth of a bud on the stem of Wisdom which carries the live marrow of the Two-Lands.

"If the child fulfils his destiny, then he will continue the spiritual lineage which allows our country to be the depository of the Sublime Knowledge, throughout all troubles, decadence, invasions.

"May we be granted to guide his unfolding wisely."

The Lord High Seneschal and Menkh bowed in respect, and the Sage withdrew.

After this, Menkh had Sita called and notified him of the extraordinary decision which released his son from the traditional bondage to give him the chance of a superior education. And Sita, aware of both the honour and the hardships this would bring upon his house, did not know whether to rejoice or to lament.

Then the Lord Menkh called for Chick-Pea: "Heaven seems to have gifted you with a keen tongue and a subtle mind. These gifts can beget both disorder and peace, according to the use to which they are put. You must learn to distinguish. . . . To every age belongs its 'master' and its 'rod'.[1] Happy the man who, one day, can become his own master and his own rod. To start with, I can be your Master . . . if you will accept my rod as well! You see, I put your destiny into your own hand, I treat you as a man free to make his own choice: Chick-Pea, son of Sita, will you leave your field and become my sandal-bearer?"

Chick-Pea trembled with emotion: free! He was free to decide for himself! The daily fetter was broken before the 'new', the unknown, he had not even hoped for. But already his new freedom disturbed him by awakening his conscience.

"In your heart I read *yes*," said Menkh, "but in your eyes, hesitation. Tell me, what is it that is keeping you back?"

"O Lord, there is Someone, and there is my donkey. He, the great

---

[1] *medu* means 'word', but also 'rod'.

Master, told me once: 'Go and till the soil.'"

Menkh smiled: "Be at peace on that account: today He wishes you to leave the soil."

Hearing this, the boy realised that for every joy a price has to be paid, and he accepted this understanding with a sigh. Repressing his emotion, he said: "If that is so, then I will also leave my donkey."

PART TWO

THE APPRENTICE

SCHOOL

Menkh's mansion looked all ablaze under a stark light: buzzards circling in the air proclaimed the middle of the day.

The Sun beat down heavily; the porter had slid down and was lying across the threshold, dozing, when a gallopade of naked feet awakened him and made him start: "Oh, it's you, Chick-Pea?"

"Indeed, it is I! Greetings, O porter, son of a porter, who shall beget porters up to the gates of eternity!"

"Greetings, O scoundrel, son of a scoundrel, who shall beget scoundrels all as unwashed as their father."

"Say that again."

"It's your Master who will say it again! Go in, under his eyes, as you are, all filthy! . . . Hurry up, run along, he has already been calling for his sandals."

"A joke heard too often wears thin. Let me pass, I'm late."

"That isn't new either. What have you been doing this time?"

"Something you've never yet done in your whole life: I've been working."

"You look more like a loafer than a worker to me. Where do you come from?"

"From a world far away from yours. . . . Down your stick and let me pass."

"First go and wash. You look red and black like a piebald hog."

"You owe me respect: I am come from school."

"I could have guessed it from your insolence. Sorry dab, who can't even hold his reed properly."

"That's no business of an ass like you!"

Ooooh! . . . The rod had no time to strike twice: a wild cat had leapt at the raised arm. Rolling on the ground the two opponents fought furiously. . . .

"Fighting like beasts!" Menkh's hard voice hit the combatants like a cold shower. . . . "No, don't move, young pedant. Go on, roll in the mud like a dog, budding scribe. . . . A fine spectacle for my servants! Now get up and collect your chattels—scrivener!"

Pale with shame, Chick-Pea retrieved the shards that had fallen from his torn bundle.

"Follow me."

At Menkh's heels he entered the high hall where servants obsequiously and busily carried water-jugs and fruit-bowls. But the Lord was in a serious mood and dismissed them with a gesture. Then he looked at the boy with mockery:

"So these are the fruits of your school-education? You, who are allowed to learn, insult the ignorant? You, the well-nurtured, despise the destitute? What have you done to deserve what you have received? Don't you know that though the gift from heaven is free, the man who arrogantly boasts of it will soon find himself in the place of him whom he despised?"

Chick-Pea bent his head. Menkh strode up and down the room in silence. Chick-Pea no longer knew where he was. The semi-darkness made the coloured shapes in the wall-panels look threatening; the deep easy-chair of the Master seemed like a tribunal. To calm his fright he tried to count the red and yellow diamonds woven into the tapestry decorating the walls.

Menkh went towards a cedar chest, took out a copper mirror and came back, sitting down without saying a word. An airhole, pierced through the wall just beneath the ceiling, shed a beam of light on to the mirror, which in the Master's hand became a lance of fire. Chick-Pea opened great fascinated eyes, the light was blinding him; with his fingers, still dirty with ink, he wiped the sweat and tears away—a picturesque scene. . . .

"Come here!" Menkh held the mirror before the spotty face. "Admire your face, Her-Bak! Do you think *Thot* will teach this clumsy monkey who cannot even master his calamus. . . ."

Before his grotesque reflection, Chick-Pea's shame changed to decision: "Oh Menkh, may your justice chastise these guilty fingers, but let not your contempt crush your servant: he did not know what he was doing."

"Ignorance, Chick-Pea, is no excuse. If the very first lessons had not taught me the importance of the 'perfect movement' I should never have been initiated into the secrets of the Craftsmen whose Master I am today. What have these twelve months of schooling taught you?"

"I have learnt the hieroglyphs and know how to transcribe them into running script."

"Show me your work."

Chick-Pea searched in the knotted rag, hesitating which of the be-smeared shards he ought to show; but Menkh, with a crisp movement, spread them all across the napkin.

"The work is worthy of the craftsman's hands. Is the scribe your master satisfied with these masterpieces?"

"He must be satisfied; he made no reproach."

"What seat in school does he give you?"

"On the first day he told me to sit at his feet and he has never deprived me of this honour."

"Are you not ashamed of usurping the seat of a good pupil? You went forth like a young lion out to hunt . . . and now, do you not rather be-have like a fawning courtier? Is your heart perhaps as sullied as your fingers?"

Chick-Pea's eyes were filled with tears; vanquished, he fell at Menkh's feet: "Lord, I do not want to be base."

Menkh bent over the table. He took the shards one by one and de-ciphered their meaning: "The noble royal scribe, Chick-Pea—The nimble-fingered scribe, Chick-Pea—He, whose every word is heeded, Chick-Pea—He, who alone fills the heart of his master, Chick-Pea—Chick-Pea, commonly called the 'good adviser'—Chick-Pea, who knows all the secrets of Heaven and Earth. . . ."

Pushing the shards aside, Menkh contemplated the schoolboy's em-barrassed expression: "Who has dictated to you these remarkable in-scriptions?"

Chick-Pea hid his face in his hands.

"You yourself, of course. Anyone can see that. Well, I shall keep these marvels as samples of your autograph, until another autograph will efface them."

"Lord, I shall soon prove that I have understood."

"And let no further boast come from your lips. Your teacher may have made a mistake, but a spoiled schoolboy can do nothing to straighten that out. Tomorrow you shall know my decision."

Dark is the Sun to the veiled eyes of remorse; and bitter the bread to the mouth of the ungrateful, for his heart knows no rest. On his way to

school, all crushed, Chick-Pea ruminated with application to himself on
the precepts and well-known texts: 'Put wisdom into practice, and all
evil will flee you' . . . "How will you find Wisdom, Chick-Pea. I think
you will have to change the means—whereby. . . ."

And lo, his steps had led him to the mound which had witnessed his
recent conversation with the Sage. A shudder shook him, and anguish
squeezed his heart: what would tomorrow be the Master's decision? Oh,
that it be not yet too late!

Menkh had quietly entered the school hall which was humming with
rhythmical muttering. The squatting pupils were busy transcribing what

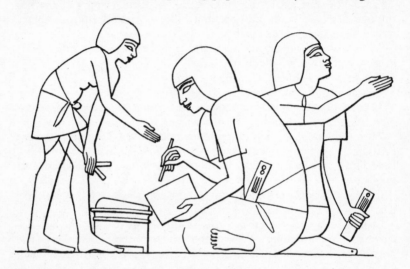

the teacher dictated: sentences of classical wisdom, rhythmically set by
the tutor to make each phrase and the spelling of the words quite clear.
The Master did not notice the Lord of the Demesne, who was listening
and observing. Menkh looked for Chick-Pea: the lesson had borne fruit;
there he was, sitting in the hindmost rank; no more arrogance on his
face, instead, grave attention, anxious effort. . . . Menkh touched the
teacher's shoulder: "Send your pupils home; I have something to tell you."

He compared the shards left by the students. "The Sage has given
Chick-Pea, son of Sita, into your care; what have you done with him?"

The scribe became worried and answered: "Lord, I have treated him as
a privileged pupil, as worthy of the interest which the Master of Wisdom
takes in him."

"Do not try to be clever. You have treated him as a vile favourite, and
you are responsible for his fall. You have spared him any criticism and
you have encouraged his vanity, and when the pupil shall have obtained
greatness, he will have no respect for you."

The scribe threw himself flat on his belly and lamented:

"How can such a thing be said against the servant-here-present that his heart has led him into causing displeasure, where he had hoped to give satisfaction."

Menkh looked at him with contempt. "I am grateful to the master whose rod, when I was a boy, inculcated in me the necessity for effort. Man pays with tears the price of conscience, if the animal has not been tamed in childhood."

"Lord, Chick-Pea knows the characters, ciphers, and formulas well enough already to be employed by a priest."

"Well then, he must now learn to forget them again and to purify himself from this poison! But he has not learnt one single correct movement, nor the respect for his tools, nor the proportions and the meaning of the divine characters which he transcribes."

"Lord, it is said: 'Man's bosom is wider than a palace, and full of divers possibilities. . . . Choose the good and leave the bad ones! . . .'"

"And you, obviously, have chosen the training of a courtier? . . . You race of slaves. If among us there were no teaching other than that of your narrow-sighted castes, O formalist scribes and profit-greedy priests, the Wisdom of our fathers would have to be buried like a treasure to save it from the profaners."

The teacher's hand trembled with fear, for he was afraid of losing his post.

"Lord, your words are forcing my heart out of my body, but look upon me as I stand before you: I shall guide the boy according to your instructions."

Menkh rose: "For everything there is a time: a time for harmony and a time for anarchy, and none can change the course of the stars. It is our wisdom to know this. As for your part, ply your trade. . . . But we shall save the good grain against the future."

"Great is the justice of my Lord. As to my beloved pupil Chick-Pea . . ."

"Forget your beloved pupil; henceforth he will be led by other hands."

Next morning, after Menkh had received his stewards and discussed the tasks for the day, he called for his sandal-bearer and said to him:

"Listen. You have swelled your memory with formulas and your heart with self-conceit. Now you will have to learn that your knowledge is spurious if compared with that of a stone-breaker, a master-carpenter, or even a nimble-fingered potter. Your hands will now have to learn that matter follows laws of its own and independent of convention; that in order to make a masterpiece from a stone one must have one's ear in one's heart and a living soul in one's fingers. For you will learn that in order to choose from the rock that flawless block which will yield a perfect obelisk or statue, the Master Craftsman needs an instinct as sure as

that which tells a wild beast of danger imperceptible to its senses, or of the plant that will cure its illness.

"Hence you will leave your scribe's robe and hand back to me your palette. You will be given a new loin-cloth and a leather apron such as craftsmen wear. From tomorrow you will go to a workshop. I have spoken."

Chick-Pea remained dumbfounded. . . . He wanted to frame an appeal, but an imperious movement dismissed him and he bowed to the ground and said as he rose:

"Lord, may your justice settle everything as it pleases. But the servant-here-present lives on the air you give him. Will he no longer be your sandal-bearer?"

Menkh softened his voice, replying: "If he is worthy of it, he will keep his post in his leisure-time. Now go."

Chick-Pea withdrew. During the day he roamed at random. On the banks of the Nile he came to a green meadow, similar to his father's; he stepped into the grass and dropped at the water-edge, prostrate.

The sky-coloured river reflected his dream, as formerly it had reflected the mirage of unknown countries . . . travel. Today he saw hieroglyphs in it, and the image of temples, which the flood was washing northward, towards other palaces, other temples, other fabulous towns well guarded behind their walls, and whose gate was still closed against him. . . .

"What mysteries can they be concealing from eyes profane? The scribes in the school did not seem to know them. The Sage would know them all, I'm sure of that. He has knowledge in his eyes . . . but what exactly do they know? You see, Chick-Pea, that is what you are not sure of. Is there anything to be known? If the scribe speaks the truth, that, excepting scribes and priests, all people are ignorant, then my beautiful dream has come to an end: my robe has been taken away. Farewell, writing reed! Farewell, ink-cups! Farewell, shards and papyrus! Farewell, above all, my beautiful pleated robe which suited me so well! It was my glory, it gave me superiority over the other boys. . . . Was I not on holiday among them like a white heron among sparrows?"

Chick-Pea thought and thought, working out a new ambitious study programme which might perhaps fill Menkh with admiration. . . .

"But if Menkh remains inflexible, could he not perhaps have chosen for me a craft with a more resplendent costume? Oh this apron of the craftsmen—it is drab and ugly. Craftsman. . . . If at least I could be a Chief like Menkh! He is great and mighty in his gala costume, with his chief's baton, his jewelled breastplate and the fine golden necklace he has received from the King. His robe is without flaw just as he is without flaw. His robe seems to foreknow every movement he is going to make, and what he says seems as if it were written on his robe. . . . But, speaking of robes, what was the one the Sage was wearing? It was white and simple, and on him I saw no jewels. . . ."

Chick-Pea thought further and sighed: "I have worn the scribe's robe and what have I done with it? I have soiled it. . . . Oh, you schoolboy, I think you are still on the wrong path.

"And about the costume, if I had been a butcher and Menkh had taken away my knife and apron, I should have felt quite as much degraded; so it is actually the trade which 'makes' the costume. . . . Oh, Chick-Pea, you were less silly when you held conversations with your ass. Indeed, you will have to return on your track."

In the flowing water new images appeared: a cobbler nimbly decorating sandals, the work-place of masons, humming like a beehive: "Catch that brick, hop, catch!" Life, rhythm, shanties. . . . A new confidence woke in the boy: "Each trade after all gives a particular skill to the artisan; and the craftsman's loin-cloth is as fine to him as the pleated robe is to the scribe. And if my former comrades come to mock me, I shall know what they are, but they will not know what I know."

In his new fervour, he ran back to Menkh:

"Lord, I will be the best of your craftsmen. I have now understood that no craft is to be despised. If through your wise judgment, I shall have to leave the workshops one day, it will be because I have conquered all difficulties which a nimble-fingered craftsman can meet there."

Menkh shook his head: "Perhaps you can start by being an apprentice?"

Chick-Pea looked at his hands in confusion: "I can! And the stains on my fingers will no longer be ink; they will be the signature of a craft: will they be good enough to efface those on my shards?"

Menkh smiled. "Go and act."

XX

POTS AND CARVEN VESSELS

HOWEVER, for the beginning of his life in the workshops, the leather apron did not become Chick-Pea's emblem, for Menkh ruled that his first apprenticeship should be to a potter. Earth and water became his material; his tools were an apprentice's hands and sweat. For before one can work the greyish clay it has to be mixed, then all bubbles must be beaten out of it, and finally it has to be kneaded into a smooth paste, soft enough to be workable, yet firm enough to hold together. And this was his first work.

That evening the weary boy sank down in the only empty corner of the workshop and looked at the countless pots drying there until they

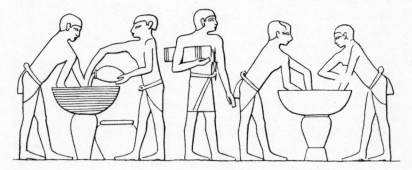

should be ready to be baked. In another corner of the enclosure sheltered by palms stood the potter's wheel and those of the apprentices, all covered with potter's clay, everywhere clay, clay even over Chick-Pea. The new workman looked at his hands . . . and laughed.

On a large jar containing drawings for pots of special shapes made to order, there was a design representing *Khnum* the divine potter, fashioning the egg of the world. Chick-Pea found it very puzzling:

"If he is a god," he said to himself, "I can well understand that he is able to model the world, but whence did he take the clay?"

Next morning, as soon as it was light enough, Chick-Pea hurried into the workshop, well before the hour when the apprentices were expected. The previous day he had not been allowed to operate the wheel: now he meant to try his hand. As he had seen others doing, he put a lump of clay upon the wheel and made it turn while hollowing the mass with his fingers. After several failures he succeeded in raising the rim as for a bowl, and a feeling of triumph swelled up in him: the form opened out like a flower, it widened, rose, and turned, turned . . . and then suddenly its shape became bizarre, a bump appeared on one side and widened into a paunch, a few more convulsive, jolty spins, and the mass crumbled like a withered flower.

Disconsolate, the apprentice began afresh: another lump became hollow and spun around . . . then the same dance, the same downfall.

The master of the workshop observed him from the threshold. Chick-Pea saw nothing except the battered pot that seemed to mock him. Furiously he turned and turned . . . alas, one after another each vessel he began lost its shape and crumpled.

The old potter's mocking laughter cut short his efforts and redoubled his anger.

"Well, you apprentice, who gave you permission to use that wheel? Do you think perhaps you can turn a pot as you can turn a phrase? The scribe may be master over his reed, but the wheel is master over the potter. The law of equilibrium is strict: it knows no pardon for departure from the true. You are a fool, if you try to turn a pot without having centred it first. Don't you know that the *axis* is the *Neter*, the god of the wheel? If you don't pay respect to it, it will fashion a monster for you; but if you give it its due, it will serve you, and make your work stable. Look."

Again the wheel was spinning; with a masterly movement the clay was cast; the well-centred mass became hollow, stretched, and rose with a regular paunch around an empty centre; the work was done by the circular movement of the wheel. The fingers hardly moved; under their magic touch the obedient loam rose in a fine layer, espoused in space the harmonious curve dreamt by the potter's fingers; and their gentle pressure, invisible and immobile, inwards *or* outwards, shaped a narrow neck or a vaulted belly.

"You see? You merely have to place the axis in the very centre."

Chick-Pea remained perplexed:

"But the centre is empty. I can't see anything there!"

Now it was the old craftsman who looked at the boy with stupefaction:

"Ah, really? And who ever, in the times of time, has seen the axis?"

That evening Chick-Pea dreamt of the axis.

Night brings counsel: next day the apprentice was full of a new idea: "Why always turn out the same monotonous shapes? Big or small, all those vessels are round: how dull."

His bewildered comrades watched him forming his clay no longer into a ball, but into a cube! The wheel began to turn . . . and lo! the mass refused the shape, under the fingers it tore away the superfluous earth, until roundness, the inescapable roundness was re-established!

Under the laughter and teasing comments, Chick-Pea tried afresh; but

neither squares nor ovals kept their shape: the wheel was inexorable. The inventor angrily submitted and silently turned out round shapes . . . like everybody else.

That day he had no further new ideas.

But after working hours he remained behind with the old potter who was selecting the vessels for tomorrow's baking.

"Tell me, master, couldn't these pots be used just as well without baking them at all?"

"No, the liquids would disintegrate them."

"But the water is oozing out from that jug there, although it *has* been baked."

"The baking has made it porous: it will have to be glazed to seal the pores."

"How do you do that?"

"You soak it for a long time in brine, and then you put it once more into the fire: and when it's ready you have a perfectly natural glaze."

"And that's how you have glazed this blue vessel?"

"No. That glaze is a secret: only he who has made a masterpiece may learn it."

"What's that, a masterpiece?"

The old potter communed with his own thoughts for a while; then he said: "The masterpiece is a piece of work which a man has created with his soul, conceived with his heart, borne in his body, from the skin into the entrails . . . which a man has lived, has carried until the time when like a ripe fruit it is brought to daylight by the fingers."

Chick-Pea was musing. "Does it take a very long time to make a masterpiece?"

"It needs whole generations to prepare it; and then it is produced by one man who is their heir."

"And what is needed to be that man?"

"To listen to the soundless voice of the Ancients, to observe and to keep silent."

To the stillness dusk added its own. The boy sighed. "So even if I had succeeded in making my square pot, it wouldn't have been a masterpiece yet."

The old creased face brightened up.

"The masterpiece was to have that idea: for by tearing away the clay that overstepped its form, the wheel has shown you the hidden power of the *Neter* in its struggle with the movement. Thus the wheel has taught you the law of round things, which you would never have learnt to *know* at school!"

"And you are explaining it to me!"

"Not at all. The explanation goes only into your head. But your *anger* has gone into your fingers, which are powerless to impose another shape. This is the knowledge that will remain yours."

"All right. But why did the '*Neter* of the *axis*' refuse this form? After all, my cube was well centred."

"The axis was not the only factor at work; another law intervened."

"But is a *Neter* then not all-powerful?"

"Within the law he rules, yes, but never beyond."

"What then is a *Neter*?"

"My boy, you roam farther than my knowledge reaches . . . strange child that you are! At your age I did not have these worries. Who has given you your wings, little falcon?"

"Oh, you won't tell me any more, and yet you know so many things!"

"You're wrong. I have told you almost all I know; and I had to turn pots a whole life long to understand this little. However, I am glad I shall return to earth with my pots, rich in my little knowledge and not with the barren arrogance of the scribes."

"But are there only bad scribes?"

"It is not their letters which are false: the hieroglyphs are divine symbols which the Wisdom of the Ancients has bequeathed to us. It is the scribe's mind that is twisted. The Sages of our temples had to pass that way, but your Master has done for you as they did: he has transplanted the sapling into good ground before it could rot."

"And you, who has taught you what you know?"

"The old traditions of the potters of yore, *the names of the pots*, which refer to their form and to that which they are intended to contain; the rites of the brotherhood, the words of the Master of Craftsmen who inspects us. The rest I have learnt from clay, water, fire, and from the wheel."

"With you, I shall be learning much."

"I doubt if you are going to stay for long with me, boy—the rhythm of your wheel is ampler and livelier than mine."

"Must one then always leave what one loves?"

"All that are pulsing with one and the same heart never really part from one another. . . . And for the rest, what does it matter?"

The old potter proved right: shortly afterwards his new apprentice was transferred to his neighbour, who carved and hollowed vessels from stone.

Never had Chick-Pea seen so many vases of varied shapes and all sizes, of slate, diorite, alabaster, granite; some polished like mirrors, others carved or engraved, others again opened like petals of a flower, while some were shaped like an animal symbol.

The wonderful patterns in the veins of alabaster excited Chick-Pea to ecstasy. Never before had the stone-carver had such an interested admirer: "And these patterns were actually within the stone, within the mountain?"

"Where else could I have taken them? But the art consists in divining aright how the veins run before one starts cutting the vase. Look at this one: carved by a negligent workman: the thread of the alabaster is broken, and full of scratches and spots, like unsound flesh; if you do such work, you'll soon know the rod and the door."

"All right! But has the workman a tongue to speak up?"

"What is there to be said?"

"Has he right to ask the master questions, so as to learn *before* he sets to work?"

The master of the workshop straightened himself as if to repel an outrage. "No apprentice would any longer believe the master, if the unskilled labourer had a right to question and know. How could one then distinguish between the arrogant newcomer and the skilled workmate who has been taught by the master."

"And did you not begin by learning?"

"I have done as you are going to do: I observed with my eyes and tried with my fingers, and if my fingers were disobedient, my back remembered and made them diligent. Your back, too, will remember, and to start with it is going to teach you the distance that lies between you and your master: come here!"

He raised the rod and administered a few vigorous cuts on the curved back.

Chick-Pea suffered the rod with clenched fists but without flinching. Then he straightened himself again and said: "How many cuts will there be for each bungled piece of work?"

"As many as fingers on your hands."

"Add the toes of the feet and give me all together straightaway and then let us forget about it."

The stone-carver looked at the boy as if he was seeing a lion-cub leaping forth from a thicket. "And why, pray?"

"I think," said Chick-Pea, "I shall work better with my mind free from threats." And between his clenched teeth he added: "And, above all, I shall have asked for them myself."

The man who listened, repressing his smile, lifted his rod again, ad-

ministered three cuts and said: "That's for your insolence. As for bad
work, I'll give you credit for a whole moon."

The apprentice's first job was to hold an alabaster egg, that was to be
scooped out into a vase. Its flawless outside was so beautiful that it hurt
Chick-Pea to see the forked drill bite into the interior.

At evening, when Menkh asked for his sandal-bearer, Chick-Pea reported on his day's work without omitting anything. Then he asked: "I
have two questions, Lord; may I ask them?"

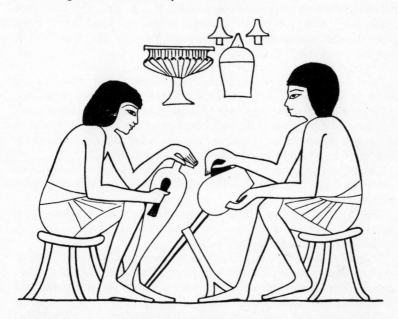

"You have my permission," said Menkh, "but one of them I can
answer straight away: the lesson of the rod has been profitable, for it has
put respect into your request and your attitude."

Chick-Pea became flustered. "Lord, you read my thought in my eyes.
Then I need not ask you . . . whether man cannot be trained without the
rod."

Menkh's face darkened with sadness. "If ever you should become Master
of Public Works, and if you have a heart, you will understand what
tragedy lies behind your question. But tell me first: do all donkeys obey
without the stick?"

"Oh! There are many donkeys, Lord, which are better than their
masters. But there are lazy and obstinate ones."

"Well, that is already an answer. But I want to teach you to think: you
are not long born and already you ask questions about fundamental

problems: hence you must also search for the fundamental solution. But listen: a lion can be tamed by the glance of the human eye, a snake by music, a cat by comfort and play, a bird by gentleness, a noble dog by voice and praise, an ignoble dog by the whip. Mankind contains within itself the whole animal kingdom: your heart partakes of the nature of the lion, your lungs of that of the bird; but every man has in his animal body some particular similarity and affinity; and if you know this you can tame men. But to be able to do this even the smallest works foreman would have to become one of those 'who know'. And there is no nation that has enough Sages to go round. The selection may be made, but the choice comes from above, and for this choice to become possible something other than the animal must awake in man: and this other something is always strangled by the animal."

"Then we ought to strangle the animal?"

"No. As little as you would strangle your donkey. But we must tame it. Man's life is short if we consider the stair he has to climb, and his brain is the most obstinate monkey there is! If his heart rules him, his conscience will soon take the place of the rod; but if not, great severity is needed to shake him up out of his inertia; severity is needed also to safeguard the honour of the trade guilds and the quality of their crafts."

Chick-Pea shook his head. "I begin to see: it's not all as simple as an ass might think. But what becomes of the man who makes some progress each day?"

"He is soon recognised and taught in the branch for which he is suited."

"Even in the Temple secrets?"

"No door is closed against him who proves himself worthy to enter."

Chick-Pea woke up, choked with joy: "Then even the least of apprentices may hope? But why has a man as wise as the potter not been given more important employment?"

"He did not 'wake up' in his youth; what he understands is the fruit of long, silent work. By ceaselessly improving his technique he has wrested its secret from the 'empty centre', and this ray of Light is sufficient to glorify his old age. Later he discovered some excellent glazes[1] and received substantial rewards, but he never felt any wish to leave the workshop which revealed this secret to him. There he continues his search for Perfection; he is the Potter of Potters; he is the 'touchstone' of the new apprentices, and many are those whom he has roused to awareness. Such people as he are the fathers of our crafts.

"And is this title to nobility not as good as any other? There are some great dignitaries who are not allowed to address me as 'my friend', but he may."

The boy remained perplexed. . . . "But in order to get nearer to the Temple, what must one do?"

[1] The technical terms in pottery are: glaze, or lustre or enamel. (Author's Note.)

"Do not talk of things of which you know nothing. Do you think the Temple ends with its walls?"

"Then there is always a little part of the Temple observing us! But who then belongs to the Temple?"

A powerful slap on his face taught Chick-Pea that he had gone too far. He kept silent.

"If you ask only questions of this kind, you may as well carry my sandals back."

"But, Lord," Chick-Pea timidly stammered, "I had another question."

Disarmed, Menkh sat down again, waiting.

"May I know, Lord, why you have transferred me to the vessel-carver?"

"If you were not so ignorant, you would know this is the only work-shop which is still working according to the ancient usages; in others, gold and silver have dethroned the stone. And it is necessary that you should know this craft."

"It's less fun than the potter's: the clay pot rises and opens under my fingers as I will it; but the stone is hard, one has to work it with a tool."

"When the curious urchin shall have tamed his impatience he will become able to think instead of asking questions. And then he will understand the value of symbols, and he will see why the *vase* is important. Meanwhile he may remember this: the potter can draw out a little mass into a vast shape; but the carver cannot hollow out a vessel larger than his block; the potter's vessel *contains the space which is given to it*; but the carver's vessel *contains that which has been taken away*."

Chick-Pea made a great effort to understand. . . . And Menkh said: "Look at these three ewers, all alike; now put them in a row and look at the space between them: it, too, has a shape that is outlined by the vessels; now which of these shapes is *the vase?* . . . For my part, I have learnt it from their name: *khent*, that is to say the relationship between the inside and the outside, that which was inside, and '*which has come forth from it*'. . . . And look farther, look at these columns: they, too, have a twofold shape: one inside and one outside, and one could not exist without the other.

"All this is a little hard to understand at your age; however, if you thus accustom your eyes to 'look' in this way you will learn to decipher the real lesson of our hieroglyphs; and only then will their name reveal our science to you.

"Go and have a good look at those vases; the water ewer, the pot '*nu*' which is round like *Nut's* sky, the porous jug, the glazed pot, the vase which contains and the vase which pours out, and the vase which is sealed. . . . Go and fashion vessels, little boy!"

Many a day later, the carver complained to Menkh: "Your apprentice spares his labour and his back. Would you praise a workman who pushes caution to the extreme of letting his neighbour do his work for him?"

Menkh repeated the reprimand to Chick-Pea, who answered by a complaint in turn: "This craft is not much fun! The stone is hard and the tool coarse; one may toil a whole day long and in the end have nothing to show for it."

"What you are doing does not matter so much as what you are learning from doing it. You will stay at this trade until you have mastered cowardice."

The boy jerked angrily: "Her-Bak will never be a coward!"

"You say so. But what has become of your promises? Have you not become weak at the first difficulty? Have you not chosen rather to waste precious time than to risk being punished?"

"But what will happen if I become a dotard before becoming wise?"

"In that case Her-Bak will have to change his name."

"Oh, my Lord . . ."

"Be still now. You have said quite enough. Even at the risk of becoming a dotard you will stay in this trade until its technique has penetrated under your skin, by dint of accidents, mistakes, and even the rod."

Chick-Pea rose, all trembling; he lifted his hand and shouted: "May it never be said again that anyone accuses me of cowardice!"

A few days later, returning at evening to Menkh, he declared: "I have cut my vase the wrong way."

"And you have been punished?"

He replied: "It was justice."

Another day he had blood on his fingers: "My drill went through the vase by accident. . . ."

And on yet another day he said: "My block today was cut badly, and to repair my mistake they had to cut the vase narrower than intended."

Yet more time passed, and one evening he came home sadly: "I was mistaken in gauging the way of the thread: now my fine alabaster vase will be spoiled."

But at last the time came when Chick-Pea appeared evening after evening with a serene expression on his face. So Menkh said: "I think it would be good to put you to some other craft."

"As you have judged, Lord, it will be good."

The next day he took leave of his master. In his farewell was nothing but gratitude. On the threshold he turned, threw a last glance over his tools and the vessels and muttered: "There is no such thing as a foolish trade."

XXI

THE TWO ASSES

WHEN Chick-Pea returned to the house of his Lord, Menkh called for him and said: "Well, what are you going to do now? Is it not rather a long time since you last saw your parents? I give you three days' leave of absence. Go and visit again the home from which you came." And he added: "You shall by no means go back empty-handed; I have had a donkey loaded with two jars, one filled with date wine and the other with fig wine for your father; and for your mother and sister two necklaces with lucky charms."

And he called him back again and added: "See that your name be spoken with respect in your home. Go, for it is sometimes useful to tie for oneself the knot of destiny. . . ."

The boy kissed the ground before his Master's feet and withdrew with joy in his heart. Impatiently he searched for that promised donkey since he reminded him of his old friend. He found him loaded with all kinds of good things, and mounting and seating himself on top of the baskets, he spurred his mount and turned towards his past.

Again it was the time when the barley was ripening, a day similar to that 'first day' when he returned happy, having made the acquaintance of the Sage. Slowly the calm waters rolled along, reflecting in their mirror the amethyst mountain and the azure sky. On the opposite bank the sandy downs were already baring themselves for the last sowing.[1]

The donkey trotted along the muddy bank, which was dotted black and white with plovers. Chick-Pea stopped and allowed himself to be held in thrall by a straw which the eddies tried to tear away from each other, passing it like a ball from one to the next, until a stronger current carried it off. He reluctantly left the river and directed his donkey along a narrow dyke at the fringe of the irrigation ditches, across the fields.

Down below there appeared the tufts of palm-trees and some low houses of brown earth. At the sight of them Chick-Pea laughed to himself: "I wonder whether my sister will not suddenly appear in the corn, as she did that other time."

And lo, he heard a loud shout of surprise, and there was Mut-Sherit running through the corn, her arms raised, as she called to her mother: "That loaded donkey there—it's Chick-Pea who's bringing it here!"

And when he found himself once more on the threshold, with the amazed Hemit, it seemed to him as if the time which had flowed since that 'other time', had made a large loop, which today was closing upon

[1] The last sowing before the floods.

itself; smilingly he traced a large *shen*[1] on the floor. As he unloaded the
ass, Mut-Sherit came running, bringing her father and brother, and all
rejoiced.

"Enter your house," said the father to Chick-Pea, "and eat and drink;
and we shall listen to what you may have to say."

And Chick-Pea replied: "Let us make merry for three happy days, for
the Lord has sent you some handsome presents, and for three days I shall
stay with you."

"Is it true," asked the father, "that you are no longer a scribe?"

"It is true," said Chick-Pea, "the Lord has decided that I should learn
other crafts."

"But," the father exclaimed, "to leave the robe of the scribe is to be
degraded. What have you done?"

Chick-Pea remained unperturbed by this question. He gave his father

---

[1] *shen*: a loop that was drawn with a cord, signifying a cycle or circuit. See Fig.
32, Pl. I.

a glance and said: "I shall tell you all you want to know; but first accept what I am bringing you."

He gave each the appointed present. His brother Fine-Speaker, having received nothing, rose with venom in his heart and left.

Mut-Sherit danced with joy before her necklace; then she approached Chick-Pea: "As you have given it to me, you may also put it on for me."

But the girl had grown faster than her brother: she had to bend down so that he might fasten the necklace, and her breast, now that of a woman, brushed against Chick-Pea as she rose again. He looked at his sister with surprise: and to his astonishment he felt a warm wave running beneath his skin like a shiver. . . . Mut-Sherit, not understanding his silence, shook him:

"What do you say: am I not beautiful like this?"

He gently stood a little away. "Oh, of course, Mut-Sherit, you are beautiful . . . but you have changed. You are no longer the 'little' one."

She burst into laughter: "Did you perhaps think you are the only one who can change?"

The father observed his children: "Well, Chick-Pea, tell us what you have been doing all this time?"

Mut-Sherit served bread-beer, and they tasted of the food sent by the Lord. Then Sita listened to the report of his son, and was puzzled:

"Of course, the Master knows what he is doing, but what does this mean, this position, in which you are at present? No school, no trade, no plans for the future? What is the matter? Has anything happened, perhaps, which you are keeping from me?"

"Father," replied Chick-Pea, "whatever I may be keeping from you, it cannot be any serious fault: even though I was sometimes a little negligent in school, I have in any case learnt all that a scribe ought to know; and, after all, the Lord is keeping me in his mansion: that should be proof enough that he has not withdrawn his trust from me."

Sita knew not what else to say, for he did not dare to criticise the Master of the Demesne; but the abnormal state of affairs gave him a feeling of deep humiliation.

"What is going to come of it? Neither my father, nor my father's father have done as much for their sons."

Squatting on the ground, Chick-Pea weighed these words within himself. He pondered that Menkh had not given him any advice on what he should say at home. . . . And now, as he was forced to explain what exactly his position was, he began to know a new feeling: he felt *responsible* for his words, *responsible* for his answer upon matters which he did not really know! What intentions had Menkh about him? Was it not against all tradition to shift from one trade to another? His brother and his comrades had their work assured; but he, what impression did he make: that of a bungler? Or of one who could not make up his mind? Actually he

had never been called upon to make up his own mind: he had done
nothing beyond obeying and he had never regretted nor doubted. . . .

And now, here, in his familiar surroundings, he was suddenly disturbed
and confused. What should he do? He could not bring himself to discuss
the orders of his Master. . . . He stopped, his heart felt cramped, and he
thought ". . . of my *Masters*".

Then he was seized by anguish: could it be that his father had a right
to interfere with his life, to tear him away from his present guides and to
force him to live within the humdrum worries of his caste?

Then Chick-Pea dimly felt the value of what he possessed: the danger
of losing it gave him awareness of it: he was just about to reply. . . . But
at this moment a gang of boys stormed into the house, Fine-Speaker at
the head of his brother's former schoolmates, and everybody spoke at
once:

"So there he is! Chick-Pea, the ex-scribe, the washout, the darling of
his master. . . . What have you done with your robe? . . . Show us your new
loin-cloth. . . . What trade are you plying now? . . . The schoolmaster
never so much as mentions your name. What on earth did you do? . . .
He has not told us any reason why you left! . . . From how many workshops have you been chucked out so far?"

Chick-Pea was choking. He shut his eyes and dug his fingers into his
ears, to overcome the desire to reply. Again he saw the whirling straw. . . .

Suddenly he remembered Menkh's farewell: "At times it is useful to
tie for oneself the knot of destiny". . . . Yes, like a *shen* which closes its
loop and then continues towards the following loop, he had come back
to his family. Then, faced with the inevitable choice, he knotted the past
and, deliberately, began something new.

Sita rose and stared at him. "On my life, you have to answer them.
Say something."

Chick-Pea, too, rose. His eyes were clear, his voice firm. "I will not
give any explanation. What my Masters have decided is the right course.
I trust in their word. I will follow their path."

And, having thus replied, he went out, leaving them in confusion.

He went to look for his donkey, the old donkey, the one he had 're-
nounced'. He found him in the stable, side by side with the new one he
had brought today. He stroked him gently and gave him some barley to
eat, and then he gave something to the new one as well.

"How are you getting on together, you two? Well? Not jealous of
each other? You are much wiser than man: no hatred in your eyes. This
is a happy day for me; but if they knew, it would fill their hearts with
rage. Tell me, old friend, do you understand me? Of course you do:
Hi-han! What a pity we cannot have a real chat together, you and I! . . .
But I'm sleepy now; be good, and I will rest an hour between you two."

And he lay down and slept.

And lo, he heard the asses speaking to each other.

Said the old donkey to the newcomer: "Don't stamp your hoof, we must let Chick-Pea sleep!"

"Who is Chick-Pea?" asked the new one.

"The sleeper between us."

"But that's Her-Bak!" said the new ass.

"No, it's Chick-Pea."

The new ass snorted mightily and said: "Let's stop it. Are we going to quarrel about it like men?"

"No," said the old one. "It is already too much that he should have thought we could be jealous."

The new ass snorted thrice as if laughing. "Jealous, indeed! It takes two to be jealous!"

"But the boy thinks we are two."

"Yes, he sees us as men do when they count their herds: so many asses, so many cows, so many dogs."

"The funniest thing of all is that men even say 'ants' and 'bees' as if there were many of them."

The old donkey shook his head. "That is just as if we were to say 'two men' for their two eyes, 'two men' for their ears, and so on."

"All right, you need not go on. It is too silly. As long as they see themselves divided up into small men, of course they will go on fighting. They think they are independent of one another."

The old donkey went on: "For us there is only one thing that has the power to separate us, and that is . . ."

"Keep quiet . . . don't mention her name!"

The old ass shook his ears violently. "I shan't mention her name; it would be unwise. She only need hear it, and might come, and then . . ."

"Then keep quiet. You don't want to name her, and yet you speak of nothing but her! We must not trouble the boy's sleep: he does not know her yet."

"You are wrong. The boy has begun to feel her appeal."

"What do you know about that?"

"I have known him for a long time," the old one said. "His blood is hotter today."

"Then we ought to warn him . . . he must not become like one of us."

"Yes," said the old one, "I know men who on this point are less enslaved than we."

"I, too, know of such men," said the new one, "and Her-Bak is in their hands."

The old one stamped his hoof. "Why do you call him Her-Bak?"

"Because that is the name they give him there."

"I like Chick-Pea better."

"That's almost the same word."

"But it seems that they mean two different things."

"What does it matter, since neither is his true name."

"That is right," said the old one, "but then men do not know the true name."

"Pronounce it then," said the new one, "to wake him up; he has slept long enough."

"No," said the old one, "he would not hear me."

Chick-Pea woke up and cried: "Say it, speak it out!"

A gentle voice whispered: "Chick-Pea . . . is that you?"

He hesitated. . . . But he recognised the voice, sighed and answered: "Yes."

Mut-Sherit remained on the threshold, brandishing a bird-trap. "Why don't you come in?" Chick-Pea asked.

She spoke with a choking voice: "You come out: father has forbidden me to look for you, so I have taken my trap as a pretext. I'm going into the fields, by the river: meet me there."

She went. He could hear her as she raised her clear voice, singing a well-known song:

Beloved brother, my heart yearns for your love.
Look what I am doing . . .
I have come with my trap in my hands;
And what happiness would there be, if you were with me when I lay my trap![1]

Chick-Pea followed her from afar; when he had caught up with her, she laughed and repeated her song with full voice. He seized her hands. "Be still, and let me look at your face; I hardly recognise you."

She laughed again. "You have known me since you were born."

"Mut-Sherit, you cannot understand that . . . but the asses are right."

She looked at him in dread. "Are you mad?" Then she saw tears in his eyes: "Why are you crying? Have Fine-Speaker and his rowdy gang hurt you? Let them have their say—I know you are right."

Chick-Pea covered his eyes with his hands. "You are not like the rest of them; it will be harder for me to leave you behind. However, it will have to be. I have not understood all of it, but I know that I shall have to become something more than an ass. . . ."

Mut-Sherit became afraid. She tore her brother's hands from his face and scrutinised his eyes. "Tell me that you are neither mad nor ill."

"No, I am not mad, but I am awaking after a long dream . . . and I am beholding you, Her, the Sister, the Woman, my Mother. . . ."

Now, in turn, he was dominating; erect and motionless he stood before her and contemplated her; while she, confused, dared neither go nor ask questions.

Suddenly he laughed out loud with joy. "Come, I'll show you that I am not mad."

[1] Egyptian love song.

They ran away like two children, towards the house of an old scribe, a friend of their father's. From him Chick-Pea borrowed two reeds and a palette. On the way he found a broken jug and stopped and drew on its belly, for Mut-Sherit's benefit, all the pots and vessels he had turned and carved. Proudly he spoke of his new knowledge, described the difficulties of the techniques, and told her the name and use of each vessel. Reassured, Mut-Sherit left him, so that he might arrive at home before her.

When he arrived and entered the low hall he found nobody at home: his father and mother had not yet returned from the fields. He looked at the furniture—a table, two stools, some jars: beer-jar, water-jar, corn-jar, barley-jar, jar for the loaves, jar for the loin-cloths, jars for the clothing. He sat down before one after the other in turn with his palette and his

reeds and inscribed on the belly of each jar the name of its contents, in hieroglyphic images.

Never had he worked with such perfection, giving so much attention to the proportions, the details of each sign. . . . He was proud of the result.

"I have left out nothing—except the spots."

As he checked the last jar, his parents entered with Mut-Sherit and were dumbfounded with surprise.

Chick-Pea quietly explained the meaning of each inscription. The father muttered: "So he has learnt something after all. . . ."

XXII

SOLITUDE

CHICK-PEA returned alone to his Lord's mansion, alone with his ass. And there he found himself alone, alone in an empty house; the sleepy porter did not even trouble to answer his questions. Apprehensively he led the ass to the stable; then he saw Menkh's steward and ran towards him.

"What on earth has happened, that the house is so sad and lonely and no one stirs in the courtyards?"

The steward was in a wicked mood. "When the master is away the varlets idle and the rod is powerless. Menkh has gone to inspect the mines; at this very moment he travels upstream, with his inspectors and accountants."

Disappointment choked Chick-Pea's throat. "What shall I do? Has he left no orders for me?"

"Plenty of time to talk them over. The Master leaves you free choice of your next trade; never has anyone been so privileged. As you wish, you may get your fingers callous with the smith, or your hands stinking with the dyer, or your teeth full of pitch with the cobbler, or you may suffocate under one roof with the weaver: the favour of your master offers you a choice of servitudes. How much more lucrative was the desk of the scribe. Now you may take your time and confer with your heart and your nose and your fingers, and when you have made up your mind, I shall introduce you into the workshop of your choice."

The boy remained stupefied where he stood. Everything was so different from what he had expected: no attentive ear to listen to his adventures; no Master to take note of his resolutions; he would have to repress the confidences he had hoped to pour out . . . there would be no reproaches and no advice for him.

His sudden freedom upset him. He went out to look for the harpist, but in vain, for the blind man was on board ship with Menkh to while away the long hours of the journey. Alone and aimless, Chick-Pea roamed through the demesne. He went towards the Nile and sat down beside a path.

Down there, beyond the cultivated fields, the mountain of the West took on the hue of a pink flamingo's back. The harshness of the rocky mass became gentler and looked smooth like feathers, as it rose in terraces towards the sky and hid in the heavy fold of the canyons the mysteries of its caverns and the secrets of its tombs. It was the mountain, naked and silent, dominating the fertile valley with the whole inertia of its sterility. No life sprang from its flanks. Dry like the breath of *Seth*, incorruptible like a skeleton, virgin in its barrenness, brooding over bones, the mountain waited.

At its feet, grassland sprouted from the mud, thickets swarmed with lives. And the shameless green provoked the mountain; carried up by the eastern wind, seeds asked for its hospitality . . . and were smothered in its dust. Inexorably the mountain denied all; but its refusal was without malice; it had the seal of the Inevitable and thus was peaceful and harmonious.

There was no sadness in its barrenness; the gentle breeze caressed it in vain, but when its mists were pierced by the rays of *Râ*, it wove, every morning and evening, veils of rosy gold which crowned it with an aureole.

And the earth of dead men seemed to irradiate light as though the Sun which it embraced each evening had left his rays in it . . . and is it not now the dankness of the fertile ground teeming with life which looks so dark at its side?

Until this day, Chick-Pea had known only this mould: was it not this that nourished him and his like? On what could he have lived in the mountain? But now his loneliness was attracted by this desert; and Chick-Pea was astounded to discover a peculiar charm in the silence that was oppressing him. . . .

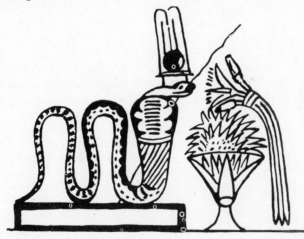

"Hey, you there, Chick-Pea, has perhaps *Mersegert* bewitched you?" The dreamer lifted his eyes towards the scribe who had called him.

"Welcome on our side of the river, oh Pa-Bak! Who is *Mersegert*?"

Pa-Bak took a look at Chick-Pea and laughed. "You have studied the scriptures and do not know who *Mersegert* is? Listen then, for I am perhaps the only one who can repeat the word he has heard from a Sage: *Mersegert* is the powerful cobra living in those caverns; she is the snake whose coils interlace in the mountain; she is the *goddess of silence*; but when her forehead succeeds in touching the sky, then her name of perfection is 'The Summit' . . . Let us see whether *Mersegert* is going to explain this enigma to you!"

And Chick-Pea replied: "I did not know her up to this very hour."

The scribe laughed again and went his way.

Chick-Pea was impressed: he contemplated the Summit with respect, as if the passer-by had given him a message.

"So there is a *Neter* of silence? . . . Is that the one who makes the Mountain so radiant? The Mountain! How can it be so much alive, when it encloses so many dead? I really must learn to know the Mountain!"

Chick-Pea considered the sum total of his knowledge: "I have known the river, I have tilled the soil, I have observed a few animals . . . moreover I have worked in stone. . . ."

And suddenly Chick-Pea understood his Master's intention. "Doubtless it is not so much a question of *choosing* a trade, but of learning with each technique the laws of Nature which it can teach. Now I like *that* much better! Let's go, there is no time to be lost."

Then he noticed the steward asleep under a doum-tree. He awakened him and said: "I want to learn to work in wood; lead me."

The steward did not stir. "What wood?" he asked. "Sticks? Timber? Door-panels? Furniture? By which of all those specialists does 'His Master's Beloved' prefer to be thrashed?"

"I do not know yet. Have each of them show me his work; after that I'll make my choice."

With one bound the steward was on his feet; but Chick-Pea did not wait for the effect of his answer: nimbler than the scribe, he was already climbing up a palm-tree, mocking the pursuer who cursed him: "May those craftsmen lengthen your ears as befits your arrogance."

"If they had free choice, are you sure it would be *my* ears they would pull, O you whom they fear more than the locusts?"

"On my life, come down immediately, or I'll set the monkey to bring you down."

"Very well then, climb!"

The scribe of the demesne became furious like a cheetah from the south; he screamed: "By the life of *Maât*: let it be rendered to you a hundred times by my hand what you are doing to me under this tree!"

"Well spoken! I have just found a book of spells which will make your wish come true without delay."

A doum nut, and another nut, and a third fell at the steward's feet.

"Let it be done as you have said! You have sworn by *Maât*: now you must give me a hundred times as many nuts as you have received! And let this be executed on the spot, or else I shall tell Menkh that you have accused him of offering me a choice of servitudes."

A servant passed. Chick-Pea hailed him: "Hey you! The scribe

Steward-general orders you to bring me here two baskets full of doum-nuts of the finest quality. And hurry."

The servant looked at the steward who grunted acquiescence; then he went away. The steward dared not risk Menkh's reprimand; so he went, according to his orders, to advise the chiefs of the workshops where sticks and furniture were made, of the impending visit of Chick-Pea. But he added: "You have no reason to congratulate yourself on a recruit who has so far been unable to keep his post in any workshop. Treat him without indulgence, this pest of a Chick-Pea, with which the Master has become infatuated to his own perdition."

However, scribes, whether chief accountant or steward, are not the craftsmen's friends: and this one's lip-venom turned against himself: when then Chick-Pea, loaded with two baskets full of nuts, presented himself to the chief of joiners, he accepted him without ill will.

"My Master," said Chick-Pea, "wants me to become skilled in a trade; the great renown of your mastery has so much enchanted my ears, that my most lively desire is to try yours. But I cannot impose upon you my lack of skill: so allow me to get the feel of wood with your neighbour, the stickmaker; afterwards I shall return to you."

The master-joiner measured the boy with his eyes.

"Indeed, is it then such a trifle, a stick?"

Chick-Pea put one basket at his feet. "Allow the servant-here-present to offer you this gift in exchange."

"In exchange for what? Do you think one can buy a master with nuts?"

Chick-Pea became confused.

"I am poor, O Nadjar, but my Lord is rich . . . and I will work."

Nadjar's sharp glance penetrated into the boy's marrow as into a young piece of wood which one puts to the test. Certainly, the fibre appeared to be sound, for the master-joiner smiled and said: "Take your nuts to my neighbour; if he is satisfied with your work, I shall see what you can be taught. Prove your mettle, workman!"

XXIII

STICKS

THE neighbour refused neither nuts nor apprentice. "On my life, you have come just at the right moment, my son. My branch-straightener has none to help him these days: let us see whether you can replace his sick assistant. You will have to learn how to strip a branch of its bark without injuring it, to warm it without burning it, to fix it into this fork, to apply the lever at the right place to curve it into the shape you wish to give it: there is work for a nimble-fingered workman. But for today your task will be to sit on the far end of the branch to weigh it down, so that when it cools off it keeps the given shape."

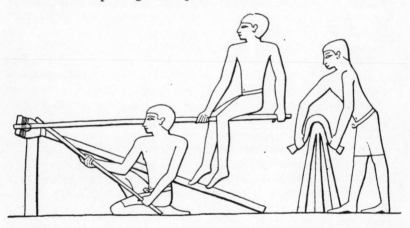

"All right. The moment has come: into the saddle, horseman!"

Chick-Pea took his seat; holding himself in a precarious equilibrium on the long branch he had leisure to scrutinise the workshop. He marvelled to see so many sticks: and that shapes which differed so widely could all be derived from simple tree branches. In a corner, they were finishing a point with an adze; in another they were truing up a pommel; here busy hands were polishing a piece of ebony; elsewhere again wood was being coated with bright paints. An artist was carving hieroglyphs; another encrusted into them ornaments of stone and metal. . . . Abit, their chief and marrow—himself a tall, meagre stick—checked the straightness and the measurements, corrected the smallest detail. His words were brief, his movements full of meaning. His nasal voice meted out to each stick the destiny of its shape. . . . He created an image by his movements, and then his body took the shape of that image, and the docile workman gave his work this shape.

From his perch Chick-Pea observed and appreciated what he saw; he burned to give voice to his admiration, and when he saw the master cutting a curve with a single movement, he screamed with enthusiasm: "Oh, Abit, truly you are the Master of Sticks!"

He was clapping his hands, but lost his equilibrium, and down he went, nose into the dust.

A curse brought the chief of the workshop to the scene; the workman checked the branch on which Chick-Pea had been sitting, but as it was already cooled it had not suffered from the shake-up the fall had given it. Abit gave the new apprentice a mocking look.

"Very young wood! Very green—too much sap, forsooth!"

But he enquired after the reason for Chick-Pea's enthusiasm . . . and friendship awoke in his heart.

That day more words (*medu*) than sticks (*medu*) were turned. The Master showed the apprentice round his workshop: "You are right to express some admiration, my son. This is no common craft. We have to adapt each stick to its use; the stick you use in the fields is one thing, simple and straight, but the tall stick for use on the marshlands is a different thing; different again is the stick on which one rests. This here is the ancient *menkh* with its rounded fork, and there you see the antique *abit*: its fork is well suited to pin snakes to the ground. And here is a rack for sticks to be used on the marshlands."

"Why do you inscribe on these the North, the South, the East, and the West?"

"They have been ordered by the Temple; I haven't been told why. Can you then read the hieroglyphs?"

"Don't you know that I have been a scribe?"

"Really? It's surprising then that you should take an interest in handicraft. But you are right: it's a good way: there is less intelligence in the accountant's reed than in the crooked stick of the shepherd. The scribe though he counts by the thousand is a block of wood whose science I for one do not envy."

Chick-Pea listened. Then he asked: "And you: what have you learnt from your craft?"

The craftsman caressed a stick that became progressively thicker and thicker towards its lower end; he leaned on it and said:

"I have learnt *what the stick means*. The speech of an animal is its cry; but in man's language his speech has become complicated, so the simplest carrier of his speech is the stick. Through the stick he expresses his gesture and his nature; with the stick he points, threatens, or punishes; with the stick he measures, on it he rests; and in the dark the stick guides him. His stick expresses his strength; his staff expresses his function. A man may be naked, provided he has his staff. . . . The moods of man vary, but his staff is unchanging; his staff re-establishes harmony; his staff imposes respect. When he sleeps, it guards him; when he is tired it protects him; and if he is tempted to forget his function, his staff calls him to act.

"A man's stick shares in his strength or in his impotence. . . . Oh, my son, what could I not say of the stick!"

Chick-Pea listened to the sound of the words. . . . Like the rhythmical pulse of the heart, the word *medu* reverberated through his veins.

"*Medu*"—speech—"*medu*"—stick. . . .

Slowly the day effaced itself; and the night wiped out the images, but that of *Abit-medu* remained for ever impressed on the boy's heart.

Chick-Pea did not want to leave the workshop. He asked for permission to sleep among the sticks while Menkh was absent. Was it laziness? Untimely zeal? Who knows whether it was not the exuberant djinn that harried Chick-Pea's heart.

Chick-Pea did not sleep: Chick-Pea was working. In a corner he had found an extraordinary staff of which Abit had not spoken to him, and there could be no doubt about it, it was the most beautiful of all. Every night, by the light of a smoking wick, his eyes glued on the model, he pruned, he cut, he shaped the new branch, paying attention to the smallest detail. . . . Then he hid his work until the evening.

The day of glory came at last. It was market day, and in the early morning he took his marvel out: a superb *was*;[1] its long-eared head was a good foot higher than his own.

"Well," he said to himself, "that's really grand: today I'm a *man*, a man in possession of *his* own stick!"

Passers-by on the market looked with amazement at the fantastic stick; two scribes guffawed with laughter; young peasants came and touched it eagerly. . . . But suddenly the scandal broke out; a passing priest rubbed his eyes, thinking it was a dream: an urchin gravely strolling about with a *was*, as if a *Neter* had descended from a stele.

Having made sure that the incredible was a fact, the priest threw himself upon the desecrator, tearing his tall *was* away from him, but Chick-Pea became indignant.

"This is *my* stick, you bandit, I have not stolen it: I have carved it myself!"

Curious people gathered; the priest gesticulated: "This wretch is usurping a sacred symbol! . . . Who are you?"

"It's Chick-Pea, from Abit's workshop," someone said.

The priest seized the culprit by the ear and hurriedly led him back to his master. He put the *was* into his boy's hand and in this pose presented him to the craftsman. "O Abit, behold this spectacle: that is how this scoundrel went strutting about in the market-place."

[1] *was*: tall sceptre-staff with *Seth*-like animal head that was usually put into the hands of a *Neter*, or, on certain occasions, of the Pharaoh.

Dumbfounded, Abit looked at his apprentice, who seemed quite unaware of his crime. "Where have you taken this?" he asked.

Chick-Pea clutched the *was* to his heart. "It's *my* stick; I have carved
it myself."

The craftsman turned to the priest. "On my life, the boy did not know
what he was doing. Let there be no anger in your heart: I will see to his
punishment."

Pacified by this promise the priest left.

Then Abit looked at Chick-Pea and burst into thunderous laughter.
"So you are strutting about on the market-place with a *was* in your hand!
This deserves punishment indeed; to ensure such a scandalous deed be
never repeated, I shall lock you up for one hour in my treasury."

He drew the secret bolt on a door and pushed the culprit into the room,
closing the door behind him; then he went back and laughed to his
heart's content in the workshop.

There he had a close look at the scandalous exhibit and marvelled at the
accomplished workmanship: to be sure, a flaw here and there betrayed
the work of a novice, but the details and measurements were correct,
the work had been done with scrupulous care. He shook his head with
satisfaction.

"Would I had such a prisoner every day!"

Again he drew the bolt and entered. The prisoner seemed to be very
comfortable in his jail; this was a foretaste of Temple mysteries. Sceptres
displayed their strange symbolism against the walls: a finely wrought
staff beside an alabaster club with pliant handle; the pommel of that
other had the shape of an onion; there, precious 'fly-whisks', and short
crooks striped with gold and blue. Oh, and those pretty three-tailed
whips with porcelain handles and coloured beads! . . . But Chick-Pea
remained speechless seeing a fine array of samples of *his* staff: what a
marvellous range of *was*-sticks in green or blue made of glazed clay, and
some of painted wood, red or black.

Abit interrupted his ecstasy. "So you little scoundrel, you are admiring
your staff!"

Chick-Pea assumed an innocent expression. "Why haven't I the right
to carry it?"

"Unless you become a *Neter* or Pharaoh, you had better hold back
from it in future. Divine symbols are not toys."

"But the King is not a *Neter*?"

The craftsman reflected. "Pharaoh, L.H.S., is the *Neter* of the Two-
Lands and their representative before the *Neters* of the Sky; when he
fulfils this role in the temple, he carries one or the other of these
sceptres."

Chick-Pea pointed towards a short stick from which issued a long
bifurcated branch. "O Abit, and this forked stick, why have you gilded
it? It is a simple tree-branch that has not even been straightened!"

Abit was slow in answering. "The Sage wanted it thus; he said it was the most beautiful of all symbols."[1]

"Ah . . . and this pretty whip, what is it called?"

"That is no whip, but one of the two symbols of royalty; the *nekhekha*; would you not say that it is like a cascade of drops that seem to issue from the stick? The other symbol is the crook: its name is *heck*; it ought to remind you of the shepherd's crook. It can catch the sheep by their wool, and hold back a lamb that might go astray . . . that at least is how I have understood it, but there are other meanings I have not been told."

Chick-Pea grew indignant. "What? You make them and don't know them?"

The craftsman sighed. "There are many steps to the stairs of the Temple."

"O my Master, are you then part of the Temple?"

A powerful kick sent the nosy questioner rolling. He rose again, grumbling: "The second time for the same thing. And for all I know this may not be the last time."

Abit looked at the boy with surprise. "Who has given you this interest in symbols? There are no priests in your family. . . ."

"I don't know what a symbol is," replied Chick-Pea.

"I can answer that one," said the craftsman. "It is the living form of a law."

Chick-Pea reflected for a while.

"Then the King ought to wear *all* the symbols?"

The craftsman bowed. "As far as our world is concerned, that is true! . . . Child, who has taught you?"

"Me? I don't know anything. I just ask questions."

"Then go on asking questions: what I know I shall tell you; but as to the rest, learn to wait. And remember *that it is better not to know and to know that one does not know*, than presumptuously to attribute some random meaning to the symbols. Well, this is enough for today."

The boy was disappointed. "You have not yet shown me all the sticks."

"You will know them little by little; let it be enough to know that every office has its emblem, and every power its symbol. I shall even tell you a secret: this long stick which seems to fit into another as into a trumpet, is the *makes*, with which the King penetrates into the temple; it is the principle of the giant fennel, whose marrow preserves and transports the fire. If you can, preserve the lesson of the *makes* in your marrow. . . . If not, may *Ptah*[2] forgive me for having mentioned it."

[1] See *Her-Bak Disciple*, Chapter 'Astrology'.
[2] Principle of the creative fire, the smith of all things. See *Her-Bak Disciple*, Index: *Ptah*.

JOINER

SOME time after this, Nadjar came to enquire about Chick-Pea's progress. He asked Abit to tell him all he knew about his apprentice.

"The nature of this boy," Nadjar then said, "is by no means common; he makes such speedy progress, that we must distinguish between him and the workman. The time has come to teach him the first elements of that which can give direction to his consciousness. Your duty now is to entrust him to me."

These words saddened Abit, who loved his apprentice; however, he did as Nadjar wished, and comforted Chick-Pea in his sadness: "When the Joiner of Joiners makes such a request, I cannot refuse. Nadjar is a master of his craft: you ought to be happy that he is willing to teach you; and don't waste those precious hours."

Chick-Pea said sadly: "O Abit, I hoped I should one day work for your treasury."

"You will meet the symbolic sticks again somewhere else; my craft is a stick-maker's; the others I have wrought for the love of art alone. Let Nadjar guide you as he thinks fit: he is a good judge."

Chick-Pea made his start in sawdust and wood shavings, no sceptres or masterpieces in sight. Nadjar seemed to take little notice of his apprentice.

The foreman was merciless. The fingers of the novice paid the penalty for his clumsiness.

When he knew how to square a wooden block with an axe, to cut and smooth the planks with the saw and the adze, he learnt to handle the bow on his drill to pierce the holes for the pegs; he learnt to cut slots with the chisel. But there was little joy in this work, for Chick-Pea yearned for his friend.

One evening, weary of trying without success to fit a tenon into a slot, he made up his mind to persevere with it and remained behind when the others went home. With small, precise cuts he busied himself with finishing the adjustment, and as the workshop was empty, he sang in rhythm with his movements[1]:

When I was a little child,
A wall opened before me:
And through the chink I caught a glimpse
Of the falcon of gold;
But the hour came to an end
And the great wall closed up again!

I counted the days by the hundred;
And there spoke a powerful voice . . .
I, a little child, played,
Did I, thus playing, offend
That powerful voice?
Who can tell me the way to it?

Many the Moons that have passed,
Then the Mountain of Silence
Poured its gold on my fingers.
My heart has guarded the treasure
Of this silence,
And my fingers have closed themselves again.

Several decades[2] have passed,
A friend has tendered me his hand . . .
A friend—is that still too much?
Who then has said:
'Leave everything and follow your way?'
Hard is the way without a friend!

A hand was put on the singer's shoulders: 'So you think you have been abandoned, my young friend?"

The surprise made the chisel miss its mark and a chip of the tenon split

---

[1] For the French text of this song, see pages 299–300.
[2] decade = Egyptian week of ten days (T.N.).

off. The boy, ashamed at having laid bare his heart, reared up: "Do I look like a weakling? And look at this: I shan't get that tenon right any more."

Nadjar took the chisel out of his hand, then he led him to the wood-store: roughly squared blocks of carob, ebony, and juniper. "Workman," he said, "pay attention to my questions: if you are ripe for a higher train-ing, you will have to solve this problem: you have drilled holes into a soft wood: what kind of wood will you have to choose for the pegs so that the adjustment may be durable and solid?"

Chick-Pea touched and looked at the blocks, as if he expected them to prompt the answer. At last he said: "Is it not true, that if a peg of hard wood enters into soft wood it may wear it out and at last make it split?"

"That is right. But now, if it is to play freely, as for instance in the case of hinges, so that it is liable to wear and tear, what would you do then?"

"Then I think, one would have to choose the hard wood."

Nadjar put his hand on the anxious head. "Do not worry, my son, you have answered well; violence is not a medium of harmony; that is why we adjust wood with wood, and not with metal. One can bind boards together with copper wire, if one wishes to leave a certain flexibility to the whole structure; but one must not pin wood together except with wood. One must search for the means of making or undoing something always *within its own nature*. But I wanted to see whether your mind was simple and open to the law of Truth. Now, look at the cut of this trunk: you can read the *medu-Neters*?[1] Can you read the age of this tree in its concentric rings?"

Chick-Pea marvelled.

"And do you know why the rib of a palm is the hieroglyph of the year? Do you know that at each New Moon a new frond grows on the date-tree?"

Chick-Pea pranced. "Then our hieroglyphs, and our crafts, and Nature, these are all one and the same science?"

Nadjar's face lit up: "Yes, my son, that is what you were meant to understand, but it is only open to him who can decipher these three books and transpose from one to the other. Tomorrow we shall start work."

Next morning the Master joiner summoned Chick-Pea into his own workshop; he bade him be seated and said:

"As you are going to study our ways of working more thoroughly, it is time to give you a few words of truth: what use you make of them will be your test. Until this day you have been a workman carrying out prescribed movements. The artisan is distinct from the workman be-cause he is aware of his *movement*, of the *instrument*, and of the *material* in which he works. But the accomplished craftsman goes further: he knows the laws of the material and tries to understand their causes; he knows the name of things and their symbolic meaning. That is the Way."

[1] *medu-Neter*: the hieroglyphs (divine words).

"And this way leads to the Temple?" Chick-Pea asked.

"Who then," Nadjar asked in return, "has drafted and wrought all our temples, statues, symbolic objects, if not the craftsmen? And he who knows the causes and the laws, is he not a pillar of the Temple?"

"O, my Master," replied Chick-Pea, "I want to become a craftsman."

"Your way," said Nadjar, "is the right way if you understand this: what you receive depends on what you give; there is what you give the craft, and there is what the craft gives you.

"The *workman* gives the toil of his arm, his energy, his exact or inexact movement; for this the craft gives him a notion of the resistance of the material, and its manner of reaction.

"The *artisan* gives the craft his love; and to him the craft responds by making him one with his work.

"But the *craftsman* gives the craft his passionate research into the laws of Nature which govern it; and the craft teaches him Wisdom."

Joy shone in Chick-Pea's eyes, as light freed from a cloud. He did not dare to shout out what was in his heart.

Nadjar put his hand on the boy's head. "Speak without fear, what do you want?"

"That I may be given your teaching (*sba*)."

"So be it; well then, let us enter by the door (*sba*)."

Chick-Pea repeated the words as if he had heard them for the first time: "*sba . . . sba*: why have these two things the same name?"

"O, joiner, my son: the craft will answer you. But what would you say about the door?"

"That it is through the door one enters into the house."

"Say rather: into a closed place."

"Yes, Master, but it is also the door that closes it."

Nadjar led his pupil in front of the door. "Now, is it really the door which closes this place?"

Chick-Pea looked at the empty entrance. "No, it is the leaf of the door."

"Measure your words, my son: the leaf is that which fills the emptiness between the posts of the door-frame; search rather for that which ensures the closing of the leaf."

"Am I blind?" Chick-Pea cried. "It is the bolt which opens and closes."

"That is why the secret of a door lies in its bolt. Do not be negligent in finding and using the right word. *Thot* never replies to inexact *medus*."

"May my Master forgive the ignoramus; is it then necessary to draw the name of a *Neter* into matters of the craft?"

"That is so," said Nadjar, "but the mere workman pays no heed to it."

Chick-Pea lowered his head: he understood the lesson. Nadjar went on:

"The door presupposes the closed place to which it is the opening, there can be no door without the closed place, nor a house without a door; now the enclosure made open by a door, is called *per-t*. If you want to make a perfect door, you must suit its measurements to that which will go through it, and the strength of its hinges to the weight of its leaf. Take care that you do not disregard the direction of the wood; like a man, wood also, having once been alive, has its proper direction, its upper and lower part. And when one works upon it, a board is by no means like a slab of stone. The art of joining pieces of the same wood which are differently directed, is one of the secrets of the craft."

Chick-Pea listened with passion. "O Nadjar, you are a joiner down to your very name!"

Nadjar smiled. "My name is rather that of the carpenter's."

"What is the difference?"

"The carpenter joins the pieces of wood in order to build the skeleton of the building *according to the limits* (*ndjer*) imposed by the fixed plan, that is a joining so ingenious that only he who has invented it can undo it."

"Is that then such a great secret?"

"Certainly, for here comes into play the conception of geometrical construction, and the working out beforehand in one's mind of the final shape."

"O my Master, will you tell me the secret of the joiner?"

"The accomplished joiner knows the nature of different woods: their essence, their resistance, and their weight. He knows how to adjust the pieces to so perfect a fit that time binds them closer rather than disjoins them. That is the meaning of your Lord's name: Menkh."

"But my Lord is not a joiner."

"He is the Master of Craftsmen, and all techniques demand a similar knowledge of what agrees and what causes disagreement and thus instability."

Nadjar rose. "Go now, and work. If you know how to listen I have said enough to you. I shall hand you over to my works master, who will teach you the laws of joining and draughtsmanship."

Some time later the demesne stirred with excitement: watchers signalled the arrival of Menkh's ship. No gazelle could run more swiftly than Chick-Pea to the harbour.

Numerous ships, ranged side by side, threw against the sky the network of their masts and cordage. Merchants of cakes, dates, and dried meat quarrelled for strategic positions from whence to tempt the appetite of the arrivals. Already could the nasal voice of the leadsman be heard and orders that were being shouted to the helmsman. . . . Chick-Pea jumped into a light canoe and wound his way between the stationary hulls. Rowing as hard as he could he reached the ship, hailed a sailor, seized the tendered oar, hoisted himself up like a monkey and climbed over the railings. Menkh stood observing the intricate progress of the ship as it approached the bank, when suddenly something rolled at his feet like a ball, clasped his knees and kissed them with mad abandon.

"Hey, what is this? Is that Chick-Pea or my monkey?"

A head looked up from the imprisoned knees. Menkh burst into laughter. "Let me observe the landing; go and wait for me on the quay and make room for my arrival!"

Chick-Pea, speechless with joy, rose and hurried away; seeing a great stick leaning against the mast he took it, jumped into the skiff and returned with the current towards the bank. There the crowd was gathering noisily; merchants quarrelled and defended their stands for displaying their wares.

"Gangway, gangway, in the name of the Lord Menkh!"

Chick-Pea brandished his stick and tried to clear the quay around the mooring posts. . . . Suddenly an angry voice cried out: "Who has taken the large staff of the Lord? Oh, you thief, son of a dog! Gangway, make way for the Lord's shipmaster!"

Chick-Pea heard it: he jumped around and, finding himself face to face with the furious shipmaster, he held the staff over his head to defend it. The merchants took advantage and immediately reinvaded the quay, while the battle was raging . . . the shipmaster tried in vain to clasp the lifted arm, Chick-Pea leapt up, and stepped aside, letting his assailant fall. The shipmaster rose again, screaming: "You will be thrashed and chased away! You have stolen the staff with the magic name, the great 'ames nefer'."[1]

"Who has dared to utter the name of this staff?" asked a severe voice. The shipmaster turned his head, whereupon he was gripped by two strong hands and hurled into the river.

Someone laughed . . . but the noise died away before Chick-Pea's grave mien. Like an ebbing tide the crowd left a void round him . . . muttering: "The staff . . .!"

A loud acclamation resounded; the rope had been tied around the post, the *Neter* had been saluted. The crowd was shouting: "Welcome!" Chick-Pea walked forward gravely, carrying the staff before him with holy awe; people made way for him, whispering to each other: "It's the magic staff . . . it has thrown the impudent one into the water! It has given might to the boy!"

Chick-Pea approached Menkh who set foot on shore in the midst of religious silence. The boy knelt down and presented the stick.

"Master, I have carried out your orders. . . . As for the *medu*, forgive your servant who acted in ignorance. . . ."

Menkh lifted him up. "Say no more and come."

The procession began to move; in the background a man climbed out of the water; dripping and shamefaced he followed the crowd under the gibes of the merchants.

That day there was great rejoicing in the demesne, and double rations of bread-beer were issued to all servants of the Master. But no bread or

[1] *ames* means the name of a stick; *nefer* means 'perfect, accomplished'.

beer could make Chick-Pea as happy as the fact that at last he was at liberty to tell his Master in confidence of all that had happened to him.

Menkh let the tide of his story flow without ever opening his lips, either for blame or for praise. "Man's words," he said at last, when he had heard all, "are incomplete evidence; the real signature of a craftsman is his work: let us wait."

At these words the boy grew afraid lest his Master might harbour rancour against him because of the staff; and he implored Menkh: "May the heart of my Master harbour no anger against me, for there was no insolence in my act! This stick to me seemed like other sticks, and I did not know it had a name."

"Know then that every thing has a name."

"But in what way was it magic?"

"It was not magic if you did not know that it was."

"But people said it was magic."

"Hence it acted upon them."

"And is it magic for you?"

"To me it is sacred, for it is my *rod of measurements*."

"And why is its name sacred?"

"Because that is its name in Truth. Now take care: since you know this, you must not profane it again!"

"O Master, your word is in my heart. But are there really magic things?"

"Certainly. But today I shall not tell you more about it. So far your attention has not been drawn to this subject. But now, since such curiosity has come to you: look, listen, and observe. . . . We shall come back to this question later on."

Chick-Pea had returned to his work; the works master rushed him through his apprenticeship, as was the wish of his Master. The boy's enthusiasm and candour refreshed the old craftsman's heart; he showed him those secrets of the trade which a nimble-fingered workman had to know; he revealed to him the traditions of the craft, adding the fruits of his own experience.

"Learn to feel the wood, my son, as you handle your tools, for the wood makes its own demands: all life is not yet quite extinguished in it—whatever the ignorant may think—unless some mistake has been made in cutting it down."

Chick-Pea's curiosity awoke. "Oh, tell me, what are the mistakes that can be made?"

"If you cut a tree after the sap has stopped rising in it, then the fibres will be empty, dead, liable to alteration and deformation in the course of time, through heat or drought."

"And does anyone know what stops the sap from rising?"

"Certain times are known, and certain circumstances; these are the secrets of the observing and 'conscious' craftsman; but one does not speak about this, my son, lest the ignorant scribes should laugh."

Chick-Pea did not lose a single word; nor did the old man tire of teaching him.

"Look at this bed, O Chick-Pea; one glance ought to show you—without trying it out—whether it is balanced or whether it rocks. The good joiner has a sure eye; he will notice whether the place for an ornament was wrongly chosen: an ornament in tradition ought to underline the power of resistance of the material; it is unwise to carve it on too frail a spot. Cut away only from a strong point, for your work must be durable. The weight of the fattest of noble princes must not make the well-adjusted armchair creak. Tenons and slots that groan under strain insult him who has badly joined them.

"A piece of furniture is beautiful if useful; it is useful if solid. Wisely follow the path of the useful, O my son; it is the sure path to success."

Chick-Pea listened to these pieces of advice, but in the evening he repeated them to Menkh, who said:

"This old man expresses his mind according to his conscience; he is an honest artisan. But the artist Nadjar would not have spoken thus: a useful thing corresponds to physical life and it is true that correct proportions give stability and beauty; this beauty, however, does not depend on their usefulness, but on the cosmic harmony by which these proportions are governed. If you want to develop your consciousness beyond that of the artisan, take heed of this: usefulness always depends on physical properties and on features of secondary importance, for *quality* in the *absolute* does not answer to material requirement. This is so true that all really perfect things are of no practical use at all, but are superfluous: wood, stone bronze are useful. Gold is not useful, but a luxury. A useful ornament is not art; pure Art begins with the Useless. The quest for perfection is not *necessary* to the earthly life; it is luxury, useless, but *divine*. That is why the meaning of the Useless is the meaning of the 'Truly Chosen'?"

"Can the workman be a member of the 'Truly Chosen'."

"If he has this sense, he will express it in his own way: then he will attract notice and be trained accordingly. This explains why we have such a great number of masterpieces; for to create these it would not have been sufficient that some Masters conceive them; we had to train a great number of understanding artists to carry them out."

XXV

THE LODGE

AND the day came when Nadjar, having observed Chick-Pea for a long time, called for him and said:

"Your apprenticeship draws near its end. You will now have to pass the test: with your own hands you will make a carved footstool for your master, and you will also design an ornamental bed. You will do this entirely by yourself, without any help or advice."

"Shall I copy from decorative models?" asked the apprentice.

Nadjar replied: "You must yourself invent the shape and fashion the details of these objects and they must comply with the rules and tradition governing their use. You will present your work by the next moon."

Throughout three days and three nights, Chick-Pea was oblivious of the world around him; he piled design upon design and sketch upon sketch. On the fourth day, having decided that he had found exactly what he wanted, he went to work. He lived and worked alone, away from all others.

When the time had elapsed and the moon had renewed itself, Nadjar sent word to Chick-Pea, saying: "Tomorrow you will present your work. My messenger will guide you to the appointed place."

The candidate spent the night putting the finishing touches to his work, and at dawn the next day held himself in·readiness, feverishly waiting for the call. At last someone came for him; Chick-Pea shouldered his work and followed the unknown person.

He was led in silence: across the river on the other bank, to the very foot of the mountain. There he descended into a small vault which might have been a tomb, but to his surprise he found in it a circle of grave men in session, like a tribunal. Light from a hidden source showed the faces and the centre of the room, leaving the frescoes and hieroglyphs of the walls in semi-darkness. He felt lost in a new world. . . .

The messenger who had brought him here pushed him into the centre of the group. There he recognised Menkh, and near him Nadjar; around them were unknown faces, but away in the shadow Abit was smiling at him. Chick-Pea breathed deeply to strengthen his courage; then he bowed before Menkh, touching the ground with his forehead.

Nadjar called his name: "Joiner apprentice Chick-Pea, come and submit your work."

Chick-Pea rose, took up his footstool and offered it to Menkh saying: "It is here; may it be found worthy to be placed beneath your sandals; I have conceived it, designed it, and wrought it, without help or advice, in accordance with the instructions I received."

"Let the Head of Joiners see and judge."

Nadjar examined the object with curiosity, then he showed it around to those present. It was a simple, sober footstool: a rectangular top, supported on its long sides by carved sidepieces of the same length, and six fingers high.

The plywood pieces had been assembled in such a way that they formed three rectangles on the top, and in each rectangle grew a lotus plant, with its flower, its buds and its leaves. On each side-piece a sun-disk extended its two wings.

The Master Joiners examined the smallest details of the work; everyone appreciated the nicety of the fitting and the good sense shown in the arrangement of the wood-pieces; for there was no flaw in this part of his work; they told each other what they thought of it, and no one uttered any criticism regarding workmanship.

But as to the chosen design, all shook their heads and remained silent.

The messenger had led Chick-Pea aside, to the door. Nadjar called him back: "Now let us see the commanded design of the bed."

As the candidate unfurled the papyrus, so that the whole assembly could see it, the judges burst into a roar of laughter, for this was what they saw: the plaited platform of the bed was supported on the elongated bodies of two asses; the two heads pointed their ears to the left and right of the board at the foot-end, whereas the four hind legs, highly cambered to lift the rumps under the sleeper's head, seemed poised for kicking, an impression emphasised by a sly look from the corner of their eyes.

Oh! what a moment of stupefaction when the artist witnessed this strange reaction to his work. When at last the laughter of the judges had died down, anger contorted his face.

Nadjar, who had been deliberating with Menkh, asked the candidate to sit down before the assembly, and spoke thus:

"As regards the test-piece, O joiner, you deserve this name, for you have shown proof of your knowledge, and your fingers have become skilful. But what a strange design you have chosen: lotus-flowers on a footstool!"

"What's wrong with that?" asked Chick-Pea, "I wanted my master to walk on flowers."

"Say rather 'on water': for where do lotus-flowers grow if not in a pool? But there are more serious faults: have you not two feet—and not three? Why then put them on a threefold bouquet?"

"Three flowers made a prettier design."

"What is wrong, cannot be beautiful. Twofold the leg, twofold must be your design. The King places the *Two-Lands* beneath his sandals, or the *two* kinds of enemies. Triplicity is Unity: and it cannot be placed beneath the duality of the feet.

"Another fault: are you crazy to allow feet to tread on the winged Sun? Is it down on the ground or up in the sky that the golden scarabæus spreads his wings?"

Chick-Pea stiffened like a stubborn ass. "And what of it! Must the artist obey the symbol even in the most ordinary things? May one not play with an idea as the mountain plays with the light? It is the variety of colours that makes the beauty of the mountain. That which never changes is dull and tiresome. It is death."

"The play of the light," said Nadjar, "changes only the *appearance* of the mountain; the colours vary with the state of the atmosphere, and this is mere *appearance*; nothing prevents the artist from playing with the appearance when he deals with the appearance. But the dance of light and shadow follows the journey of the Sun; the rays from the East light up the mountain of the East, and thus the shadow step by step follows the progress of the Lord of Light: this in relation to the Earth is a *reality*. And in the same way do numbers and symbols impose their law upon the artist."

Chick-Pea listened thoughtfully. "Am I to become an *artist* or a *copyist*? If things are like this, I don't see the difference."

Menkh rased his hand, and Nadjar's answer stayed on his lips. "I shall answer this question myself," said Menkh. "Listen first to your master's judgment."

Nadjar resumed: "As regards the design for a bed which you have shown us, I allow you to defend your choice; since you want to play, let us play: why have you taken the ass as carrier?"

Chick-Pea rose and replied to the whole assembly: "As I have been ordered to speak, I shall speak . . . but what can I say? A dog does not speak his master's language, and I fear that I do not know yours! . . . I was told: 'Take care that the symbol remains truthful.' Well, as it happens, your beds are usually carried by a lion; but which of the two images is more truthful as carrier of a man's body: lion or ass?"

Nadjar smiled. "Be it so. Let us play. But we still have to know for what stake we are playing. If the stake is everyday common sense, you win; but if the stake is *consciousness of the Indestructible*, you lose, for our symbols reveal the invisible by means of the visible and give the notion of their relationship; but this they cannot do if employed incorrectly. Moreover, you are confusing *image* and *symbol*; but now is not the time for me to speak of this."

Menkh showed his satisfaction. "Be praised, O Nadjar; you have spoken well indeed."

Nadjar bowed before the Master of Craftsmen and resumed his interrogation. "Can you now explain why you turn the feet of the man towards the head of the animal? This is not in keeping with usage."

"O my Master, this donkey carries the man towards the land of dreams, and if my donkey carries me to market, do I face his ears or his tail?"

"Listen then to what as yet you do not know: that which you behold in one manner while you are awake, you see in the inverse manner in sleep. They are two separate worlds, one reflecting the other as in a mirror. But we have other reasons for placing the sleeper upon the back of an animal head above head: when the soul is carried away by sleep, the inert body remains identified with that of the animal; hence it is no longer *carried* by the animal, and that is why we put it on four legs, as if there were his own support. Thus in this bed Chick-Pea identifies himself with the body of an ass."

"But am I not nearer to the ass than to the lion?"

Menkh laughed, and the whole gathering laughed. "I am no judge of that," replied Nadjar, "but the lion is a Royal animal, while the ass is a servant; and such beds are not given to servants, but to men whose function it is to lead."

"Besides," added Menkh, "the lion is the *solar* quadruped of the Earth: he lives on the border between our Red Earth and our Black Earth, he comes and goes from one to the other; hence it is right that he be the guardian of the human body, while the soul is wandering from one world to the other. These words are not for you, little boy, but for the others who understand, although you may preserve their crumbs in your heart. . . .

"And for your benefit I shall say: the ass *begets* and *forever perpetuates* himself; he is the endless circle of this Earth, and his punishment is to carry burdens *perpetually*. . . . But he is without pride and obedient to the voice; he knows the secret of sound, and his large ears are his reward. What more do you want?"

The boy's features were drawn with fatigue and emotion. "I think I am loaded like my donkey," he sighed.

A sign from Menkh stopped the incipient laughter. "It remains to be seen whether you can pass beyond the animal; if you can overcome your weariness and formulate clear questions, I will answer them without making mysteries."

Chick-Pea closed his eyes and made a desperate effort to think. Someone told him to sit down. The silence deepened and the boy felt as if he were being engulfed in an abyss . . . but then his confusion melted away; a fraternal bond established itself between the candidate and his judges, and, without raising his eyes, he spoke:

"O my Masters! Something in my heart hears what you say, but something else revolts and cries 'slavery'! . . . My question is: what is the difference between a simple copyist and the artist who is the slave of measurement and symbols?"

"The copyist," Menkh answered, "reproduces the models without understanding them. The artist must know the various meanings of the symbols; hence he has the choice between equivalent expressions."

"O Lord, an artist who is not permitted to invent, must certainly strangle the life of his heart."

Menkh protested: "Everyone may invent what pleases him, witness the humorous shards. But that which is to *remain* for future ages must not be allowed to teach errors; hence we destroy without mercy all inscriptions that are not flawless."

"Then are those who work with the aim of teaching condemned to forgo all initiative? Where is then the pleasure of novelty? Where is the pleasure of expressing one's dreams in one's work?"

"Nadjar has replied very well on this point," said Menkh. "Everyone finds that which his nature attracts: if you seek *phantasy*, you will find in it your *pleasure*; but if you search for the *laws of Harmony*, you will find *Knowledge*.

"The artist, as you understand it, looks through Nature at himself; but he who listens to our Masters seeks the *Neter* in Nature . . . and meets them within himself."

"Is it then impossible to teach phantasy and Harmony *together?*"

"Oh, you insatiable boy! Man's life is limited, and each people has its destiny. We have to teach according to our destiny, and according to our Time. Other Times will come, when man will have lost the Wisdom of his Heart; then he will turn to phantasy in order to escape from the sterile ground of dialectics.

"To our Sages the world is *translucent*. Our symbols allow the Causes to shine through even the most concrete facts. He who seeks in silence will perceive them there, and his life will never be long enough to exhaust their riches; but from the windbag and the pretentious scribe this treasure is hidden."

"Yes, Lord, what you are saying is very well for the pupils of the Masters; but as for the artisan confined within his craft, who repeats each day his task which is determined beforehand, what joy is his? What has he gained? What part does he play in this scheme?"

The gathering listened to Chick-Pea with great sympathy.

"Look at the mural paintings," said Menkh. "What do you see?"

Chick-Pea was disappointed. "Oh, these are pictures of very ordinary folk: wood-sawyers, branch-straighteners, joiners who fit a bed, workmen as I see them every day."

"Yes, that is what they would say, all those who have not yet been introduced into 'the heart of the House of Wood'. (Note that the word *khet* means both wood and thing.) But these small personages, the precision of whose movements, whose technical skill, and whose workmanship are admirable, and whose every detail, every word, are in themselves a lesson, well, ask any one of us what meaning these minute people convey on this wall."

Menkh looked towards the youngest of the Master joiners. The man rose, approached the candidate, took him by the hand and led him to the wall, where he asked him to observe the tiny size of the workers compared with the enormous image of the Master.

"Listen to what they have to say, little brother:

'See, we are working for our Master. We are very small, and our Master is very great. Our Master *knows*; he is supremely intelligent; and we, his servants, are also intelligent in our own way, for we are practical, absolutely practical; in our technique there are no mistakes, and we understand to perfection the intent of the orders we are given. We know the value of the right movement, and this knowledge is our glory. And behold, we do not spoil the material entrusted to us.

'You who are contemplating us, do not believe that we feel humiliated by our thraldom: we are like the bass notes of a melody. The higher notes speak of things beyond our understanding, but this does not worry us, for we are part of the melody as a whole. The Sages in their wisdom have devised *simple* instruments; and one day, when one of us tried to improve on them, we were told: "Do not change anything, for your Masters have devised these tools with the help of eternal symbols; the highest abstractions have helped those Masters to find you the best tools." They were wise indeed, those who have given us the shape of our furniture, the shape of our vessels; those who have translated for us into physical form the underlying idea. . . . *For we are living in a world of form.*

'Be not surprised on hearing us speak like this: while still on earth we should not have been able to, but now since we are "on the wall", we have become the *Soul* of the craft; we know what gives the craftsman his joy, a joy he does not analyse, but which makes him sing at his work and gives rhythm to the strokes of his axe and the blows of his hammer. Little brother, little brother, there is no sadness in our toil! The rhythm of the tools is part of the symphony in which the blood of each worker becomes aware of some movement in the life of the Universe.' "

"Did they really think all that?" asked Chick-Pea.

A Master answered: "What matters is not that one should *think* it, but that one should experience and live it."

"That is so," Menkh confirmed. "Man willingly submits if the work imposed upon him gives him not only toil but enthusiasm. Those who *know* train others to become ardent for perfection. Then there is the magic of the songs; the humorous side of the craft; the pride the brotherhoods take in their activities, and the teaching they receive by implication from their rites."

"True," muttered Chick-Pea, "we are never sad in the workshop." Full of curiosity, he went towards the other walls, but Menkh reprimanded him: "What more are you looking for, you inquisitive cat? Will nothing ever cure you of your curiosity? It is late—have you any other questions?"

The boy hesitated. "What shall I say now? I don't dare any more . . ."

"Speak," said Menkh, "this evening all shadows must be lifted."

"It is this," stammered Chick-Pea, "I feel shame at seeing the people's poverty. The artisan makes such beautiful things; why does he never make any for his own use?"

Menkh turned towards the gathering. "This question is a sign of the Times, O friends! There is no going against the time-table of Heaven.

"Hearken to these words, little man: it is with deliberate intent that our Sages reduced the needs of daily life to a strict minimum. Luxury and superfluous comforts would soon have become indispensable; they would have complicated life, increased material worries, and made ever more different crafts necessary.

"The structure of society was organised by our Masters to suit the needs of this country: they imposed discipline upon the passions of the human masses that inhabit our fertile Black Earth—our much too fertile Earth, with its far too easy life, where the blessings of the Sun can be drawn upon as if by sympathetic magic.

"Here one ends by forgetting one's soul, by forgetting everything, as there is no need for any effort; here more than anywhere else in the world one is tempted through inertia towards animality. . . .

"It is in order to save our people from this inertia that our Masters have instituted our particular form of society, whose object is the study of human nature, and this study is an exact science and a fine art. Crafts have been divided as far as necessary but not farther. For every craft all the 'causes' have been assembled and each has been accorded its proper importance. No lawless improvisations are permitted; each man has to learn and to persevere in his craft through which he will become able to understand the universal order, which would be too difficult for him if he had only the human order to start from. The æsthetics of the craft were defined in such a way that everybody can learn to think for himself, if he first learns to think as the others do; but æsthetics of sensual satisfaction have not been allowed for: *they have been disregarded*. There are the *laws of proportion*, and if these are rigorously applied, Beauty results. In this sense 'regulated' imitation is necessary.

"But the sympathetic bond between men and craft develops, despite everything, a certain ingenuity in applying the Symbol. Then there is the pride of craft, the intoxication with craft, the graces of the craft; and if these awaken the spirit of 'quest', the craft will lead man beyond toil towards nobility. This theme of 'craft' is engraved on the stone or depicted on the fresco, *unalterably*. The drawing is frozen movement: it signifies both Movement and Man. It is simultaneously magical and a descriptive sign.

"Later, if you persevere on this road, you will have explained to you the rigid laws of the canon. Today you have passed the first threshold, and what you have received is very heavy for your age. But henceforth you may return to this place, my child: here you will find again the forgotten Words: these walls are impregnated with them.

"And now go and greet your Masters and your brothers, and may your joy this evening be complete."

Chick-Pea trembled with weariness and emotion. He approached those present, and one by one they embraced him, and taught him the gestures of brotherhood, and he felt among them like a young and well-beloved brother. And while the Masters formed a circle around him to carry out the ceremony of farewell, he dropped heavily to the ground, overcome by weariness, and fell asleep while the dark rocks resounded with the appeal to *Ausar*.[1] . . .

[1] *Ausar:* one of *Osiris'* names.

XXVI

THE SUMMIT

It often happened now that the Master of Craftsmen, when visiting some workshop, would call for Chick-Pea to accompany him.

Once, having to order a piece of cloth of great value, he went to a highly skilled artisan. The workshop was a low hall which blinded their sun-filled eyes with its obscurity. Then they saw the large looms, spreading high over the ground the sloping surface of their coloured threads; bowed women operated the shuttle, carefully checking that the cloth emerged flawless.

But Menkh did not stop here; he merely passed through this hall: in the neighbouring room two high looms carried their weft of fine linen with wrought seams like white sails. These marvels were the work of the master of this worshkop himself and of his son. Menkh gave them his orders; then he told Chick-Pea to admire the complicated texture of the fabrics on the loom; he asked the weaver to allow his sandal-bearer to stay till the evening so that he might see the manner and reason of their work.

But father and son were sparing of words. When Chick-Pea returned to his lord he tried to learn from him the lesson he had not gathered from the silent craftsmen.

Instead of replying, Menkh asked him: "Perhaps they had nothing to tell. Do you believe you can find a weaver who can explain his symbols? A person who knows these mysteries would hardly waste his time at the shuttle?"

"By what right then might I, the servant-here-present, know them?"

Menkh gave no reply. After a very long pause he said:

"The work has been done under your eyes: what have you seen?"

"I have seen threads stretched from top to bottom and kept taut by terracotta weights; I have seen the shuttle go to and fro, left and right between those stretched threads, and thus a cloth was made."

"Very good," said Menkh, "what more do you need?"

"That my Master reveal to me the lesson of weaving as he has done for the other crafts."

"As much as you are capable of finding out," Menkh replied, "that much you will know, nothing more. You may leave Nadjar's workshop for three days; go, roam about freely and look around for yourself. We shall see whether you will discover how to meet the *Neter* of weaving."

So Chick-Pea set out, his heart filled with joy, his eyes ablaze with enthusiasm. To be sure, he would do what Menkh had told him; advice from his Master could not but be excellent! Still, his was a very strange command indeed: "To go out to meet the *Neters*. . . ." However, if Menkh thought him capable of such a quest, could he, Chick-Pea, entertain doubts of himself? Had he not learnt several secrets before? It was entirely up to him to prove his worth by finding the key of a mystery!

But where should he look for this key? . . . No time was to be lost; each hour ought to bring him nearer to his goal.

Chick-Pea set forth as a conqueror. He went out into the fields, and once more saw the familiar landscapes, till he came to the banks of the stream. There he sat down, observing the movements of the ships plying to and fro. Some moved out of sight and others drew near, upstream, downstream; their sails drew towards each other, crossed, and parted again . . . until the next encounter.

The coming and going of the ships reminded him of that of a shuttle across the thread of the warp; but these shuttles left no thread in their wake. He lifted his eyes: some little wisps of cloud were running from west to east over the blue sky, leaving no track. He felt his quest was adrift like those clouds.

"*Where* are the *Neters*? *What* are the Neters? . . ." At harvest time he had learnt of *Rennutet* and her stone image. Of *Thot*, the *Neter* of science, he knew several symbols; and the potter had said that the *axis* was the *Neter* of the potter's wheel. Are there *Neters* without image? What had Menkh said: 'Go, run along in freedom to search for the *Neter* of weaving.' I am not very familiar with the ways of *Neters*: if I met them, would I know how to recognise them? I have not seen them in the fields or on the river. Do they perhaps hide in the mountain? . . . When Pabak the scribe told me of the Summit, did he not speak of the mountain?

Advance-bastion of the Theban chain, the 'Summit' dominated the valley of the dead, raising the symbol of its pyramid over the Royal tombs. Chick-Pea contemplated its regular shape which seemed to have been carved from the stone by giants. Fascinating in the halo of its legends, the mountain seemed to conceal in its flanks the mystery of the Sky in the Earth and that of the Earth in the Sky. . . .

When he rose to seek the ferry-boat, his heart was heavy with projects.

On the other bank he walked to Pabak's house. The young scribe was very busy, for the 'Valley Festival' was imminent, and he was discussing with his comrades how best to show their zeal. "Let us make a special effort," he said. "On the occasion of this festival many appointments will be made; it might well make the favourable oracle *Amun* has given me come true!"

Chick-Pea was strongly intrigued. "What oracle? O, Pabak, tell me the story!"

The ambitious scribe did not have to be asked twice: "It happened at the last festival of the 'God's Procession'; as usual we had written questions on the shards and presented them as the procession passed by. For my part, I had asked whether the 'Chief Reader' would take me into his employ at the next time of appointments, and *Amun* inclined towards me and said 'Yes'."

"But, Pabak, a statue cannot speak!"

"The statue inclines towards one side to say 'Yes' and towards the other to say 'No'."

"But a statue is not alive!"

"It is animated by the god!"

"And you believe that?"

They looked at him with contempt. "Should one not believe what happens under one's eyes? When a man was robbed by his neighbour, *Amun* confirmed the name of the thief that was written on the shard."

Chick-Pea, who knew nothing of all this, was astonished. "And there is never a mistake?"

"The *Neter* cannot be mistaken. Once there was quite a fight about it, when the accused protested he was innocent."

Chick-Pea thought it over. "And *Amun*," he then asked, "whom you carry in procession, of what is he the *Neter*?"

The scribes cried out with one voice against such ignorance and each of them uttered one of *Amun's* titles:

". . . the King of the *Neters* . . ."

". . . the foster-father of the Universe . . ."

". . . the Bull of his mother . . ."

". . . the *Neter* of Wast (= Thebes) with *Mut* and *Khonsu*.[1] . . ."

"Are there other great *Neters* in this country?" asked Chick-Pea.

One of the boys became angry. "Go and get yourself taught in school, and leave us in peace to finish our business!"

Chick-Pea rose. "As you wish; but tell me one thing: which is the right way up to the Summit?"

Pabak was amazed. "You are mad! The Sun is entering his mountain; don't say you want to pass the night with *Mersegert*?"

"And if it were so, have I not the right to?"

The boys looked at Chick-Pea with surprise. "That shows great daring! But one does not go there without expecting some wonder, and woe to him whom the Goddess does not protect."

The ignoramus suddenly turned hero meant to maintain his prestige. "Don't worry about that; just tell me the way."

They described to him the two possible paths; the one that wound itself up the eastern flank, and the other which ascended westward, through the valley, skirting the dark canyons.

Pabak's mother, all the while preparing the sweet beer for the festival, had been listening to the young men's conversation. Now she called Chick-Pea: "Do you really want to go on this risky adventure? You can-

[1] *Amun*, his spouse *Mut*, and their son *Khonsu* are the divine triad of Thebes. See Pls. V and VI.

not possibly go without some preparation. You must stay here this night; you can carry out your intention tomorrow."

"What should I fear, O Mother?"

"Jackal and hyena will be on the prowl; and there are the KA[1] of some famished dead who might suck your marrow; you risk being driven mad by the spectres, or emasculated by the harpies. Listen to me, my son: you need protection against all those enemies. This night, when the moon rides high, I shall lead you to an excellent magician: he has charms against all such dangers: and tomorrow you can face the Summit."

A low house of brown mud, half sunk into the rock, so that the back-room was a cavern. There a man was sitting before a wood fire; a copper kettle was heating over the half-burned logs.

Two shapes were squatting, motionless . . . the fire reddened their contorted faces. At the man's feet lay two beheaded ducks, their blood staining his legs. He accompanied his incantations with rhythmical swaying. He bent down, took a piece of cloth, and drew a figure on it. Then he put it on his thigh, stretched out his hands and continued his incantations:

"The Earth is in flames, the Sky is in flames, man and the gods are in flames. If thou recitest these conjurations against all this, *They* will come in their true name, *They* will deliver thee from the flames of the horizon."

The sorcerer cast into the fire a powder which threw up vivid green flashes; the faces became livid like those of corpses. . . .

"Aroynt thee, who bringest thy face, thy soul, and thy corpse, and all ye that bewitch by your looks, O ye Spirits, thou Deadman, thou Deadwoman, ye enemies male and female, aroynt ye for the space of one night!"

The throaty voice rose to a wolflike howl. Then he ordered the boy to approach the flame and to crouch down by it; he put the cloth on his knees. "This will remove the spectres from thy path. . . . But what do I see? Thou wouldst challenge a *Neter*? . . . Bow thy head, young daredevil, and regard the vessel!" He threw various ingredients into the pot, from which arose a suffocating odour. . . .

"Breathe in the bile of crocodile, breathe in the magic frankincense, breathe in the frog's head. . . . *They* will come and *They* will speak."

The acrid smoke and nausea brought Chick-Pea's heart into his throat. . . . The sorcerer seized his shoulders with gnarled hands; sinister laughter rumbled in his throat: "Thou! Jackal's heart! Thou wilt not venture far into the night!"

Chick-Pea stiffened. "Whatever happens, I'll go."

"So be it! Take thou these four white threads, take thou these four green threads, take thou these four blue threads, take thou these four red threads; with them make a knot and hold them in thy hand. . . ."

---

[1] The references here is to inferior KAs which, being unable to find their salvation, become maleficent.

He took a hoopoe from a basket, cut its throat, and let the blood flow over the fingers which held the threads. From a jar he took a scarabæus, drowned it in a jug of milk, and then told Chick-Pea to finish the operation.

"Pull the solar scarabæus out of the black cow's milk; bind its body with the threads washed in blood; and now wrap it into the cloth on thy knees." Again his throat emitted some incantation. Then he took the magic parcel from the boy, tied it with a string of seven knots and hung it round his client's neck.

"Now go. My charms are all-powerful! Go through the night! Go through the rocks! Go through the earth! Thou wilt fear neither spirits nor demons. And bear the incantation well in mind: *They* will come and *They* will speak!"

Pabak's mother raised a timid voice: "May it please the excellent Magus to write down my request so that I may entrust it to the pilgrim?"

The sorcerer inscribed her demand on a large sheet which he boiled in broth; then he gave the woman and the boy each half of it to drink. "Behold! he himself will now be thy prayer."

The woman rose, dragging the staggering Chick-Pea to his feet. Outside a fresh breeze revived them; Chick-Pea turned his eyes towards the Summit and sighed.

As the morning came, Chick-Pea left Pabak's house, well provided with onions, loaves, and cakes.

All day long he roamed through the fields, asking the peasants to tell him what legends they knew of the Summit and sharing his food with them. When the old peasants heard of his intentions they shook their heads.

"Are you sure you know what you want from *Mersegert*? It costs him dear who trifles with her!"

"I know what I want to get."

Chick-Pea's determined attitude impressed them. One, however, seeing how young the boy was, said: "Be careful; one scribe who doubted her has been struck blind."

Another told of a strange sickness that had befallen a blasphemer.

"Has anyone ever seen *Mersegert*?"

"No. No one has seen her; but they say there is a snake inside the Summit."

"They say she strikes like a lion . . ."

"They say that she casts a spell over the impudent . . ."

"They say that to her faithful she gives the gift of vision and the power of fascination . . ."

"They say . . . they say. . . ."

Chick-Pea listened quietly to everything, as one word fell over the other in contradiction; and the mountain there, before their eyes, no doubt it was listening, too.... Fear, or respect? Gods, or demons? Sorcery, or wisdom? . . . More undecided and worried than ever before, he rose as a friend of Pabak's, Ipy the scribe, happened to pass.

"Hey you, Chick-Pea, so tonight is the night, eh?" Then he saw the little bag on his chest: "Very good, very good indeed, you are even wearing an amulet! Well, tomorrow you'll have some adventure to tell us."

Chick-Pea turned away without answering. He walked towards the sands, waiting for the day to end. Little by little the elfin glow of the sunset waned; the whole landscape was unified in tones of grey; then in turn the silvery crescent illuminated the mountain, picking out clearly the sinuous line of the path.

Chick-Pea watched how the wood-fires on the fringe of the fields died down, and the dim little points of light in the houses faded one by one, all these eyes closed for the night, and the silence around him grew heavy, until the mountain pilgrim at last found himself in one vast isolation . . . with the mountain looming ahead, crushing in its mystery; what was there in store for him on his journey? The answer, or hostility?

He felt wrapped in absolute calm: no fear, no fever; he smiled and remembered the amulet: would it be effective? If so, he was armed: his way was assured. He began to walk joyfully. As the path turned, he noticed that he was actually winding his way round the left flank, instead of ascending towards the pass. He retraced his steps, searching for the way that lost itself among the stones. He continued to ascend slowly, sitting down now and then to contemplate the plain as it lay beneath the blue light. He ascended, then stopped once more, as if to preserve a last link with the inhabited world. . . .

Quite near was the pass which separated this living world from the valley of the dead; there began the mystery: on his left the steep flank of the Summit; on his right and all around him a desert of stony hillocks; and in front, the shadow of threatening chasms. . . .

Suddenly he heard a loud challenge; he had been forewarned: this was the watcher of the guard. . . . He flattened himself against a knoll and waited motionless for a long time. Then he slid towards a hillock, searching for the path to the Summit. The moon cast its shadow on the stones, he grew afraid he might be seen and crept more than he walked; the beating of his heart seemed unbearably loud. Again he stood up to search for the way. Around him there was nothing but solitude and stones in a new and unfamiliar pattern of landscape. Already the moon hung low and brightened only one side of the Summit, its light picking out the phantom circle of neighbouring mountains. Chick-Pea guessed that there would be a gulf between him and their crests, but what gulf? He did not dare to approach.

Why did the moon decline so quickly towards those crests? Suddenly he became aware of the vastness of his solitude, as if he could actually measure it. He closed his eyes in order to regain strength. What then was he seeking in this darkness? Which secret? Which *Neter*? A lion? A snake? . . . Doubt seized him: suppose all this were nothing more than a fairytale? Menkh's word came back to his mind: a test, no doubt? What had he made of this test?

A cloud covered the moon, casting a veil of darkness. And in the anguish of the night there rose a horrible cry, a rending cry of murder, the cry of a being in the throes of death. The boy, pierced to the marrow, cowered lower. "The killer comes! Now he is here. . . ." But it was a bird of prey, almost touching him with its wing as it passed, and the pilgrim straightened himself again, shame in his heart. The moon had now emerged from behind the cloud and Chick-Pea quickly found the right way: in a short while the moon would darken again and return no more.

What was that again, that raucous cry, this shrill yapping laughter? . . . Why that fear, coward? Don't you recognise the jackal? . . . Hyena or jackal? . . . Instinctively he touched the amulet. . . . A soundless laughter rose to his throat. . . . Yes, just laugh, you fool! Where is your magical power? Where is your courage? You search for mystery, and a jackal makes you tremble! . . . He tried to advance; the light was waning: too late to attack the Summit! Step by step he made his way forward, face to those crests, and behold! the line of shadow broadened, and the gulf revealed itself: a few paces ahead, the precipice! . . .

This was the end of it. The mountain swallowed the Moon. Now the night was mercilessly complete. Distress overcame the lonely pilgrim . . . seized by giddiness he surrendered and let himself fall to the ground, where he lay shivering.

The silence reigned complete: no animal cry, no breeze, nothing alive save he alone. . . . Where was he? . . . Could he be sure that he was alive at all? There was nothing now to be seen, and nothing to be heard but the humming in his ears. . . . He was engulfed in a complete void . . . and terrifying fear rose and paralysed him, a fear of 'nothing', a vertiginous fear, *Fear* itself. . . . Oh! was there not something to come and wake him . . . an animal, a spirit, anything whatever: *something*! . . .

A spirit?—the amulet. . . . It created a strange feeling of unease around him. He did not dare to make use of it, nor to throw it away either. . . . But this concrete thought checked the vertigo; the 'void' took shape. He had touched the bottom of fear and now from this fear, little by little, rose shame; the shame of his overweening conceit. That which he had *believed he knew*, that which he *had wanted to will*, his ambitions, feelings, and dreams, took shape and moved like living images. Successive aspects of Chick-Pea walked past him, a procession in which the person was always the same, but the expressions changed. Once more he saw the enthusiasm of his 'first day', his childish ardour, his confidence, . . .

But whence came this changed aspect of the later Chick-Peas? Whence
arose this shadow in their eyes? They were saddened by defeat, exalted
by success. Why did they stubbornly exhibit this susceptibility which cast
shadow upon their light? Why did their glances express doubt?.... If one
did not *know* anything, was it not absurd to *believe* or to *doubt*? . . .
Where was the joyful expression of the 'first day'?

The boy *found himself again*. He looked at himself, he smiled at that
innocent ardour and compared it with the latest face, whose smirk of
vanity disgusted him.... And now a new face began to take shape, a face
shining with the candid smile of the early times, yet with its gaze firmly
fixed in one direction. And Chick-Pea accepted it and little by little made
it his own, step by step, as those more recent faces in shame grew thin
and vanished.

The fear had gone. Chick-Pea stretched and shook himself; if he dared,
he would sing for joy! What would he not dare at this moment?

But lo! from the depth rose a murmur, a murmur that grew more and
more into an urgent appeal. . . . It was a human voice. Whence did it
come? Chick-Pea listened, now without fear; he found his bearings and
realised that the voice came from the bottom of some chasm in the valley
of the dead, quite near him. He crept through the dark, cautiously,
groping along the ground as he advanced; and there, at an elbow's length,
was the void.

The lamentation grew louder and more urgent. Chick-Pea put his
hands around his mouth like a trumpet and called down: "Who are
you?" In the chasm his voice assumed a sepulchral hollowness, and from
rock to rock was repeated by the echo: "Who are you?" . . .

"Speak: what is your name?" he insisted

Then came the answer, trembling with hope: "O Goddess, you then
deign to hear me! I am Pantha, the perfume vendor, and I come in
supplication!"

From above, the hollow voice reverberated once more: "You are well-
known, Pantha, you thief. You tamper with your scales, you adulterate
your oils: what hope dare you harbour?"

Hearing these words echoing eerily, the voice of the pilgrim below
shook with emotion: "O Goddess, if you will perform the miracle, I
shall restore the right weight; *ben* oil will be *ben* oil, and my scales will be
the scales of *Maât*!"

The pilgrim above listened to the pilgrim below, and his joy knew
no bounds. He increased the volume of his voice: "What is your
request?"

"O Goddess, hear my prayer: an evil spirit has tied a knot into my leg
for years and makes me limp with pain. O Goddess, I beg of you to
cure me!"

The pilgrim above was greatly embarrassed. But after all, what risk did he run with a thief like that? It would be a harmless farce. . . . He did not resist, but declaimed his oracle:

"It lies in your own power to cure yourself: if your promise is true, you will run like a gazelle! . . ."

There was a long silence.

And then there rang shouts of joy from a voice hoarse with emotion: "O Goddess, O Mighty One, my leg is unknotted! You have wrought the miracle. . . . I can walk. . . . I can walk!"

The pilgrim above held his breath, stupefied. Was this possible? This once more threw into confusion all he could understand. A miracle? And the other believed in the goddess! If ever he found out the imposture. . . .

Chick-Pea was gripped with fear: was there imposture in this? Of course he had never *intended* to impersonate. However, he could not bear this lie; he bent down, he opened his lips to cry out the truth. . . .

But at this moment out of the dark an image rose before his eyes: the face of 'Him-who-knows' was looking at him, and his finger, laid across his lips, commanded silence. . . . Was this a dream?

The boy stayed motionless until the image faded; he closed his eyes, and listened. He obeyed the dream of Wisdom which counselled him: "What matters the cause of the marvel, if it cleanses the soul, and the leg of the thief? He is too small to understand. . . .

"Besides, which marvel is the greater: to heal a limpfoot, or to *bring light into the vanity of an intelligence that is newly born, through candour which has become conscious.*"

And the pilgrim above fell asleep with a smile.

A radiant dawn awakened him. He rose, and then his eyes alighted on the Summit, and he remained standing for a while, perplexed. At last he happily shook his head. "What does it matter? I shall understand it all later. It was a wonderful night!"

He made ready to leave, when he remembered Pabak's mother: he had forgotten her request! He thought for a moment and then uttered solemnly: "May be done to her the good she meant to do to me."

He descended the slope singing.

He avoided the houses of the village and went straight to the fields; meadows and palm-trees vibrated with the chirruping of birds. He ran to the river and down the bank, he took off his loin-cloth, untied his amulet and threw it into the current, which washed it away; then he plunged with delight into the water.

As he emerged from his bath, Ipy the scribe came past. "Hey, Chick-Pea, have you seen the miracle? Pantha, the limpfoot, has been cured by the Summit."

But the pilgrim, thus addressed, did not move. "No, I don't know anything—I have spent my night far from the Summit."

H.B.— M

"Well, what did you do? What did you see? Where is your amulet?"

"The amulet? An afrit has eaten it."

"An afrit? . . . 'Pon my life, what did he look like?"

"His face was exactly like yours!"

The scribe went away cursing.

THE LAST DAY

CHICK-PEA stretched like an awakening cat and started counting on his fingers. "My last day for finding that *Neter*! . . . Up, Chick-Pea, and on with the hunt!" He had come back across the river, and as he passed the garden of Menkh, he heard Mesdjer's arpeggios filling the air with enchantment. This harmony was indeed more beautiful than anything else in the world, more peaceful, more joyful, more vibrant with life. Never had a love song been more moving, more passionate, more triumphant. He ran, entered the garden, and looked for the harper . . . who broke off his song.

"O Mesdjer, never have I heard the like! What song have you been singing?"

"I shall tell you later. But speak, Chick-Pea, you are quite out of breath. What do you want from me?"

"It's this: I must give Menkh the reply, and I have not found it yet, and this is my last day!"

The blind man shook his head. "The last day. . . . Let us put it to good use."

Chick-Pea told him of the visit to Pabak, to the sorcerer, to the Summit. "The Summit," he said finally, "has taught me a great lesson . . . but it has not shown me the *Neters*?"

"Which *Neters*?"

"The *Neters* of weaving, whose name I must find. . . ."

The harper smiled. "You have obviously been searching for a phantom. . . . Don't be sad about it; whether you want to or not, you are going to make this mistake over and over again. One goes the same way often and often, but each time the eyes are a little wider open."

"What shall I do? I shall have to bring my Lord an answer, otherwise he won't tell me anything."

The blind man moved his fingers silently over the harp. . . . After a few moments he said: "It would be best for you to search alone, and I ought to keep my mouth shut; but as it is your 'last day', I shall put into your hand the end of the thread . . . *listen to this*:

"When Chick-Pea was so small, that he was still in the nest (*sesh*), then Chick-Pea, the little falcon, was under the protection of the goddesses. His mother had woven his garment—designed (*sesh*) by *Seshat*[1]—with the shuttle which *Neith* helped her to guide (*seshem*). That is a secret (*sheta*) of *Seshat*; it is a secret of *Neith*. And Her-Bak will become the escort (*shemsou*) of him whose name he bears (Horus = *her*).

[1] *Seshat*, the *Neter* of all that is writing, drawing, etc. See Pl. VI.

". . . It is enough to find the *shuttle!*"

Chick-Pea opened his eyes, mouth, and ears. "O, Mesdjer, is this a game? All these words which are so similar to each other."

"If you wish: it will be what you make of it."

"Explain . . ."

"Nothing more, my child."

Chick-Pea tried to repeat the words he had heard. . . . "And with these words," he asked, "can I find the *Neters* whom I seek?"

"If you are searching for a *Neter*, observe *Nature!*"

Chick-Pea regarded the blind man with admiration: "O Mesdjer, does my Master Menkh know that you know all these things?"

Mesdjer had a happy smile. "Am I not his 'brother'? Have I not my image in his tomb?"

Chick-Pea started. "But Menkh is alive!"

"The 'House of Perpetuity' must be built during the earthly life: *it is not always a tomb.*"

"I do not understand . . ."—but while he was still uttering these words, Chick-Pea remembered the 'House of Wood'[1] . . . and he broke off.

"Yes," said the harper, "it may be what you are thinking of."

The boy seized the blind man's hand. "O Mesdjer, you can read in my heart? You can hear without words?"

"Since the veil of my body has already almost gone. . . ."

"Oh, why do you speak like that?"

"There is no sadness in it. Horror, when the end comes, is there only if one finds oneself clutching the earth with dragon claws. But if we have woven our wings in our body of clay, then we take our flight with bliss. I am old, my child, and the mountain is calling me. . . . I will dedicate to you my last song."

"Oh, Mesdjer. . . ."

"Don't speak, my son, *listen in peace.*"

The prelude from the harp impregnated the atmosphere with harmonies so serene that they soothed Chick-Pea's trouble; and then rose Mesdjer's song:

> *The child that rises towards the East*
> *Carries exuberant joy*
> *Like an aureole,*
> *But soles of lead on his feet.*
>
> *And the endless, haunting day*
> *Divides him, tears him to pieces.*
> *Skywards stretches his crown,*
> *Earthwards his heavy weight.*
> *Hard, hard is the struggle*
> *Against that which divides.*

[1] See Chapter XXV, 'The Lodge', page 149.

Degree by degree he ascends
Towards his zenith.
Oh, hour of glory! Hour of love.
He stretches out his arms to embrace her
The well-beloved. . . .
Oh terror
To find himself suspended in the void!
Oh tragic destiny of man, ever crucified.

Oh twilight! Oh great hope
Of drawing together . . .
A word spoken about a glimpse of peace;
An embracing of Sky and Earth,
Fusion in which rejoices
—In the peace of the divine Amen—
The exuberance of dawn!

Oh night, fertile and luminous;
Night without shadow,
Where Appearance disappears.
Oh serenity of love
At last known!
O saviour, thou hast conquered
The vain hope, the weight, and the Divider!

I find thee at last again, O my young desire,
Candid child!
In thy joyous beginning,
My radiant end is heralded.
Thou carriest me towards the Light
Where evening and morning unite:
A ring of gold
Without seam, without end.

O desire, thou art no longer! O Love, thou and I are one!
In Thee, Mediator,
Conqueror Horus takes his triumphant flight![1]

The singer had ended. He laid his hand on the boy's forehead and urged him to continue his pursuit:

"Rise now, my son, and go! . . . Go, and *do not forget to look for the shuttle!*"

[1] For the French text of this song, see pages 300–301.

XXVIII

WEAVING

WHAT was there to be done but to obey? Chick-Pea went off, carrying the song in his heart.

Where should he go? He turned towards silence and shade. A palm-grove sheltered some mud-huts; it was deliciously fresh there and he sat down at some distance from the houses. He began to search for the 'end of the thread' in Mesdjer's mysterious sentence; he found and recalled the words, but did not succeed in unravelling the skein. As he began to despair, children passed by playing; something fell from their hands; Chick-Pea collected it: it was a bird's nest, plaited from supple twigs. He marvelled at the skill with which the bird had interlaced the sprigs, with only its beak for tool; he gave a cry of surprise: the name of the nest (*sesh*) resembled the name of the 'guiding' needle of the thread (*seshem*). Then he opened his eyes upon *Nature*; near him a young palm-tree grew its leaves into a bouquet; the base of each one was hidden in fibrous tissue which wound around the trunk; Chick-Pea thought he could see a work of Nature which was identical with the weaver's.

He studied the texture of the palms. Their leaves had a part in the texture of the trunk: at their bases they tapered out at the rim into fibres similar to those of the sheaths; one 'force' rose out of the Earth and stretched its threads: this then was the *warp*. But from whence came the thread of the weft? And what shuttle guided it?

Many hours later, when the last ray of gold had been extinguished in the palm-trees, Chick-Pea returned to the lordly mansion, where he was soon called before Menkh.

"Lord," were Chick-Pea's first words, "you have granted me three days; now I bring the answer."

"Speak then and give this answer."

"O my Master, I do not know the *Neter* of weaving, for I do not know what that is, a *Neter*; but I have found in Nature various examples of weaving. Here is a nest built from interlaced twigs: who taught the bird this work? Here is a network which enveloped the base of a palm; the threads of which it is composed seem to be arranged like the threads of a piece of material. Then I looked at other plants and saw that leaves, too, could be woven, since there are plenty of threads crossing each other."

Menkh took the fibrous shred into his hands. "Your eyes have seen what you *believe you know*: this way one finds no truth at all. How is the weaver's material made?"

"There are threads stretched lengthwise: that is the warp; and one thread carried by the shuttle interlaces them, from right to left, and from left to right: that is the weft."

"Your explanation is quite right; but now look at the network of the palm: is that made in the way you have just been describing?"

Chick-Pea, having observed more closely, was astonished.

"O Master, it is as you say: this is another way of working; here the threads of the warp rise in angles, first to the right, then to the left, alternately. There is no *weft*. It is the superimposed layers which inter-cross, and sometimes interlace, thus giving the impression of being interwoven."

Menkh approved.

"Now your eyes have seen without error; but even though these threads actually should interlace, it would still be no weaving, since there is no thread of weft: it is the threads of the warp which by their alternating direction produce this illusory effect."

Chick-Pea looked attentively at the fibres; then he raised his eyes to his Master. "Then there is no weaving at all in Nature?"

Menkh smiled. "Know, on the contrary, that the shuttle of Neith never stops. The error you have uttered lies not in the principle, but in the application you have made of it. The character of the tissue is the inter-crossing of the *Mobile*, the thread (*nu*), across the *Fixed*; its function is the come-and-go of this Mobile carried by the shuttle; the *Motive* is that which fixes the warp and gives it its tension."

"O Lord, the fixing of the warps is done by the earthenware weights (*ta*) which hang under the loom!"

"There is great truth in the word. But tell me, what, in a tree, is the fixed thing?"

"That must be . . . that which remains in the ground: the root."

"Well answered, for it is the root which causes the shooting forth and rising of the fibres and the vessels which are the *warp* of the trunk. The *weft* is the *substance*, the mysterious work of the shuttle, or, if you prefer, of the two arrows of *Neith, for she is the true Neter of weaving. Neith* gives the thread (*nu*), the shuttle carries and guides (*seshem*) it. *Neith* is the great weaver of the World. Two things are to be noted in her work: substance and movement. Just as your chest expands and contracts, thus the two arrows of *Neith* give the double principle of its form."

"But, my Master, arrow and shuttle are not the same thing."

"Certainly, there is a difference between them: the arrow settles in the target. The shuttle on the contrary never settles: it imparts movement: it passes (*sesh*) across the fabric, comes and goes, guiding the thread, de-posits it and withdraws having done its work; but its signature remains through the pattern it has left in the fabric, the plant, or the animal.

"But do not ponder too long today over problems of which you do not yet possess all elements.

"The study of the structure of our words is actually the key to our teaching. Our language is built up on a deep knowledge of the Laws and functions that determine the structure of everything that exists. The name given to each thing is its definition, expressed through the value of the sounds which make up its name and the signs which write it. That is why one single word can replace a description or express a theory. It is not a language for idle chatterers; it is a language of Sages who *know* the analogical relations between the visible and the invisible, and who teach the abstract through the concrete.

"But if you would gain access to this key, you must accept a gradual moulding which is the 'ascent towards the Temple'. Your present stage is the realising of the existence of a deliberate affinity in the structure and the significance of a group of words. Just keep in your memory the examples of which you caught a glimpse today, as a signal that will awaken your attention.

"Now tell me what happened to you during these three days; speak, and omit nothing."

Chick-Pea gave his tongue free rein, and the tale of his adventures rejoiced the heart of Menkh.

When the boy had ended, his Master congratulated him.

"The time of these three days has certainly not been wasted! The Summit has taught you a great lesson; but you have made one mistake: he who wants to rise to the Summit must seek its base in the cavern. Weigh these words with great care; and when you have understood them, do not tarry: go back to the mountain, but this time spend a night in the depths of the rock. Still, do not go without letting me know beforehand."

Chick-Pea's heart was heavy with questions, but Menkh refused to hear any more. "Do not squander your treasure. Exuberance is a good stimulus towards action, but the inner light grows in silence and concentration."

XXIX

THE VALLEY FESTIVAL

THE stream was furrowed by numerous boats, transporting the faithful to the beautiful 'Valley Festival'.

What a crowd there would be on the other bank! Peasants, scribes, food-sellers huddled together, overloading the boat; a perfume-vendor revived the embers of his incense-burner to tempt the buyers; the smoke of the resins blended with the stench of garlic and onions. No breeze came to clear the atmosphere; heavy effluvia rose from the black land. But the fever of expectation, the hope for 'no-one-knew-what', was smouldering in all hearts like a fire beneath ashes.

A scribe had climbed upon a pile of baskets to keep his white robe clean. Chick-Pea stole near him and asked: "I have seen *Amun's* procession towards his Apet of the South: will this procession be like it?"

"There will be the same boats, but today they travel towards a different goal: today *Amun* pays a visit to the *Neters* of the West, to the Kings and the deceased Nobles."

"How can *Amun* visit them?"

"His boat will stop at each of their funeral temples in turn; after that it will continue upstream to the sanctuary of *Hathor*, to spend the night there, on the summit of the great temple Djeser Djeserou."

"But *Amun's* ship is immense, it is like a floating island; no one can carry that."

"They carry the small golden boat which is in the naos of the large one."

"But what is the point of taking a boat to those graves?"

"Because the *Neters* of the West, the Kings and the deceased Nobles expect from *Amun* the water of rejuvenation."

"But all those dead are in their vaults?"

"Certainly, but then one sprinkles their statues."

"But their statues are not alive!"

"They say that their spirits profit from the water."

"I don't understand that. . . . You have spoken also of the *Neters*: how can *Amun* rejuvenate them?"

"*Amun-Râ* is the King of the *Neters*."

"Your answer isn't clear at all!"

A snarling voice broke in: "It is only too clear for a profane mind like yours!"

Chick-Pea gave the man with the shaven skull a glance; then he said: "If you are a priest, isn't it your job to teach the people?"

"People need not *know*: it is quite enough for them to pay the tithe and to make their offerings."

"I don't understand that. You have so many *Neters*: have I not the right to know and to choose the one to whom I want to bring my offerings?"

"The ignoramus who starts questioning stops obeying the laws."

"Well then, to stop my questioning, teach me. Why are there so many gods, a different set for each stretch of the river, for each town, and for every time of the year?"

"Isn't it fair that the clergy of every temple should receive in turn the benefits of the offerings which are brought to their own *Neters*?"

"*I don't understand that*; is the *Neter* there to serve the priest, or is the priest there to serve the *Neter*? . . ."

Luckily for Chick-Pea, the boat struck land at this moment. The tumult of the disembarking separated the speakers; Chick-Pea made a passage through the crowd, but the angry priest did not let him out of sight.

Groups formed, invaded the quays, and scaled the sepulchral mounds, the trees, and terraces, so as to enjoy for a longer span the spectacle of the boats on the river, then on the channels, and up to the stations of the procession.

But now another procession came to meet them; the statues of the royal patrons, the protectors of the necropolis, advanced on sledges drawn by ropes, milk being poured on their path to facilitate the gliding.

The brotherhoods and the clergy of the western bank accompanied them singing. The two processions met, *Amun's* golden boat, lifted by forty carriers, joined the royal effigies which had been awaiting this day in their mansions in the Amenti. Frantic joy . . . acclamations! Prayers of all families in the name of the occupants of all funeral vaults, the most humble as well as the most exalted.

And then began the long circuit from stage to stage which was going to bring each 'sleeper' the divine water of rejuvenation. And in this torrid season when the Earth was all dust like those mortal remains, it was the tombs that inspired men with the hope of spring. For to the tombs were dedicated all those flowers, grown and guarded for this day, near the royal temples as well as near the small pyramids of the common dead; their gardens and pools were brightened with posies and chaplets of flowers. The visitors thronged around the offering tables, and each tomb awaited the divine visit.

The halts made near the sumptuous temples were lengthy; all along the route gatherings formed to partake in common of the traditional repast. Groups roamed about, headed by copious libations. Somewhere rose a quarrel; indignant shouting . . . snarling voices. . . . People gathered around the focus of the disorder: the ludicrous dispute between a priest and a boy. While the spectators commented on the cause of the conflict, backing one or the other of the belligerents, the crowd was parted by two men forcing a passage . . . and then Chick-Pea emerged firmly held by powerful hands which dragged him away from the curious.

Finding himself seated before a table with plates of fruit and cake, the confused combatant did not dare to ask questions of his two companions, who seemed to observe him with a kind of friendly irony. He looked at them and was sure that he had seen their faces before . . . and did he not remember their insignia? Where then had he met them? He risked a question, but was ordered to keep silent: "Eat . . . and hold your tongue!"

What a strange day . . . what a strange festival! Death and life, mourning and rejoicing, a funeral cult which was a vibrating song of renewal. . . . Hymns alternating with drinking songs; no sadness, but life! A life, however, whose ill-assorted elements collide with each other without any apparent common bond. . . .

The older of the men observed the tense frown on the boy's face. He gave him a smile and his words pacified the atmosphere:

"The KA of the food is for the KA of the dead; the food itself for the living; and thus, through the food, the living unite with the dead."

XXX

THE CAVE

In the evening of that same day, Chick-Pea arrived before Menkh like a cheetah from the South. "Lord, the servant-here-present begs a favour from you."

"Since it is the first time you make such a request I will not refuse."

"Hear then: may my Lord deign to answer *in truth* to my questions!"

Menkh glanced at Chick-Pea with surprise. "Where is the favour in this? Have I not always done so?"

"By no means, O Master; whenever I asked questions about the Temple it was my backside that received the answer."

Menkh laughed. "You have taken me by wiles; but be it so; I have promised. What do you want to know?"

"Lord, what is a priest?"

"A temple official."

"There are a great many priests; have not all the same function?"

"Not at all. There are as many priests as there are functions; the business of some is to receive and count the offerings, others busy themselves with the maintenance of the temples, again others with sacred objects, and others again with the animal sacrifices. . . ."

"And they are men like the rest of us?"

"Certainly; they often have wife and children, and not all of them live in the temples; there are for instance the lay priests, who serve on certain days and at certain hours and for the rest of the time live elsewhere and ply another trade. But what connection is there between this question and *the Temple*?"

"Is it not the Temple which teaches the knowledge of the *Neters*? And are not the priests their servants?"

"O Chick-Pea, do not confuse *the Temple* with the chapels of the cult, nor the cult with Knowledge, nor the priest with 'those who know'."

"What then do the priests know?"

"They know what concerns the *discharge* of their office. Those who are qualified to know more do not remain slaves of cult and office. Will you tell me why you ask these questions?"

Chick-Pea hesitated; then he allowed his resentment to boil over. "That holiday was an ill-starred day for me: I had a dispute with a priest in the procession."

Menkh gave him a severe glance. "I know: I had to defend you against your accusers, but I am not going to do that again. Really—how old are you? Will you spend the rest of your life quarrelling? Had you perhaps been drinking like the rest of the crowd?"

"And what if I had! Should I allow a priest to ill-treat a 'defenceless one'? Those priests and scribes permit themselves any outrage on the strength of their robe and their name: must the people suffer it without protest?"

"If robe and office cease to be respected for what they represent, anarchy will soon reign in the country. I know how they misuse it, but have you the right to make yourself the judge of it? . . . What at present is your aim: to correct others or to develop yourself? Can he rectify false weight whose own scales are uncertain? . . . Can you enlighten your neighbour while you yourself have no light?"

Chick-Pea lowered his head. Menkh continued:

"Don't let what you have seen dishearten you: have you not already received abundantly? Don't let these gifts go to your head. This festival was a stumbling-block for you: its popular aspect can no longer satisfy you and its true meaning you do not yet know. . . . Don't you think you ought to pay another visit to *Mersegert*?"

"If you want me to, I shall go tomorrow."

"Not if I want you to, but if you yourself wish it. You must please yourself."

Chick-Pea deliberated a long time with himself, then he rose and declared: "Lord, tomorrow I shall go to the mountain."

"If you want to carry out this intention, then keep away from the crowd and the wine-bibbers. Stay the whole day at the entrance of the valley and rest; enter it towards evening; I will lend you my seal, so the guards will allow you to pass; then seek shelter in the cavern and spend the night there."

Chick-Pea was about to kiss the ground before his Lord, but Menkh raised him and embraced him. "Go, and be neither weak nor boastful."

"Lord, I shall do everything as you have told me."

Dry stones—the world's end. A pathway crept precariously between the bare rocks; the stark stone slopes squeezed it together, threatened to crush it, then relaxed their grip but bent it into endless meandering curves. No sound; no breeze; silence.

In the wan light the silent pilgrim walked stealthily along. . . . Where was the crowd? Where was Life? . . . Was there anywhere a world that was not silent, a world of people who talked, lived, struggled? . . . The steady rhythm of his steps drugged his senses, like the intoxication of sweet wine. He allowed himself to be lulled, to be carried away. . . . The silence filled him like food; he could have walked on and on, tireless and endless, on this road of absolute peace, on this crumbling earth that seemed so dusty, so light. . . .

Suddenly the path took a sharp turn and came to an end: he faced a narrow circle of overpowering rocks; on the left the thick folds of the rocky wall formed dark chasms; the feet of numerous visitors had marked the path.

The wanderer was dragged out of his beatitude by the necessity of making a choice: this, no doubt, was the goal. He approached the cavernous crevices; he hesitated, groped his way. There was one that was deeper—no doubt it had served as hermitage, for a few bricks were piled up to form a little bench.

Chick-Pea decided to remain in the rock which hemmed him in like a prison. He touched its walls, as if to assure himself that he was alone and isolated. Then he sat down on the bed of bricks and tried to clarify to himself the aim of his pilgrimage.

The enchantment of silence was drowned by the violent inrush of disorderly memories. The scenes of the procession invaded his solitude; again he saw the enthusiasm of the crowds, the impressive calm of the dignitaries. Everything stood out in sharp contrast: the splendour of the costumes and the poverty of the people; the humble faith of the worshippers, and the arrogance of the priests; the dignity of the Masters of the guilds, and the servility of the scribes. He recalled Pabak's story, the questions, and the statue's answers. Was this oracle or trickery?

The way trust was being misused revolted him. In the name of what power was it permitted to dupe the ignorant? If the oracle was real, how could the *Neter* allow his servants to oppress the faithful?

Chick-Pea became indignant, but then he accused himself: he was living happily and under protection, while the people were exposed to tyranny. Was he not an egoist, a profiteer like the others? . . . But who were those 'others' whom he was incriminating? He reviewed those who had been his Masters:

There was MENKH, steadfastly leading his people; what a certitude in his ways! And ABIT, full of joy and love of his craft! And NADJAR, who knew the secrets of matter. And finally MESDJER, the ever serene!

Why did all these not intervene to educate the people? . . . But actually, had they not educated him, Chick-Pea? But why this favouritism? Why lift some up and let others fall? Why tolerate the injustice and harshness of the scribes, the hypocrisy of the priests? Why were the temples opened to those who bought their office by theft and corruption?

He recalled stories of scandalous lawsuits, of depredations, of vengeances. His rancour piled up, he challenged the *Neters*:

"If they are present, let them answer me. But if their image is mere make-believe, what use to wish to know them? What good is it to serve them? What good to follow their advice, their precepts? It would be as well to live in pursuit of one's pleasure, to laugh and drink with the heedless! . . .

"No one! No one replies."

Pressing his fists into his eyes to stop his tears, Chick-Pea had cried his anguish aloud and his appeal resounded under the rock. . . .

"Chick-Pea! Here I am!"

Choking, he opened his eyes: at the entrance to the grotto a tall silhouette stood out against the moon. He! Was it possible? Was this not another mirage?

But the Sage approached, he put a hand on the boy's forehead: "Be in peace, my child."

Overwhelmed by the shock of surprise, Chick-Pea crumpled up at his feet, in tears: "You, you have come."

The Sage lifted him up; he sat down on the bed of bricks and drew the sobbing little creature to his knees. "What does this mean? The crowd rejoices, and you weep?"

"Those who rejoice are brutes—they drink, they sing, and suffer the priests to deceive, to fleece, to bully them! . . . And I am ashamed for their cowardice."

"Calm yourself, my child, and try to look at things without bias: do you really think that when the people are honouring their gods, their joy is not genuine?"

"Most of these peasants know nothing of the Temple, except the tithe they have to pay! Those who know the names of the *Neters* know only of their demands; out of fear of those *Neters* do they bring their offerings, out of fear they resort to sorcery."

"You, Chick-Pea, see only one aspect of these matters: be wary of judging without real knowledge. The priests—that is *those priests of which you speak*—are subject to the same passions as the people; that is why they are able to make an impression upon them, to bring them to heel without scruples, often by means of fear and superstition. It is a decadent caste, fallen because it has retained power without Wisdom.

"However, there are other priests, of whom you do not know, because they do not mingle with the crowd, and these priests pursue activities which are fully worthy of your respect. But these priests cannot impose upon the people the laws they obey themselves, for they are too austere, nor their ideas, which are too abstract."

"But why do those who are wise not intervene to change the others?"

"Oh, you inexperienced child! One cannot change a man as one changes dough into bread. To do that, a new kind of leaven would be needed. . . . The Time has not yet come."

"Master, what does this saying mean?"

"The epoch in which you live is the end of one Time, hence it is already a *decadence*; but of the new Time you will know only the premonitory signs, for a long famine is needed to draw down the rains of Heaven!

"In order to act wisely in these difficult periods of transition one has to know the rhythms and the Laws of the cycles. But this forms part of the true Temple, and it is not child's play. It would be unwise to say more about it at this moment."

"And in the meantime, must we leave the people without help?"

"What do you know of the needs of the people? Do you know them at all? . . . Chick-Pea, what do you want? Do you want to live with that crowd, share in its pleasures, and suffer with its sorrows?"

"Oh no, how could I do that? What gives them joy, leaves me cold; and they are indifferent to what makes me suffer. . . ."

"Well then, *why do you desire that which you deny and deny that which you really seek?*"

"Because doubt has entered my heart, doubt about the things which are said to be sacred: the oracles of the god in the procession, are they real or trickery? People tell me of *Mersegert*: but I have seen nothing, be it divine, serpent, or *Neter*!

"They venerate the Summit; but the Summit is a mere heap of stones."

"True: the Summit is the apex of the mountain's height, but there are both *Summit* and *Valley*; hence something exists *which causes both*. And equally there is within you that which wants to *lift itself* despite the animal instincts, and also that which wants to *remain earthly* so it can profit from these instincts.

"*Summit* and *Valley* are two powers manifested; if there were not *these two* there would be only *One*: the absolute *Neter*. . . . But its name would be no longer '*Neter*'. But since there are *two* there are also all the others which spring from these, the other *Neters*. It is better to know them than not to know them . . . if one wants to attain the knowledge of the One, the Absolute, the Eternal."

The boy remained silent for a long time. . . .

"You say nothing, Chick-Pea; do you understand me?"

"I don't know: besides, what is 'knowing' good for?"

"For nothing, unless the heart hungers for Light. Chick-Pea, cease playing about: answer in truth: *if you can renounce 'knowing', then say so: renounce.*"

Chick-Pea began to tremble; a violent emotion distorted his features. . . . "Master," he cried, "I cannot renounce!"

"Then, my child, be sensible, and stop feeding this volcano. The night is now full; leave behind anguish and fear . . . and may peace come and be with you until the light returns. Sleep, my child."

Chick-Pea offered no further resistance. He curled himself against the feet of the Master, and, under his soothing hand, fell asleep.

And now the Sage entered into his own silence, into its very depth.

And Wisdom within him spoke:

"May he who 'guides' beware of error. The child has begun to feel the 'duel' but he has not yet touched the bottom of his revolt. . . . His experience is too young to put the 'question' in such a way that it makes necessary the supreme answer.

"However, the drama has begun. . . . If you allow the thought un-bridled to become his master before he has learnt true 'understanding', his reasoning intellect threatens to choke the truth within him.

"The boy who has spoken incarnates the spirit of this Time, with its elements of contradiction that are going to cause the tragedy. He who still sleeps bears a consciousness superior to this Time; hence *he will be able to help the people of his own Time.*"

"But if I awaken him too early to his own Reality, will he still keep aware of the suffering of his contemporaries?"

"That is the danger: but he is of such a precocious lucidity that the sight of traditionally sanctioned errors may shock him and deal him a fatal injury, if he is not guided towards understanding the sequence of things; then he might become a Rebel, and, no doubt, leader of rebels. . . ."

"Is it then not a mistake to precipitate the time of awakening?"

"He himself has given the answer: he *wants to know.* As to the rest of the way, not the greatest Master can go even one step for his disciple; in himself he must experience each stage of developing consciousness.

"Therefore he will *know* nothing for which he is not ripe."

The Master meditated for a long while, identified as it were with the disciple, measuring the progress made, the present difficulties, the struggles to come, and forging already in his mind the weapons that should ease the way. . . .

But before the weapons, the test. However great his love for this chosen being, he would mercilessly sharpen his consciousness.

Here now the first struggle was drawing near its end: what would the outcome be? Would instinctive nature want to triumph by personal effort, violence, in revolt against the errors of the epoch? Or would it be conquered by the 'will towards Light' in impersonal effort which no longer served individual will but obeyed the rhythm of Wisdom?

The Master rose and went out to contemplate the serenity of the night.

When the first light of dawn broke the darkness, he returned to Chick-Pea.

"Her-Bak, awake! It is time!"

The one who was thus drawn out of his sleep opened his eyes with surprise; then he shook off his torpor and knelt at the feet of the Sage. "Here I am, O Master!"

"Yes, Her-Bak, but now you must give me your answer. Listen: the struggle waged in the Earth's bosom between the two hostile brothers[1] bears richer fruit than the peaceful beatitude of the 'enlightened ones' around the Summit . . . provided one knows the means of delivering *Horus* of *Seth's* fetters, by weakening his guardians.

[1] *Horus* and *Seth.*

"The falcon can soar sunward; but it can equally turn cruel and re-belliously attack the living heart of things. . . ."

"O Master, what do you mean?"

"You will know soon. I offer you the choice: I can teach you to be-come a Leader, holding in his hands the power, the armies to hold the frontiers, the laws to chastise injustice, *as he pleases*. Or I can place you in the shadow of the Temple, where you will seek, in secret, to penetrate the mysteries of the gods . . . if they allow it. In that case there will be neither action nor glory, but often reproach, and non-understanding from men. . . . Choose! But do not speak without consulting the deeper will of your heart."

After these words, the Sage left the boy alone, withdrawing even his thought from him and his decision.

When he returned, Her-Bak walked towards him, regarding him firmly. "Master, I wish to find that which is true and real, even though it be in silence. . . . But you, teach me to curb my impatience!"

The Master took the boy by the hand, drawing him with him on the path leading upwards.

They reached the plateau with the first rays of dawn. The world was rising from its slumbers and recovering its colours: the Summit, the stones of palaces and temples, the green of the gardens. Palm-trees brought life into the torrid earth, giving shelter to the mud-huts which opened themselves to the light. . . . And the gold of the morning flooded over all miseries.

The Sage made a halt, looked at his companion, and embraced him, saying: "Her-Bak, my disciple, may your choice then be accepted! How-ever, before going farther, I wish that you engrave in your mind the *vision of the valley*. . . . When one travels in unknown territory, each parting of the ways throws the pilgrim into confusion and indecision; each mirage, each illusion threatens to lead him astray; but if he has chosen wisely, his glance takes bearings from his horizon, and he will no longer confuse the ways. Look at the valley; from the most destitute to the wealthiest, each man there spends his days, one after the other, in the narrow daily round of his passions, his greed, his hatreds, his desires, his particular satisfactions.

"If you want to abandon this road, I do not say that you should *abandon these pleasures*, but rather 'Let your desire be at the same level as your goal'. If you aspire to superhuman joy, accept the superhuman struggle in a very human body, and know that the abyss is always near neighbour to the summits.

"Do you understand me, Her-Bak?"

"Oh most certainly, Master; this is the happiest morning of my life!'

"Be it then! All right: let us go ahead without looking back."

"But must I not notify my Lord?"

"Menkh knows the scale of values; he will understand."

"But I must thank Nadjar. . . ."

"Do you think Nadjar is far from the Temple?"

"But I must tell Mesdjer. . . ."

"Mesdjer is resting, leave him in peace. Understand me well: I am by no means saying: 'leave these duties alone', but I say: 'tread your path', for one must never let the moment go by. Later on you will pay what you owe."

Her-Bak happily put his hand into the powerful one.

"And now, my son, come: let us go to the Temple!"

XXXI

HER-BAK

At the foot of the mountain where Chick-Pea, now Her-Bak, had at last found his Master, there was an ass, guarded by a servant, waiting for him. And Her-Bak was deeply moved, for this ass was like the one that had belonged to Chick-Pea.

And the Sage said to him: "Is it not fitting that the 'carrier' which, on the first day, led the unwitting child,[1] today brings him back again after his free choice has been made? . . . The donkey will carry you to the river bank; there you will find me at the embarking quay."

The contagious enthusiasm of the rider had urged the mount into a gallop; the impatient legs whipped the flanks of the ass, directing him along the ditches across the cultivated fields.

But although Chick-Pea's movements had reverted to their familiar rhythm, his heart had grown beyond it. Could choosing a new direction in life thus change the look of things? The rider had the impression that the heart of Her-Bak was observing the body of Chick-Pea and his ass. . . . Instinctively he kept a tight hold on the flanks of the animal, but his eyes searched the opposite bank of the river for the walls of the Temple.

The Temple, his desire, his goal, his conquest! The Temple that would free him from the life of routine; the Temple with its majestic mystery, the world of marvels into which he was going to penetrate. . . .

The Temple of his dreams ennobled all that touched it, and peopled itself with divine beings, resplendent and haloed with all excellent qualities. . . .

A green tuft of grass tempted the donkey to slow down its course. Absent-minded in his contemplation the rider urged him on; a stone provided a welcome obstacle for the animal: it stumbled under the heels hammering its flanks and abruptly lashing out it threw the rider off like a troublesome burden.

The dreamer picked himself up, angrily. Never had he been thus insulted. And his anger increased as he heard within himself the mocking laughter of the 'observer'. Brought 'back to earth' against his will, he once more bestrode his mount and tried to keep awake to his surroundings by observing the fight of a crow with a buzzard.

Into the blue a falcon stretched the crescent of its wings, immobile, hardly quivering, master of the air that bore him like a weightless being. . . . One beat of his wings, and suddenly he dropped like a stone,

[1] See Chapter I, "The First Day".

'heavier than his own weight'; and again he soared, rising in a straight line into the light, as if the sun drew him upwards. . . . Was this a chase or a game? . . . Cruelty or prayer? . . . Chick-Pea observed the symbol of his new name;[1] what was its true meaning? Sun-bird, or merciless hunter, slaying the dove in full flight to drink its blood?

This problem had not been solved by the programme the Sage had prepared for him so that he might earn admission to the Temple. . . . Chick-Pea had tilled the fields and watched the animals; he had studied 'matter' through various crafts; his adventures had shown him some flaws in human nature and his own weaknesses. . . . As he left this imperfect world, how would he manage to adapt himself to the perfect life of the Sages? . . . How would he, the ignoramus, be accepted by the learned teachers whom he imagined to be the custodians of the secrets of Nature, by these sublime beings who stood above all human miseries? Only yesterday, had he not been the shy and wayward child, Chick-Pea the proud, impatient, curious, the impetuous and rebellious? One might think that the Sage had thrust back all his past and awakened Her-Bak from a long sleep by uttering his new name; the night in the cavern had conquered all his resistance and thrown him at the Master's feet. . . .

At this evocation, the luminous image once more took bodily shape; Her-Bak intoxicated himself with his name: was he not the Master's adopted disciple? His enthusiasm expanded and drove out all fear and with triumphant joy he covered the distance still separating him from the quay.

Meanwhile the Sage, carried in his chair by his servants, approached the river by another way.

His meditation turned upon the consequences and possible repercussions of his action: the adoption, against all rules, of a disciple who had not passed through the test of the preparatory lower degrees! In the scales of Destiny his conscience balanced the daydreams of the candidate. . . .

Of course, being the undisputed Master of the Council of Wisdom he had the right to impose his will without justification. But he was aware that both past and future would bear witness for or against his choice: for the living Wisdom of Egypt was a constant Presence throughout all Time. And the new disciple, if he was to be a 'link in the chain', had to show himself worthy of his predecessors; he who had chosen him would be responsible for him.

The child was obviously predestined and this could justify the choice: the experienced eye of the Sage had thoroughly scanned the transparent shell of this chosen being and gauged his worth. Her-Bak, son of a simple farmer, had all the characteristics of the race of Masters:

—the piercing eye of the falcon who gazes into the light with cool blood;

[1] Her-Bak: Falcon-face.

—unrelenting search for that which is 'truest';

—keen sense of Quality;

—inborn nobility which declares its mistakes and squarely attacks its errors;

—altruism and consciousness of responsibilities;

doubtless there was a flame of life capable of burning away the defects of Chick-Pea? . . .

But meanwhile, how would he react to surroundings so different from the imaginings of his heart? . . . For, unfortunately, he would have to pass through complexity in order to exhaust the various possibilities until the awakening of the consciousness which leads towards simplicity: would he be able to bear the intermediate phase between his dream and reality?

PART THREE

HER=BAK

THE PERISTYLE OF THE TEMPLE

XXXII

ADMISSION

THE barque had crossed the river and drawn alongside the eastern bank.

As on the first day[1] they walked towards the Temple, the candidate's hand in the hand of his Master. They passed along the canal leading from the river to the landing-stage for processions; the road was lined by huge sphinxes.

"Why so many stone animals, Master, and all alike?"

"They are not quite alike: each differs from the others in some detail, according to its place, that is its number; and all together they reveal a Law."

"Do all priests know this Law?"

"Each of them knows what he can decipher."

"Master, does one need images and stone statues to learn what one must know?"

The Sage listened to the question ... to which the sphinxes themselves, with their immutable symbolism, were the answer.

"Listen, my child: a day will come when mankind will know how to worship God in the spirit; then they will no longer need temples, nor myths to symbolise the working of the divine thoughts; no longer will they need statues to represent the various states of His power; nor will they need mysterious scriptures to tell the secret meaning of the divine Science to those who have eyes to see and ears to listen.

"But mankind has not reached this stage yet, and you, child of mankind, are still in need of all this."

Her-Bak heaved a sigh of regret. "How beautiful is all this."

The Sage allowed him to contemplate for a while the magnificent avenue; then they turned back, and walked along the wall of the outer precinct until they came to the entrance of a village inhabited by craftsmen. Here they passed by workshops in the service of the Temple, stores, schools for the training of specialists, a hustling horde of workmen, buzzing like a bee-hive. A door opened into the second enclosure, a maze of alleys inhabited by priests and scribes.

"Here you will live, Her-Bak; during the first stage the scribe Pasab will look after you."

Her-Bak remained dumb; his heart was running on the path of discovery; his imagination broke through the walls, opened closed doors, conjured up mysteries. ... But the Master dragged him back into reality.

From the alleys they passed through doors, into courtyards and chapels,

[1] See Chapter I, 'The First Day'.

where, among statues, there was a busy coming and going of scribes and officials.

Some priests were checking offerings which had just arrived; others supervised the correction of a mural inscription; sculptors were changing a name within a cartouche; painters were retouching hieroglyphs. In front of a statue, students sat meditating; some were copying the inscription on its pedestal. Farther along a group of musicians was passing by; from a little neighbouring temple sounded the chanting of a psalmody.

Who could have suspected from outside what an intensive life was going on here?

But Her-Bak's curiosity was violently roused by a large wall covered with hieroglyphs[1] and sculptured images; a wooden door wrought with gold shimmered in the sunlight. Alas, the Sage passed on. . . . He followed closely the curve of the wall through an endless corridor which at last opened near a less sumptuous entrance: a large door of plain wood, guarded by watchmen. There the Sage halted at last.

"Do you really wish to pass this threshold, Her-Bak? Think well before you answer: this is the first step in a teaching that commands your respect. To enter here is easy; it will be harder to find your exit through the narrow door to the inner Temple; many are those who, content with appearances, end here!"

"Master," protested Her-Bak, "I want that which is the most difficult! I want to know all that one can know."

"In that case you stand in danger of never knowing that other door: such is the lot of the talkative and curious."

Her-Bak bowed before the Sage. "Your will is mine, Master."

"Be not hasty in your judgment; what you really want, you will know when faced with your deeds; we do not judge men by their words. Enter, Her-Bak."

The door opened before them and gave into a large courtyard encircled by colonnades. In the shade of the galleries formed by columns and walls, the white robes of the scribes shone against the vividly coloured background of sculptured inscriptions.

The students had been notified of the impending visit of the Sage and were awaiting him, passing the time conversing with their teachers.

The Master and his disciple slowly advanced over the paved court and through a cross-fire of curious glances; the Sage steered towards the colonnade, and immediately all foreheads were lowered before him. He raised them again with a gesture; then presented his candidate. Surprise and envy closed all lips: the favourite of the Master of Masters! What jealous hatreds, what intrigues, what fawning servilities were born in that moment! But 'He-who-reads-in-the-hearts' cut out the unhealthy roots:

"He is the least among you; he knows nothing; he shall receive

[1] In Egyptian: *medu-Neter*.

nothing he has not earned; he shall be forgiven no weakness. Pasab, you will take him into your custody."

Pasab's deep eyes took stock of his new pupil with sympathy.

A very young schoolboy approached the novice. "I am Awab," he said, "since you know nothing, I will be your friend; come."

The Sage kept him back. "Listen to me, all of you. Her-Bak knows nothing whatever of gods and their sanctuaries; you must teach him; who will earn my praise by giving the best definition of the Temple?"

Awab looked at him with his candid eyes: "The Temple is the House of the god."

The Sage gave him a smile, then an accountant-scribe pushed the boy aside: "Let those speak who know. The Temple, O Master, is the place where the riches of the Two-Lands[1] are accumulated for the All-powerful Master."

The Sage threw a glance at the well-rounded paunch: ". . . and for the bellies he feeds! Remeny, what does the Temple symbolise for you?"

"Is it not," the teacher Remeny declaimed, "the god's castle, where this god, like the King, wears his crowns and receives the tributes from his faithful?"

"That is a description of appearances alone," said the Sage, "and you, Smôn, what have you to say?"

The assembly parted, and a tall gaunt body was pushed forward, all the while trying to keep in the background. Smôn's meagre neck sprang from narrow shoulders, like that of a vulture.

"Well, Smôn, give us your opinion."

"He won't give anything," a scribe whispered. "He is so mean, he even hoards his thoughts away."

Smôn heard this and shot a glance of defiance at the scoffer. "I will speak albeit," he said. Then, with great effort, he uttered:

"Thesis: the Temple can be the expression of any science: astronomical, cosmical, numerical, analogical, anagogical, or the like. Supporting evidence: the assertions of certain people who call themselves initiates and spread this hypothesis.

"And the antithesis: it is improbable that the temples are records of anything but ritual gestures, historic facts, and royal enactments. Supporting evidence: the systematic destruction of monuments from preceding reigns and anterior cults, the usurping of royal cartouches, the modifications of shapes and measurements—quite inadmissible measures if the plans and symbols are ordained by a systematic science."

"And of all that," the Sage impassively asked, "which do you advocate? Thesis, hypothesis, or antithesis?"

The gathering, uneasy, repressed their smiles. Smôn stared vacantly

[1] Upper and Lower Egypt.

and bit his reed. The Sage insisted: "Do you believe in this 'numerical, analogical, anagogical science, or the like'?"

The irony released the laughter! Smôn's lips moved and gave forth an indistinct sound. "Did he say yes or no?" someone asked. The Sage turned his back on him and his voice lashed out like a whip: "Who has the courage to give a definition of the Temple?"

The audience stirred; some teachers stepped forward.

"Master," said Renf-ankh, "it is written that *Ptah*, when creating the world, brought the gods down to Earth by fashioning their bodies in all kinds of wood, stone, and metal, in whatever manner pleased their heart. The gods entered the statues and the place where these are preserved is really a replica of Heaven, or—with reference to the Sun-religion —of the celestial horizon."

Smôn gesticulated. "I protest! The Ancients did not have sufficient knowledge of Astronomy to conceive the idea of the horizon."

He was answered by a great burst of laughter. Renf-ankh went on: "The sanctuary doors are called 'the gates of Heaven'. Now on our walls the King is represented as a live man; whereas the gods are of stone. . . . To my mind the only satisfactory explanation is that priest and priestesses represent the divine personages at the festivals. . . ."

"That is an opinion," the Sage interrupted, "not a definition."

Renf-ankh explained: "Well then. What is the Temple? However, since the Temple stands in relation to the Heavens, let us ask first of all: what are the Heavens?

"When the gods still reigned upon Earth, before the Heaven-Above was organised, when the men were their subjects . . ."

The Sage stopped the orator: "This would lead us too far! O Renf-ankh, you have recorded ideas which come near to reality, but your utterance is of nebulous uncertainty. Dare to seek the thread which links all our sanctuaries together, and you will find a peace-bringing harmony."

A priest's voice rose from the background: "I will give a clear definition of the Temple."

"Who was that?"

"The teacher Amenatu."

"Let him step forward; we listen."

Oozing with joviality, his powerful jaws disguised by an unctuous smile, Amenatu expressed himself with great heartiness: "It's quite simple; actually all of you are right; but I think one must not lose oneself in argument over imaginary subtleties! The Temple is the palace of a god with his servants, courtiers, stewards, and the managers of his demesne; each of them plays his part, just as in the house of a nobleman: there is the levee of the god, dressing and breakfast, he is washed, dressed, and adorned with jewels . . . ."

"I appreciate your sense of humour," the earnest voice cut in, "and I am sure that it is merely the modest cloak for a deeper understanding!"

The teacher Neni stepped forward. "My answer will be simple: temples are the eternal houses of the *Neter*."[1]

"Do you speak of the Temple, or of temples? Every temple had a beginning: therefore none of them is eternal."

"Still, O Master of Wisdom, the word *hehe* means eternal!"

"No. *Hehe*[2] or more exact, *nhehe*, means duration for centuries of centuries. But this needs expounding in a way that would lead us too far at the moment."[3]

The Master's eye steadily fixed one by one all those who had answered. Then he spoke: "Each of you has defined the Temple with an obvious concern to stress its utilitarian and human aspect. Each of you is free to express his own opinion, since we are not going to inscribe it for posterity. The teaching of the outer Temple shows only the shell of the fruit. It has reference to the 'effects', and in no way to their deeper 'causes'.

"Many of you are deceived by the triviality of our inscriptions when studied from this angle. There is no shame in mistakes made because one lacks some essential elements. Your personal observations enrich the material to be studied by others; all conscientious research disposes the intellect to the clear formulation of problems which then deserve to receive a solution.

"Note that this solution would be unintelligible to those who are accustomed to rely on appearances only, and who have not cultivated their 'wisdom of the heart'. This is another way: it can be offered but never imposed, for it demands a suitable mentality. But the understanding of our inscriptions depends on it.

"You cannot reproach us for this: this discipline was established in olden times through the very way in which our Masters expressed themselves, and we merely continue their tradition."

Pasab, the oldest of the teacher-scribes, kissed the ground before the Sage: "There can be no resentment, since this knowledge is offered by the ancient Masters themselves, and each seeker can take of it according to his own capacity. But would you deign, O Master, to give us a true definition of the Temple?"

"The simplest definition was given right at the beginning," said the Sage, "it was: 'the House of the god'. That is correct as much as the statement: 'the body of man is the House of the god', is correct. That is why it is said: 'Man, try to know thyself'.

"Knowledge is a spherical vessel of pure crystal, filled with Wisdom. In this lens the whole universe is reflected, then gathered into one beam, and projected in images on the surface of the walls. But when reading these images, everything, the proportion of those surface planes, of the columns, halls, enclosures, as well as their arrangement and orientation all this helps to guide the thought.

---

[1] *Neter*: God; the *Neters*: the gods.   [2] See Fig. 1, Pl. I.
[3] *nhh*: the older form.

"Such is the Temple, the Royal Temple, which encloses the places where the Whole is taught in the part, and the particular in the Whole. All this is merely a preface to the definition of the Temple, but the ears of those who listen today would be unable to receive more."

Pasab thanked the Sage. "Master, your words have thrown a ray of light upon our walls; may this boy be blessed for having provided the occasion.

"The years have whitened my hair without bringing me the joy of crossing the inner door. I do not complain of my lot; but, having engraved in my heart all aspects of our divine characters, it happens at times that I see their secret analogies: shall I stifle this vision in me lest I overstep my domain?"

"O Pasab, the star under whose protection you are is the Lord of Time[1]; those who are under his influence share in its slowness, but also in its patience and depth.

"True teaching is not an accumulation of knowledge; it is an awaking of consciousness which goes through successive stages; each consists in discovering the key to the following door; your qualifications have placed you as 'The one of the door'; you have fulfilled your role to perfection. Sab, the jackal, who gave you his name, holds the first of these keys; he lives in the dusk and in the night; yet he can become the 'Opener of the ways'[2] and even the 'Guardian of the secret'.

"If you have found the first key, then remember this word: 'The man who knows how to lead one of his brothers towards what he has known may one day be saved by that very brother.' Come, let Her-Bak become acquainted with his fellow-students."

They went in silence, but when the large door had closed behind them, a noisy group formed around the new candidate. The teachers, in a group apart, put their heads together and discussed the unforeseen event; they agreed that it was a scandal: not one of them had been consulted!

Her-Bak, bewildered, remained silent under the crossfire of questions; Smôn watched him out of the corner of his eye and counselled caution. "Wait and see! Let us first of all hear what he has to say for himself."

From the shade where he had reflected with half-closed eyes, a priest who so far had observed a diffident silence now came forth; a gloomy, meagre silhouette whose salient cheekbones underlined the rings around the searching eyes and the bitter fold of a disenchanted smile on the lips; Seth-Mesy raised his voice to support Smôn's view: "I, too, think circumspection is good counsel. Who knows? He may have some high personage for his protector . . . he might be a kinsman of the Royal House. . . ."

Amenatu went over to the group of students, with a winning smile and outstretched hands: "Children, children, you are scaring him. Sit down.

[1] Saturn.   [2] See footnote, page 273.

Her-Bak, welcome among us! Your father must be beloved by the *Neter* since his son has been allowed to enter here. Is it his hand that has led you to us?"

"I don't know."

"Your tongue is prudent like that of a serpent! Speak freely—you are among friends!"

Awab slipped to his side and smiled. "Don't you know where you have come from? Who has directed you to the Temple?"

"*Mersegert.*"

A vague pout of pity flew over the scholars' faces.

"Another one of those shady visionaries."

"Or trying to outsmart us . . . let's be careful."

Amenatu leaned towards them. "Harmless mystic. Don't worry." Then aloud: "What do you want to be, Her-Bak: a priest or a scribe?"

"I don't know."

Jibes from every corner: "He plays the fool!"—"No, his Naos is empty!"[1] "He is a waster relegated from school that they've sent us!"

Awab protested: "The Master has said that he does not know anything. How can he answer? He just doesn't know the answers!"

Amenatu raised his hand: "Give him a chance. He does not know us yet."

"Now I recognise the scribes," said Her-Bak; "they are like those I have known."

"You have been a scribe?"

"Yes. But not a priest. So I cannot tell."

New outbursts of laughter, while Awab replied: "A priest is a servant of the *Neter.*"

"Aren't all men servants of the *Neter?*"

Surprise and silence . . . several teachers took offence. "What insolence! Why has the Master brought us this rebel? That's a dangerous ferment of disorder! Keeps a queer sort of silence. Might be a sorcerer's apprentice for all we know."

"I'll see to this," Seth-Mesy reassured them; "let me tackle him."

He took Her-Bak aside and asked him to sit down. "Listen, my child, the priest is a temple official. The service of the *Neter* entails a number of different functions: there are the superintendents in charge of the reception of offerings, those in charge of the service of the divine statues, of the maintenance of his house and the objects of worship; there are those who arrange and supervise ceremonies, processions, festivals; some are attached exclusively to the religious services; many others—and not the least important among them—manage the temple revenues, and supervise the work of scribes and novices: that is my function."

"Where are the scholars?"

---

[1] Naos is the inner sanctuary of a temple; priest slang for saying: there is no brain in this skull (T.N.).

"What scholars?"

"Those who know the 'Laws of things'."

The priest's answer was lost in the outcry of the scribes: "What science are you looking for if not ours? Isn't it the scribes who have the old inscriptions in hand? Don't you see here masters of scripture, arithmetic, of liturgical texts? And of medicine? And the study of stars? And land-surveying, the science of ground-measuring which gives us so many privileges?"

Each scribe extolled his own talents: "I can tell you the names of 90 towns in the Two-Lands!" "I am unsurpassed at Cretan names!" "I am an expert in formal correspondence!" "The scribe has all the power; he is exempt from serfdom!" "Nobody bothers him!" "We are lords over the uncultured masses, everybody depends on us!"

The shrill voice of Smôn pierced the uproar: "For all that one still has to know what one wants; perhaps this genius wants everything at once."

Seth-Mesy observed the novice. "There is some ambition in this young man; but I am not displeased with that. A priest who learns diligently may obtain the highest posts; he does not remain locked away in the temple; he may be called to manage a large demesne and fill important offices in the house of the Great, even perhaps of Pharaoh, L.H.S."

"Are the others locked away in the temple?"

"Some have strictly religious functions and have to carry out certain rites and practices every day; those are the permanent servants of the sanctuaries and their gods; others share their life between their particular tasks—during fixed days and hours—and their social functions: one priest may be a chief registrar with a treasury, another, a workshop manager; some prophet of Ammon directs the allocation of waters."

A young teacher sighed: "Luckiest are the incumbents of a rich funeral temple foundation!"

"No doubt, no doubt," Seth-Mesy agreed. "They are safe from all worries! But in any case, all priests are people of repute and unquestioned authority! Not counting the profits from the offerings to the god and many other privileges."

Her-Bak absorbed and weighed every word. Then he asked: "Is it permitted to search for Science . . . without privileges?"

Uneasy silence all round. "It is a mystic," muttered Renf-ankh, "and if not a mystic, then a humbug. Don't let us judge him without knowing for sure."

Smôn called the pupils back. "Leave the newcomer in peace and let him take his place in the ranks like everyone else."

The groups reformed around the teachers; Her-Bak was assigned a place in Seth-Mesy's who opened a papyrus he held in his hand, and read out its title aloud:

"The Knowledge of all that exists, that *Ptah* has created, and *Thot* has written: the sky with its stars, the Earth and what it contains, what the mountains have thrown up and what has issued from the Ocean; what concerns all things upon which the Sun sheds light and which grow on Earth."

This promising title made Her-Bak's heart leap. Amenatu handed him the papyrus. "Let us see whether you can decipher it."

Trembling with emotion, Her-Bak began to read: "*pet* (sky), *àtn* (disk), *iâh* (Moon), *sah* (Orion), *meskhetyw* (Great Bear), *iân* (constellation of the dog-headed ape), *nekht* (constellation of the 'strong one'), *rrt* (constellation of the sow). . . ."

Patiently, Her-Bak deciphered the tedious list. At last, disappointed, he stopped. "Is that all?"

"What more do you want? This list will teach you how to write all that is needed."

"I had hoped for something different."

"You are reading quite correctly, continue."

The sulky voice enumerated the apellations of court officials, of various professions, social classes, human types, towns, districts, and buildings. At last followed a list of beverages and various sorts of meat. . . .

The supervising scribe gave the sign to stop reading, for the hour of the meal drew near, and immediately the imposed discipline gave way to noisy relaxation.

Amenatu bade silence. "Let us recite the final prayer of thanks to *Ptah* for his blessings."

Tablets, shards, palettes and reeds were hastily collected; and the scanded phrases resounded under the colonnade, while buzzards, hovering in the blinding light, with cries proclaimed the middle of the day. . . .

The prayer finished, pupils and teachers scattered, leaving the novice behind in bewilderment. A student, having conferred in whispers with Smôn, came over to Her-Bak. "I liked your answers: you're neither a courtier nor a coward; I will help you with your work."

Her-Bak glanced at the angular face, the hard, intelligent eyes, the sharp, narrow lips. He hesitated. But the friendly manner swayed him. "What's your name?"

"Asfet."

"You have come, seeing that I am alone. Oh Asfet, I will be your friend."

Pasab, who had returned unnoticed, separated the two students. "You will meet again tomorrow. Her-Bak, the Master has entrusted you into my care. Come, I will introduce you to your new life."

XXXIII

TEACHERS

HUBBUB under the colonnade: pupils and teachers had deserted the study rooms to witness the novice's first lesson. All welcomed this diversion from their daily task, for, after consulting the other teachers, Amenatu had declared that it would be unwise to enrol the newcomer without testing his knowledge first. "Let all teachers question him to their liking, and may our hearts feast on their learned words."

The pupils formed a circle in front of the masters, and Pasab told Her-Bak to sit down in the centre. "Speak without hesitation," he then said: "What is a student's first duty?"

Her-Bak took a look at his examiners and answered with firm voice: "To know that he knows nothing, and to take his Master's advice. May I therefore be allowed to ask for some advice from the learned Amenatu?"

The priest was flattered in his heart; he gave the novice a smile and spoke to him with unctuous words: "You have given a perfect answer; if you persevere in this way, yours will be a prosperous career.

"Beware of foolish pride and dangerous innovations; in everything be moderate: stray not from the well-known paths! Repeat untiringly the maxims which we have found satisfactory. Do not utter thoughtless words. Let your answers be cautious; people bring about their own undoing through their tongues; beware of causing yours! And remember this last piece of advice: be skilled and persevere in the scriptures and if one fine day you find yourself among pretty girls, don't swear that those learned writings are no good at all!"

A laugh was smothered in the audience and someone whispered: "It is also said: 'Don't say: I am free of sin!'."

The orator heard it but without reacting turned to Smôn, inviting him to interrogate the novice. "I want to know," said Smôn to Her-Bak, "whether you know the rules for arranging the characters; describe in detail some writing by any pupil of mine, to support your demonstration."

Her-Bak picked a shard at random and read aloud: "I am lazy and dissolute; I send myself a thousand slaps."

"Who has written this absurdity?" Smôn was angry, but Amenatu asked for leniency: "Has the writer not punished himself already? Pick another shard, Her-Bak!"

The novice obeyed; he deciphered the inscription and then commented: "The letters of this word are arranged as if framed by a square. In this other instance, the letter *t* in the word *Mut* is placed before the bird instead of behind it, as is usual."

"Don't you know the reason for that? Don't you know that the letters are arranged in quadrates sometimes in order to save space, sometimes for the symmetry of the design?"

Pasab interposed. "May I be allowed to object that I have often found in the disposition of the quadrates or their, apparently irregular, inversion[1] an intention to imply another meaning, which modifies the apparent sense of the text."

Smôn answered testily: "Is that the talk of serious teachers? I should not distort the mind of my pupils with phantasies of this kind."

"I have," replied Amenatu, "deciphered certain mysterious[2] scriptures, and I must acknowledge that their meaning sometimes remains hidden from us. But I think, that if one tries to navigate in uncharted waters one runs the risk of shipwreck."

Smôn continued his interrogation: "Can the novice speak about the first letter of our alphabet?"[3]

"It is twofold," said Her-Bak, "when written in the form of a bird, it represents the vowel *a*; when written in the form of a reed it is pronounced sometimes *a* and sometimes *i*.[4] Pasab has told me the reason why the bird '*a*' is sometimes pronouned *al*, which makes it a divine character."

"What does this mean?" Smôn asked sternly.

Pasab explained. "In long years of study I have arrived at this conviction: the first letter is twofold, because it expresses the principle of the first breath. In its bird form it is the breathing in, and as such would be unpronounceable and divine; in this interpretation it is sometimes pronounced as *al*; whereas in its reed form, it is the breathing out and the active, concrete sense of the first letter, of which the other is the negative or abstract sense. That is why I suppose that the reed is pronounced *a* when it refers to the Creative Origin, and *i* [= English *ee*—T.N.] when it has a particular meaning."

Renf-ankh showed astonishment. "An interesting hypothesis; but it would have to be confirmed! If what you think about the twofold movement of breath, *àa*[5], is right, then it would be proper also to find out whether there is any correspondence between the letter *f*[6] and breath. Amirenf, what can you tell us about the letter *f*?"

Without hesitation Amirenf replied: "It is the animal represented by that sign."

"It is a viper," said Asfet.

"Viper?" the teacher of natural science protested. "What viper?"

"Is it not the horn-viper?"[7] muttered Awab.

"It looks rather slimy . . ." objected Her-Bak. "If it were meant to

---

[1] Metathesis.   [2] Cryptographic.
[3] See *Her-Bak Disciple*, Comm. I, §2.
[4] See the two aspects of the letter *a*, Fig. 2, Pl. I.
[5] Fig. 3, Pl. I.   [6] Letter *f*, Pl. IV.
[7] See *Her-Bak Disciple*, Comm. III, §2.

represent the horn-viper, it would hardly be depicted as coming out of the water and climbing up a papyrus-reed, as I once saw in a picture."

"It might be a snail that has left its house," suggested Awab.

Pasab intervened. "Don't you think we are making a mistake in ascribing some definite animal to this sign? It is not the only sign whose form does not exactly correspond to any species we know. Would it really be absurd to assume that here some mythical animal has been put together and been given such characteristics as symbolise the functions it was meant to represent?"[1]

The shrill voice of Smôn tried to cut short the debate. "Aren't you ashamed to embark on such a sea of phantasy?"

Ignoring this remark, Pasab continued: "To Renf-ankh I would reply that the animal of the letter f[2] seems to express the sound of breathing, as it were, the manifestation of the expiration, of which the double letter *àa* is the origin. One might also say: 'it is the *carried* breath', and even '*that which carries* the breath'—carrier and carried being in this case one and the same.[3] For f is no longer the indeterminate breath of the origin: it is the *emitted* breath, governed by the lips; it can be warm or cold, according to the manner in which it is emitted. It is this double nature which is indicated by the horns of the animal—horns which sometimes look like ears."

The natural scientist gave a grunt. "Ears? What ears? Whoever has seen the big ears of a viper?"

"Precisely," said Pasab, "that is just what gave me the idea that they must have some symbolic meaning. I studied the nature of breath and finally came to this conclusion: the breath emitted by a living being has already enlivened its blood; but it is this enlivened blood that *makes* the flesh; for without the blood, the flesh could neither build itself nor live; flesh is therefore the carried breath, and since this flesh is the primary substance of any living being, it is understandable that the letter f—symbol of the carried breath—should serve also to compose the name of flesh *af*: that which is made by f (breath) and carries this breath, *fa* (carry)."

Neni turned to the teachers. "What do you think of this theory? I might at a pinch admit the choice of an animal whose breath gives the sound f; but as to the rest . . ."

Pasab interrupted. "That would not be at all absurd, for the Ancients have named several animals according to their cry: 'mioo' for the cat, 'roo' for the lion. But this stands in no contradiction to the rest."

Khabes, the dean of the teachers, became impatient. "I thought, gentlemen, that we were examining a novice, and not a teacher. Speak, Her-Bak, what are the *medu-Neter*[4]?"

"They are divine signs which serve to form the words."

---

[1] See *Her-Bak Disciple*, Comm. III, §1.   [2] Letter f, Pl. IV.
[3] See *Her-Bak Disciple*, Comm. III, §2.   [4] Hieroglyphs.

"Why do you say 'divine'?"

"Because they are 'Symbols' which have a divine science for origin."

Smôn rejected the answer. "You are not asked for a philosophy, but for precision! Asfet, you give us a good definition."

Asfet declaimed: "They are conventional signs which serve to form words with which one expresses thought."

Again Pasab intervened. "No more than that? Can you tell us, oh Asfet, why the sign med[1] is the sign of the stick?"

"Because it serves to pronounce both: word and stick."

"And Her-Bak, what do you say?"

Her-Bak hesitated. "Perhaps because the word is supported by these signs like a man by a stick?"

Smôn raised his hand. "This is no nursery, that we should have to listen to such childish nonsense!"

"I think," Pasab replied, "the Ancients took their inspiration from life when choosing their symbols. Now a stick is a piece of wood from which the sap that flowed through it has gone; it is dry, but, except for the sap, it still preserves the vegetable form. In the same way, the word preserves the form, although not the life; this life will be added by the intonation, the ring of the voice."

"I do not deny," Neni declared, "that the Ancients had a keen sense of observation; but I cannot agree that they had an abstract philosophy! Surely their constant preoccupation with material necessities—which shows itself even in their inscriptions—left them no interest for philosophical speculation."

"The fact," Pasab answered, "that the word medu is followed by Neter proves, however, that there was some intention of giving this term a more exalted sense than the literal one."

"How do you interpret it?" asked Amenatu.

"Just as a stick is the vessel of the sap," said Pasab, "just so can med be the carrier of a Neter-function."

Khabes grew angry. "Anybody can read anything into anything."

Everybody gave their views; Amenatu raised his voice. "Friends, friends! You argue as over a pot of beer! Quiet, please. Let everybody speak in a way befitting an assembly of teachers such as we are. You, Smôn, have uttered nothing but reproaches; can you not define the medu-Neter?"

Everybody was silent in eager expectation of the answer, but Smôn remained mute. At last he uttered in a professorial tone: "A letter represents a sound, and a conventional meaning; the assembling of letters conventionally forms the words."

"Allow me to ask a question," said Pasab, "a convention is something arbitrary: Smôn therefore affirms that it would have been possible to attribute to a letter a meaning different from the one actually adopted."

[1] See Fig. 4, Pl. I.

"It is obvious," answered Smôn, "that the sign *md* is a stick!"

"And that Smôn is a goose!" added Awab.[1]

Outbursts of laughter were immediately smothered by a glance from Pasab; Smôn hid his anger under a smile of pity; then he continued: "As for seeing a relation between the word *medu-Neter* and the name of the stick, that seems as far-fetched as to see a relation between the words *àb* (*ib*), heart, and *àb*,[2] to be thirsty."

"And I, Pasab, believe that such a relation exists: does the heart not drink without ceasing the flow of blood, and then empty itself to refill itself afresh? Is it not the most perfect symbol of something insatiably calling for the liquid without which it would cease to beat . . . and to live?"

There was a stir among the listeners, who gave voice to varied opinions. Amenatu put an end to the debate. "We are wasting our time! I suggest that each teacher begin his lesson according to our daily usage."

They obeyed and rose; the pupils grouped themselves around their teachers; some silently changed over and sat down near Pasab. Khabes, seeing this, shrugged his shoulders. "Poo! Poo! There will always be those who look for revelations."

Her-Bak caught the remark, and his heart grew indignant. "Why don't you answer him, O Pasab?"

"Remain in peace, my son, this debate has lasted far too long already; it is very good that there should be sceptics."

Asfet shook his head. "Pasab is a fool!"

"No, Pasab is not a fool! . . ."

All eyes looked for the source of this answer. Seeing a new arrival, the students shouted his name: "Abushed! What's he doing here? We haven't seen him since he passed into the inner Temple!—Abushed, who has sent you here? Do you come back to us?"

Abushed went to Pasab: "Nobody sends me; I happened to pass and heard your controversy. It's a rare enough occurrence to surprise me! But what I have said is true: the fool is not the one you think."

Smôn's voice rose over the tumult: "He hasn't changed a bit. Still the same insolence!"

"Why do you call him a fool," asked Abushed, "the man who has seen a little ray of light?"

The students pressed around him, flowing over with questions. "So you, too, dream of these crack-brained notions? You, the sceptic, the scoffer, have they succeeded in outwitting you?"

Abushed waited until their mockeries had run out. "I do not dream," he then said, "I know. I have seen evidence that has dispelled my previous errors. Blessed is Pasab who has believed without having seen."

---

[1] The *smôn*, a goose sacred to *Amun*, is the most vicious of all waterfowls. See Chapter XXXVIII, 'The Sacred Animals'.

[2] *àb*, thirst, is written with a picture of a kid. For the phonetic spelling see Fig. 5, Pl. I.

A hostile group joined them. "Do you mean to say that our Masters are teaching us errors?"

"In this precinct everyone teaches what he believes."

"Well, if there is another truth elsewhere, why hide it from us?"

"Judge for yourself what reception you give to what passes beyond your little daily rounds?"

"Who then has opened to you the gate of another teaching?"

"My dissatisfaction."

Abushed took advantage of the growing din to leave with Pasab, and he said to him with laughter: "Who would have believed it? Has enthusiasm unlocked the lips of the cautious Pasab?"

"Have I said too much? Their blindness provoked me into answering."

"Why should it matter to you? Leave him in error who loves his error. Do you not know that it is written: 'O you who will be on earth ... O all you scribes who know how to unknot the difficulties of writing and who are skilled in the hieroglyphs, O you who launch yourselves into research for knowledge, O you who in bliss enjoy the acquired results....'[1] It is for those that the texts of the Sages were written, and for those who know to deny, with nobility, the errors of routine in order to find truth. But for the others the truth has been veiled under trivial forms. That is why you must measure your words."

[1] Appeal to the living, engraved at the entrance of the inner chamber of the funeral chapel of Khaemhât at Thebes.

XXXIV

THE JACKAL

In the evening of the same day, at the hour when the sap slows down its flow, a mysterious link was forged between two beings.

Daylight already stood under the invasion of night: *Râ's* final amethyst reflections still held the veil on the lights of *Nut*. The mirror of *Mut's* lake, shaped by the Sages like a crescent, reflected the lunar barque.[1] The novice and Pasab were contemplating it in silence.

The peace of dusk bade a truce to the feverish activity of man. Whatever had risen active and full of fight in the morning was now preparing its rest. The spectral shadows of the first bats were dancing around the lake, while a jackal furtively skirted the pool, Pasab quietly pointed him out to Her-Bak.

"Look, my animal form is coming out there from between the old stones. Don't scare him away—he will come near: this is his hour; it is also the hour of my birth."

The jackal stopped before them and examined them curiously.

"You are a man, Pasab," whispered Her-Bak, "why do you speak of your 'animal form'?"

Pasab kept his eyes on the jackal, who tarried fearlessly, feeling at home in this place where he prowled along the walls in quest of prey, alive or dead, to fill his larder.[2]

Then the man spoke softly, attuning his voice to the peace of the evening. "This hour among all others is favourable for the communion between speaker and listener. . . .

"Let fall the day, let rise the night. The leaden shade smothers all colour; its veil of greyness flattens the mountains; for whereas the crudeness of the day defines and separates, dusk fuses all things into one; the soul of the beings reveals itself as soon as our eyes no longer delimit their shapes.

"Happy is he who does not refuse himself to this obscure union: the Master of this hour will teach him the scripture of the gods. Listen to his teaching.

"Nature is one in her cause; numberless in her creatures. Her creatures above are the stars of *Nut*; her creatures below are men and animals, plants and minerals; and each of them bears a signature which *Thot* has

---

[1] In this latitude the first quarter moon crescent lies on its back in winter, like a barque.
[2] The jackal tears his prey into pieces which he buries so as to let the flesh rot in the ground.

inscribed at its birth, and *Seshat* keeps in her records all these names, the features and properties they represent.

"Each signature corresponds to a *function* which reveals its essential nature—that is to say, one of the *Neters*."

Her-Bak opened astonished eyes. "Then every being wears a signature of the *Neters*?"

"That is what Wisdom has taught from the most ancient times. As to man, he is a summary of the Universe, but the determining conditions prevailing at his birth[1] imprint on him a character which belongs to the same signature as that of some plant or animal, and this makes for a similarity of inclinations; and between them there develops invisible sympathetic currents . . ."

Her-Bak interrupted him. "Why then does such an animal not search out its man?"

"Because the ignorant resist this link; those who *know* cultivate that sympathy by protecting that animal species; and, reciprocally, the *Consciousness of that Species* will protect its protector."[2]

"Your friend the jackal has given you his protection?"

"More than that: he has made me conscious of my nature through being conscious of my name."

"Then your name is not a mere coincidence?"

"This name that is both mine and this animal's[3] becomes the expression of a symbol; the letters which form it must express its nature: hence one can also through its nature divine the sense of the letters of its name."

"O Pasab, what a wonder!"

"Thus I began to seek for the way."

"Have you found the means by yourself?"

---

[1] See *Her-Bak Disciple*, Chapter 'Astrology'.
[2] The totem principle. See Chapter XXXVIII, 'The Sacred Animals': cf. *Her-Bak Disciple*, Comm. V, §2.   [3] *pa-sab* means the jackal.

"No. Observing my efforts, the Master directed my search."

"But once one has found all this, it ought to be easy to understand the rest?"

"It is not possible without a guide: the thought of man goes easily astray; it judges 'things' by their appearances, without taking account of the *invisible Neters*. Now Nature and *Neters* cannot exist without each other, and their relations form the tissue of the Universe. He who does not know them walks through the night without a guide."

"And one cannot know them through one's own research?"

"Man's existence is brief, and this science is hidden from them through their own mental and moral errors."

"O Pasab, teach me how to seek!"

The teacher silently measured the pupil's understanding so that he might suit his answer to it.

The last glow in the Amenti[1] had died; the victorious moon showed silver on the water of the lake, its slanting light cast oblong shadows on the ground. Man's little lights spangled the penumbra with minute ruddy fires. The jackal reappeared, restless—some suspicious noise had scared him ... he suddenly leaped forward and ran on, a fine silhouette lengthened by its plumed tail.

At last he vanished and the scribe explained: "It is by observing my 'Symbol'[2] that I have understood the first step: the jackal is a devourer."

"He is a cruel beast!"

"He obeys the law of Nature whereby the death of one gives life to another; he devours flesh which has become rotten; he cleans the highways. The jackal's *function* is digestion, transforming putrid flesh into life-giving nourishment; what for other beings would be infectious poison, in him becomes an element of life, after the destructive element has been transformed."

"Does not the vulture, too, devour dead things?"

"Yes, but the vulture is a huge bird; his element is the air; whereas the jackal lives on earth and in his burrow."

"Why is his name also that of a judge?"[3]

"Have I not played this role in the mob of students who remain in the Peristyle?[4] For it is I who selected elements capable of evolving, and separated them from the intransmutable elements of the mass. No easy role! For this discrimination is not the work of the *intellect*, but an *experiment in life*; that is pure to the jackal which can be transmuted into his own nature. Happy the seeker who has understood this!

"But never must he confuse his *true* nature with the extraneous tendencies heredity and outer influences have brought about."

"What then is my 'true nature'?"

"That which has *caused* your birth at such a moment and in such a

---

[1] Occident.   [2] See *Her-Bak Disciple*, Comm. II, §2.
[3] *sab* = judge, and also jackal.   [4] Outer Temple. See Chapter XXXII, 'Admission'.

place; but this you will learn from others. This evening learn the meaning of the word *wâb*, pure:[1] *wâb* means the widening of an individual nature freed from all alien additions; hence the name of the 'Wâb priests' who have worked out their 'nature' in such a way that each of them finds himself in perfect harmony with the function that has been advisedly entrusted to him, whatever the importance of this function, great or small."

"Then every Wâb priest is a perfection?"

"By no means. Human endeavour must always remain short of perfection; besides, no one will ever weed out the tendencies innate in his particular nature; the point is to change their force into life power."

"Tell me, what are my true tendencies?"

"You will learn them at a propitious moment; can you not study some principle without having to relate it to your own self?"

"Be at peace, Master, I shall transform myself into *wâb*."

The night hid Pasab's laughter. "May *Thot* take a hand in it!" he replied. "Such a transformation does not come about without struggling: that is why the horn, meaning attack, has been introduced into the word *wâb*.[2]

"Few pupils have the courage to allow their corruptible elements to be destroyed; for every man is rich in excuses to safeguard *his* prejudices, *his* instincts, and *his* opinions!"

"O Pasab, why do you speak of morals instead of science?"

"Because science is not the same as Understanding. To know means to record in one's memory; but to understand means to blend with the thing and to assimilate it oneself, as the bread which you eat is assimilated by your body; but *prejudices* stand like a screen between the *thing* and the man, and what the 'seeker' succeeds in seeing the screen distorts.

"Some keen intelligence will be blind to the *naturally obvious*; some attitude of specious criticism closes the door to naïve intuition; certain mediocre virtues remain petrified and supine.

"The role of a 'judge-*sab*' therefore consists in discerning the Real from the artificial and in selecting for the 'House-of-god' those elements which can become incorruptible."

"Shall I be one of those?"

"That will depend on your choice: realities or appearances? There are two kinds of error: *blind credulity* and *piecemeal criticism*. Never believe a word without putting its truth to the test; discernment does not grow in laziness; and this faculty of discernment is indispensable to the Seeker.

"Sound scepticism is the necessary condition for good discernment; but *piecemeal criticism is an error*. By this word I mean the dissection of a lesson into its elements and the scrutinising of each *separately*.

"The Wisdom of our Masters is a synthesis, and everyone of its ele-

[1] See Fig. 8, Pl. I.
[2] See Fig. 9, Pl. I; cf. *Her-Bak Disciple*, Comm. VII, §13.

ments, even a simple letter of the alphabet, is in itself a living synthesis; you cannot understand the full meaning of a hieroglyph unless you consider *simultaneously* its symbolic shape, the *nature* of the thing represented, its number, and its resonance; and all their teaching is of this kind.

"If you dissect an animal, you will not know the living relation between its organs; if you separate matters in a state of digestion, you will make them unassimilable; and this holds true for research into the great Laws.

"Dissection or analysis causes decline of thought:[1] it is the *wrong application of the digestive principle.*"

"But have you not told me yourself, O Pasab: 'Never believe without discussing'?"

"First you must listen, but listen in your heart, so that you hear *the meaning intended by the teacher*. Then you must call to mind the arguments against, provided they attack the *whole idea*, and not its separate elements; for it is the living sense that gives the various elements their value. Do you understand, Her-Bak?"

"It is hard. . . . I think what you are advising me to do is not to cut into pieces the living word of a Master? But what shall I do if a lesson itself is made up of small pieces only?"

"If so, that teaching is false, for in it is no living sense."

The pupil's eyes sparkled with mischief. "Of course, I shall hardly risk hearing such an abomination in the Temple."

The Master ignored the irony. "And if it did happen to you, what would you make of it?"

"I should have to be judge and jackal and discriminate between good and bad teachers!"

The scribe nodded his head. "You are quick to learn! However, beware of making enemies around you. Don't let your talents make you arrogant. And do take heed of this: those who will teach you will not all have the same horizon; take advice from the ignorant as well as from the learned, until your own judgment has become sharp enough.

"If some day it be given to you to pass into the inner Temple, you must leave no enemies behind."

This word deeply stirred Her-Bak; he threw himself at the teacher's knees. "O Pasab, you have spoken like the Master; now I know that you speak in his place; I shall obey."

[1] See *Her-Bak Disciple*, Comm. VII, §6 and §7.

XXXV

THE THREE

THE ducks and ducklings among the pink lotus flowers on the large pool wisely shunned the border where six nervous legs were dangling.

Quack-quack on the water . . . argument on the edge . . . and the beams of *Râ* shining indifferently over both. Those on the water were united: a group-soul of fowls held together by identical appetites. But those on the edge were divided: one 'would fain' the other 'fain would not', and the third in the middle hesitated between them. Her-Bak, remember the jackal!

Her-Bak felt worn-out and sighed: "Is life in the Temple always like it was yesterday and today?"

"I don't see how you can complain since it's all your own doing," Asfet retorted bitterly. "We did not call you. And none of us argued against what they teach us as our daily task."

Awab defended his friend. "It was Pasab who argued, not he."

But Her-Bak did not want to be excused. "No, Asfet is right: it was I, for I back my Master."

"And I shall defend mine," said Asfet, "after all, what weight has your opinion? What right has an ignoramus like you to sit in judgment over his teachers?"

"Has then the search for Truth no place in your syllabus?"

"Truth has no doubt been waiting for you to be its mouthpiece."

Awab cut in: "What Pasab said was like air to my lungs; to you the words are dead, but he makes them come alive."

Asfet gave a contemptuous laugh. "You believe without thinking, as a dog swallows a fly!"

"Does one have to think to know whether one loves or not?"

"Love is one thing, Knowledge another. To you it gives pleasure to liken the heart to a thirsty young goat. But I seek out all cases where these words have been used, the various ways in which they have been written; I think of the possible predilections, omissions, and mistakes of the scribes, which may have led to the differences; then I carefully reason it out to decide which is the best version. You see: I am taking into account what part intelligence has played in the progress we have made."

"So you set yourself up to be the judge of your predecessors' mistakes?"

"Not I—our teachers. Must one not explain the divergencies in the scriptures? Only reasoning can sort them out."

"And you are all so clever that you are sure you overlook nothing?"

Her-Bak listened to the debate. As Asfet did not reply, he spoke:

"I take up your arguments, Asfet: assume the descrepancies in the scriptures really arise from the negligence or predilection of scribes. If so, how can we explain that the priests of the inner Temple—who are said to be so strict about the exact copying of inscriptions—have not corrected these errors? You don't know? And what do you think of the words and word-roots which are spelt alike but have different meanings?"[1]

"It's the poverty of the language."

"You would have done better, no doubt! But tell me why the determinative sign of the word *àb*, thirst, is a kid that is leaping . . . like the heart? Moreover, the same word means also dancing, leaping."

"Yes, that has been noticed."

"Your teachers and you, Asfet, accept what you understand and reject what you fail to understand. What right has an ignoramus like you to sit in judgment on the builders?"

"These builders . . . are people from many different epochs and classes; you are not going to tell me that they have always followed one and the same guiding principle according to laws which they have kept hidden?"

Awab replied to Asfet. "Pasab has taught me that between epochs of Wisdom our history has known long periods of darkness when this Wisdom lay asleep; but he said also that afterwards our gods always sent some Masters who were in possession of the secrets. And he maintains that those Masters allowed nothing to be preserved that had not been worded in accordance with the sacred law."

Asfet laughed. "Pasab imposes upon your simplicity! What King or nobleman builds for his private life is destroyed, because his sons, too, will build for themselves. Might one not say as much for the public monuments?"

"Pasab says that temples, statues, and steles conform to the teaching that must be bequeathed to future times."

"What does Pasab know?"

"He believes what the Master told him."

"Belief is nothing: proofs are needed."

Her-Bak spoke again: "They tell us that the monuments teach the mysteries of the Heavens."

"What is mysterious about them? Sun? Moon? Stars? Does not everybody see them rise and set?"

Her-Bak laid his left hand on Awab's shoulder and his right on Asfet's. "Awab, you are *àabet* (the Orient); Asfet, you are *àment* (the Occident); *àment* is the end of the day; *àabet* is its beginning. I have learnt that the child starts crying the moment it is born, and then begins to breathe air. Now what does Pasab say? This first cry, the cry of the beginning, is that not the *à*[2] of breathing out? And his breathing in, is it not *a*[3] which takes in the breath without which the heart *àb*[4] would cease to beat?"

---

[1] Homonyms.   [2] Letter *à*, Pl. IV.
[3] Letter *a*, Pl. IV.   [4] See Fig. 10, Pl. I.

Awab could no longer retain his joy: "Listen to that, Asfet, that is proof!"

Her-Bak replied: "Listen to this, Awab: Pasab also said: 'One must search for the proof *before* making an affirmation!' For me the proof has been brought; Pasab has understood what the Ancients thought about the twofold primary letter *àa*[1] and for *àb*, 'heart and thirst'."

Asfet hit upon a cunning answer: "If such were their subtle thoughts, why then have they given on their walls and steles only monotonous formulas of offerings and foods, war stories or favours bestowed upon them by the King?"

"The food," Awab replied, "is for their father, *Amun*. . . ."

"No, Awab," interrupted Her-Bak, "that is no argument! Asfet's question looks quite sensible. However, everybody speaks of their secret knowledge. . . ."

"Precisely," said Asfet in his most ingratiating way, "as Smôn has said, if it is here that the error lies, then, just because it is so widespread, one has to know and to fight it. It is absurd to believe that people in such ancient times were capable of creating concepts that went beyond the concrete and material!"

Her-Bak reflected. "However, O Asfet, the Sage said that those inscriptions have a second meaning for those who know the key."

"Who can say that this is not an illusion? The ancient inscriptions are shorter and less clear than those of our times. If there were such a wonderful science, why hide it from us? Are we not well advanced over the Ancients? In the early times only Kings had the privileges of rites and funeral services; little by little the nobility came to share in this privilege; now even the common man has all these rights: there is evidence of progress!"

"Asfet, do you know what they teach in the inner Temple?"

"Those who have entered it do not tell us; but if some lofty science had really been revealed to them, don't you think they would be quick to show it off?"

"Abushed said he had found proof of it!" cried Awab.

"Abushed would see stars in bright daylight if he could thus prove that there is a circle of initiates!"

"And why have your teachers not entered the inner Temple?"

"Favouritism no doubt, or some private interest, which admits some and excludes others. But these are insolent questions: we may be merely 'outers', still from our ranks come priests, expert scribes, and influential officials."

"Sages as well?"

Asfet's answer was so violent that the frightened ducks all began quacking at once. "True Sages are those who give what they have, without meanness and without secret!"

---

[1] See *Her-Bak Disciple*, Comm. I, §3.

"O Asfet, secrecy irritates only the talkative!"

"For an intelligent man there is no mystery."

"That is a vain man's word: to him the Sages close the door."

"Door to what? To a mysticism of halfwits and degenerates? What good are these maunderings about an arbitrary symbolism? The scribes who count the thousands have a surer sense of reality!"

"And you think that all this fantastic toil to erect these monuments and cover them with inscriptions served no better purpose than to proclaim banalities?"

"You are a pack-ass! There is no sense whatever in that body of yours!"

The quarrel became bitter; Awab interposed: "You know it is said: 'Do not shout in the House of the god.'"

Asfet rose in fury; he held forth, his threatening fist calling to witness his gods, his teachers, and his friends, that their school was in peril if such arrogance was to be tolerated.

"The insolence of this beginner is the ignorance of the gullible! It is the death of progress, the beginning of decay! The return to slavery! It is an aberration that will engulf us finally into imbecility!"

The noisy dispute roused attention; conversations stopped, people came near, and Asfet's anger doubled; with wide gesticulations he stepped backward and fell into the pool, from which the ducks flew up with loud squawking.

Everywhere bursts of laughter rose. Asfet was a poor swimmer, he splashed and floundered painfully under the mocking eyes of the spectators; Awab threw off his robe and dived in to help him.

They reached the steps where Her-Bak was waiting for them, and the three combatants looked at one another, sobered and somewhat ashamed.

Her-Bak took the 'drowned man's' hand and led him away from the crowd; drying his robe and prestige in the Sun, Asfet declared: "It does not matter; on the contrary: the water of this pool has a purifying effect!"

Her-Bak masked his laughter under a shocked expression: "What are you saying there, my friend? Aren't you being engulfed in the mysticism of degenerates?"

XXXVI

THE HEAVENLY *NUT*[1]

MOONLESS night. On a roof-terrace covered with mats, two shadows are sitting side by side, legs crossed, hands on knees. Surrounded by the serenity of the sky, they speak softly, not to disturb it.

"Why do we not come here every night, O Pasab? The nights are sweeter than the days!"

"Your voice is heavy with regret, Her-Bak! Does the day not bring you the teaching you seek?"

"Not the teaching which I desire. O Pasab, you who have succeeded in perturbing my teachers and whose answers have warmed me like a flame, now you no longer set right their errors! Ever since that day you teach like the others: where is truth now? Must I become 'judge' over even your words?"

Pasab replied gently: "If it had not been the Master who entrusted you to my care, I should not speak before the pupil had acquired a sense of respect! However, I will answer this thirsty young goat, but at a propitious moment of which I shall be the judge. But is this all that this serene hour suggests to you?"

Her-Bak lifted his eyes to the stars; their twinkling fascinated him, and little by little calmed his boiling impatience.

For a pastime he began to count them . . . it proved impossible and this roused his apprehension. Was this the first time that he really saw the sky? His ignorance confounded him, and he burst out: "Pasab, what are the stars? Pasab, what is the sky?"

For an answer he heard Pasab laugh. "Her-Bak, what is Light? Her-Bak, what is Nature? Such a question deserves another: do you expect a definition? Are you trying to force me to speak to you in the manner of the other teachers?"

Her-Bak, confused, apologised. "O Master, must I not ask questions about what I do not know?"

"The Sage has taught me that an answer brings no illumination unless the question has matured to a point where it gives rise to this answer which thus becomes its fruit. Therefore learn how to put a question."

"Our teachers don't teach like that. They dole out their knowledge as one loads a burden on an ass; there is no room for reflection; a good pupil is he who commits their lists and formulas to memory!"

"A faulty method is a touchstone to the students: the sheep submits;

[1] The name of the goddesses *Nut* and *Mut* (French *Nout* and *Mout*) are to be pronounced with a long vowel, as *noot* and *moot*, to rhyme with *route*, *loot* (T.N.).

the fox turns it to his own ends; the cat takes advantage of it to remain lazy; the lion relies on his own strength."

"The lion knows how to find a track; I, Her-Bak, do not know how to seek."

"Learn, then! First of all you must achieve *curiosity*."

"But is Asfet not curious? He scoffs at hidden teaching, but listens eagerly for its feeblest echoes."

"That is a kind of indiscretion; curiosity is something different: it is a sponge made for absorbing water, but dry; in other words, it is thirst for knowledge, it is a poverty of which one is aware.

"Now the soul knows everything, but it does not formulate. If one becomes conscious without knowing how to formulate, then one is poor, restless, thirsty, curious."

"Then it is necessary to dare to admit that one is poor?"

"That is the first condition. That is why vain people know only the unhealthy kind of curiosity: to snap up, copy, and repeat what others have formulated."

"Ought one not to study the scriptures of the Sages?"

"Certainly, they are excellent for orientating and guiding one's *inner research* which alone gives Understanding. That is why *healthy curiosity* draws out of itself the elements of all problems and creates *by its desire* the contact with the thing it wants to know."

"What then have I that I could draw out of myself? O Pasab, I am poor!"

Pasab laughed. "Very good! Everything of which you have become aware in your varied trades and experiences is a real acquisition: it is memory of the soul and not of your brain. Awaken this consciousness so you can extend it to that which you wish to understand; in Nature everything is linked with everything else, and you are part of this Nature; observe outside, observe inside: you will be surprised when you begin to see the relations between things, and little by little their living interplay.

"Then do not be impatient, go on listening . . . and then begin once more, until the acquired consciousness can be formulated without effort; *thus you will understand* what you have *known*."

"O my Master, will I have so much patience?"

"If your thirst is not intense enough, leave it, and remain 'like the others'!"

Her-Bak gave an angry grunt. "You certainly have said all that needed saying! Now I shall begin; I will try to understand the sky."

He crossed his hands on his knees, but his Master said: "Not so; lie on your back and contemplate in silence."

He obeyed. His nape to the ground, face to the sky, Her-Bak observed intensely the countless golden dots: they twinkled like eyes winking at him . . . their multitude upset him. What was there to be found in the sky?

"What is the sky? . . . I no longer see the 'sky', I see stars: small dots of light. What are they? . . . Oh! a shooting star falling down! So they can move? . . . There are too many. I am at a loss! Everywhere they are. . . . Everywhere? But for how far? Is there anywhere an end to them?

"What are the stars? Between the shining points I see nothing: is that 'the sky'? . . . If the stars are lights, why don't they lighten the 'black'? . . . On what are they fixed? Or do they hang in the void?

"It is frightening, that big dark hole . . . everywhere, everywhere 'black'. Where am I? In the 'black'? . . . The Earth is solid, but if I were to fall from the Earth I should fall into that very 'black'! Where to? . . . I cannot: one does not fall 'upwards', one always falls to the Earth. . . . Why don't the stars fall? But they do fall: I have seen it. . . . There is another one falling! Where does it go? I no longer know. . . . Oh that emptiness. . . . I am afraid!

"All these twinkling dots of fire—is that fire? They move . . . they turn . . . no, it is I who am turning! One would say they're coming nearer. . . . That blue star, it has become larger . . . it is coming down . . . it is going to fall upon me. . . .

"*I am afraid!*"

His eyes blinked and he shivered; giddiness gripped him . . . his chest heaved painfully. . . .

"What is the sky? Fires? Holes? One hole? Emptiness? . . ."

His resistance was flagging; his lids fell over his eyes. . . . And he sank into sleep, in the midst of stars that were falling.

Pasab, who had observed him in silence, drew a mat over him, and sat down near him. Then he kept vigil, alone, in the night.

And now his pupil's problem, to which he had postponed the answer, returned again to his mind. Her-Bak's complaint stirred the memories of his own suffering: why was he teaching what was contrary to his conscience?

He recalled his earlier studies, his patient meditation, his laborious researches, the joyful revelation when the letters of the alphabet came to life, when the symbols took form and incarnation. Was it his duty to preserve silence, or to share his treasure? Abushed had warned him not to say too much; he obeyed, he was keeping to the trivial formulas: but was that not tantamount to lying?

What happened when he disclosed his vision: some were fired with hope, others revolted; each took offence at the other; the result was trouble and confusion. . . . Was the revolt caused by the *mystery*?

"Can one abolish mystery? What reveals itself to me ceases to be mysterious—for me alone: if I unveil it to anyone else, he hears mere words which betray the living sense: profanation, but never revelation. What is one to do? What was the Master's attitude towards me? He listened to my questions without answering directly; but he set right my mistakes, he modified my way of seeking; he simplified my thought; he taught me to become problem-conscious. . . . Why did I resist for so long a time? Can I blame others?"

He meditated deeply, seeking the reasons for the obstinacy of mankind, and measuring the value of the various forms of Knowledge.

In the last hour of night he became aware of a twofold reality:

The first concerning the 'Secrets': *all cognition comes from inside*; we are therefore initiated only by ourselves, but the Master gives the keys.

The second concerning the 'way': the seeker has need of a Master to guide him and lift him up when he falls, to lead him back to the right way when he strays. But where is a Master who could compel the proud to prefer what is 'Real' to appearance and to his prejudices?

Pasab felt powerless to pass beyond the present stage. And from this consciousness sprang a cry of appeal: *the irresistible outcry of the hungry*.

Her-Bak's face emerged from the mat; the freshness of dawn awakened the sleeper; he sat up, confused: "So I have been unable to keep awake! Day already?"

The grey dawn had not yet dimmed out the stars; Her-Bak looked for them anxiously. "They have changed their place: these are different patterns, and yet it still is the same sky. . . . What is the sky?"

Pasab was silent.

"You did not sleep, Pasab, did you?"

"The night is propitious for the gestation of the light, and the day for its formulation. I will answer your reproach, Her-Bak: why have I ceased to teach what I have understood? In other words: *is it good to attack error among those who are not prepared?*

"And I, I am asking you: *who* has falsified the teaching? Our hieroglyphs are the same for all; to all eyes signs and words offer evidence of the philosophy from which they sprang; nevertheless, you have seen how the teachers revolted!

"Don't let this astonish you: people's first reaction is selfish; they are afraid of changes which might upset their habits; they are too vain to admit that there is a Wisdom which they do not possess. He who points a new way out to them is a troublesome intruder, and all those who allow themselves to be limited by that which they have professed in the past rally themselves against him. It is hard to be made to eat one's own words. *Only the sincere seeker is capable of doing this.* Few are the worshippers of *Maât* who dare to deny themselves for her sake! To uphold their own doctrine those who teach will resort to scoffing and subterfuges *at the risk of deceiving the young.* . . .

"Remember, however, that this is the outer Temple, the testing-ground for that which is to be possible."

"And you, my Master, why then did you stay here?"

"I had to fulfil my part and my destiny. But the hour of the jackal will soon come to an end."

The dawn had blanched the earth; the break of day coloured the sky. "The stars are going out," said Her-Bak. "The last one has become so pale that one can hardly distinguish it; where are the others?"

"Where should they be, if not in the sky?"

"Is it possible? They remain up there, invisible, the whole day long?"

"Yes, like points of light within light. . . ." Pasab said, and then added: "Let it take body, that which has been conceived during the night. There is a time for everything. Come back this night. And then come again . . . so that *Nut* herself may yield her secret to you."

From the neighbouring temple arose a murmuring; Pasab looked towards the Orient, he bowed low, and with emotion repeated the words which the priests were speaking at that moment.

Her-Bak's second night was spent in solitude. However, he knew from Pasab that on one terrace of the temple priests were passing the hours of night studying the sky; and though he could not see them, the knowledge of those other 'seekers' stirred and stimulated him.

He had made eager preparations for this vigil. He had asked Asfet questions, but Asfet had mocked him. "You . . . you don't even know what they teach us, and you want to tell your teachers what's what."

Her-Bak had kept his mouth shut and made no reply: he had learnt his lesson. He had spent the whole day deciphering inscriptions, his nose lifted to the walls to spot symbols; and Awab had told him with simplicity all that he had been taught. But Awab's explanations perturbed him.

In vain did he now interrogate the star-spangled ceiling: it contained nothing to confirm the legend he had heard. "Is it true that *Nut* is a woman whose body is the sky with its constellations? Is it true that she assumes the posture of a cow, 'on all fours'? They teach that she swallows *Râ* every evening, to give birth to him again at dawn? But I cannot see *Nut*, and the Sun has descended below the mountain; is then *Nut beneath* the earth? . . . That would mean that she is not in the sky I see.

"And another thing I don't understand: as she is called *Râ's* daughter, how can *Râ* become her son every morning? Awab said also that she is the mother of the five great gods: *Osiris, Isis, Nephtys, Seth* and *Horus*; and I have read the words of a scribe on a stele: 'Between the arms of my mother *Nut*. . . .' Are all men and gods her children?

"Why do they put a vessel on her head? It is the vessel *nu*[1]; it is round like the sky. . . . A vessel is made for containing water: is there water between the stars? But the water I drink is called '*mu*': what then is the water for *nu*?

[1] See Fig. 11, Pl. I.

"How many things there are to be learnt!

"The symbol of the sky[1] is a flat top resting on two triangles: the sky seems round, for the Sun issues from the Earth every morning, he rises into the sky, and returns into Earth every evening; but I don't see any triangles! They say the sky is supported by four pillars: are those perhaps the two feet and two hands of *Nut*? I don't understand it! . . .

"Regarding the Sun, I know he gives light and heat; and he is round. The Moon is not always a disk: why? . . . She travels fast, she passes in front of the stars: *who* pushes her forward like that? I don't know anything: how can I seek?"

Her-Bak had the impression of butting against a wall: he felt shut in, stiff, dry. What was the matter? Why could he neither understand nor feel? . . . He went for advice to his past. He searched his experiences for a trace of light: the lesson of the potter, the warnings of Menkh, the revelation of the Summit.[2] He delved back to their cause: at the source of each he found a fault, an error the removal of which opened out a joyful vision. What obstacle was holding him this time?

His schoolboy rancour gave answer. He listened to his griefs; he gauged his ignorance. . . . And the scales did not tilt in his favour. "At bottom I am proud: I know nothing and yet want to set the others right! It is no fun to see one's own failings; but it is even more annoying to remain bogged in them." And lo, a ray of hope dissolved his bitterness; he dared to look into the black void; were the stars no lights? And the Moon, and the Sun always lights? . . . Then man was never quite without light?

The darkness appeared dazzling to him; the joiner's old word once more took body: *sba*[3] star, *sba*[3] door. . . . "Is a star a door in the sky? A door through which passes the light? Why is its name almost the name of the soul: *ba*?"

The night became alive; the boy who so far had not 'recognised' his mother,[4] felt enwrapped by an immense Mother, a *Nut* who fed every one of the stars. And he, minute creature in their midst, he laughed with joy at sensing his infinite Mother, and, comforted, settled to sleep in her arms.

Next morning the teachers were surprised to find Her-Bak eagerly at work. No arrogance, no sulking; he listened with deference, he repeated the texts, he committed the formulas to memory. Asfet had to smile at his eagerness, and called him after the lesson:

"Well, Her-Bak, are you tired of playing the ass? Take my advice, you'll find yourself all the better for it: cut out the day-dreaming, the fantastic theory that has only the remotest bearing on the reality of facts! Learn the well-known formulas, and don't look for anything beyond

[1] See Fig. 12, Pl. I.   [2] See Chapters XX, XXIV, XXVI, XXX.
[3] See Fig. 13, Pl. I.   [4] See Chapter XI.

them, unless you want people to say 'He is a fool', as they say about Pasab."

Impassively, Her-Bak replied: "Don't worry, I shall learn the formulas."

The third night reunited Master and pupil on the high terrace; and again *Nut* took possession of Her-Bak, and no longer did Her-Bak ask: "Where is *Nut?*"

The 'seeker-apprentice' made an intense effort to put together the acquired knowledge of the two previous vigils; he did not glance at the sky, but endeavoured in the darkness to evoke the twofold vision: that which was 'up there' and the symbols of 'all that'. Little by little these two entered into a relationship; he did his utmost to express this relation, and speaking to himself he softly translated his thoughts:

"If I say 'sky', I imagine that which I have seen; but if I am writing its symbols, I do not imagine the sky I have seen. If I say 'stars', I imagine the luminous dots I have seen; but if I draw five-pointed stars, they are no longer the luminous dots I have seen.

"Now since our Masters have decided to represent these things by signs which are not exactly their images, the reason must be that they wanted to express other things for which one must not look outside with the eyes, but inside with the heart."

Pasab deemed that the hour for reply had come.

"Your conclusion is perfect; you have spoken to yourself, but it is as well that I overheard you. You begin to understand how to formulate a problem; now express clearly what you have understood."

Her-Bak summed up the three nights; Pasab approved of his pupil. "There you have excellent food for thought! True teaching is given in the covered Temple; we, alas, are in the Peristyle. But your way is the right one for finding the door; I can merely help you to seek it.

"Our Sages knew the movements of the stars, the meaning of the decans and the months. Do you know the full meaning of the month? It is one of the first things one ought to know. You have seen the Moon when she is full?"

"Yes, she is round; she is *meh*."[1]

"Beginning with that day she diminishes until she is no longer visible, and then she begins to grow again.

"The first evening you see her crescent, that is her first day: the last morning you see her crescent before it vanishes, that is her last day but one. Now then, from the first to the last day is a *lunar month*: *àbed*.[2] And now, Her-Bak, answer me, what is a *day?*"

"A day is all that happens between sunrise and sunset."

"No; for while you are sleeping, the Sun continues its course through the night. A day is the time from one rising of *Râ* to his rising on the next day. Hence, whereas the Moon *makes* the month, the Sun *measures* it.

[1] See Fig. 14, Pl. I.   [2] See Fig. 15, Pl. I.

"The Sage once told me: 'It is thus that everything is measured.' . . .
But I do not yet understand him."

"Does the Moon take the same path as the Sun?" asked Her-Bak.

"She lags always behind, and each month the Sun catches up with her.
When she is farthest from him, it is full Moon. The Temple priests
measure time by the stars.

"*Nut* is the image of the Heaven's life. The symbol of the sky is a
secret.[1] The four pillars of the sky are the four directions: if you lie down
on the ground you have the Orient to your left, the Occident to your
right; your head points to the North, and your feet to the South whence
comes the Nile."

"All this is not hard to keep in mind!" said Her-Bak. "Shall I learn
any more in the Peristyle?"

[1] See Fig. 12, Pl. I.

"You will learn what everybody may know, but not the 'secrets', for which one has to be prepared."

"The 'secrets'!¹ I have upheld them, on principle, against Asfet, but I must confess that the idea of 'concealment' annoys me."

"I know, my son; I too suffered from it until that day when I began, dimly, to discern some more abstract meanings of the *medu-Neter*; then I understood why it is important: the sages told me, and my own experience confirmed it, that mankind would badly misuse those secrets if they were generally accessible, and I learnt to keep silent. Besides, the judgment of Heaven often comes to confirm the legitimacy of secrecy: the man whose heart is not prepared feels something like a wall rising before him, and the mysterious meaning escapes him."

"O Master, I have experienced that in my second night, and my pride fell."

Pasab smiled. "You are too ignorant to have the right to revolt. You have judged your teachers unfairly: these men have worked hard. Mere compiling? Agreed! But for some it has been desperately hard work. You, who have done nothing so far, how dare you raise your voice? . . . From them you can learn their ideas about the world of appearances: that is what senses and memory record; hurry through that stage; then practise the art of formulating. It will be a blessing for you, if the insufficiency of this kind of 'knowledge' gives you the courage for a greater effort! Then you will be ripe for another kind of research: that which explores the *driving power* behind a thing and its *living meaning*. No longer will you ask 'How?' but 'Why?'."

Joyful peace illuminated the novice's face as he asked: "How can one know the teaching which is given through the images?"

"Be praised for this good question; the reply will be the way you will have to follow: it will teach you *why* one teaches through images."

¹ See *Her-Bak Disciple*, Comm. II, §2.

XXXVII

THE VISIT

SINCE the enrolment of the novice there had been no further break in daily routine; one month was like another and one day's story was very much the same as the day following. But one lucky morning the Peristyle stirred with unaccustomed liveliness: a party of students from the temple in Memphis (Hat-Ka-Ptah) had come for a visit, and their fellow-disciples of the outer Temple received them joyfully.

The news of their arrival had been greeted with a general cry of joy, and the boat was met with shouts of welcome. From their very first glimpse of the port, the visitors had not ceased to marvel, for *Amun's* town (Nut-Amun) stretched along both banks until it was lost to sight. They were led to the city of *Mut*, where the school gave them a reception, and the journey through palm-groves, through villages of serfs and artisans, through workshops and gardens fulfilled all expectations.

Servants carried their presents: pieces of linen for the temple of *Mut*, wine for the temple of *Khonsu*, terebinth resin for the great temple of *Amun*, and good things of all kinds for their fellow-disciples of the South. An old man from the inner Temple of Apet-Sut[1] presided over the reception, greeted by Pasab as Nefer-Sekheru.

Her-Bak listened eagerly to all the Memphians' replies to courteously asked questions: they were showered with compliments on the reputation of their sanctuaries and described them with enthusiasm: the glorious past of Memphis, the splendour of its court, the fabulous wisdom of the great Sage Imhotep. They described Hat-Ka-Ptah with its golden, jewelled gates, the statue of the *Neter* made of gold and precious stones, the two royal effigies, kneeling statues of silver and gold presenting offerings; the chased silver tablets engraved with the official decrees; the mysterious Naos made from a monolith of granite from Elephantina, which in its interior sheltered the divine triad *Ptah*, *Sekhmet*, and *Nefertum*; the countless vessels, cups, and sacred objects, all of gold or silver; the court of Aneb Sebek, planted with trees of myrrh and frankincense. The Memphians were proud of the countless treasures which issued from the 'Golden House' whose workshop was close to the temple, and from the houses of the craftsmen and perfumers, and the storehouses overflowing with produce from the Two-Lands.

They were listened to, complimented, and avidly asked for the details of their beautiful journey; and their stories, full of the life of the well-beloved river, revived in Her-Bak the nostalgic dreams of Chick-Pea.

[1] Karnak.

But now these dreams centred around more powerful goals: the un-known sanctuaries he heard described: Heliopolis, Memphis, Abydos.[1] His heart surged with emotion towards this new vision. His head swam, he was gripped by doubt, and felt shaken. So far 'his' temple had been *the* Temple and centre of the world, one Temple, and one horizon limited by its two mountains; one earth, his; one Master, the Sage. . . . And now the world was suddenly full of other temples whose marvels he heard praised! The earth unfolded itself into Southern and Northern Land. Other places were named and other Masters: the words had an unfamiliar ring; the names of the sacred animals were different.

This multiplicity troubled his harmony; he listened in silence, straining towards the new conceptions. Should he not know, too, what the others knew? The students discussed; Awab asked questions:

"You called *Ptah* the master of the gods. Now we, too, have a temple of *Ptah*, but we learn that *Amun-Râ* is the King of the *Neters*, *Mut* is his spouse, and *Khonsu* his son."

The Memphian Ptah-Mosis replied: "*Ptah* created the world, but eight primordial gods contributed; his work in Nature continues unceasingly: hence *Sekhmet* is his spouse, and *Nefertum* his son."

Awab wished to parade his knowledge: "We know that *Sekhmet* is his spouse, but here, in his sanctuary, he is accompanied by Imhotep . . ."

Nefer-Sekheru interrupted Awab: "What are you saying there about Imhotep?"

"We know that he is a son of *Ptah*."

"Say 'I know'; not 'we know'. Don't involve others in what you don't know."

Neni spoke reproachfully. "Have we not a right to affirm our teaching?"

But the Old Man bade him be silent. "Should we not invite speech from our guests?"

A Memphian brought out the relationship between the teaching of Heliopolis and that of Memphis.[2] "Heliopolis teaches the history of the Sun god who was *Atum* and became *Râ; Atum's* children, *Shu* and *Tef-nut* brought forth *Geb* and *Nut*, who in turn gave birth to two couples: *Osiris* and *Isis*, *Seth* and *Nephthys*. These gods together are the divine company of Heliopolis."

Another Memphian intervened. "The priests of *Thot* teach us that *Râ* issued from the eight primordial gods, for they formed the cosmic egg from which the sun was hatched."

"We know these eight gods," Neni replied. "*Atum* belongs to them under the name of *Ur*."

"*Ur*," said a Memphian, "is the name of the creative *Neter*."

"In Heliopolis," said another, "it is one of *Râ's* names."

[1] Iun, Aneb-hedj, Abdju. Iun (Heliopolis) is the *On* of the Bible.
[2] See Documentary Appendix, v, § 2.

"That is true," said Ptah-Mosis, "but it is equally true that he has the same standing as *Ptah*."

A visitor broke the silence to prove that there was no contradiction in this. Everybody put forth his own arguments; the discussion became general. Her-Bak, abashed, held his breath.

"These abstract theories about divine creators," said Asfet, "are play of the intellect; I prefer the beneficent gods who are accessible to men and give them prosperity: our *Rennutet* of the harvests, *Khnum* of the weddings, *Tueris* of fertility, and even our *Osiris*, the protector of the dead."

"You should see Abydos," a visitor exclaimed, "if you want to know *Osiris*. It is there that he reigns as master over the deceased."

"Have we not, too, *Osiris*, the first of the Westerners, the principle of resurrection, in our mountain of Amentit?"

Her-Bak risked a timid remark: "In our mountain we have also *Mersegert*."

"That is a local goddess, she cannot compare herself with the great gods."

"How can a god be local? Is the *Neter* not everywhere?"

Awab tried to help him. "Certainly, but every *Neter* has a specific function: *Osiris* and *Thot* look after the Moon, whereas the star Sothis is *Isis* who with a tear makes the great waters overflow."

Everybody gave his opinion. Neni called for silence and addressed the visitors: "I apologise for our little ignoramus: he mistakes symbols for reality. We scholars would not commit this error. We see in such symbols the spontaneous imagination of the 'primitive' Ancients who move in mystery with ease, because they reduce phenomena, which they cannot explain by logic, to their own scale by bringing them down to the human plane."

The oldest Memphian introduced a discreetly reproachful note: "This theory bears the hallmark of a sceptical modernism from which we so far have kept free. I am surprised to hear it uttered in the domain of all-powerful *Amun-Râ*!"

"These young people speak for themselves," Nefer-Sekheru explained. "None of them has as yet received any theological instruction."

"Intelligence makes up for that," said Asfet under his breath.

There were whisperings among the listeners; a young visitor turned towards Asfet. "I like this independence; I should love to stay here."

The Memphian Ptah-Mosis bowed before the Old Man and asked with great respect: "What must one do to receive your secret teaching?"

"What one must do in your temple, my son: bow one's head and open one's heart!"

Amenatu rose. "I am afraid, my children, you are giving your fellow-students from the North a rather unfortunate impression; listening to you they might almost think you are unbelievers, and, by the life of *Amun-Râ*, nothing could be farther from the truth.

"All you who are listening, children of North and South, you are servants of the King, L.H.S., who is ever living with us. He is the *Neter* that gives breath to our nostrils; let us join His Majesty in our hearts, and we shall live! There can be no divergencies between us, since He unites all creeds as He unites the Two-Lands. Know this: it is not the words that matter, but docility to the principles of wisdom. Put those into practice, and things will be well with you. Follow the path of virtue; distrust the depraved. Teaching brings life to the house, but be on guard against words that deceive: men bring about their own undoing with their tongues; beware of causing yours. Follow the path of custom: it is safe and free from traps.

"Make offerings to the *Neters*, and avoid what displeases them. We, the priests, do the thinking for you, fix the boundaries of your path! Serve the *Neters* by your obedience to our precepts, your attendance at our festivals, your generosity in your offerings: and the *Neter* will give you all you need."

Her-Bak stifled a resigned yawn. Seth-mesy turned to his pupils. "My children, will you give our visitors a demonstration of your knowledge of the precepts of Wisdom."

The students of *Mut* obeyed, and each eagerly recited some of the well-known verses:

"The virtue of a man, whose heart is just, is more agreeable to God than the oxen from the doer of injustice. . . ."

"Do the work of God, and He will work for you in return. . . . God knows those who work for Him."

"To let people benefit by your possessions is the duty of one whom God favours. . . . Don't be a miser with your riches: they are yours only as a gift from God. . . ."

"Celebrate the festival of your God when its day has come, for the god is angry with the negligent; song, dance, and frankincense are his food. . . ."

"Say your prayers with a loving heart, and let each of your words be hidden. The *Neter* will provide what is needful."

"Make offerings to your God and beware of what displeases Him."

The guests politely listened to the well-known precepts; but Her-Bak poured into Awab's heart the bitterness of his disenchantment: "If you are my friend, tell me the truth: am I doing wrong? Am I a coward? These precepts make me rage like a cheetah of the South. The virtue they preach imprisons my joy in a cage! This dictated perfection chokes me! Virtue! Virtue! What is virtue?"

This flood of fury terrified Awab. "Virtue is what pleases the *Neter*."

"What do you know about it? Who has ever spoken with the *Neter*? Who knows him? In the fields I could believe . . . but here? Priests, stone statues, and jealous people! But *Neters*? Talk, talk, talk about them, all the time, but I can see them no longer!"

The frightened Awab tried to hush him. "Listen rather to what Nefer-Sekheru is saying. Do you want to miss such an occasion?"

The Old Man was suggesting a visit to the principal temples and the

Memphians responded enthusiastically. People rose and crowded around him, when Seth-mesy took Her-Bak by the hand. "Stay with me, my son: I will guide you as we visit the houses of our gods."

The Memphians listened as Nefer-Sekheru explained: "You are now in the Peristyle of *Mut* in Asheru.[1] Asheru is the water of the 'black river', or the lake shaped like a crescent—or, more exactly, like a stomach where death begets life. The name of *Mut*, which means 'mother', is very near to the word *mut* (death) for all life is born from the death or decomposition of a germ.

"*Mut* is the mother of our novices, in her inner Temple she brings to birth those who will be the great servants of *Amun-Râ* and those worthy to become disciples of *Thot* and *Maât*.

"Note that *Maât* has a sanctuary just opposite ours, north of *Amun's* great temple; for *Maât* chooses and brings to perfection the elements whose nature is being defined in *Mut*.

"*Mut* assumes various shapes according to the phases of the function which she represents and the various states they cause in the substance transformed by her. Greet her here under the name of *Sekhmet*, the lioness-woman whose face is circled by flames like a Sun eclipsed—the drinker of blood and mistress of the dark when Light will revive again. Is not her name[2] that of a sceptre,[3] and also that of a power?"

The worshippers of *Ptah* admired the majestic image of his spouse—or rather his 'merit'[4]—the sitting *Sekhmet*, her severity deepened by the sombre granite. Noticing how impressed they were, their hosts led them around the temple through a corridor which was full of these statues.

"It is amazing," said Ptah-Mosis to the Old Man, "how all these statues of *Sekhmet*, although carved in the same epoch, are not cut from the same granite; how each statue differs from the others in colour, from the palest grey to blue-black; and the veins of the stone—now white, now red—cutting strangely across the forms. . . ."

"Does that not confirm what I told you of *Mut-Sekhmet?*" replied Nefer-Sekheru, "every moment of transformation is represented by one shade. And the veins: can one believe that works of such perfection could carry the traces of mistake or accident? I can show you the statue of a queen whose breast is encircled by a red vein:[5] the stone was intentionally chosen to stress the specific function of this image.

"It is worth while to seek the causes of these small differences, as of each detail of our sculptures!"

In the south-western corner of this corridor, the Memphians were shown a kneeling statue of Senen-Mut holding before him the knot of

---

[1] The lake of the temple of *Mut* in Karnak. Cf. *Acheron*, the (black) river of the Underworld in Greek mythology.
[2] *Sekhmet*.   [3] Sceptre = *sekhem*, see Fig. 126, Pl. III.
[4] See *Her-Bak Disciple*, Index: *merit*. The French 'aimant' means both 'loving' and 'magnet' (T.N.).   [5] This bust can still be seen in the temple of *Mut* at Karnak.

Isis and on it the head of *Hathor* wearing a sistrum.[1] The coincidence surprised Ptah-Mosis. "Will you tell us, O Nefer-Sekheru, whether there is some relation between this name Senen-Mut and his place in the temple of *Mut*?"

"Who could doubt it?" replied the Old Man. "Senen-Mut (brother of *Mut*) the guiding Sage of a feminine reign (Hatshepsut), the great Major-domo of the Royal Maid (whose 'foster-father' he is called as well) . . . Senen-Mut carrying the symbol of the double feminine function '*Hathor-Isis*' (or rather *Hathor-Mut*, for this knot is equally the symbol for one of the functions of *Mut*), this Senen-Mut guards the corner-stone of the goddess *Mut*; and should that be mere coincidence? But who does not want to believe is free to doubt!"

These explanations were missed by Her-Bak, who listened to the legend of *Sekhmet*, how *Râ* had her intoxicated with beer (red with earth from Elephantina) so as to stop the bloodshed among human beings.

"How much truth is there in this story?" asked Her-Bak. "Are the gods cruel? Is that permitted to the gods which is forbidden to men?"

Seth-mesy smiled good-naturedly. "One must not scrutinise the private life of gods or kings too closely. One obeys what is powerful and bows before the 'strong one'! The power of the *Neters* demonstrates itself every day—what more is needed? Worship them and beware of disobeying; do good, shun evil, practise virtue, and you will enjoy their favour."

"What is Evil?"

"What the *Neter* forbids."

"And how does one know what is forbidden?"

"We priests translate their will; be pious, be pure, be obedient!"

Her-Bak did not reveal how much his heart was perturbed; silently he followed the priest. They took an outer way to pass around the crescent-shaped lake into which the sanctuary of the temple projected like a pestle into a mortar. This disposition greatly surprised the Memphians. The Old Man listened to their questions with a smile.

Black and white plovers dipped their red feet into the edge of the muddy water. Nefer-Sekheru asked his guests to note each detail. "All these symbols ought to be living words to the scribes of the *medu-Neter*: every shape has its reason, as has every colour; but there are several meanings to one symbol.

"Let us now go towards Amenti (the Occident), if you wish to study the history of *Khonsu*, the fruit of *Mut*, in the various stages of his evolution."

On their way to *Khonsu's* temple they met with an ever-thickening stream of busy people: the approaches were alive with noisy activity: draughtsmen and engravers, painters and sculptors were putting the final touches to the interior decoration and the monument in the wing that had recently been modified.

[1] See Fig. 143, Pl. III.

Ptah-Mosis, observing that the building-material was brown stone and red sandstone, said to Nefer-Sekheru: "How do you explain that the same Pharaoh who built with white limestone in our part of the country should have chosen brown stone for your temples?"

"No doubt," said someone, "because one or the other stone-quarry was nearest."

"If that had been the reason for his choice," replied Nefer-Sekheru, "why should the red stone of Elephantina be carried to Memphis, or the stone *biat*[1] from Heliopolis to Thebes?[2] Or why should different stones be used for the same monument? Why pieces of limestone inserted in a wall of sandstone, as can be seen in some dilapidated temples?

"Those students of the inner Temple who have learnt there to observe without prejudice so as to be able to decipher the mysterious symbolism of the Sages, might answer these questions."

"What a lesson," exclaimed Ptah-Mosis, "is this scrupulous observance of symbolism even within the walls, where it cannot be seen!"

The Old Man agreed: "Every piece of stone, every vein is chosen with the same care, from the moment it is broken from the quarry; for each part of the monument the right stone is chosen, even if it is later to be painted, carved, and sometimes to be covered with chased metal!"

Everyone listened to Nefer-Sekheru's words and reflected upon them in silence.

They approached the entrance, passed around the austere bulk of the monument and entered the temple through a side door. A priest of *Khonsu* received the guests and showed them the beauties of the *Neter's* house. Walls and columns, covered with inscriptions and relief scenes, were resplendent with rich colour, gleaming with precious metals. Sumptuously decorated statues, vessels, votive tables—a treasure-house filled with silver, gold, enamels, and glittering gems.

"In *Mut's* temple," said Her-Bak to Seth-mesy, "green and blue predominated, but here the colours are so varied that one is dazzled by this mountain of marvels."

"It is only right that this temple should be one of the richest, since *Khonsu* is the son of our god."

"Are then the gods covetous?"

The priest burst into laughter.

"Covetous or not, they bless in direct proportion to the generosity of the faithful!"

He asked the novice to admire the magnificent door, its gold-covered framework, its uprights and leaves decorated with patterns encrusted in gold; he enjoyed impressing him with the fabulous weight of gold that

[1] *biat*: a crystalline sandstone whose colour, according to quarry, ranged from yellow to red.   ~ [2] Wast.

had been used for all this decoration, the beauty of the precious woods, brought as tribute by foreigners from the eastern mountains.[1]

While they were discoursing, the priest of *Khonsu* showed the Memphians the different representations of the *Neter*, and several expressed surprise at the variety of his forms. As the priest gave no reply, one of the guests insisted:

"All swathed up, as he is in this picture, *Khonsu*[2] looks like the image of *Ptah*[3] except for the headgear and the arrangement of the emblems. ..."

"*Ptah*," replied Nefer-Sekheru, "is in the beginning; *Khonsu* succeeds him as son of *Amun* in becoming. Therefore as the royal heir he wears the curly fillet. In this form he still is 'fettered', though he already carries the sceptre of various powers; but further on you see him unfettered, in movement, and crowned; this other picture gives him the face of a falcon to express his Horian nature.

"Do not forget that *it is the hotep of Amun which makes Khonsu. ...*"

The guests were led to the top of the tower through a narrow stair built into the eastern wall. The Old Man pointed out that for the walls of this staircase certain blocks[4] had been chosen from a temple of *Amun* built by Amun-hotep Neb-Maât-Re,[5] and later destroyed. The Memphians noted this fact and how it bore out Nefer-Sekheru's last remark.

Ptah-Mosis observed that the decorations on these stones fitted in well with the symbolism of the place.

They came to the passage over the door, and then to the top of the western tower. From four gold-sheathed masts of pine, pennants streamed in the wind.

From the narrow terrace in a wide panorama stretched the splendour of *Amun's* domain, extending beyond sight towards the South. The Old Man pointed out how the heart of Mut-Amun (the town of *Amun*) threw out like rays its avenues of rams and sphinxes, the longest leading right up to Apet-Reset (Luxor). He pointed out the canals coming up to the landing-stages and thus connecting the enclosure of the temples with the river which fed the Two-Lands. He pointed out where exactly on the two banks stood the ancient sanctuaries and the new ones, giving for each the principal elements of their teaching. His words gave the northerners the impression of a gigantic net, forming patterns apparently as irregular as the constellations of the skies, and yet regulated like these according to a plan prearranged long ago.

He allowed his listeners to follow their dreams in silence. Then he called them back into reality, the relativity of this world, and stretched his arm towards the Amenti.

---

[1] The wood in question is mainly the famous wood of the fir *ash*, whose trunk, perfectly straight and very tall, was used for masts and temple doors.

[2] See *Khonsu*, Fig. 13, Pl. V.   [3] See *Ptah*, Fig. 25, Pl. VI.

[4] These blocks can still be seen today in that staircase.

[5] Amenophis III.

"All earthly glory must come to an end. . . . And there is the barrier: the mountain of the last teaching where the bones of our Kings await the blanching and the water of renewal. . . ."[1]

One by one, the pensive students went down the stairs in the hollow wall. Not one word broke the enchantment.

Awab looked for Her-Bak and to his surprise found him near the threshold, his hand in Seth-mesy's. His sulky face bore witness to his disappointment at having been kept back. His expression upset Awab, who went to tell Pasab of it, but Pasab merely replied: "Don't worry about Her-Bak."

They now turned towards the temple of *Amun*, through a maze of pathways, between chapels, shady pools, and gardens in which flowers abounded like sand grains on a beach. The northern students were as a signal favour allowed to cross the courtyards so as to penetrate straight into the heart of *Amun's* city. Colossal statues of black stone, limestone, or pink granite reigned in each court, reducing the guests to the size of pygmies. The sun cast blinding brightness upon the yellow stone; the walls were all iridescent with coloured images; gold sparkled everywhere, and white-robed priests and scribes moved over the white flag-stones like white birds in a palace of jewellery.

Through a side door the great temple of *Amun* opened its peristyle, and with deep emotion the Memphian guests beheld the venerable goal of their pilgrimage: the royal seat of the *Neter*.

Having performed the rites before the votive altar, they were led into the pillared hall, where a feeling of the grandiose overwhelmed them, taking their breath away and closing their lips.

Immeasurable height forced them to raise their heads. . . . Depth, further deepened by the enormous shafts of this forest of stone; the magic play of the Numbers in the moving patterns of avenues marked off by columns. . . . Masses outlining space as a vessel encloses emptiness; shimmer of colours giving life to the chiaroscuro: all thought was thrown into confusion by the gigantic conception and multiplicity of the symbols.

Each column was a book, and puny man would have had to circle unceasingly around it to read the contents. No column was independent of the others; each shifting of position revealed a relation of measurements or orientation between them.[2]

Not knowing where to turn in bewilderment, the guests looked to their guide to give them a clue to the interpretation.

Nefer-Sekheru spoke. His calm, deep voice seemed to emanate from the very stone, and to imbue the temple with life.

---

[1] See Chapters XLI, 'Funeral Rites' and XXIX, 'The Valley Festival'.

[2] Some features and fluting of the columns of the temples reveal this precise intention of orientation.

"What was your aim in this pilgrimage? To satiate your curiosity? To fill your eyes with images and your hearts with memories? Or did you come to commune with the heart of the Masters, who conceived these temples as projections of Heavenly Principles in their action on the Earth?

"Has our temple not been called Apet-Sut, of which one meaning is the place of the Number?[1] If such was your aim, then know that you must abandon your own thoughts for the moment, so that you may surrender yourselves to the message of the builders; surrender yourselves to the genius of the temple which creates a reverent state of mind. For the science of true symbolism has here been carried out to the smallest detail, and this science constitutes a magic which has the power to awaken an understanding of the heart such as no discourse could evoke.

"The eye follows as the shape directs it, much as a march accepts the impulse of a rhythm. Through sound and form it is possible to compel our body to make certain gestures, or to rouse in us certain reflexes, or to provoke certain reactions which correspond to the intention of the directing idea; a statue whose proportions conform to the play of Numbers of the Principles which it represents will act on the deeper consciousness of the contemplator; the pointed top of the stone fingers, our obelisks, calls down the heavenly fire.

"Nature—even in human beings—obeys such gestures and forms as are executed according to its laws, provided it is not thwarted by the will of the brain. It is thus that we act upon the KA of Human beings, so as to grant them cosmic harmony and to educate their consciousness.

"Decipher *simply* the teaching of this temple:

"Raise your eyes if you seek to know what relates to the laws of the Heavens; look around at our walls, to study there the Principles—or *Neters*—of Nature. And if you want to learn about the part played by the Earth, how it conceives and brings forth from the ground all vegetation, then seek the relevant symbols near the base of our columns and walls, and even on pavements and foundations.

"Thus through its roots the plant draws nourishment from the Earth; thus through its top—be it shoot or flower—will it seek its life-principle in the sky; and thus our columns will speak to you.

"Since *everything* is built upon the laws of *analogy*, you will thus be able to find there the threefold teaching which is inscribed in all our temples."

The Old Man advised the Memphians to fill themselves with this vision; he allowed them to wander among the columns, leaving each to find there the echo of what he was seeking. Then he let them go out by the northern door near which Seth-mesy was waiting with Her-Bak and his other pupils.

They went round the wall of the pillared hall; then followed the paved

[1] See *Her-Bak Disciple*, Comm. VI, §5.

path punctuated by statues, sycamores, palm-trees and fragrant shrubs. A sky of lapis-lazuli cheered the northeners. The gold of the monuments glittered in a splendour of light.

Ptah's faithful were eager to see the temple consecrated to their god. They entered, prostrated themselves, while a priest recited a prayer before the heavily bandaged *Neter*, who in his closed fists held all the symbols of creative power.

"Here is *Ptah*, your god . . ." Asfet said.

". . . and *our* god, too," said the Old Man. "Without him there could be no creatures."

"Why is his temple so small?" a young Memphian exclaimed.

Nefer-Sekheru answered, echoing: "Why is the *naos* the smallest part of a sanctuary? Why, amongst so many *Neters*, is the Great *Neter* called the only and hidden god?"

Everyone sought in himself the sense of these words. Asfet triumphed: "I knew well that there wasn't very much behind the 'secret'!"

Her-Bak, lagging behind through no fault of his, listened to Seth-mesy's explanations: "Our guests are amazed at the disproportion between this small temple and that of Hat-Ka-Ptah; but isn't it quite natural that their god recedes into the background here, and leaves all glory to our god *Amun*!"

Her-Bak was not satisfied. "How can one god be Lord over the others in Memphis, and another one here?"

"My son, be a little intelligent: a god is worshipped with greater fervour, if his name is mighty and his temple grandiose; it is only just to distribute them over different places, so that each country having his main god might benefit from the abundance of the believers."

"What is a believer?"

"A man who observes our precepts and rites and does not argue all the time as you do. Passing one's day in idle dreams fills neither head nor belly! The favour of the Mighty does not go to him who questions their orders. To be independent is not to set a good example! Obey, be virtuous, be pure, and you will prosper."

The visit drew near its end. Her-Bak managed to break away and sought Awab. He ran, he elbowed his way through the crowd; his blood boiled like a tumultuous vortex; he called his friend, panting rather than speaking: "Come along with me, I'm choking! . . . Awab, what is man? Is he a clay doll moulded to pattern? Or an *Ushabti*[1] which answers for someone else? 'Do this, and things will go well with you! Obey! Be prudent! Be mediocre! Be pure! Shave off all your cravings like a priest's skull!' Let's go away from here! I want to get away from the temple! I want to eat and drink with the boatmen! I want . . ."

[1] *Ushabti*: statuette, originally made of Persea wood, later of stone or varnished earth, serving as 'mouthpiece' for the defunct; *shubty* or *shwabty*, meaning originally 'she who is of *shub* (Persea) wood', has by pun given *ushabty* 'mouthpiece'."

Awab held his breath. "Are you mad? You've got a sun-stroke! Go and rest a little. Go to Pasab."

"No, I won't go! I want to seek life, a healthy life, without *Neters* and fault-finding priests. Their virtue clutches my heart like a claw! Ah, the Sage had other words. . . . But by the time he summons me they will have emptied and flattened me out like a dried fish!"

While he was thus complaining to the unhappy Awab, he did not notice that a young man, Aqer, unknown to him, was listening to his outburst. Aqer ran quickly to Nefer-Sekheru, telling him what he had heard; they had a few words with Pasab; then the Old Man softly gave instructions to Aqer, who left to join the rebel.

Her-Bak made for the round walk with long strides. His rage searched for a pretext, like lightning seeking where it might strike. To the counsels of virtue his animal instincts replied with defiance. A snarling litany marked his course: "Be pious! Be pure! Be pious! Be pure! Be pious! Be pure! . . . *Wâb! Wâb! Wâb! Wâb! Wâb! Wâb!* . . ."[1] He passed the rear entrance, where the watchman looked at him with surprise: "*Wâb?* Already?"[2]

He passed by, ran, came to a canal, and looked into the muddy water. . . . Then, with sadistic glee, he dived in, in his white robe!

Aqer had tracked him and joined him at the moment when the mud-streaked mummy climbed up the bank. He showed no sign of surprise but called: "Where are you heading for, friend? It's hot and I'm thirsty! Will you come with me? Near the river I know a tavern which has excellent sweet beer."

"I'm Her-Bak; what's your name? Who is your Master?"

"My name is Aqer; I am free." Without showing the slightest trace of irony, he added: "Take your white robe off, let us go together and make a merry day of it."

The '*wâb*', a little embarrassed, obeyed. They went along the canal, then took a path through a palm-grove. Sounds of song and laughter led them towards a low-roofed house where a cheerful 'welcome' greeted them.

A smoky wick shed yellowish light on the blurred faces of the drinkers. People made room for them, and they were served sweet beer and honey-cakes. Her-Bak did not have to be asked twice: he had set his mind on carousing.

The boatmen were squatting or sprawling around on mats, singing lewd songs, while watching the antics of a mountebank and his monkey. As reward for his capers the animal grabbed the cakes and drank freely of the spectators' beer.

Heads became heated. One drinker spilled beer on the ground, swearing: "By all the *Neters*. . . ."

---

[1] *wâb*: pure; designation of a priest-class.
[2] *Wâb*-priest. See Chapter XXXIV, 'The Jackal'.

"Shut up!" screamed Her-Bak. "Don't mention the *Neters*! I am free, I am a man who wants to live! Let's dance! Sing! Drink! It's my birthday!"

He led them on, doing his best to eat and drink more than anybody else.

A woman took the floor, a dancer and acrobat, naked under her open robe, shaking her voluptuous hips. A *'Bes'*[1] was tattooed upon her thigh.

An almost ritual dance began; now with feline, now with jerky movements, she shifted her gestures and postures, in monotonous repetitions and nerve-racking contortions. Her supple fingers snapped, spoke, and gave life to the meaning of each gesture; and the drinkers, clapping their

hands, beat the rhythm; and the rhythm marked the flow of time . . . of a long time. . . . A long time, while the shameless female was offering herself, while the pangs of desire sharpened. . . .

Carob-wine was poured out; Aqer, without himself touching it, filled the cup of the novice, who drank silently.

The monkey, his belly full, began to lurch about. The half-drunken boatmen cracked rude jokes, laughing with raucous voices, spitting, and teasing the monkey and the woman. She stopped before Her-Bak, performing her most lascivious postures under his eyes, until two men brutally caught hold of her, each trying to knock the other out of the way and have her all to himself.

Her-Bak, intoxicated, already dreamy, wavered; he wanted to drink more . . . but Aqer refused. Dead drunk, he collapsed on the mat.

Aqer lifted him into his arms and bore him away.

[1] See *Bes*, No. 5, Pl. V.

THE SACRED ANIMALS

THE raven cawed his warning, for the dawn had dispersed the darkness of the sky. A fresh breeze cleansed the atmosphere of all nocturnal life, driving away the smell of wild animals; blotting out the memory of murders done by night.

The morning star[1] had 'bathed the face of *Râ*' preparing for his birth on the horizon; the owl withdrew to its stony shelter where, standing at the entrance of its hole, it watched the gates of Sky and Earth being opened.

Now the air was rent by the strident trill of the buzzards, signal of liberation from silence and shade. Shy chirpings gave answer; word went around in the shrubs: 'Light breaking!' And then from everywhere the twittering broke out. . . . The cries and noises of the day returned. Blinded, conquered, the owl plunged among the stones.

"Her-Bak, do you not hear the call of the psalmodies?"

Through the narrow window a ray of gold threw light into the dancing dust. "Her-Bak, wake up!" But leaden sleep held the sleeper! The ray of light was tenacious: it glided nearer, it brushed over the sleeper's eyes. "Her-Bak, your comrades are already assembled. What are you doing here?" Like a lance, the ray pierced the lids, which opened. . . .

"Who struck me? Where am I?"

Sitting up with a start, Her-Bak held his heavy head; his coated tongue explored a bitter mouth. Memory returned with the awaking senses: it replied to his question first with a vacant snarl, then with apprehension. Who had brought him back to his house? Who was the unknown fellow-drinker? Did Pasab know of his escapade? Of course he did, for otherwise he would have tried to rouse him from his slumbers.

Her-Bak called out for his Master. . . . No reply. This was the time when Pasab was teaching about the *medu-Neter*. Had he disowned his pupil?

Her-Bak felt a gnawing at his heart. He tried to collect his thoughts. It was late; every moment made his case worse. To rise and run to the Peristyle and take his place at the Master's feet? That meant appearing before his judge!

Seeing himself afraid, he revolted. "Are you a coward? Who will judge if not yourself? The escapade was your final misdeed. . . . Up, Her-Bak!" He stretched his limbs, then fetched some water from the jar to wash away his torpor.

[1] Venus.

Suddenly he realised that he had lost his robe! Stupefaction crushed him; his escapade—which he had wanted to forget as one brushes away a dream—compelled recognition; it gave evidence of itself; its consequences could not be concealed. It *was*, and its presence altered the atmosphere of the room: was this the stale smell of drunkenness? . . . Could a deed that was past never have been? Or, if it could be thus, would he want it? "Don't try to deceive yourself, Her-Bak, you are not sorry for what you have done, except that it has to have a sequel, and that the sequel is so inevitable."

The inevitability upset him. "What I have seen and what I have done repels me: it is brutal, gross. I have yielded to my lusts like an ass; but have I done wrong? I don't know. I am not happy in my heart about this escapade, and yet it still exerts some attraction over me. Why do I feel no shame? My desire was true and strong, and I obeyed it without guile; and is not *Maât* the Truth? . . . Does *Maât* exist? What is Truth? Can a virtue that lies be truth?"

A breeze whispered in the palm-trees; it swept the sand into a whirl, rushed it into the door and lashed the dreamer's skin. This lash hastened his decision. His fists clenched, he ran off towards the temple and entered the Peristyle as if it were the Hall of Justice. Would this lesson be his last? . . .

He stepped forward, feeling naked under the startled glances of his comrades; naked in his narrow loin-cloth against their white robes. He went to his group, the blood humming in his ears; he slid among them; how strong was the wish to be invisible! All his comrades were sitting around Nefer-Sekheru; he remained upright, his head high, thus listening to the Old Man, who, apparently unaware of his presence, finished his discourse:

"I shall not repeat what I said, that is, the lesson we have drawn from yesterday's events. Everyone takes the Light where and how he can. But let everyone—if he has ears to hear with—listen to the counsel of Wisdom which is: 'Cast your heart ahead on the chosen way; then go and retrieve it, and let your steps loyally follow its voice.'"

The perturbed novice had kneeled down; but like the others he had to rise when Nefer-Sekheru proposed to visit the sacred animals. Her-Bak looked towards Pasab, who left without seeming to notice him; he followed the group; some scribes abused him; others asked him to go away. "You make yourself ridiculous; without a robe you don't belong to us." He did not answer; walking, he listened to his thoughts. "Because I am naked they push me away: am I then different when in my robe? Is the robe a virtue? Does it give some special knowledge? All it did was to proclaim me a scribe, it distinguished me from the illiterate. Yesterday I had my robe, today I am naked . . . yet I am wiser than yesterday. Men take pride in learning; what a queer thing is learning: a few drops of beer and the learned rolls round like a beast and knows no longer what he knew. . . .

What is knowledge? Yesterday I did not know what I know today: but it is not from the scriptures I've learnt it!"

They had come to the sacred lake. A building near the bank was dedicated to the birds of *Amun*.[1] The priests who served as their custodians displayed them proudly. The birds were fat, handsome, and enjoyed the freedom within their domain, where no one would dare to disturb their gambols. A visit was paid to their larder, where the baking of cakes and pasties could be seen. What peasant ever feasted like those birds?

Sycamores cast their shadow on the banks of the lake; *Amun's* geese left the shade to disport themselves on the water, to the great fear of the other fowls who flee the rage of the *smôn*, the most vicious of all water-fowls. Her-Bak wondered what reason there could be for the worship they were paid.

"What is there sacred about them? They are no gods, they are not even human, and they don't even know that they are worshipped; for whom are they paid all that homage? For *Amun*? What then have they in common with the great god? . . ."

"Our sacred animal," said a Memphian, "is the divine Apis; he, too, has a house, servants, and priests to look after him, to adorn him with trinkets for his great processions; his herd of cows is the finest there is and their offspring are paid all respect. He is given a magnificent burial; he gets all the honour meet for a beneficent *Neter*."

Once more a storm growled in the novice's heart. "However sacred to the *Neter*, the animal drinks, eats, and drops its dung exactly like any other animal. How then can it be divine? Is it not debasing oneself to worship an inferior creature? Beasts are animal, and men are human; divine are only . . ."

Her-Bak stopped, surprised at his own thought: "Divine?" Why did he now affirm what yesterday he had denied? He examined himself: this word had sprung from his heart . . . his thoughts became confused; he would have liked to have a moment to clarify them. But Nefer-Sekheru had given the signal to depart. At this moment Asfet went up to the Old Man and said aloud, pointing towards Her-Bak: "Master, forgive my boldness, but this boy is a scandal among the scribes: he is naked."

The Old Man looked the 'scandalised' accuser up and down. "Yes, yes, he *is* naked, much more 'naked' than you think; and you, alas, are not! . . ." Asfet withdrew in confusion, at loss for the meaning of this answer. Awab ran towards his friend: "You cannot stay with us as you are; come —I'll lend you a robe."

Her-Bak did not know what to do. . . . He glanced towards Pasab, who nodded and said: "Go."

[1] 'High temple' dominating the southern quay of the great basin of Karnak and sacred to the offerings to the god and to *Amun's* birds. It is surrounded by dependent buildings—grain stores, resin stores, and so on, and enclosures for the birds, particularly the riverside geese.

On their return they found their comrades in a temple garden. Dates,
cakes, carob-bread, and beer were served, and, as a special homage to the
northern guests, the harpists had been called. One of these was singing
the old poem of past times:

All shape born of a womb must disolve and pass away,
Thus it has been from the time when first there was a god.
Generation after generation rolls onward to its destiny.
Waters stream to the North,
And the northwind blows to the South,
Every man passes onward to meet his fate,
Rejoice and be merry. . . . Do not trouble your heart,
Nothing, nothing is worth while that you should trouble your heart with
*   sorrows.*
While you are in this life, draw not upon your heart;
But rejoice and make merry—often, and often, and often.[1]

Her-Bak, yielding to the melancholy of the song, listened to the echo
within himself and was surprised at his inconsistency. Only yesterday
pleasure had been his truth, his aim, his goal: today his horizon had
changed! His heart was full of reproaches for his 'beastliness' and demanded something different. But what? . . . This 'divine' something which
yesterday he had denied, today he almost called a 'necessity'; was he
One-who-does-not-know-his-own-mind, a 'weathercock in heart'?
When would his heart be centred upon one thing?

How could it shock him that 'divinity' should be attributed to sacred
animals, unless it was something real? If he, Her-Bak, had no divine soul,
whence this dissatisfaction with human pleasures? An animal does not
reject what gives it pleasure. . . . What then was the motive of his own
unrest? What the reason for this reversal?

It was the story of the sacred bull that had perturbed him; had he perhaps failed to understand the meaning of the geese and the bull? Shyly he
approached the Old Man. "O Nefer-Sekheru, may the ignoramus ask
you a question?"

"Ask it."

"Master, perhaps you have given the explanation while I was absent,
or perhaps I missed your words: I fail to understand the meaning of the
sacred animals."

"Be in peace," Nefer-Sekheru replied, "I did not explain it; but all dis-
quiet appeals for an answer, therefore listen to this:

"Every animal is the incarnation of certain characteristic aspects of a
function; it is this which causes the diversity of the various species. Birds
fly, that is they depend on the air; but some among them have special
power in breathing, so their lungs are particularly strong and their flying-

---

[1] For French text of this song, see page 301.

power is very great; such are the falcon and the swallow. Others express Breath by singing.

"Some birds are denizens of the water as well as of the air: such as the duck; or of the earth, as the goose. The duck dabbles in the marshes; the goose prefers the banks. Though it can fly it keeps to the place where it has built its nest; its hatching time is twenty-eight days, and it never lays more than twelve eggs.

"The feathers of the goose *smôn* are of varied colour, like the high plumes of *Amun*. It is this particularity that has led to its choice as animal sacred to *Amun*, that is to say the numbers and tendencies which govern its life are caused by the numbers and impulses characteristic of the Principle which we call *Amun*.

"The animal in which these characteristics are incarnate to such perfection is therefore more than an image: it is the living symbol[1] of the *Neter*. For the same reason it may be said that our bull and the bull of Memphis are incarnations of *Ptah* in certain functions, for *Ptah* gives life to and designates this animal specimen, more particularly so inasmuch as certain patterns and spots of colour add to the exactness of the symbol in details."

Pasab remarked that the nome of Thebes had four bulls.

"These are the four aspects of *Montu*," Nefer-Sekheru explained. "Each of them represents one particular characteristic of the same function."

Her-Bak listened eagerly: "And of all this I knew nothing. However, I still do not understand why they are worshipped: they are not divine!"

"It would be profitable to the critic," said Nefer-Sekheru, "if he carefully studied the sense of the words and gestures through which we express what homage we render to the *Neters*, and then brought them into relation with the transposition given in common speech.

"As you know, the two essential terms denoting what you call 'worship' are *iau* and *dwa*. Try to penetrate into their true meaning. The earthly being 'doing his *iau*'[2] to the divine Power *identifies* himself with the Property or Function emanating from it. Animals, who obey the impulses of Nature without resistance, commune with her instinctively; the songs of the birds, the gestures of monkeys at sunrise and sunset, the mewing of cats, and the howling of dogs beneath the Moon, all are expressions of being in tune with the life of the Heavens which in turn gives life to the Earth. That is why we say that monkeys 'perform their *iau*'. It is true praise from the creatures to the creative Power and life-giving forces whose properties and activities they at all times express. *Iau* therefore is related to the functional life of the Universe.

"The action *dwa* brings the creature before the life-giving Principle to which it addresses itself. In *dwa* there is dualism: giving and receiving.

See *Her-Bak Disciple*, Comm. II, §3.
In Egyptian, function is expressed by *iaut*.

"*Iau* is fusion of life natural with life divine.

"*Dwa* is the manifestation of the creative—animating—life and the acknowledgment of this manifestation by the creature. That is why *dwa* is the name for the praise given to the Sun appearing triumphant over darkness.

"Hence all our manifestations of worship, veneration, or praise express the consciousness of an interdependence between abstract and manifest properties, between causes and their effects.

"As for the cult of veneration[1] which we pay the sacred animals, it is rendered to them as to earthly expressions of a cosmic functional property. Note also the difference between the two aspects of animal worship. The first is meant to carry into effect the wholesome harmony resulting from the natural affinity between some animal species and the inhabitants of the region that is its favourite dwelling.

"The second aspect serves to educate man towards becoming conscious of the universal functions incarnated through each of those 'species'.

"Now for every teaching we seek an expression through something concrete that will produce an effect in spite of mankind's inertia and lack of intelligence. Thus we increase the influence of an animal 'type' in the locality that corresponds to it, by protecting the animal through rigorous laws and by giving a place of rest and respect to the bones of their corpses and even to their mummies."

This explanation gladdened Her-Bak. "So that is the reason, why from all Egypt corpses of cats are brought to Bubastis, and those of ibises to Hermopolis? . . . Pasab has spoken to me of the 'affinity of tendencies', but today I understand their importance better!"

"Understanding develops by degrees," the Old Man answered. "You will still have to acquire knowledge of the structure of the human being before you can really interpret the second object of the animal cults; for this object is the development in man of the ideas, and later the consciousness of natural functions, so as to teach him the path of their total Consciousness, of which he will finally have to become aware within himself.[2]

The more a man is still an animal, the more useful it is for him to relate himself to the 'functional type' corresponding to his own nature. As his superior Consciousness progresses, it makes him more and more independent of the inferior states and their influences, and finally he will have to acquire complete domination over them. The human élite discerns this progress in the transformation of animal cults, when man seeks to replace them by human images[3] until he at last arrives at the idea of the Spirit without images or formulas."

[1] See *Her-Bak Disciple*, Comm. IV, §5.
[2] This is the aim of animist religions. See *Her-Bak Disciple*, Comm. V, §2.
[3] Thus was born the Greek and later Christian anthropomorphism.

Only Pasab and Ptah-Mosis had heard the Old Man's teaching. The others were comparing ancient and contemporary poetry. Views differed; and the arguments became heated. Nefer-Sekheru intervened.

Someone repeated the conclusion of the song:

> *Intoxicate your heart from dawn to dusk*
> *until there comes your day*
> *for landing at the other world,*[1]

and deplored its materialism, sign of degeneration of a past epoch. Nefer-Sekheru cut in:

"Don't be mistaken: this is the recurring phenomenon of the revolt against the stranglehold of dogmatism. Overmuch stress put on the outer forms and acts of worship, and intellectual complication of symbolism always provokes a negative reaction. Spiritual denial and unbridled search for pleasure in turn produce disgust, despair, and a call from the soul to return."

"Ought we to be sorry or glad about this?"

"We are not masters over this; every individual existence is brought into rhythm by a pendulum, to which the heart *àb* gives type and name, there is a time for expanding and a time for contraction; one provokes the other and the other calls for the return of the first.

"But between the two Phases, Nature pursues her function of gestation—a world is formed, a world destroyed; beings arise and vanish, some into light, others into darkness. . . ."

Ptah-Mosis sighed: "It is not agreeable to live in the period of darkness."

"Never," replied Nefer-Sekheru, "are we nearer to the Light than when the darkness is deepest! The time when this materialist song was written was followed by a rebirth of which we feel the benefits today. The Sesostrises and the Amenemhats who built at Apet-Sut there inscribed the wisdom of their Time.

"A long period passed by, followed by new darkness; and now our predecessors have tied once more the thread of tradition, giving the teaching appropriate to our Epoch in the temples and monuments which our great Pharaohs had built towards the end of the last black period. And these Amenhoteps have destroyed what had to be destroyed in order to rebuild in conformity with the law of the new Epoch; but they have piously 'salvaged' the stone blocks from the old temples to serve as foundations for the new ones."

Ptah-Mosis listened with admiration. "Master, your words seem to imply that our Sages could foresee the return of those periods?"

"You speak truly: they could, and always can; and the names which they give to our Kings are evidence for it. But this is not the moment to speak of it."[2]

---

[1] For French text of this song, see page 301.
[2] See *Her-Bak Disciple*, Comm. VI, §5

Ptah-Mosis thanked him and withdrew, great joy in his heart, taking his companions away with him.

Seeing them go, Her-Bak approached the Old Man and kissed the ground before him. "Oh, Nefer-Sekheru, you have calmed my unrest with the teaching you gave us! True, I am not worthy of it, for yesterday I misbehaved and was rebellious; hence I am ashamed to receive today the marvellous reply which I have not deserved."

The Old Man gazed at the novice for a long time in silence. "I know you, Her-Bak," he finally said. "The Sage has spoken of you to me. Every single word you have just uttered contains an error: you have no idea what shame is; for that there is too much pride in you. We know what you have done; the cognition you have acquired through this deed has been an excuse for it in your eyes: but it has in no way touched your self-satisfaction!

"As to deserving, know that the gift of Heaven is free; this gift of Knowledge is so great that no effort whatever could hope to 'deserve' it. But for receiving it, man must be freed from his fetters, he must become transparent as a crystal; this is the work the seeker has to do.

"As to my words, they clarified that towards which you were heading without knowing: I have merely given you the key. But I have another key to offer you. Let Pasab go with us."

They made for the landing-stage and followed the canal to the Nile. There Nefer-Sekheru began to speak. "Look at that boat without sails floating downstream. What moves it along?"

"The current."

"What is the current?"

"The force which makes the river flow towards its end."

"Very good; thus everything is carried towards its end. But now look how this barque moves without effort upstream along the bank. How is this possible?"

Her-Bak observed attentively, then he answered: "There is a current ascending upstream along the bank, and the barque takes advantage of it."

"That is right; the bank offers an obstacle to the flow of the water. It causes it to flow back, and thus a current in the opposite direction is formed. This shows the law of *reaction* and gives you, O my son, the first lesson of Wisdom. You, Pasab, listen to my words, and do your utmost later to get your pupil to assimilate them:

"Every natural cause has an effect; this effect is the direct consequence of this cause. If you judge the facts according to their appearance, you will be deceived as to the true workings, and your reasoning will be erroneous.

"In reality the effect is always indirect, in the sense that the cause must be thrown back by a resistance of the same nature; this will provoke a transformation of the two forces, and this transformation will give birth to the effect. It is thus that the seed acts on the substance of the ovule, and the two will annihilate each other so as to give life to a new being.

"Thus this effect is the consequence of a *reaction* of the resistance which has transformed the causal action. In other words, Nature produces its phenomena by interplay between complementary forces, the active force provoking resistance from an opposing force; and it is the reaction of this latter which will give rise to the phenomenon.

"Human will may transgress this law, and impose its decision directly: but sooner or later it will suffer the recoil. The mass of mankind is subject to this law without understanding it, but every teacher must know it, lest he achieve the opposite of his intention.

"Direct action is the action of the savage who smites in order to dominate by violence. The action of an intelligent gardener or physician is different. The gardener will not impose on the plant excessive fertiliser which forces its growth but leads to swift exhaustion of both plant and soil a little later. The physician will not treat an illness by brutal repression of the symptoms, nor by directly compensating the humour, the excess of which has caused the pain: physician and gardener must find the *indirect* means which will provoke the vital reaction in the organism in such a way that plant or patient be induced to produce within themselves—or to pick up from Nature—the principle of which they stand in need.

"This mediating action cultivates in the individual thus treated organic consciousness and vital liberty; the direct action atrophies the consciousness of the individual and makes him the slave of the force."

Pasab thanked him, deeply moved. "O my Master, this is a revelation and a path."

"It is the first great lesson Egypt has for this child. Listen to this, Her-Bak. Presenting to man the virtuous aspect alone is to awaken the attraction of the bad aspect: forcing him to do good provokes the will to the contrary; and equally giving without compensation, helping and thus removing all need for effort, creates envy and revolt rather than gratitude."

"I think," said Her-Bak, "that I have understood that one must never create opposition through direct action that *wills* the thing, without taking the rebound into account, which is as inevitable as that of a stone I throw against a wall."

Pasab was surprised at his pupil's sagacity. Nefer-Sekheru replied:

"This law has no exception. If you want good, consider the possibility of evil, and listen to the reaction of your heart towards the good. And know that neither the one nor the other is ever absolute[1] . . . except one Evil alone, the rejection of the Light."

The novice's heart began to find its bearings; Her-Bak obeyed it and gravely affirmed: "O Nefer-Sekheru, you have destroyed my revolt and mapped out my way."

[1] See *Her-Bak Disciple*, Comm. VII, §13.

XXXIX

AKHENATON[1]

THE next day was dedicated to a visit to the temple of Hatshepsut, Djeser-Djeseru[2] in the western cliff. Everybody looked forward to it, for no ear was ignorant of the praise of its beauties, its flights of stairs ascending into the sky, its terraces from which a panorama could be seen stretching for more than four miles.

Nor were they disappointed! But in vain did they ask the Old Man about the symbolism of this temple and its mysterious queen: no answer came from his lips.

From one of the terraces, along a passage built by Hatshepsut, they went to visit the temple of *Hathor*, where *Amun's* statue comes to spend a night during the beautiful Valley Festival.[3]

"Note this," said Nefer-Sekheru to the Memphians, "this temple of *Hathor*, erected on the mountain, is bounded to the North by Djeser-Djeseru, to the South by the pyramid of Mentuhotep."

Her-Bak obtained as a favour permission to conduct his fellow-disciples to the Summit;[4] he spoke to them of *Mersegert*, and, as he spoke, he felt once more the emotion of his first visit. As on the first time, fervour was born from his doubt and revolt, and his heart was flooded by a wave of enthusiasm.

The silence of *Mersegert* descended upon all lips. When they had listened to Her-Bak, everyone went down the desert path, sealing the memory in his heart.

They passed groups of houses and cultivated fields, until they came back to the river bank where they took a barque for the return journey to the City of *Mut*. The wind drove the boat towards the quay of the Apet Reset.[5] The enclosing wall gave an indication of the size of its temple, of which nothing could be seen, except the masts over the tower.

The boats in the harbour, roped to the bank, hull to hull and oar to oar, sent a forest of masts into the sky, a sight which gladdened all hearts. The Memphians expressed their wish to land and visit the renowned sanctuary, but Nefer-Sekheru refused. "It is not for me to introduce

---

[1] Also called Ikhnaton (T.N.).

[2] 'The Sublime of the sublime,' a temple situated high up on the slopes of the Theban mountain.

[3] The visit of *Amun's* barque to the Theban necropolis. See Chapter XXIX, 'The Valley Festival'.

[4] A pyramid-shaped summit in the Theban mountains. See Chapter XXVI, 'The Summit'. *Mersegert* = goddess of silence.

[5] Temple of Luxor.

you; but I will convey your wish to him who has the authority to do so."

They were carried downstream by the current. Some Memphians sitting in the prow conversed softly. Hearing them mention the name 'Akhenaton'[1] he asked: "Which of you worries about Akhenaton? Speak without hesitation; there is nothing wrong in this. What did you say about Akhenaton?"

"We were wondering," a visitor replied, "whether anything of that Pharaoh's works was still extant hereabouts; but we were afraid lest it might be indiscreet to mention the mysterious dissidence of that reign."

"May your heart be at rest; we have no sacrilegious dissidence! Your curiosity is legitimate, but an answer would be useless unless given at a suitable time—and place.

"Make use then of the present moment, contemplate *Amun-Râ* in his fulfilment before he leaves the earth of the living. You have seen the west of Thebes; engrave this vision upon your hearts and ask *Mersegert* to reveal to you her secret."

Next morning, as dawn blanched the earth, Pasab awakened the Memphians, bidding them to follow him. With him were Amenatu, Her-Bak, and Awab.

They were heading northward by a path outside the wall enclosing *Amun's* great temple. When they had arrived due·east of that temple, they saw Her-Bak fall at the feet of a man of tall stature and kiss the ground before him. It was the Sage, who was awaiting the guests. They approached to pay homage, but he stayed them. "This is not the moment for compliments—it is the hour to greet the Master of the world, who will appear presently."

He turned his face to the East where the first rays of the Solar glory began to colour the horizon. "He, the *Aton*, who comes to gild all earths and to spread life in profusion."

To the great surprise of his audience he chanted the hymn to the solar disk, using its name *Aton*. Then, turning back towards them, he observed the reaction to his behaviour on their faces. All were reflecting in silence. . . . At last Amenatu dared to give voice to his surprise. The Sage raised his hand and replied:

"Hear and understand before you allow yourselves to feel shocked, for behold, it is well for mankind to listen.

"I summon you to this place to assemble for the rising of *Aton* on the very spot where was once a temple erected by Akhenaton and by him named 'The horizon of *Aton* in the pillar of the South'.[2]

---

[1] Akhenaton (Amenophis IV) obliterated most symbols of *Amun*, and replaced them by symbols of the cult of *Aton* (the solar disk). Modern historians believe that this was done in connection with a religious revolt instigated by Akhenaton.

[2] The 'pillar of the South' does not designate Ermant as has been believed, but ought to be located in the region of Thebes.

"He built it outside the wall enclosing the temple of *Amun*, as befitted the emblem of a phase 'outside the normal law of *Amun*'. No more than other Pharaohs was he free to act according to personal will; he had to submit to the law of his time.

"It is not within our rules to expound this law in the outer Temple. However, I will show you one of its aspects. Nature has produced two sexes, one male to beget, the other female to gestate; such is the normal course of organised life.

"But in the series of functional manifestations of a genetic cycle exceptions are found, and these are symbolically expressed in the legends of the scarabæus and the vulture, of the scarabæus who, without female, has his seed conceived and gestated in his ball[1]; and of the vulture who conceives without male from the north wind.[2]

"Now it so happened in the succession of our Periods, that the period immediately preceding ours personified this exception in its two aspects: a masculine queen, Hatshepsut, and a feminine king, Akhenaton. Their temples stand facing each other: one on the mountain to the west of *Amun*, receiving there the rays of the morning, the other to the east of *Amun*, receiving there the evening rays on low ground.

"Both had to play their part as two accidents necessary in the natural Osirian lineage; both had to disappear when this role was accomplished, so that obedience to *Amun's* law[3] under his proper name *Amun-Râ* should be restored. However, each of them left the necessary evidence of the exceptional 'phase' he or she had to represent.

"For Hatshepsut, her Sage—Senen-Mut—reveals one aspect of the mystery of her reign on her statues, name, titles, in the development of her functions and in a special symbol which he vaunts that he invented."[4]

"Is this symbol not merely a pun on the name of Hatshepsut?" asked the sceptical Amenatu.

"Don't you know," asked the Sage, "that important secrets must be hidden under an apparently trivial aspect? Now Senen-Mut attracts the attention of the seeker by saying explicitly that this symbol 'has not been found since the Ancestors', by which remark he wants to indicate that it corresponds to the particular case of this 'moment'.[5]

"I do not want at this moment to develop the whole meaning of this symbol, but I may tell you this much, that this Sage confirms in it the androgyny symbolised by the Queen Hatshepsut who, for a period of her reign, takes upon herself the role and aspect of masculinity, whereas name and role of Senen-Mut, by a curious crossing, gives to this Sage—although he was a man—a feminine aspect in his role as foster-father of the royal maid."

"I know a statue of Senen-Mut," said Pasab to the Master, "which

---

[1] See Chapter XI: 'The Gods'.   [2] Horapollon, Book I, 11.
[3] See *Her-Bak Disciple*, Comm. V, §7.   [4] See Fig. 144, Pl. IV.
[5] The word 'secret' here is to be understood in the sense of 'key'.

seems to confirm this character of his. There he is represented sitting on his heels; and his robe, hemming in his knees, forms a cube out of which emerges the little head of that royal child."

The Sage approved of this remark as much to the point, but he refused to enlarge further on the subject. Instead, he explained the relation between the scarabæus and Akhenaton.

"The scarabæus conceals his ball in the earth until the time comes for the seed to be hatched: then he brings it out into the light and plunges it into the water, where his progeny will be born. And in exactly the same way the preparation for the 'moment of *Aton*' is done in darkness; and when the Time of *Amun-Râ* shall have been completed and accomplished, then the Solar fruit of his Spirit will come forth from the darkness under the sign of a new star, as a divine fish in the ocean of the sky."[1]

The Memphians grew restless and muttered among themselves: "Obviously he is prophesying. But what can be the meaning of these words?"

The Sage was sensitive to the unrest this strange revelation had caused. He asked his listeners to sit down and explained. "The movements of the sky govern the future of mankind; our cult and history are the image thereof.

"The second period of this history had the character of the *Amun cult* in its occidental and lunar aspect. Its third period[2]—which was to correspond with the beginning of the royal Solar Principle—started with a last affirmation of the Lunar Principle, symbolised in the Pharaoh *Iahmes*— Ah-mes—(born of the Moon), conqueror of the Hyksos, then by the first Amenhotep (Amenophis I) who began the *hotep* (or end of the accomplishment) of Lunar *Amun*, whose passing into the Solar *Amun* was announced by the transformation of the fourth *Amen-hotep wa-n-Râ* (first of *Râ*) into *Akh-n-Aton wa-n-Râ*.[3]

"This shifting of one nature into another—whatever the kind of genesis[4] in which this transition takes place—is always marked by an inter-

---

[1] See *Her-Bak Disciple*, Comm. III, §13.
[2] The period beginning with the eighteenth dynasty.
[3] Amenophis IV, who became Akhenaton.
[4] T.N.: The term 'genesis' is used here with a special meaning that cannot be easily derived from English definitions. There is no English equivalent. It appeared best to keep the term and, by way of explanation, to anticipate here part of Commentaries III, §13, from *Her-Bak Disciple*:

"The Greek origin of the word 'genesis' gives it the meaning of *becoming, production*. The *Dictionnaire philosophique* by Lalande defines it in very clear terms: 'The genesis of any object of study (e.g. a being, a function, an institution) is the way in which it has become what it is at the moment in question—that is to say, the sequence of successive forms which it has taken—considered in their relation with the circumstances in which this development has occurred.'

"The genesis of a thing therefore implies the existence of successive states or 'modes of being', and transformations.

"Becoming, production, mode of being or of transient form, transformation. . . ."

vention of a spiritual nature, which remains a mystery: or the cerebral intelligence or intellect, being comprehensible only to the spiritual intelligence, the understanding of the heart.

"This transition, which constitutes the characteristic feature of Akhenaton, appeared twice within the succession of reigns in this third period,
so that both principles necessary for the advent of the Solar King should
find their manifestation.

"The first instance was the theogamy of the Queen *Iahmes* (born of the
Moon) with *Amun* in the shape of the first Thotmes[1]; their product was
the Queen Hatshepsut.

"The second instance was the theogamy of the Queen *Mut-m-uia*[2] with
Amun in the shape of the fourth Thotmes; the result was the third
Amenhotep who in turn begot the fourth (and last) Amenhotep, who
became Akhenaton—that is, the emergence of the Solar disk from out of
the Lunar medium.

"It must be noted that the transition of one 'nature' into another is
carried out through the mediation of a mixed principle, so to speak
androgynous, as is the case with the characters Hatshepsut and Akhenaton.

"The history of these two transitions aims to convey a twofold teaching:

"The evolution of human consciousness through experiencing two
natures—female and male—in order later to achieve a whole;

"And the revelation of the character of the most mysterious 'moments'
in the genesis of mankind, through symbolic episodes in the history of the
Pharaohs.

"This history is placed in Time at each moment where it corresponds
to an analogous passage in the development of some genesis, be it an individual, a nation, or the whole of mankind.

"As is our custom, we do not write any theoretical treatises on the
subject, but teach it through the names of our kings and of the personages
entering upon the scene with each king, or through symbols and riddles,
such as those of the scarabæus and Senen-Mut's vulture.

"About this last symbol[3] Sen-n-Mut was quite right when he said that
'it had not been found since the Ancestors', for the case had actually never
arisen since the beginning of the era headed by Mena.

"As for the scarabæus, his luni-solar nature makes him a splendid
symbol[4] which we make use of at each epoch characterised by its func-

The commentary goes on to show that the Egyptian equivalents of these words
all derive from the name of the Scarabæus, and concludes:

". . . the Egyptian meaning of 'genesis', and that given it here . . . is the very foundation of Egyptian teaching. . . . It teaches the idea of successive states of being, and
of transformations which are one of the essential themes of the funeral inscriptions."

[1] Thotmes = born of *Thot*.
[2] *Mut-m-uia* = Mut in the barque.
[3] See Fig. 144, Pl. IV.
[4] See Chapter XI, 'The Gods'; and *Her-Bak Disciple*, Comm. III, §13.

tion. Its chief meaning is the transformation achieved by gestation, of which the dung ball—which contains the seed—represents both nature and fruit.

"The various phases of a gestation are symbolised in our pictures by colours; the phase for which the scarabæus mainly stands is the black phase. Now the third Amenhotep, whose reign corresponds to a black phase preparing for the advent of the Kingly Man, built his palace on the western bank, in the city called 'The City whose People live in Darkness'. The Master of his time, Amenhotep, son of Hapu, has given special development to the theme of the Kingly Man in the conception of his colossi."

"But Akhenaton," said Pasab, "must doubtless not be taken to represent in himself the principle of Solar Royalty?"

"Akhenaton and Hatshepsut," answered the Sage, "are intermediate principles, necessary temporarily to prepare the advent. The Solar Royalty comes to fruition in progressive stages, through the Rameses[1]; the essential episode of this fruition is *Khonsu*.

"However, this Royal Solar Principle is still a principle of the human level. . . . The advent of the Sun of the Spirit belongs to a Time much more remote."

Amenatu hardly knew any longer where he was standing. Never before, never, had he been upset by such perplexity. "Master," he said, "never have we heard the like! But if under an apparent error such truth is hidden, why do you not reveal it?"

"Is this not just what I have done for some of you now? The masses cannot understand the teaching about certain causal laws; in that case silence is better than profanation."

"But, Master, is not this silence the reason why Akhenaton's work has been judged a blasphemous outrage, an arbitrary setting up of a reformatory cult?"

"Only the ignorant have interpreted thus."

"But the ignorant are the majority. Why should they be left in error?"

"Better error in human concerns than a profane divulging of the Laws Divine."

Amenatu thought it over. "However," he replied at last, "there must obviously have been a will to destroy the monuments and symbols of *Amun*!"

"If Akhenaton's revolution," replied the Sage, "had been born from personal hatred against a clergy or a principle, would it not have destroyed completely the temple of Apet-Sut, who was the heart of *Amun's* cult, instead of merely obliterating his symbols? That would have been a decisive destruction, and much easier to execute than the hammering away of symbols, which was carried out with such care that the shape often can

[1] Ramses.

still be discerned. . . . What work that must have been for the initiated supervisors, who checked the tiniest details of all those monuments, walls steles, obelisks, so as to preserve those signs which were to be respected? I could show you some stele where one aspect of a *Neter* has been obliterated, while another is preserved, so as to suit the symbol to the characteristic 'moment'. Whoever wants other proofs of this can find them in countless numbers. Did not the Queen-Mother Tii have her palace in Akhenaton's town? Would she have resided with her son if there had been a conflict between him and his father Neb-Maât-Re, who himself lived for a time in El-Amarna? Did not Tut-ankh-Amun first live at Amarna under his name of Tut-ankh-Aton, thus forging a link between the periods of *Aton* and *Amun-Râ*?"

Amenatu shook his head disapprovingly: "May your wisdom take no offence at our scepticism, but can it be denied that there is hostility in someone who relentlessly obliterates the name and image of the gods so that his chosen *Neter* may become exclusive?"

"When the end of a Period arrives," answered the Sage, "one must know how to abandon that which sets its characteristic boundaries, so as to give free access to the Light of the new Period; one must know and hand over to destruction that which is corrupt, so that only what is indestructible should subsist.

"Akhenaton performed a necessary act: to obliterate temporarily the expression of principles which were to make room for the function personified in him, and to eliminate everything connected with the cult representative of the obsolete functions."

"O Master of Wisdom," Amenatu exclaimed, "we cannot doubt your word, but who can understand this? . . . Why should Akhenaton have built a sanctuary in this very place, within *Amun's* territory, when he built the great temple of *Aton* in Amarna?"

The Sage smiled. "Note that both these centres of worship bear the same name, Akhet-Aton, and that both are on the eastern side. Just as Amenhotep Neb-Maât-Re[1] had already hallowed the name of *Aton*, thus Akhenaton now instituted the first positive evidence for *Aton* beside the temple of *Amun which he did not destroy*.

"But he indicated by his departure a change in orientation towards the East, after the completion of *Amun's* Period."

"Master, I have seen the remains of the sculptures and decorative work done under Akhenaton; looking at the composition of those pictures, at the shape and attitudes of the personages represented, one can no longer recognise our technique in them, so different are they from that which was before and that which came later! A pious man's heart takes offence, for One[2] has transgressed the rules imposed since ancient Times, One has scorned canons, proportions, and measures; One has no doubt said to the craftsmen: 'Draw what your eyes see and what gladdens your senses'."

[1] Amenophis III.   [2] Pronoun of respect designating Pharaoh.

The Sage rose. "You are speaking with sincerity: I shall reply as befits. Follow me."

He led them to a workplace of reconstruction where the frusta of columns and carved blocks were stored in order; certain stones had been recarved to render some motive more conspicuous; others had been hammered down, until only one sign or phrase was left in isolation. Everything was prepared and arranged as for a well-defined purpose. Ptah-Mosis noticed it and made a comment. The Sage replied:

"It is as you say, truly: these stones have been selected and broken from certain monuments, to be incorporated into new buildings, where they will serve as record for the guiding idea of these: some will be corner-stones and show the essential principle of the new temple; some will be used in the foundations, where they will be the basic seed-ideas. Some will even serve to 'fill' the inside of a pillar or wall, expressing thus the inner motive—or agent—which caused the formation of the principles expressed on the outside of the wall.

"Among those selected stones you may see quite a number taken from *Aton*'s temples. They are preserved like the others, and will be used in certain monuments as base, or filling, according to the meaning of their symbols; some have recently been incorporated into a pillar of *Amun*. This is not the moment to go more deeply into the reason for this; I have said enough to allow you to find it out for yourselves. Only know this: that nothing is left to chance, nor to the builders' fancy. What is to be demolished is demolished in the exact way which befits the meaning of this demolition and the future use to which the piece will be put."

"May it be permitted to me," said Amenatu, "to revert to the question asked by Ptah-Mosis: Is it not true that Akhenaton violated the canonic law of measures and proportions, forms and gestures? Is this violation not sacrilegious?"

"No sacrilegious violation has occurred," replied the Sage, "merely a temporary but necessary change in rhythm, so as to correspond to this 'moment of exception'.

"Since the olden Times our Masters have studied Nature, its analogical relations, and the continual variations in the aspects of the sky—and their untiring study has borne extensive fruit: they have learnt to deduce from these aspects of the sky the succession in the phases of what constitutes our history, just as it is possible to know the phases through which a child must go while forming in its mother's womb. Thus they were able to find out in advance what characters and symbols were to express or personify each phase."

"Then every builder, every sculptor is compelled to obey their directions in his work of building or decorating?"

"Yes, he is indeed under that obligation. It in no way lessens the skill of the craftsman; but he is forbidden to follow his own interpretation of what he thinks may be beautiful or true.

"The theme is always prescribed, including its measurements down to the slightest details (for every detail has its importance), and even the technique: for intaglio-engraving has a meaning different from that of relief-work; even the smoothness or harshness of the relief has a significance. All this may render our work cold as regards emotion, but we never sacrifice anything to the pleasure of the senses: the dignity of the aim forbids it.

"However, this very austerity and precision of balance give our works a beauty which will never be equalled, because they obey a necessary order, which is that of the 'becoming'."

"But is then," replied Amenatu, "a brutal change like Akhenaton's not a disturbing element in all this harmony?"

"It may be found," the Sage replied, "that the theme of a Period demands a change in expression; then we obey that necessity, as was done for the 'moment of Akhenaton'. Look at this statue. The anomaly—or perversion—which it represents is indicated by a wilful exaggeration of effeminate forms: waist, hips, and belly are stressed, sometimes to the extent of becoming grotesque."

Ptah-Mosis failed to see in the decorations of the Period *Aton* anything but arbitrary fancy. "Not at all arbitrary," answered the Sage; "they are the correct symbols for that 'phase'. The moral theme is first of all inversion, even the composition of the decorative designs is inverted: you will find birds near the ground, and plants near the tops of the walls; secondly, there is the flaccidity and lasciviousness; and finally there is the characteristic fact that all scenes from that period are preoccupied with purely human affairs.

"The Era of which Akhenaton was a very early forerunner will be the Era of *man*, when human emotions will predominate. That is why his pictorial annunciation abandons, for this period, the hieratic rigidity and expresses—in a sensual, almost bestial way—that human susceptibility to emotion which in the foreshadowed future Time will have to take a loftier form."

"Ought one," asked Amenatu, "to look upon the independence of thought as an ennoblement of man or as a servitude?"

"What is nobility, if not the liberation from slaveries, hence from error?"

Ptah-Mosis and Pasab were delighted by this definition. "O Amenatu," the Sage continued, "I have answered your question: if the Master teaches what is error, the disciple's submission is slavery; if he teaches truth, this submission is ennoblement. You yourself in the outer Temple, are you not a slave to your own doctrines—that is, of the deductions made by your logical ratiocination?"

"O Master," replied Amenatu, "how could it be otherwise?"

"It could be otherwise, if you were willing to recognise that Cognition is not a fixed doctrine but a fusion which is gradually accessible to the seeker, once he has repudiated his false science."

The Sage said no more. Each listener tried to record in his mind what he had heard. Ptah-Mosis went up to the Master and thanked him for this wonderful revelation. The party of Memphians followed him, voicing the common impression that this was a marvellous teaching which certainly had never been given since the ancient Times!

"That is not correct!" the Sage said aloud. "It has always been taught in the secret of the Temple,[1] but today certain things must be revealed with a loud voice!"

Her-Bak had registered each word in his heart. Looking at Amenatu, he saw bitterness in his face and said gently: "It is your questions which have brought us these wonderful answers. I should like to talk them over with you. Do you know when this new Time, of which the Sage has spoken, will come?"

Amenatu rested his hand on Her-Bak's forehead and answered with melancholy: "You must not ask me, but Pasab, my child."

[1] See *Her-Bak Disciple*, Comm. VI, §5.

XL

TREASURE-TROVE

Her-Bak's joy knew no end when the Sage agreed to accompany them to the temple of *Mut*. The time of the journey was shortened by enthusiastic confidences, the Sage listening to the novice, and while listening, observing him. "O my Master," Her-Bak asked at last, "when shall I become your disciple?"

"I think," replied the Sage, "that moment is drawing near. However, you have not attained yet. . . ."

Her-Bak trembled with emotion. "What do I lack, Master?" he urged. "Tell me, and I shall seek for it!"

The Sage smiled. "Do not worry, my son! That which you lack is found when one does not seek it. . . ."

In the outer courtyard they met Asfet, who had been waiting for their return; with him was his brother. Asfet kissed the ground before the Sage: "O Master, my brother has come to submit a request to you: when walking on the eastern mountain he has seen crystals which look like Amethyst. Our hearts know no rest, so great is our desire to dig in that rock that we may find a treasure worthy of our temple."

"I have never heard of Amethysts being found in this region," replied the Sage. "Besides, these crystals grow inside almond-shaped gangues; it would be very unusual to find them in isolated crystals; however, an almond may have been broken. . . ."

Asfet's brother Kuku threw himself at the Master's feet, affirming that he was certain of his discovery, and begging him to allow Asfet and some of his comrades to go with him. Her-Bak and Awab could hardly await the reply, for the expedition tempted them with promises of novel pleasures. "Oh, Master," said Her-Bak, unable to keep his eagerness in check, "how wonderful it would be if we should really find Amethysts which could be added to the treasure of this temple. And what a privilege to take part in such an expedition! Please, allow the servant-here-present and his friend Awab to go with them."

The Sage realised that this diversion would be good for the novice. "Be it as you wish," he said. "You will set out tomorrow at dawn; choose yourselves what tools you may need."

"Be praised, Master," Asfet shouted joyfully. "Certainly we shall leave nothing undone."

They were already discussing what they might need, when the Sage interrupted them. "Is your brother sure," he asked Asfet, "that he can find the place again, where he made his discovery?"

"He has built a cairn at the approaches to that point," Asfet replied; "he knows the mountain well."

"Very well then," said the Sage, "go, but keep together, and when you have found the spot, divide the ground between you, and let each search within his allotted part. Who finds the greatest treasure will receive a reward from me: this is the prize," and he showed them a trinket he wore on his arm, a golden bracelet inlaid with blue enamel. A cry of joy rose from four breasts. They thanked the Master and took leave of him, and then went to make everything ready for the early start.

By the first light of dawn the four prospectors had already reached the outskirts of the cultivated area. They had brought a donkey along, who carried three jars of fresh water, some loaves, two baskets for the 'treasure', and the tools—hoes, wooden hammers, and bronze tools for detaching the stones.

They walked briskly; the daylight found them already on desert ground. But now the light revealed hundreds and hundreds of tracks, some parallel, others radiating towards every point of the mountain. They had to choose. . . . Kuku took his bearings and pulled the ass on to one of the tracks. "This is the way! Straight ahead now!"

In these deserts, where the ground is a mass of sand, of gravel, stones, and pieces of calcareous rock, full of sandy hillocks, there is no such thing as a straight line. The track snakes its way between the mounds, broadens, disappears, reappears, splits at the foot of a hill, and finally peters out into a mass of rubbish. The yellow flatness is deceptive! Any moment it may go up a little round hillock; or one hillock may hide another. . . . A dune was found to camouflage a wadi: they went down the slope, and crossed a ribbon of pebbles. At the bottom of the wadi a group of small dry bushes was dying for want of moisture, stuck as they were in what once had been a puddle and now had become a mere sediment of cracked mud. The mountain seemed to be quite near.

But when they had reascended the opposite slope, once more the desert stretched before them.

The eye reassured itself by firmly glancing towards the unmoving goal. But the mountain spread along the horizon, and still they failed to see the cairn which Kuku had mentioned.

With the Sun rose the heat; shadows shortened, while the way stretched. Flies, too lazy to use their wings, settled upon them.

Another wadi! "Onward, onward!" Kuku shouted. "From the other edge I'm sure we'll see the cairn!"

Down the slope. They hurried, their feet scorched by the pebbles. The wadi was wider than they had thought.

"Look," said Her-Bak, "gazelle footprints!"

On the other edge a long-eared hare scuttled to its hole. Kuku observed the mountain, but could not find his bearings. Her-Bak intoned a rhythmical chant; his magic soothed the fatigue and rekindled their ardour.

They went on through the dazzling yellow. A cloud of sand rose and formed into a whirlwind; others formed, pursued each other, veered around, came back, blindingly! Feet stubbed against the little hillocks which had become invisible since there were no shadows. The ass stumbled at each step; it lagged behind, stopped at the smallest tuft of thorns, cropped it, and was deaf to all calling. Awab tried to drag it on—it was holding up the whole expedition. Kuku had gone ahead. Asfet put his hands to his mouth like a trumpet, to hail him. Now they could see Kuku on a higher hillock and hear him shout, joyfully.

They hurried up. Triumphantly, Kuku pointed towards a white spot on the side of the mountain: "The cairn! In less than one hour we shall be there!"

At the foot of the hill, another wadi. "This heat is killing," said Asfet, "but we cannot stop here, if we want to do the job before nightfall. Let's eat something and then go on quickly."

This they did, handing out the water parsimoniously.

But when they tried to go on again, the ass refused to move. They shouted and pushed, but neither word nor stick made any impression. Having tried every trick, Kuku said: "That's enough! We cannot tarry any longer, one of us must stay behind and look after the ass, the others will take over the load."

As none was willing to stay, they drew lots: it fell on Her-Bak. . . . Hurriedly each took his tools and the baskets; Awab shouldered a yoke and carried two jars, and off they went, leaving ass and guard behind.

Her-Bak resentfully watched them move off and disappear. He sulked: how unjust the lot had been! Was it not he who had obtained the permission for this expedition? He congratulated himself on this favour; obviously his companions had underrated his importance: the Sage would rebuke them!

Nevertheless, it would be one of them who would earn the trinket, the bracelet worn by his Master: that, more than its beauty, made it precious. Her-Bak bit his fists in anger, trying to find some excuse to rejoin the others. . . . Suddenly, the Master's words came back into his mind: "Keep together!" No other argument was needed: he leapt up, ran to the ass, untied its halter to serve as a hobble, took a third jar and went off.

He ran, he flew—no hill, no stone, could stay him; the mountain came nearer, the cairn drew him like a magnet. . . . The white spot grew under his eyes. . . . Now he had reached the foot of the djebel! Would he manage to rejoin the others? No track? Well, then, the rock! He did not stop to think, he allowed his aim to swallow him up, he hoisted himself upward; feet and hands bleeding, he clung to the overhanging rocks, he moved around a chasm. . . . And suddenly, on this very detour, he saw his comrades approaching the cairn. What was that? Awab, a little behind, was running: he fell, the jars broke and spilled their water on to the ground.

Her-Bak could not help laughing: no doubt was possible, *Amun* saw and protected him! Certain now of a good reception, he felt more at ease in his mind as he rejoined his friends. The three prospectors stood before the cairn, arguing. When they saw him, they were amazed: "What have you done with the ass? Is it not bad enough that we have lost our water?"

Handing them the remaining jar of water, Her-Bak reminded them of the Sage's orders. They stopped arguing: it was late and they made their tools ready.

"I don't know exactly where it was," said Kuku, "but it was somewhere near this outcrop; so let's divide the ground in four parts and draw lots."

This done, they went to work. Each dug as he pleased, clearing away the soil, breaking pieces of rock. Nothing was heard but the metallic clang of the hoes and the thud of the hammers. The stony ground was broken by countless fissures, and every fissure was a hope!

But time passed and drained the diggers' strength, without anything to show for it.

Her-Bak's allotment adjoined Asfet's, both lying to the right of the rocky projection, which separated theirs from the area allotted to Awab and Kuku. Noticing the decline of the Sun, Asfet sighed: "Only one hour more of daylight! I will go and see whether the others have had better luck." He went and was soon lost to sight.

Her-Bak had lost all hope of finding any crystals in the stony ground. Asfet's territory seemed to hold better chances. Prompted by curiosity he cleared a rocky corner of his neighbour's ground . . . and behold! There shone a brilliant prism! A rosy transparence with mauve reflections. Her-Bak no longer knew where he was: his heart hammered within his chest . . . in a flash he saw the hand of the Sage and the trinket: desire rose in him like a whirlwind, blinding, stunning, becoming a frenzy, and nothing was left in him but the 'will to possess'! He bent down, tool in hand, to break the crystal loose . . . when the hammer slid from his hands and the mirage lost its power.

He rose with haggard face, wavering, feeling as if beside himself; a state of hesitancy as unbearable as the feeling of helplessness in a nightmare! . . . Mechanically he stooped again and threw a handful of earth over his find. Immediately afterwards he heard Asfet's steps returning.

As Asfet emerged from behind the rock, he saw Her-Bak sitting on a boulder, hiding his head between his knees.

"What is the matter, Her-Bak? Giving up? The others haven't found anything either. I shall have a last try, then we must go!"

A few moments later the mountain resounded with his happy shouting: "Come here, all of you! I have found some crystals! It is too late now to do anything more. Come along and help me: let us carry away what we can and bury the rest: if this sample has any value, we can come back and dig out all there is."

Her-Bak helped his comrades without saying anything. The dusk had not yet turned to darkness when they arrived at the wadi, where they started worrying about the ass. Glad to have an excuse to get away from the others, Her-Bak went ahead to look for the beast. He could not bear the company of the others; he could no longer endure their glances. Solitude might free him from these, but another glance was still pursuing him!

"Her-Bak, what have you done? Don't say you have resisted temptation: your fate may have saved you from doing the deed, still the deed was conceived within you; you were even prepared to do it. . . . What kind of deed? Treachery, theft, stealing from a comrade? Is it possible, that you, Her-Bak, should really have intended to do that? What prompted you? Desire for that trinket? No, it wasn't that: it was the fact that the trinket was worn by the Master.

"This or that, what does it matter? The fact remains: you were possessed by this passion, your hand stooped towards the larceny, this hideous thought is part of yourself! If another had acted thus, what name would you call him?"

He was sick with sudden disgust; clenching his fists, he began to run, as if to chase the obsession away. . . .

"Her-Bak, are you not trying to run away from yourself? To what end? Can you deceive your heart? Remorse will run beside you like a shadow. . . ."

"I don't want to feel remorse! It hurts. I'm in pain. . . ."

Her-Bak had come to the wadi. He let himself fall, face down, to the ground, and wept.

A long-drawn raucous cry tore the air: the ass brayed to make its presence known. Her-Bak dried his tears and rose. He found the ass and freed it from the hobble; seeing Awab near, he handed the animal over to him, and then set out again by himself, ahead of the little party.

The moon threw light upon the smallest details of the way, giving shadow to each stone and to the fragments of broken jars which lined the path. The cool night air swept away all fatigue; Her-Bak walked more and more briskly in order to remain by himself. But someone was going with him, the very one he did not want to see, who showed him another reflection of himself. . . .

"Well, who is he, that impetuous one, that 'headstrong' one, that arrogant fellow always ready to rebel? And this hand? Oh! this hand which stretched forth towards larceny. . . ."

"No! No! It wasn't for the sake of the treasure—it was because I love the Master so much!"

"A fine love, which leads to such an abomination! No, Her-Bak, be quiet, seek not this excuse! Touch it not; not He is the 'cause', but that which is within yourself. The passion of the beast has spoken: there grows no wheat where there is no grain! Take notice of its presence, admit that it is there. . . . You don't dare? Are you a coward?"

Like a sleepwalker he went on; the others could hardly keep up with him. But the ass pulled them along, trotting as only an ass can, who is returning to his stable; and no one guessed that Her-Bak was carrying within himself a heart all seared by fire!

"What is remorse?—A fire you vainly long to quell! Do all criminals feel remorse?"

No longer did Her-Bak try to run away from himself: instead he searched for the root of this remorse. He dug into his heart to find the bottom of the abyss, he touched the live flesh: his suffering put him in contact with himself; he saw himself as he was, so different from what he would have liked to be! . . .

. . . And it was a new Her-Bak—ashamed of his true image but at one with it—who entered Pasab's dwelling to sleep heavily into the morning, despite all his desire to keep awake.

Asfet had to rouse him. "Hurry! The Sage will see us; the others are waiting for you, and you are still asleep!"

Her-Bak sent him away: "You go ahead. I'll catch up."

With memory the burning pain returned, and the anguish of the guilty one who goes to judgment; and this anguish strangled him. But suddenly he realised that no one was accusing him: no one had the slightest knowledge of his fault. . . . Why then create a drama that did not exist?

Reaction quickly followed; no longer did he seek excuses of his own deceitful image; the sentence of the copyist came to his mind: "I am dissolute; I send myself a thousand slaps." He gave himself a powerful slap on the face and then hurried off to the Peristyle.

The Sage was examining the sample crystals. "My children," he said, "I am sorry to have to disappoint you, but these are no Amethysts, only worthless pink gypsum such as is commonly found in these parts. Don't be sad, you still have had the pleasure of the excursion. Which of you made the find?"

"Asfet found it," said Awab, when Her-Bak threw himself on the ground before his judge, crying: "No, it was I! Master, I do not deserve to be your disciple!"

Asfet stared at him as at a madman. "Stand up, Her-Bak," said the Sage, "and speak the truth."

Her-Bak remained prostrate, crushed by dreadful shame: it was the first time that he did not dare to lift his face. He closed his eyes, called out to the Master in the silence of his heart, and then, with a great effort, he spoke, accusing himself: "Master, I have committed an infamy."

The Sage stopped him. "Stand up, I said! You prostrate yourself in veneration, but if you are guilty it is upright that you must bear your fault and dare to admit that which you dared to do. However, you are under no obligation to speak in presence of the others."

Her-Bak rose. "If one has become vile in one's own eyes, one may as well be vile in the eyes of others, too. This is what I have done." And he told what had happened, leaving out nothing. Asfet gave a cry of indignation; the Sage called for silence and asked:

"Can you say what exactly prevented you from doing it?"

"I don't know."

"You are sure that you were not aware, at that moment, that Asfet was coming back?"

"I was not aware of it, but that takes nothing away from my shame! I might have committed the theft: that is enough to make me unworthy of the Temple. There is no excuse for my fault!"

For a moment, which seemed a century, the Sage did not open his lips. He looked at Her-Bak, and Her-Bak, utterly crushed, felt his heart melt in his breast. . . .

At last the Master spoke: "You have told the truth: there is no excuse for your fault. Go!"

All the limbs of the novice were seized with violent pain; he gathered his strength in order not to faint, kissed the ground at the Master's feet, rose again, and went, the taste of death in his throat. . . .

Asfet looked after him with contempt; Awab began to weep. Her-Bak had reached the door, when the Sage called him back. "Come back, Her-Bak, take your place at my feet, and listen to my words."

Her-Bak hesitated. . . .

"Obey! And all of you, listen to what I have to tell him.

"The urge which prompted you was evil; but do you think you are guiltier today than you were before the excursion? Is the filth carried within no filth unless one thinks of it? But one wants to ignore the filth! And do you think this is the only filth within you? How many animal instincts are there in you? . . . The wise man learns to subdue them; but before one can subdue them, one has to recognise them. You were more impure while you were still so satisfied with yourself.

"What makes a man unworthy of the Temple is the cowardice which prompts him to avoid the experience of shame, for this avoidance breeds oblivion."

The Sage took the trinket from his arm. "I have promised this prize to him who would find the greatest treasure: it is yours, Her-Bak, for shame accepted is the greatest treasure."

"O Master, I shall never be able to wear it!"

"Wear it, if you wish to become my disciple, though not as a reward, but to keep alive the memory of a wound. It is pointless to keep alive a remorse that has borne fruit, but that fire which springs from remorse is precious. Beware of neglecting it!"

Her-Bak was overcome; surprise strangled his voice. He stammered: "Master, how can one bear the humiliation of shame?"

The Sage fixed his eyes upon those of Her-Bak, and said to him: "O novice, the Door will open before you when you have understood this: the only thing that is humiliating is helplessness. The cause of such helplessness lies in ignorance of your errors; awareness thereof, on the contrary, attracts to you the power of your god. . . .

"If you deny the existence of the fault or error, it will strengthen its hold over you;

"If you recognise it, your awareness will destroy it. He who rejects this will never know the entrance to the Temple."

Her-Bak fervently kissed the hands and knees of his Master, who lifted him up.

"Stand up, Her-Bak, and go! This is your 'second day'[1]."

[1] His 'first day' was the first encounter of Chick-Pea with the Sage. See Chapter I.

XLI

FUNERAL RITES

"WHY are you weeping, Her-Bak? When a just man enters Amenti, is that such a great calamity? Nadjar was your Master in the woodworking craft;[1] that craft gave him mastery: every mastery is a form of awareness, and by that awareness he lives! But Nadjar was also a Brother to us, who received you into this lodge which will become his tomb; and yet we do not weep: for we know that he dwells with us in *Maât*."

Her-Bak listened to the Master-joiner who whispered these words into his ear, while the barque in which they were followed the funeral procession.

"Dry your eyes, Her-Bak! Are there not sufficient women here to lament? It is the women's task to moan and lament, so that the KA may not escape and so that the reunion may be accomplished.

"It is the task of the hired mourners, the weeping women, with their streaming hair, who surround it with tears in order that the 'feminine principle' should not escape; that is the role of the two heavenly sisters, *Isis* and *Nephtys*, whose tears shall be the water of resurrection. . . ."

[1] See Chapter XXIV, 'Joiner'.

The boats touched land; upon the bank the procession formed itself; Her-Bak, who had been privileged to accompany the Master-joiners, helped with the unloading of the coffin, which was placed upon a sledge drawn by four oxen. Libations of oil and milk were poured upon its way. Servants carried the chattels of the dead man: bed, vessels, chests, sticks, as well as his favourite tools.

And the heart of Her-Bak was cramped in pain at this sight.

"These things Nadjar has loved—never will he touch them again: his skilful fingers lie firmly tied with bandages! Never again will he come and teach the apprentices this knowledge he has acquired! This is the journey on which no friend can follow him; it is pitiless separation. . . . And every man lives under its threat. . . . What am I saying? Threat? No, certainty! How can one live in happiness while waiting for this to happen in the end?

"And yet his Brethren, who are surrounding me, seem to remain unaffected; they are grave, but their faces show no pain. . . ."

The procession arrived at the foot of the mountain where the Western Goddess received them in front of her chapel; then they turned obliquely towards the North, despite the efforts of a servant who grasped the ropes of the sledge and tried to turn it back to the South.[1]

Along the entire route followed by the procession the priests protected the mummy with chants and burning incense. Relatives and friends redoubled their lamentations, and the wails of the weepers grew ever louder. Only the 'Brothers' of Nadjar seemed at peace and softly spoke the ritual words.

At the entrance to the tomb, the last farewell. The coffin and the dead man's effigy had to be handed over to the funeral priests whose function it was to perform upon this image the liberating rite: the opening of mouth and eyes before the descent into the grave. Her-Bak, who had seen the animal sacrifice only from a distance, was no better placed for observing this Mystery, and what he saw of it seemed like a comedy and perplexed him.

"This is not Nadjar, but only his image, whose mouth and eyes the priest is touching with an adze and then with scissors. How can this semblance give him back the use of an organ or a sense? . . ."

After the consecration of offerings followed countless unctions, censings, and libations; at last the friends of the deceased were invited to carry the coffin into the tomb, where further rites in the diverse symbolic phases were to be enacted. Her-Bak helped from outside with the formation of the procession led by the officiants. He saw the coffin disappear, preceded by the great mourning woman representing *Isis*, and followed by *Nephtys*, the small weeper. Of all this symbolism he understood nothing, nothing except that this was the final parting.

At this moment the oldest Master-joiner approached Her-Bak: "Was

[1] Ritual ceremonies.

it not you who drew a bed with the head of an ass? Why did we never see
you again among us?"[1]

His eyes misty with emotion, the former apprentice answered: "The
Sage has taken me into the Temple; I hoped to meet Nadjar there, and
now he is dead!"

"His body is dead, but his soul and KA will come back to us."

"I do not know anything of either soul or KA!"

The old man looked at Her-Bak in silence. "Have you already been accepted into the covered Temple?" he asked at last.

"Perhaps I shall be soon."

"In that case, I understand that they have sent you to us to help with the
funeral rites! Have you ever seen this ceremony before?"

"No, it's the first time . . . and I don't understand any part of it!"

"I cannot explain it to you, not being your Master; it is a great lesson,
but one has to know many things if one wants to understand it! Moreover, the ceremonies are not the same in all cases."

"Do they not always perform the opening of the mouth?"

"That is part of the essential rite; but the other acts of the ritual vary:
there may be changes in the details and the place for the animal sacrifice;
or it happens that one performs the entrance of the defunct into the skin
of an animal, to be reborn with it into a new life: that is what is called the
tikenu. Sometimes the mummy is led into the tomb on a dummy barque,
as if it were a sea voyage."

"But why," asked Her-Bak, "is the opening of the mouth performed
upon the statue of the dead man?"

"It is not always a statue. It may be the effigy of his mummy, and often
both; it may even happen that there is neither statue nor simulacrum of the
mummy; each of these variations corresponds to the special case of the
defunct, to his nature, his name, his spiritual state, or to what he sym-
bolises."

[1] See Chapter XXV, 'The Lodge'.

"Will I know the meaning of these symbols some day?"

"They are not only symbols: the magical action of gestures and words comes in, too. Whether you learn to know them rests with yourself; but I have no right to anticipate the instruction which you will receive in the proper time and place. Hurry to prepare yourself for it, O neophyte, for it is the best means of losing the fear of death."

"What is death?"

"A transformation; but my answer is worthless for one who does not know its elements. Work, my child; become so determined that nothing can discourage you."

The reply bore its fruit. Her-Bak rose, went without turning his head, and resumed his way towards the East.

XLII

WOMAN

Some time later it happened that Her-Bak began to linger every evening near the dwelling of an artisan. It was not that the novice was curious about his weaving, but this man's wife and daughter, who were employed at the temple of *Mut*, went past and returned towards the fall of night. Pasab, who had observed his pupil, went out with him one evening and led him towards this very place.

When the women passed by, Her-Bak hardly knew any longer where he was. The mother was a figure of beauty, more beautiful than any other woman; the daughter was plain and without charm, but her provoking eyes clearly held a challenge for the spectator. "For which of the two," asked Pasab, "do you come here every night?"

Her-Bak was confused. "Is it not natural that man's desire should go towards woman?"

"If this woman is another man's wife, she will be punished, and you will know the truth of the word: 'A little moment, the duration of a dream . . . and death is the penalty which pays for the pleasure!'

"As regards other women, you may choose among them a wife if you want to take your pleasure, as do the men of the Earth; in that case, listen to what has been said: 'If you want to found a home, take a wife while you are young, so that she may give you a son; love her sincerely; see that she has raiment and food; and make her heart rejoice as long as she lives; for she is like a fruitful field to her master.'

"But as regards the man who wants to know the secrets of the *Neter*, from him it is first of all demanded that he learn to master his animal instincts, lest he fall into the nets of a woman: 'for woman knows how to set traps, she is like a deep water, whose twists and tortuous currents one does not know'. He who has fallen into such a trap runs the danger of becoming false to his vows: he may work his undoing with his tongue."

The novice's face darkened: "Oh Pasab, all my desire is towards the Temple more than towards any other thing! But if the ass becomes too strong in me, what shall I do?[1] If I am forbidden a pleasure, don't you fear that the desire for it may become an obsession?"

"In that case you have to decide whether you want to be Chick-Pea or Her-Bak! Has the Master not told you that there were two ways: the broad way of the herd; and the very narrow which leads towards Wisdom? Between those two you have free choice."

The novice did not reply.

[1] See Chapter XXI, 'The Two Asses'.

Mother and daughter returned to their house; Her-Bak followed them with his eyes until they had disappeared. "Is there not a danger," he said at last, "that man deprived of woman should become like a cheetah of the South?"

"Oh novice, novice!" Pasab laughed. "You need instruction on this subject; listen therefore. The animal joins with his female to reproduce himself, and Nature fixes the mating seasons. Man is not limited by these Times because he has other ways of provoking this rut; these means are the contrivances of imagination and the guiles of seduction.

"The error caused by the 'contrivance' does not lie in the sexual act, but in the illusion of union mistakenly connected with it; for it is in the nature of sex to affirm *dualism*, whereas Knowledge[1] is fusion, hence *unification*: the man who seeks after Knowledge must therefore avoid the illusion which would draw him away from the path of Union.

"This illusion is maintained by the will to possess and the artifice of seduction; all this is the game of the herd which wants satisfaction. Now woman, left to herself, wants satisfaction and artifice, for these are the trap that attracts and captures the male. And this is man's downfall."

"Are all men subject to this downfall?"

"It is not a downfall for the man of this world, any more than for the animal; many priests have wife and children! A downfall it is for him who has heard the call of the *Neter* and who feels that he must answer that call. Now I have orders to speak to you as to one of these."

"O Pasab, what do you know? I have committed some villainies. . . ."

"If you fall, that is your business; our duty is to show you your signature."

"But haven't the priests heard the call of the *Neter*?"

"The priests carry out the various functions of the Temple; these functions correspond to their nature and their aptitudes. Independent from all this is the personal Wisdom, or mastery, which leads to Knowledge.

"The call of the *Neter* is that which compels a man to seek the narrow path leading towards this Wisdom. Few are called to it, very few follow it truly."

Her-Bak listened to these words; surprise widened his eyes; he said to Pasab: "In order to be among those, one surely must find the strength to bring one's instincts to heel!"

"Let not your heart be troubled over this; the disciple of Wisdom is not condemned to reject the appeal of life, he will merely respond by different means."

"At this moment you are my Master: can you not tell me of these means?"

"Certainly not! It is not my task; but those who direct us know the human heart: they have trained women to be assistants in our temples.

[1] French: *connaissance* (T.N.).

These women set no traps, they never seek to capture the hearts of the men; they have pledged themselves to the 'service' of the *Neter*. With them the disciple can find the necessary moments of life, of a life that does not spell death; for it is not a question of smothering this ardour: on the contrary, it must be increased . . . but in a different direction.

"O novice, listen to me: a living Fire animates man; a sexual fire reproduces him. These two fires are one at their source. Man can either drain this fire for his pleasure, or he can sublimate it into a divine force.

"This is what you had to learn today in order not to commit a fateful mistake."

Her-Bak began to recover his spirits, seeing a solution to the problem which obsessed him; his relief found expression in a deep sigh: "O Pasab, have then the Masters thought of everything!"

Pasab only laughed in reply. But the pupil remained serious. He whispered: "This is all very well; but who can tell me whether it really is the call of the *Neter* which I have heard? Do I then know the *Neter*? . . ."

LITANY

THEY noiselessly entered the anteroom of the chapel of *Hathor*; each found his place in the semi-darkness . . . the individual was engulfed in the atmosphere, drowned in the mist of ecstasy . . .
    things lost their name,
    all desire was melting into indifference
    or serenity . . .
    the ear yielded to delight and the senses surrendered to the subtle spell of the heavy fumes of incense. . . .
    Bodies swayed like corn in the wind, abandoning themselves without resistance to the pervasive rhythm. . . .
    The strumming of the sistra pulsated through the air. . . .
    Drums throbbed and resounded with a stifled voice. . . .
    Vibrating harps whose vibrations soared,
    striving till exhaustion to reach most distant harmonies. . . .
    Waves of sound, bearing on the fervent appeal of worship,
    widening, ever widening to fill sphere after sphere;
    Murmuring murmurs of monotonous hymns;
    And all this humming, rhythmically held together, stirs into sympathetic vibration the Mistress of the Spheres.

> *She listens, the Countenance divine;*
> *She responds, the Giver,*
> *The dispenser of grace;*
> *Mother of the gods, Hathor, House of Horus,*
> *Golden House, vessel of Light,*
> *House of Heaven and of the Countenance,*
> *Mother of Love and of Harmony,*
> *In her lives Maât, the mirror of Justice,*
> *The seat of Wisdom;*
> *Mother of the terrestrial Sky,*
> *Womb of the Man divine.*
> *She is one,*
> *She is twofold, for she is*
> *Two in one . . .*
> *She is mother without bearing children,*
> *For she is the womb of the Origin,*
> *Which she brings to its ultimate end.*
> *United from the Beginning with her creator,*

She is the Medium, the perfect balance,
And the Accomplishment.
O Maât, daughter of Râ! Râ, Lord of Maât!
O Râ, living in Maât! O Râ, attracted by Maât!
O Râ, growing in Maât! O Râ, glorified in Maât!
O Râ, nourished by Maât! O Râ, strengthened in Maât!
O Râ, illuminated by Maât! O Râ, united in Maât!
Maât spouse of Râ from her beginning! . . .[1]

The magic of the litanies enthralled Her-Bak and carried him away; no longer did he think; he saw . . . no longer did he hear; he vibrated in unison with the atmosphere vibrating all around him; the chanting plunged him into a sensation of delight so that he expanded beyond himself. He drifted, floated, he allowed himself to be carried farther and farther away by the intoxication of ecstasy . . . until he was drawn back to earth by the skilfully graduated decline in resonance.

When it had died away, his exultation was followed by frenzy. Her-Bak trembled with ardour, he felt capable of immense achievements . . . which, however, remained vague; there were no limits to his capacities! Nothing could stem his grandiose hopes! Exalting himself, he dreamt dreams of achievement in cloudy realms, losing himself among nebulous schemes . . . which melted away the moment he found himself back 'on earth', leaving no trace in the ensuing silence except the sting of pain.

On the evening of that day the novice said to Pasab: "This wonderful hour has made of me a new man; I was happy, I was as in a different place; I felt light and powerful, as if I were rising towards the Heavens. . . ."

"Don't you know that it is written: 'Song, dance and incense are the *Neter's* food'?"

"O Pasab, why is it not made a daily duty?"

"Everything must be done on the days and at the hours that are favourable," replied Pasab.

The ardent nature of the novice had found a new passion; he had tasted exaltation, and now he sought it, waited for it; every hour during the day the intoxication of the rhythm called to him. He trembled with impatience when his teachers lectured beyond the hour, for fear he might miss an occasion. . . . And yet each session left him dreamier and more disappointed with the monotony of his existence. Work seemed irksome; the once active pupil became melancholic. . . .

Pasab reproached him with it. "What is happening to your good name? Your zeal for the studies has cooled! For three decades you have done nothing. Your eyes are full of dreams. Do you know what your teachers say? 'He is deaf to what he hears; he passes by, oblivious of what is pointed out to him.'"

[1] For French text of this song, see page 302.

"Three decades," replied Her-Bak, "is that so much? I have now been twelve months in the Peristyle, twelve months studying what the whole world may know! Is that not sufficient time spent on it? A caged lion loses his strength, and these barren thoughts are a cage to my heart!"

"So the lessons of your teachers are barren?"

"What gives no life, takes life away. I seek life."

"And how is your quest prospering?"

"I have found a way out of my cage. During the chanting I escape, I am free, I live."

"Yet, when you come back from that dream you are morose and in-active; you have lost the taste for work."

"Beside this intensive life everything else is insipid."

"Life is no dream: it is a task."

"The studies have never given me such joy, such satisfaction."

"Satisfaction is the pleasure of an animal: it is not the joy of the heart; true joy is the fruit of liberation from slavery."

"O Pasab, that is excellent; but that is just the effect the chanting has on me."

"Do not allow yourself to be deceived; you have merely fallen from one slavery into another, which has become an obsession. Outside it you are inert; your soul no longer inhabits your body: that is the error."

"But that is perfection for me, if thereby my soul meets the *Neter*!"

"The *Neter* you can find only within yourself. O novice, do not tread the path of illusion! True joy and life are active forces increasing power and inclination for work, not diminishing them; you may seek the *Neters* in plant and animal, if you find their correspondences within yourself; but you will never find them in the clouds."

"Why then is it written that dance and song are the *Neter's* food?"

"They are, if your *Neter* has awakened in you; otherwise this is the great illusion!"

"What *is* the *Neter*? . . ."

XLIV

THE NIGHT OF THE *NETER*

AND once more began the life of everyday, as the student had known it before the first chanting, for he did not want any more complaints brought against him. He worked harder than anyone else, to make up for the time lost; but his heart remained unsatisfied.

One day, when he felt even sadder than usual, Pasab led him before the chapel of *Hathor*. "Here you have tasted the power of rhythm and the magic of sound; the clever man uses them to learn to know the 'Word';[1] the ignorant allows them to carry him away into illusion: that is what you have done. But by renouncing this error you have set your foot upon the threshold of a door. Are you prepared to force it open?"

The novice's face brightened; he answered without hesitation: "Nothing will be too hard for me, if it leads to the inner Temple!"

"That remains to be seen," Pasab said gravely. "Know this well: no trick will open that door; your knowledge and skill will be of no avail. But *Anubis* may carve the way."

"How would *Anubis* act for me?"

"Is not he the force that selects the indestructible by eliminating the destructible? However, it is you who will have to play the part of *Anubis*: there is no *Neter* that might intervene . . . except one only whom you will have to recognise yourself.

"Tonight you will be introduced into a secret place, where you will spend the night, without sleeping, until dawn."

"What shall I do there?"

"Whatever your heart may command."

"What will happen?"

"Whatever your fate may decide. This test will be decisive; you may refuse, if you think the hour has not yet come."

Her-Bak conferred for a long time with himself, weighing his strength and his desire. "What have I to fear," he said at last, "unless it be that I might let the hour pass unused? . . . I shall go whither I shall be led."

Pasab sent him back to their dwelling: "Go, rest until the end of this day—but take no food."

It was near to the New Moon; when the night had blotted out all earthly forms, a priest came to fetch the novice.

The darkness and the mystery of the journey increased his anguish. At last, after a thousand deviations, they arrived, finding a guard standing

[1] French: '*Verbe*' (T.N.).

near a low door which opened into a long, narrow passage . . . barred at the end by a heavy door with a complicated bolt.

The priest drew the bolt and thrust the novice into a room with hieroglyph-covered stone walls. The flame from the wick of an oil cup on a very low stand feebly lit a naos which stood against the wall. The novice hardly dared to raise his eyes.

"The *Neter* is in his naos," said the priest. "You will spend the night alone before his Face; may he deign to manifest his presence!"

Her-Bak no longer knew where he was. "What shall I do?"

"Entreat the *Neter*; pray that he may reveal himself to you."

"But I should not know how to speak to the *Neter*. . . . What can I say to him?"

"All that you desire, all that you feel; to show your respect to the god you will say everything aloud; you must not go near any wall nor try to read the inscriptions."

The priest took a vessel from the small stool. "Drink this wine, which is offered to you by the *Neter*, so that slumber may not overcome your eyelids."

The novice drank, and found himself strengthened.

The priest approached the naos, which was a closed box somewhat taller than he; he opened two small folding panels in the upper half: in the opening the yellowish light disclosed the face of *Ptah*. The priest bade Her-Bak go through the gestures of worship; then he went, leaving the neophyte face to face with the god.

Her-Bak heard how the bolt was replaced; then he was alone. . . . And now, suddenly, he felt something like doubt; as his eyes became used to the dim light, he scrutinised the floor paved with flagstones: there was no well, no trap-door, but the stone beneath his feet was worn. How many had prostrated themselves here before him? . . . His glance roamed over every wall, into every corner: nowhere a fissure; only in the ceiling a narrow aperture through which a star could be seen sparkling. It was forbidden to read the inscriptions on the walls: it was not forbidden to look at the god. . . . He approached shyly; the stone statue well-nigh filled the hollow of the naos: no man could hide there! There was nothing else in the room, except the little stool for the offerings, the god and himself. . . .

The *Neter* and himself! . . . But was it the *Neter* or merely his image?

He remembered his promise, and repeated aloud: "The *Neter* and myself. . . ." How difficult it was to speak in the void! He painfully finished his sentence: ". . . The *Neter*? Or merely his image?" The words struggled to come over his lips; he no longer recognised his own voice; never would he be able to utter his thoughts! He wished to obey, he tried: "Never shall I be able to utter . . ." The thought, expressed aloud, came back to him like an echo; he became confused: "Never shall I be able . . . Never shall I . . ."

His throat contracted. Exasperated, he sat down on the floor; stopping his ears to escape the sound of his voice, he shouted: "What use is my anger? I want to force the door! I shall say a litany, so as to get used to it."

He found some phrases from a chant and forced his lips to intone the words. . . .

And lo, little by little the rhythm steadied his voice, he became familiar with the sound . . . his confusion waned. He stopped chanting, and now expressed himself without reticence:

"I have loosened my tongue; is that a victory? What shall I say to the *Neter*? What I desire? But I do not know; and I am angry that I cannot feel anything. . . . No doubt it is a great honour to keep vigil before a naos; am I unworthy? I do not feel the presence of a *Neter*! Who is this statue? Is there any life in it? . . . Tell me, who are you? *Is there any life in you?*"

He shivered at his own audacity; he scrutinised the face of the god for any reaction. The vacillating flame lent life to the stone image. . . . He spied, anxious. . . .

"What glimmer has sprung from the eyes? A mere reflection! . . . Has not the mouth opened? . . . What was that noise? The wing of a bat! And that shadow on the naos? It's my own arm!"

Uneasiness stirred him; his exacerbated attention amplified the slightest movement. The dim little oil wick blazed like a torch; the semi-darkness became alive with strange shapes. . . . What menacing horror was there squatting in the darkness of that corner? . . .

His imagination wandered; fear drew his eyes towards the gap aloft: "What threatening face will appear in that opening?"

He was creating that face, his imagination prepared to give it a shape. . . . Dread paralysed him and compelled him to wait for this 'thing' to appear . . . but it failed to come.

"Whatever it is that threatens me, let it come! . . . So that my fear be not that of a coward, so that my fright may have a reason!"

All expectation, lying in wait for the smallest phenomenon, every sense on the alert, he did not dare to move, so as not to provoke the 'thing' into appearing. . . . But time passed . . . and nothing came.

"But this fear of mine, whence does it arise? What then have I to fear? What danger is there more unbearable than fear itself? . . ."

He turned to the *Neter*: "If you are a living god, you will protect me; and if you are not, what can you do against me? Why have they brought me into your presence? To obtain a favour? What can you do for me?

"What I want to know is the true *Neter*: are you his image?

"There are so many images. . . .

"Divine statue, are you divine? . . .

"I obey, I am speaking to you, and yet you give no answer. . . .

"How could you answer? Your lips are stone, your ears are stone! And still the Sages bow before you and call you the Creator of the World!

"All-powerful *Neter*, where are you? If you are human, you live on earth. What man has known you? . . . If you are not human, why should they have given you human appearance?"

Her-Bak had fallen on his knees. Sitting on his heels, hands stretched towards the naos, he implored: "If you have a face, feet, hands, you can die like myself. I want a god that cannot die! . . . If I worship you here, I am worshipping something like unto myself! And I am not powerful, I am not good: I want a god who is better than anything in this world. . . .

"What good is wanting? I shall not change anything of what there is. . . . *But what is?*"

Chin in hands, he pondered deeply . . . losing himself in vagueness: he escaped from the vagueness, and his deepest 'depth' led him into himself. He heard the beating of his heart, and this gave him a bearing: "This is; my heart is; but anything else? I don't know anything!

"You, I do not know you! Whether you be in the stone, in the earth, in the sky, if you are god, you know everything. Answer me! If you are all-powerful, why have you given me eyes that cannot see you? Why have you made me ignorant?

"Why are images allowed which are less true than myself? I think, I speak, I suffer, my heart is more alive than your statue—why should I worship you? I have the right to know since they force me to kneel before it! What is there in it that is sacred? . . . *What in the world is sacred?*

"Why have I knelt down? For You? For the statue? Are you the statue? . . . Do I believe in it? . . . Do I believe in You?"

Shuddering with anguish, Her-Bak had risen. He firmly faced the statue. Clenching his fists he stared into its face, he provoked it, solemnly adjuring it, challenging its dumbness:

"Speak! Reveal yourself! I repudiate your image! I want the true *Neter!*"

He approached . . . and with a dark impulse to force the issue of his doubt, he spat into the god's face!

The storm was followed by complete silence. Reaction shook Her-Bak in every limb. Trembling, he glanced at *Ptah's* impassive face. . . .

And suddenly he burst into sobs; turning his back upon the naos, he threw himself down, forehead against the ground, crying:

"I worship Thee, *Neter* of the world, against whom there is no spitting! Oh! Reveal to my heart Thy true face; I am calling Thee! . . ."

"Very well, my son!"

Her-Bak started at the sound of the well-known voice. He rose on his knees—before him stood the Sage.

"O Master, I have . . ." The Sage interrupted him: "I know what you have done. The *Neter* you are seeking is within you! You are his true Temple. But in order to know this it was first necessary that you should have the courage to deny all that is not His Reality. That you should distinguish between the destructible and the indestructible.

"The image is destructible. Few human beings, however, can do without it; it is sacred to those who set their faith upon it. For those we render it more efficacious by the power of magic, for it is meet to help man according to the quality of his quest; the reaction of the herd is not that of conscious man. Blessed is he who renounces superficial satisfactions in order to find the Absolute!"

"I do not yet know what I am seeking: I want what is truest. . . ."

"That is enough. Her-Bak, the way is open before you, the way of the covered Temple, where all questions will find their answer, once you are accepted by the Masters of Wisdom. But before undergoing their examination, you will have to face the 'piercing eye' of the Master of the kingdom, for I am responsible for you to His Majesty.

"This is an honour conferred upon you; what feeling does it awaken in you, joy or fear?"

"Does my Master really expect a reply? . . . I know nothing of Pharaoh, and why should my heart tremble before a man?"

The Sage smiled. He went out, leaving Her-Bak to his uncertainty. When he returned, Pasab was with him.

"Thank your teacher," said the Sage to the neophyte, "for having brought you up to this point, for today you will leave the Peristyle. And you, Pasab, thank your pupil for having listened to you, for today you

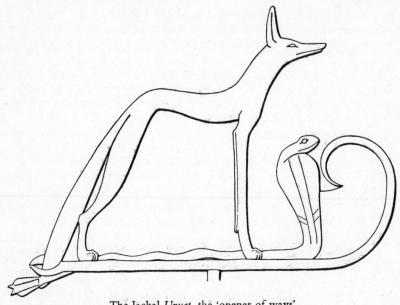

The Jackal *Upuat*, the 'opener of ways'.

will enter the inner Temple; and your name will no longer be Pasab: you shall be known as Upuat.[1]

Pupil and teacher, overwhelmed with joy, kissed the Master's feet; but while the pupil's joy was exuberance, the unhoped-for fulfilment of a beautiful dream, the mature man's joy was mixed with grave apprehension of a drama as yet unknown. What new problem was about to surge up on the other side of the threshold? . . .

And the novice trembled at the possibility of failing in his examination. And the teacher grew steady at the prospect of a fruitful struggle.

[1] Upuat (Fr. = Oupouat), *the 'opener of ways'*, is one of the forms of Anubis. (The scientific transcription of this name is 'Wepwawet'. The modified French form has been retained as easier to pronounce. T.N.)

PHARAOH

"Is this really a King's palace, O my Master? These narrow passages, these plain chambers? . . ."

". . . Are the Great House of Pharaoh, L.H.S., and the place of His Majesty's throne!"

The low voice of the Sage replied to the halting voice of Her-Bak. The presence of guards, the semi-darkness, the waiting, everything combined to make the disciple feverish. His questions pressed upon each other brokenly.

"What a contrast to the splendour of our temples! . . ."

"Temple and Heaven, Pharaoh and *Neter*, everything has its proportions."

"Is he not the powerful Master of the Two-Lands?"

"The whole kingdom is his palace; the hearts of his subjects are his resting-place."

"I do not know Him. What shall I say to Him?"

"You must stand in awe before Him."

"But I feel no awe!"

"You will be overwhelmed by the fear of His presence."

"I shall not be able to simulate what I do not feel."

"You will have to, because such is the prescribed ceremonial."

"Pharaoh is only human! . . ."

"He is *The* royal *Man*, the Man consecrated by the *Neter*!"

"O my Master, lead me away! Do not bring me into the presence of Him before whom I shall not be able to tremble."

A stir in the waiting-room. . . . Ten palace servants advanced, surrounded them, bowed before the Sage and preceded him, thrusting the disciple before them up to the audience hall. There ushers seized him and forced him to kneel down: and behold, against his will Her-Bak kissed the ground before the awesome door.

They raised him again from the ground, seized him, and dragged him along. There was no need to simulate fear: he was seized by a stupor, which shook his body with trembling, blinded his eyes, and paralysed all his limbs . . . it was a man without consciousness that the ushers threw on his belly before the platform beneath the throne!

The shock of his forehead against the flagstone brought him back to consciousness. He half opened his eyes but dared not raise his glance above the gilded step. The Sage, having prostrated himself, was rising to introduce his stricken disciple to Pharaoh.

And His Majesty said: "Let him rise and speak to me!"

Under the hand of his Master, Her-Bak recovered his spirits and tried to obey. With closed eyes, he evoked within his mind the royal image sumptuously adorned, his state costume, his imposing headgear, his loin-cloth and belt glittering with jewels, the necklaces, pendants, and magnificent trinkets. . . . Pharaoh's voice drew him from his torpor.

"Speak, Her-Bak! Speak! . . ." .

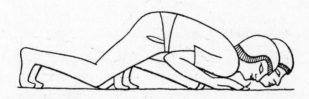

It was an order. With an effort, Her-Bak rose, his eyes ascended one by one the steps to the platform; he beheld the gold-wrought feet of the glittering throne . . . and, on that throne, the plain robe of the Pharaoh, almost as plain as that of his Master! One necklace, two bracelets, and frontal Uræus were all his ornament.

The mocking smile on the royal Face revived, whiplike, the pride of Her-Bak, who uttered, with effort, some words:

"O Master of the entire Earth, the servant-here-present is over-whelmed by Your Majesty . . . he does not know what he could say or do. . . ."

The King laughed, unleashing the laughter of the courtiers. "This servant-here-present," he said, "has not always been so tongue-tied! My Majesty knows him, for This One sounds the heart of the good as well as of the bad! Have I not seen you, Chick-Pea, on the market-place, carrying, stick-like, a tall *was* sceptre? . . .

"Have I not seen you in Menkh's garden, letting a monkey make water over a scribe? . . .[1]

"Have I not seen you, Her-Bak, in the tavern, where you got drunk among the sailors? . . ."

[1] See Chapters XXIII, 'Sticks'; XVI, 'The Garden'; XXXVII, 'The Visit'.

The laughter of the Pharaoh and his household brought the disciple's confusion to a climax, but he let nothing of this be seen. Upright before his Sovereign, he tried to live down the memory of his collapse; he steadied his voice:

"Your Majesty knows what It wishes and does what It pleases. . . . Its power is so great that It has shattered the insolence of the servant-here-present and filled every limb of his with a dread that is no pretence!"

Bravado or innocence? . . . All eyes were watching the impassive Face for a sign of wrath, ready to expel the impudent one. The royal silence closed all lips. The knitted brows beneath the frontal Uræus sheltered a piercing glance. Eyes fixing eyes, Sovereign and subject took stock of each other. . . . A contagious tremor ran down the audience. . . .

Without lowering his lids, Her-Bak slowly fell upon his knees. Pharaoh bent towards him.

"Her-Bak, do you know how to lie?"

Into the silence the answer rose like a challenge:

"May Your Majesty forgive me, not yet!"

Scandal, ready to break out, awaited the slightest gesture. . . .

Pharaoh turned round, fixing one by one each of the courtiers. "Who among you will undertake to teach him?"

One sentence, one single gesture from the royal hand and imminent scandal recoiled, drawing in its wake the stupefied assembly.

The hall was empty around throne, Master, and kneeling disciple. Pharaoh had risen; he descended the steps, embraced the Sage and offered him an arm-chair beside the throne.

But the Sage bowed. His hand came heavily down upon his disciple's head and prostrated him before the empty throne. Imperiously and solemnly, his voice commanded:

"And now, Her-Bak, kiss the ground where His Majesty has walked! Venerate the 'Presence' on your knees! Your pride confuses form and Reality! . . .

"The Presence is a Light veiled by the body's shadow; human stupidity judges the shadow and loses the sense of the Presence, the sole sovereign power!

"This throne is the summit of Power on Earth; the gold covering it is the quintessence of earthly riches. The man of the Earth kneels before this gold. . . . The 'living' man disregards the form, but he venerates the gifts of Heaven poured upon the throne and the royal Person.

"For the King stands in need of Heaven, as the Earth stands in need of the King; by the force of Heaven His Majesty is *sut*, He, the Person, the royal type of the human person.

"Through the virtue of Heaven, His Majesty accumulates and renews *ankh*,[1] the power of Life individualised.

"Through Heaven, It received that superabundance which makes the

[1] See *Her-Bak Disciple*, Comm. VII, §5.

King *udja* for the kingdom, which makes Him the provider of the poor, the granary for the hungry, the sustenance for all mouths, and the source of that which stills all hearts.

"Through Heaven, He becomes *snb*,[1] healthy in his body which is imbued with life by the union with his KA, he becomes the Master balanced like the gold of *Maât*.

"His Majesty (*hem*) is the womb (*hem.t*) which gestates the evolution of his subjects.

"It is the rudder (*hemu*) which modifies the direction.

"It is the yeast of his people, the salt of his kingdom."

Pharaoh stepped forward and raised up the disciple, whose face was bathed in tears. He laid a friendly hand on his shoulder, saying: "Yes, Her-Bak, My Majesty is all that . . . provided that It is truly the slave (*hem*) of the *hepu*! But the one who knows the *hepu* stands here."

He bowed before the Sage, took his hand, closed it around that of the disciple and said:

"He is the just voice of *Thot*, the 'prophet-channel' of *Maât*; he is 'He-who-knows', he is the Master. . . . You are fortunate, Her-Bak: you will never be King! You can free yourself from the slavery of the Earth; your kingdom will be superior to mine . . . if you go your own way!"

---

[1] The formula *ankh-udja-seneb* (life, health, strength, abridged to L.H.S.) often follows Pharaoh's name. Cf. Fig. 49, Pl. II.

END OF HER-BAK, CHICK-PEA

PLATES I to VI

1 hehe = *h h*

2 *a à* (or) *a i*

3 *à a* (or) *i a*

4 medu = *m d*

5 *à b* (or) *i b*

6 sab = *s a b*

7 wâb = *w â b*

8 wâb

9 wâb

10 àb (or) *ib*

11 nu = *n u* (= *n w*)

12 pt (or) *hry*

13 sba = *s b a*

14 meh = *m h*

15 àbed (or) ibed = *à b d*

16 her = *h r*

17 àrt = *à r t*

18 shert = *sh r t*

19 r (or) ra = *r*

20 mesdjer = *m s dj r*

21 shu = *shu*

22 shuty = *sh u t y*

23 Ptah = *p t h*

24 hotep = *h t p*

25 âsha = *à sh a*

26 shâ = *sh â*

31 senedj = *s n dj*

32 shen = *sh n*

33 ren = *r n*

34 nedj = *n dj*

35 enty = *n t y*

36 àn = *à n*

37 ner = *n r*

38 nefer = *n f r*

39 qed = *q d*

40 neter = *n t r*

41 âa = *â a*

42 ur = *u r* (*w r*)

43 sut = *s u t* (*s w t*)

44 sa (or) za = *s a*

45 saa = *s a a*

46 sa = *s a*

47 sa = *s a*

48 sep = *s p*

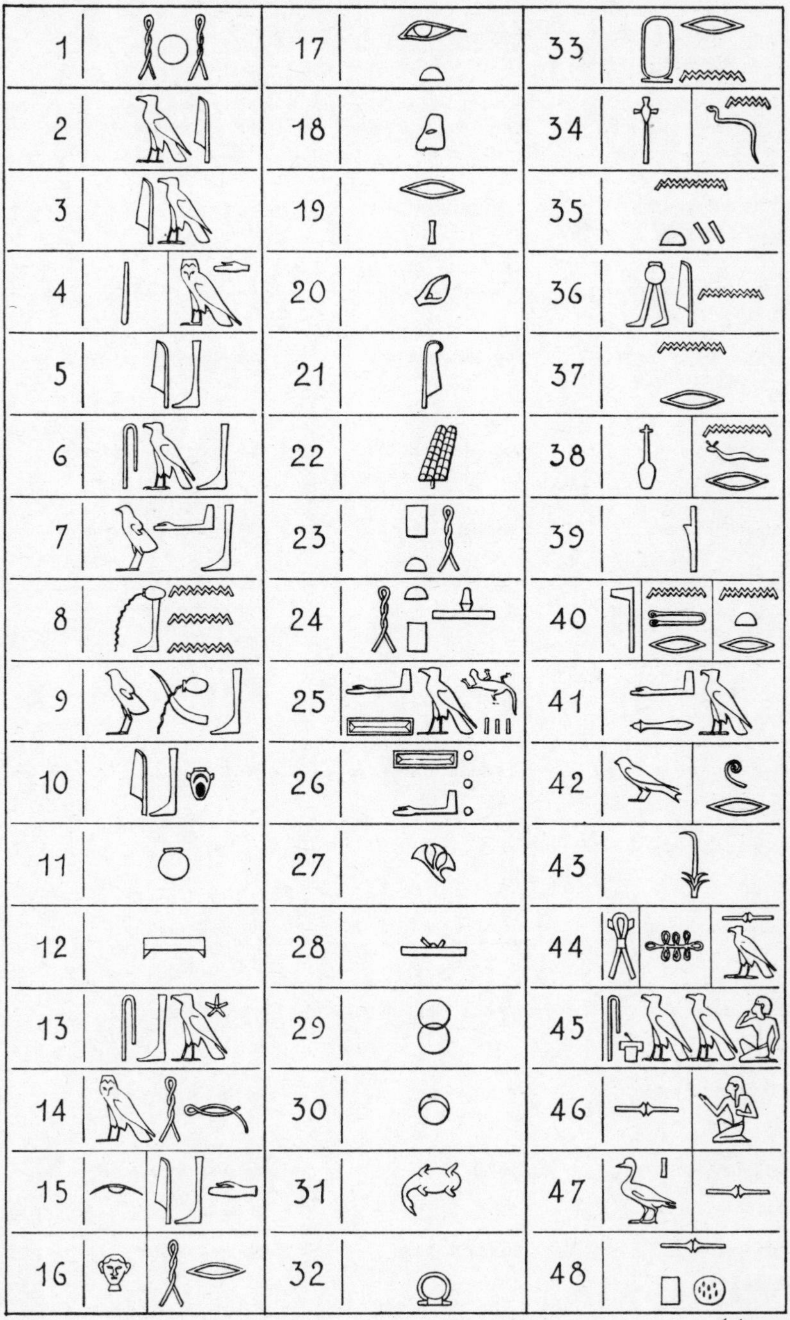
1
2
3
4
5
6
7
8
9
10
11
12
13
14
15
16
17
18
19
20
21
22
23
24
25
26
27
28
29
30
31
32
33
34
35
36
37
38
39
40
41
42
43
44
45
46
47
48

L. Lamy

49 ankh udja seneb =
   ankh udja (*s n b*)

50 seneb = *s n b*

51 sut = *s u t*

52 bit = *b à t*

53 heqa = *h q a* (or)
   heq = *h q*

54 per âa = *p r à a*

55 per = *p r*

56 per. t = *p r t*

57 kheper = *kh p r*

58 kheper = *kh p r*

59 neper = *n p r*

60 imyra = *i m y r*

61 nes = *n s*

62 sen = *s n*

63 hery = *h r y*

64 pet = *p t*

65 tep = *t p*

66 àten = *à t n*

67 nef = *n f*

68 senef = *s n f*

69 sma = *s m a*

70 sma tawi =
   s m a ta wy

71 hat = *h a t*

72 peh = *p h*

73 her = *h r*

74 hathor = *h t h r*

75 àr = *à r*

76 dà (ou) di = *d à*

77 rdà (or) rdi = *r d i*

79 ais = *a i s*

80 sia = *s i a*

82 nut = *n u t* (*n w t*)

84 aker = *a k r*

85 ter = *t r*

86 heru = *h r u* (*h r w*)

87 ruh = *r u h* (*r w h*)

88 nub (or) neb = *n b*

89 *r h*

90 *h r*

91 wadj = *w a dj*

92 maât = *m a â t*

93 maât = *m a â t*

94 maât = *m a â t*

95 wast = *w a s t*

96 was = *w a s*

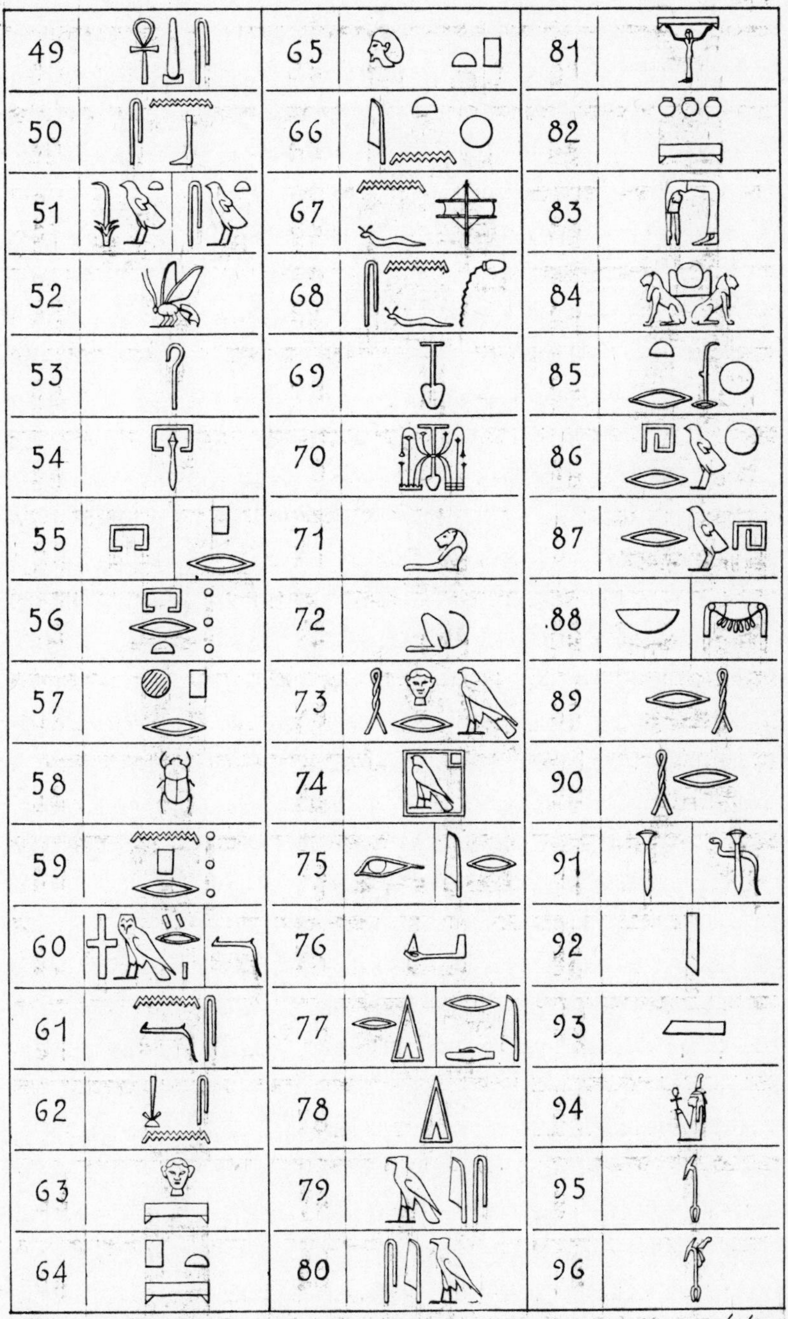
49
50
51
52
53
54
55
56
57
58
59
60
61
62
63
64
65
66
67
68
69
70
71
72
73
74
75
76
77
78
79
80
81
82
83
84
85
86
87
88
89
90
91
92
93
94
95
96

L. Lamy

129 ânkh = *â n kh*

114 mes = *m s*   130 udja

115 hem = *h m*   131 nekht = *n kh t*

116 àn = *à n*   132 khen = *kh n*

101 bit = *b à t*   117 ka = *k a*   133 ut = *wt*

102 ba = *b a*   118 meska

103 akh = *a kh*   119 wâ = *w â*   135 ut

104 akhet = *a kh t*   120 khnem = *kh n m*   136 tut = *t w t*

105 akh = *a kh*   121 user = *u s r*   137 djed = *dj d*

106 akhet = *a kh t*   122 Sefekht's symbol   138 djed = *dj d*

107 iuâ (or) iwâ = *à w â*   123 sefekht = *s f kh t*   139 tt

108 iaau = *à a a w*   124 mer = *m r*   140 shems = *sh m s*

109 au = *a w*   125 khem = *kh m*   141 kherp = *kh r p*

110 rekh = *r kh*   126 sekhem = *s kh m*

111 kher = *kh r*   127 hem = *h m*

                         128 tekh = *t kh*

Pl. III

97		113		129	
98		114		130	
99		115		131	
100		116		132	
101		117		133	
102		118		134	
103		119		135	
104		120		136	
105		121		137	
106		122		138	
107		123		139	
108		124		140	
109		125		141	
110		126		142	
111		127		143	
112		128			

L. Lamy

Pl. IV

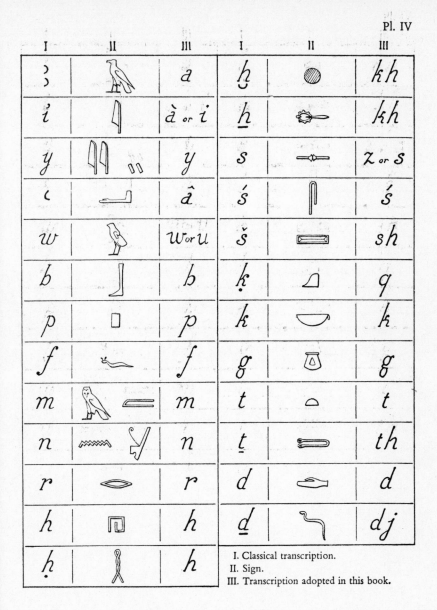

I	II	III	I	II	III
ꜣ		a	ḫ		kh
i		à or i	ẖ		kh
y		y	s		z or s
ꜥ		â	ś		ś
w		W or U	š		sh
b		b	ḳ		q
p		p	k		k
f		f	g		g
m		m	t		t
n		n	ṯ		th
r		r	d		d
h		h	ḏ		dj
ḥ		h			

I. Classical transcription.
II. Sign.
III. Transcription adopted in this book.

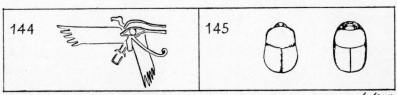

144

145

L. Lassy

NAMES OF THE NETERS

1—Amun	2—Anubis
3—Atum	4—Apet
5—Bes	6—Shu
7—Children of Horus	8—Geb
9—Hathor	10—Horus
11—Isis	12—Khnum
13—Khonsu	14—Maât
15—Min	16—Montu

Pl. V

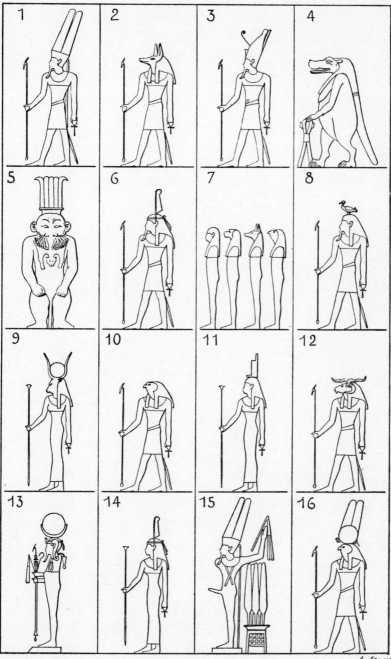

L. Larny

NAMES OF THE NETERS

17—Mut	18—Nephtys
19—Nefertum	20—Neith
21—Nekhbet	22—Nut
23—Osiris	24—Wadjit
25—Ptah	26—Rennutet
27—Seshat	28—Sekhmet
29—Selkis	30—Seth
31—Sobek	32—Thot

Pl. VI

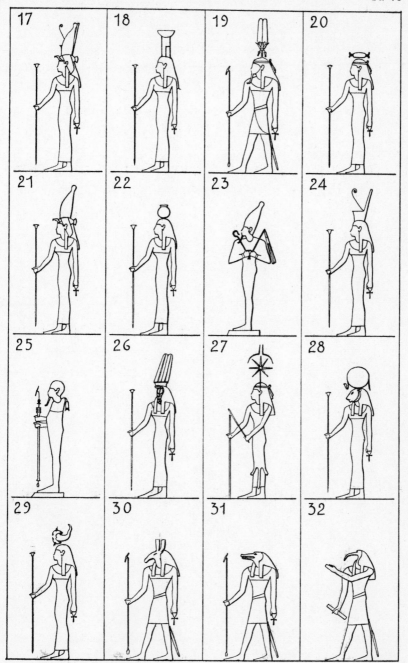

L. Lamy

THE SONGS IN THE ORIGINAL FRENCH

I

Chapter II, page (13), Mesdjer's first song.

Pourquoi rire, pourquoi pleurer?
Pourquoi voyager sur le fleuve?
Pourquoi chercher la joie
Au-delà de son horizon?
Désert, montagne et plaine
N'ont-ils pas la même lumière?

Maître du soir et du matin,
Serviteur et roi des Deux-Terres,
O toi qui détermines,
Pour chaque lieu, son horizon!
Celui qui te cherche en lui-même
Trouve sa royauté
Libre de toute servitude!

2

Chapter II, page (15), Mesdjer's second song.

Je chante ton repos,
Je chante ton amour,
Terre aimée, terre aimante,
Amante du Soleil,
Ta-ourit, ô Kemit, ô Apet!
Ventre prodigieux . . .
Toute semence tu l'acceptes,
O maternelle!
Point de choix;
Qu'importe le cobra,
Le vautour ou la tourterelle?
Douceur et venin fraternisent;
Tes mamelles nourrissent en jumeaux
Les frères ennemis!
Terre aimée, terre aimante,
Je chante ton amour!

3

Chapter VIII, page (39), Song of the Nile.

Nous te saluons, ô Hapi, notre fleuve
Issue de notre Terre,
Auteur de tous les dons.

Nous te saluons, ô rénovateur,
Porteur de toute essence, puissance de toute sève;
Tu es le désiré des produits de la terre.

O lumineux, issu du gouffre de ténèbres!
O magicien qui conduis vers la lumière
Tous les germes vivants que tu as apportés!

Conducteur des semences, nourricier des grains,
Multiplicateur des greniers,
Pourvoyeur de toutes mamelles!

Mâle fécond, tu t'engendres toi-même,
Et tu gestes comme une femme;
Jeune et vieux, sans âge, immortel.

Fleuve de vie, nul être vivant ne t'ignore;
Rosée du ciel, tu fertilises les déserts.
O Roi et Loi de ce que tu animes!

Le mouvement de ton flux régit, dans les Deux-Terres,
Le 'devenir' et le destin des germes;
Ton cours harmonieux met les rives en joie.
Ton trouble crée le trouble; ta colère épouvante et provoque Typhon;

Le rejet de ton flot pétrit la terre aride en un limon fertile;
Par toi, Sobek—le crocodile—est fécondé.

La terre irradiée met au jour la verdure;
Tout être terrestre est vêtu par la pleine mesure de tes dons.
Par toi, la barque flotte au-dessus des bas-fonds.

Tu sépares et tu assembles;
Tu relies les deux rives inconciliables;
Tu apportes et tu animes la terre noire.

Ta croissance est le signe de toute réjouissance;
La terre tressaille jusque dans ses moelles,
Et ses os arides, mêmes, sont émus;

Car tu désaltères le plus avide,
Et le plus dénué est comblé de tes dons;
Mais celui qui est rassasié t'ignore.

Tu régis toutes les fêtes des Neter,
Et tous les sacrifices de leurs prémices,
Et la mesure de toutes leurs offrandes.

O toi qui ne peux être dénombré!
O mystérieux qui jaillis sans cesse de l'abîme
Sans pouvoir s'épuiser!

Nul homme ne connaît tes cavernes secrètes;
Aucun écrit n'a jamais révélé ton nom.
Mais tout fruit de la terre porte ta signature!

Par toi il se nourrit et se transforme.
Et voici:

Il arrive à son parfait accomplissement.

4

Chapter X, page (49), Chick-Pea's song.

Fauche ma faucille, fauche tout le champ!

L'orge chevelue, tu l'as abattue;
Les épis levés, tu les as couchés;
Fauchez, compagnons, chantez avec moi!

Fauche ô ma faucille, fauche ô ma faucille!

Un bon artisan creusa ton bois dur
Semblable au croissant de la jeune Lune.
Il y incrusta les dents de silex.

Fauche ô ma faucille, fauche ô ma faucille!

Tu es belle à voir, faucille nouvelle;
Tu passes en coupant, tranchant les épis,
Comme le bateau passe, fendant l'eau.

Fauche ô ma faucille, fauche ô ma faucille!

Puissant est l'épi: son grain me nourrit.
Plus forte est ma faux, plus forte que lui,
Car l'esprit du grain s'enfuit devant elle!

Fauche ô ma faucille, fauche ô ma faucille!

Que soit préservé le Neter Nepri!
D'épis en épis, la faux le pourchasse
Au dernier abri: la gerbe finale!

Fauche ô ma faucille, fauche ô ma faucille!

Faucheurs, épargnons la gerbe sacrée!
Tressons ses épis! Neter *du* neper,
Nous te sauverons des mains du vanneur.

Fauche ô ma faucille, fauche ô ma faucille!

Nous te garderons au 'double grenier';
Ranime nos grains, rappelle l'esprit
Qui s'est envolé au vent du vannage.

Fauche ô ma faucille, fauche ô ma faucille!

Parfaite sera la moisson prochaine,
Nombreuse en épis, féconde en semeneces;
Gerbe de la fin, protège Nepri!

Fauche ô ma faucille, fauche ô ma faucille!

5

Chapter XIV, page (70), Song of the Tavern-tent.
       (The following lines are repeated over and over)

             Un cabaret est préparé,
             Sa tente est tendue vers le Sud.
             Un cabaret est préparé,
             Sa tente est tendue vers le Nord.
             . . . .
             Buvez, matelots de Pharaon,
             Aimé d'Amon, loué des dieux!

6

Chapter XVI, pages (81–83), The guitarist's song.

Qu'elle vienne à l'étang des lotus
Ma belle aimée,
Dans sa chemise transparente
De fin lin.
Qu'elle se baigne en ma présence
Parmi les fleurs,
Que je la contemple en ses membres
Sortant des eaux.

—J'ai deja entendu ta chanson
Sur d'autres lèvres!
Il est vrai que l'amour est, partout,
Toujours le même.

—*Non, depuis que la terre existe,*
Nul n'a connu
Un amour tel que mon amour
Pour sa beauté.

—Pauvres petits hommes sur terre,
Quelle pitié!

—*Je chanterai sous tes sarcasmes*
Outrecuidants!
Je dirai l'amour de ma belle
Malgré les sots,
Les envieux, les vents, la foudre,
Malgré les dieux!

—Fais vite par pitié pour nous:
Mieux vaut affronter le péril
Que la menace.

Si je l'embrasse elle s'enflamme,
Elle m'enivre!
Je suis un hòmme heureux sans bière
Et sans vin doux.

—Sauf le vin doux,
Un autre a dit cette paroic
Trouve plus fort.

—*Si je la vois je suis en vie;*
Quand elle ouvre son œil mes membres rajeunissent,
Loin d'elle mes forces dépérissent,
Je ne reconnais plus mon propre corps.

—Hé! beau chanteur, si tu plagies,
Fais donc que la copie
Soit meilleure que l'original!

—*Point n'est besoin du chant des autres:*
Je dirai mes propres paroles.
Jamais on n'aura entendu
Tel chant d'amour:
Quand elle baigne son beau corps,
La couleur de ses membres
Fait pâlir le lotus;
Nul poisson ne s'ébat avec la même grâce
Que son bras s'agitant
Comme un aile d'oiseau.

—Oh! Choisis pour ta bien-aimée
Ecaille ou plume . . .
L'amour n'est point si exigeant!
. . . .
Qui n'a pas vu ma bien-aimée
Ne connaît point la Lune
En sa splendeur.
Sa lumière brûle mes yeux,
Et la chaleur de son étreinte
Est charbon ardent pour mon cœur.

—Lune brûlante, ô Lune ardente,
O cataclysme insoupçonné!

—*Que le récit de ses beautés*
Ne te hante jamais
Pour la voler à mon amour!
Point de torture
Assez grande pour ton châtiment!
En son absence
Il n'est point de souffle à mon nez,
Pas de remède à mes membres tremblants.
Mais elle ne veut point, mon aimée,
D'autre ivresse que mon ardeur,
D'autre lien que mes bras amoureux.

7

Chapter XVI, pages (83–84), Mesdjer's song.

Le chant d'amour du jeune amant
Est fièvre d'attente et soupirs,
Désir d'étreintes,
Triomphe de possession,
Communion des corps, lui et elle.

Le chant d'amour de la veillesse
Evoque souvenirs et regrets,
Impuissance, désillusion.

Moi je chante l'Amour
Sans mensonge et sans leurre,
Qui connaît en toute saison
La passion et sa maîtrise;
L'Amour, appel et réponse
En lui-même;
L'Amour qui ne dédouble pas,
O Nature, partout tu divises!
Ton amour est combat et mort.

Je chante l'autre Amour,
Qui ne cherche ni lui ni elle,
Qui donne sans exiger
Aucun échange.

Ainsi, Lui possède en lui-même
Son univers,
Elle n'est plus séparatrice:
Elle est en Lui; son univers
Est rempli d'Elle.

Tel un soleil
Qui se nourrit de sa propre chaleur,
Tel Il rayonne au-delà de l'objet.
Et sa propre substance
Devient Lumière et passion.

8

Chapter XXIV, page (138), Chick-Pea's song.

Lorsque j'étais petit enfant,
Un mur s'est ouvert devant moi;
Par sa fente j'ai entrevu
Le faucon d'or;
Mais voici: une heure a passé . . .
Le grand mur s'était refermé!

J'ai compté les jours par centaines;
Une grande voix a parlé . . .
Moi, petit enfant, j'ai joué!
En jouant, ai-je effarouché
La grande voix?
Qui saura me guider vers elle?

Beaucoup de Lunes ont passé,
Et la Montagne du silence
A versé son or sur mes doigts.
Mon cœur a gardé le trésor
De ce silence,
Et mes doigts se sont refermés.

Plusieurs décades ont passé,
Un ami m'a tendu la main . . .
Un ami est-ce trop encore?
Qui donc a dit:
Laisse tout et suis ton chemin?
Le chemin est dur sans ami!

9

Chapter XXVII, pages (164–165), Mesdjer's song.

L'enfant qui monte à l'Orient
Porte sa joie exubérante
En auréole,
Mais à ses pieds des semelles de plomb.

Et la durée du jour,
La durée hargneuse, l'écartèle.
Vers le Ciel se tend sa couronne,
Et vers la terre sa lourdeur.
Il est dur de lutter
Contre ce qui divise!

Il monte, degré par degré,
Vers son zénith.
Heure de gloire! Heure d'amour!
Il étend les bras pour l'étreindre,
La Bien-aimée . . .
O terreur
D'être suspendu dans le vide!
Homme, ô pauvre crucifié! . . .

O crépuscule, ô grand espoir,
Rapprochement . . .
Parole de paix entrevue;
Embrassement de Ciel et Terre;
Confondement
Ou s'éjouit
—Dans la paix de l'Amen divin—
L'exubérance de l'aurore!

Nuit féconde, nuit lumineuse;
Nuit sans ombre
Où l'Apparence disparaît.
O sérénité de l'Amour
Enfin connu!
O Rédempteur, tu as vaincu
L'espérance vaine, et le Poids,
Et le Séparateur!

Je te retrouve enfin, ô mon jeune désir,
Candide enfant!
En ton joyeux commencement,
Ma fin radieuse s'annonce.
Tu m'emportes vers la Lumière
Où soir et matin sont unis;
Anneau d'or
Sans brisure et sans fin!

O désir tu n'es plus! O Amour, tu es moi!
En toi, Médiateur,
L'Horus vainqueur prend son vol triomphant!

10

Chapter XXXVIII, pages (234) and (237), The old poem of past times.

Toute forme née d'un ventre est appelée à disparaître, et cela depuis le temps du premier dieu. Les générations s'en vont à leur destin. . . . Les eaux coulent vers le Nord, l'aquilon souffle vers le Sud; chaque homme va vers sa destinée.

Prends donc du bon temps. . . . Ne trouble pas ton cœur, en rien, en rien, avec tes soucis. N'use point ton cœur pendant la durée de ta vie Prends du bon temps, beaucoup, beaucoup!

. . . .

Enivre ton cœur du matin au soir, jusqu'à ce que vienne le jour de l'abordage dans l'autre monde.

II

Chapter XLIII, pages (265–6), The Litany.

> *Elle entend, la Face divine;*
> *Elle répond, la Donatrice,*
> *la dispensatrice des grâces;*
> *Mère des Dieux, Hathor, Maison d'Horus,*
> *Maison dorée, vase de Lumière,*
> *Maison du Ciel et de la Face,*
> *Mère d'amour et d'Harmonie.*
> *En elle vit Maât, miroir de Justice*
> *et siège de Sagesse;*
> *Mère du Ciel terrestre,*
> *Matrice de l'Homme divin.*
> *Elle est Une,*
> *elle est double, car elle est*
> *deux en une . . .*
> *Elle est mère sans enfanter,*
> *car elle est la matrice de l'Origine*
> *qu'elle amène à sa dernière fin.*
> *Unie dès le Commencement avec son créateur,*
> *elle est le Milieu, l'Equilibre,*
> *et l'Accomplissement.*
> *O Maât, fille de Râ! Râ Seigneur de Maât!*
> *O Râ vivant en Maât! O Râ qu'attire Maât!*
> *O Râ qui s'accroît en Maât! O Râ glorifié en Maât!*
> *O Râ nourri par Maât! O Râ affermi par Maât!*
> *O Râ qu'illumine Maât! O Râ conjoint en Maât!*
> *Maât conjointe de Râ des son commencement! . . .*

DOCUMENTARY APPENDIX

THE LAND OF EGYPT

THE HISTORY OF EGYPT

CIVILISATION AND SOCIETY

THE TEACHING OF EGYPT

THE EGYPTIAN RELIGION

DOCUMENTARY APPENDIX

I

THE LAND OF EGYPT

1. The Names of Egypt

THE word *Egypt* can be derived from the Greek word *Aigyptos*, a transcription of *Haikuptah—Ha-Ka-Ptah*—the name of *Ptah's* temple at Memphis.

In the Egyptian texts Egypt was known by several names.

—*Kemit*, 'the black one'; that is, the black earth. This name was known to the Greeks as *Khemia* or *Khimia*. All arable land does, indeed, consist of Nile mud with its characteristic grey-black colour.

—*Ta-meri*, the 'beloved earth', or rather the 'magnetic earth'. The word *mer*, meaning love, affinity, attraction, magnetisation, invests the earth, *ta*, with the function of a magnet drawing to itself the vital forces and 'gifts' of its *Neters*: *Hapi*, the Nile; *Râ*, the Sun; and *Nut*, Heaven or Sky.

—*Ta nutri*, 'land of the *Neters*', land of the gods.

—*Mizraïm* is the name which the Hebrews gave Egypt, and this name passed into the Arabic language as *Misr*.

—The '*Two-Lands*' is the name given to Egypt in numerous inscriptions, to describe the whole of this country, composed as it is of two parts, the North and the South, allied like two complementary powers under the same Pharaonic authority, each of the two preserving her particular crown and symbol.

The 'Land of the North' consists of the territories within the Nile delta from Memphis to the Mediterranean. Its symbol is the papyrus; its sovereign wears the red crown; his attribute is the bee, or wasp, or honey-fly.

The 'Land of the South' stretches from Memphis to the southern border of Egypt. Its sovereign wears the white crown and his attribute is the reed *scirpus*. This reed and the papyrus, united in a monogram (which leaves to each its place and its individual character) represents the '*Two-Lands*', North and South.

The Pharaoh, 'Lord of the *Two-Lands*', wears the double crown, the *pshent* (*sekhemty*=the two powers), which consists of the white crown supported by the red crown.

2. The Nile

In Egyptian: *atur*, 'the river'. The Nile is Egypt's only river, and her 'life-artery', flowing through her from south to north.

According to Diodorus of Sicily, the original name of the Nile would have been *Aegyptos* (from *aegypta*, Greek for vulture). It would have received the name *Nile* from the king Nileus.

Its length is 4,000 miles. Issuing from Lake Victoria Nyanza at an altitude of 3,620 feet, it forms five cataracts between Berber and Aswan.

North of Memphis the Nile used formerly to fan out into seven arms, spreading towards the Mediterranean. Today only two arms of importance remain: the Phatmetic, which reaches the sea at Damietta, and the Bolbitine at Rosetta; between those two stretches the delta is irrigated by numerous canals.

The Nile begins to rise at the summer solstice; its first waters, green and foul, are the 'green Nile', followed by the 'red Nile', which carries a thick reddish slime. The level reaches its greatest height between September 30th and October 10th, after which it gradually subsides again. In order not to create disaster by inadequate or excessive flooding, the floods have to reach a height of at least 20 feet and at most 27 feet.

During the period of inundation the Nile is called *Hapi*. It is symbolised by an androgynous figure: a masculine body with the breasts of a nursing woman and the womb of a mother. On the head he carries a wisp of papyrus, and in his hands the cross of life, with the 'gifts of the Nile': vessel filled with water, fruits, lotus, etc.

3. Egypt as Organised in the Image of Heaven

Text, Hermes Trismegistus to Asclepius: "Do you then not know, O Asclepius, that Egypt is the copy of Heaven, or rather, the place where here below are mediated and projected all operations which govern and actuate the heavenly forces? Even more than that, if the whole truth is to be told, our land is the temple of the entire World" (A. J. Festugière, *Corpus Hermeticum*, collection Budé, Vol. II, p. 326).

4. The Nomes

The country of Egypt was divided into squares, and the determinative sign of the nome is a rectangle divided into squares. This symbol is akin to that for the character *p*, which is used in writing the name of heaven, *pt*. The Egyptian word for nome is *spt*. The root *sp* in Egyptian means specification, and actually it can be established that the nomes, through their emblem, the name of their capitals and through their *Neters*, specify certain functions, as if the nomes of Egypt were the dwelling-places of organic nodes, both terrestrial and celestial. . . .

There are 20 nomes in Lower (Northern) Egypt, and 22 in Upper (Southern) Egypt, which gives a total of 42 nomes, and 42 is also the number of the assessors (or functions) of Osiris, who is the *Neter* of Nature.

Each nome had its 'standard' consisting of an emblem on top of a kind of perch; it had its metropolis, and one or several *Neters*, who were its 'patron-saints' more or less symbolically related to the emblem. The lists of nomes specified for each its principal irrigation canal, its subdivision, the nature of the soils and their confines, and sometimes the length of its local cubit.

5. The Towns of Egypt

The names of the towns of Egypt are determined by the fundamental characteristic of each place; there is therefore a relation between them and the symbolism of the nomes, since each nome corresponds to one *organic* function in the body of Egypt, which claims to be organised in the image of Heaven.

Principal towns (listed alphabetically according to the name most commonly used):

Abydos	Kom-Ombo
Aswan	Memphis
Asyut	⎧ Earth of the Bow (Nubia)
Busiris	Philæ ⎨ The Bow, the 9 Bows
Buto	⎩ The land of Cush
Elephantina	Saïs
El-Kab Nekheb	Tanis
Heliopolis	Thebaïd
Heracleopolis	Thebes
Hermopolis	Thinis or This
Hierakonpolis-Nekhen	

ABYDOS, or *Abdju* in Egyptian: capital of the 8th nome in Upper Egypt, not far from the ancient Thinis, and near the present town of Girgeh.

Tradition placed the tomb of Osiris in Abydos. The present large temple contains some construction bearing this name. At all times Abydos was the goal for funeral pilgrimages; even the living had a stele or a cenotaph erected there for themselves. Abydos was already a sacred town under Pepi I; his temple was restored by Ausar-tesen, embellished by the kings of the XIIIth dynasty, then rebuilt by Seti I and enlarged by Rameses II, who added another smaller temple.

The journey of the dead, who were brought in barges to pay a visit to Osiris, was considered as an almost compulsory rite.

The temple, of white limestone, was built by Seti against the holy mountain into which Osiris was reputed to retire every evening.

At Abydos the great 'mysteries' of the passion of Osiris were celebrated every year, lasting until the festival of *Khoyak* (end of December).

ASWAN is the modern name of ancient *Sunu*, the *Syene* of the Greeks. Aswan forms the extreme south of Upper Egypt; Philæ lay on its frontier with Northern Ethiopia.

Towards the Saïto-Ethiopian epoch, *Sunu* replaced the ancient *Abu* (Elephantina) as capital of the 1st nome of Upper Egypt.

It is said that at Syene there was a well, into the shaft of which the sun-rays fell vertically at the moment of the summer solstice; but this well has never been found.

Evergetes I and Philopator built a little temple there, dedicated to the Isis of Syene; this temple was never finished.

The characteristic feature of Aswan is the striated reddish-pink granite of its quarries which from the remotest ages supplied the Egyptians with materials for their temples, obelisks, sarcophagi and statues. There can still be seen today an obelisk, a colossal statue of a king, and sarcophagi, none of them finished and still in process of excavation.

ASYUT (*Lycopolis*), the ancient *Siut*, is the town of the 'wolf-jackals', sacred to Anubis.

In the mountains of Asyut numerous small wells have been found which are filled with mummies of wolves and jackals.

Siut was the capital of the feudal princes of the XIIth dynasty.

Its nome and that of Unu were replaced, under Akhenaton, by a new nome which had *Khut-n-Aten* (Tel-el-Amarna) for capital.

BUSIRIS, the Greek name of *Pa-Ansar* or *Bus-Osiris*, was written *djedu* in Egyptian (the hieroglyphs containing the pillar, *djed*, of Osiris).

Busiris, in the 9th nome of Lower Egypt, was the most ancient sanctuary of Osiris; its original *Neter* was *Andjty* (wearing a headgear of two feathers with a ribbon falling down his back, and carrying the hook, *heqa*, and the flagellum, the symbolic sceptres of terrestrial royalty.

Andjty became Osiris, who represented the same principle with a more Occidental character, and with the same symbols.

The temple of Busiris was also sacred to Isis mourning over Osiris. The Osiris of Busiris was therefore the *Neter* of the *Amenti*, also personifying the Sun in his nocturnal journey, with the principle of perpetual return to Earth.

BUTO, in ancient times *Per wadjet*, sacred name of the metropolis of the 19th nome of Lower Egypt called *Ammt*, 'the town of the eyebrows'. It is mentioned in the Bible.

The town of Buto was divided into two parts (or districts), *Pe* and *Dep*, whose inhabitants used to battle with each other on certain symbolical ceremonial occasions, such as the re-erection of the *djed*.

Buto lay on the Sebennytic branch of the Nile, and was important because of its temples and its proximity to the famous island of Shemnis, which, according to Herodotus, "lay against the temple of Buto, in a deep, wide lake, and was said by the Egyptians to be floating". The legend of the island floating among the swamps (where Horus is reported to have been born) is the same as that of Latona, who gave birth to Apollo on a floating island, which after this event became fixed. In Buto, by the way, these two legends link up, since in that town there was also a temple of Diana and Apollo, which contained a chapel dedicated to Latona "made all of one stone; its height, width, and walls are of equal dimensions, and no less than forty cubits in each direction. The roof is made of another stone and projects four cubits" (Herodotus, Books II, CLV, CLVI). Herodotus says again, "among the Egyptians, Apollo is called *Horus*, Ceres: *Isis*, and Diana: *Bubastis*" . . . (hence Bubastis or Bastit is here the *lunar* cat, since Diana is the Moon).

At Buto there was also a famous oracle of Apollo—or Horus.

ELEPHANTINA is the largest island formed by the rocks of the first cataract and lies opposite Aswan. Its name derives from the Egyptian name *Abu*, meaning elephant, alluding probably to its round grey rocks.

Between the VIth and XIth dynasties the Egyptians of Abu colonised Northern Nubia. Abu was then the capital of the nome *Ta qunset*. whose other principal localities were *Senen* (the island Bigeh), *Pa lak* (the island Philæ) and *Nubit* (Ombos). *Suan* or *Syene* (Aswan) played only a subordinate part at that time.

Today only a few ruins remain at Elephantina, the sub-foundations of a sanctuary, built under Trajan with stones taken from other buildings, and still bearing the names of Thothmes III, Thothmes IV and Rameses III—and a cemetery of sacred rams.

A temple of Amenophis III and another of Thothmes III were entirely destroyed at the beginning of the 19th century.

In the north of the island there is a nilometer of ninety steps.

The *Neters* of Elephantina were *Khnum, Anukis* and *Satis*.

EL-KAB, in Greek Eileithyias, is the ancient town of *Nekheb*, capital of the 3rd nome of Upper Egypt, containing the temple of *Nekhbet*, 'The White One', whose symbolic animal is the large vulture which can still be seen flying over that region.[1]

Nekhbet is *Mut*, the gestating one, after she has passed the black stage of *Mut*, the destroyer; she causes the flower to spring from the seed (*nekhbet* = the lotus bud risen from the water). *Nekhbet* brings the growth of the embryo, which *Mut* has gestated, to a good end.

Nekhbet is the protector of all 'growing and developing things'. Hence she can be seen overshadowing the images of the Pharaohs, or spreading her protecting wings on the ceilings of corridors in tombs and temples.

Her temples are decorated with scenes from agricultural life.

Opposite El-Kab, on the eastern bank of the Nile, lay *Nekhen* (Hierak-

---

[1] cf. *Her-Bak Disciple*, Comm. III, § 15.

onpolis), a town and temple sacred to the swaddled Horus, the symbol of embryonic Horus.

HELIOPOLIS (Greek for *Iunu*) lay roughly where El-Matarīya, near Cairo, lies today. It is the *On* of the Bible, whose High Priest's daughter married Joseph.

It was *the* solar town; the *Neter* of its temple was *Râ*, and in its priests' school the highest philosophy was taught; Solon stayed there to study theology. Herodotus affirms that "the inhabitants of Heliopolis passed for the most learned among the Egyptians".

An avenue of sphinxes led to the temple; at its end stood two obelisks (built by Sesostris I), one of which can still be seen at Matarīya.

HERACLEOPOLIS MAGNA, in Egyptian *Hakheninsu* or *Akhenas*, was the capital of the nome of *Naru* (from the rose-laurel or oleander), and lay on the Bahr Yussef, south of Lake Moeris. During the IXth and Xth dynasties it was the capital of all Egypt, and gained importance once more under the XIXth dynasty.

Its name (*Herakles = Hercules = Khonsu*) explains the double aspect of its temple: both solar and Osirian (the funerary Osiris, the Sun of the night, that is, the Moon).

Today Heracleopolis is the large village of Ahnasieh.

HERMOPOLIS. There are two towns of this name. *Pa Tehuti*, 'the one of Thot', was the capital of the 15th nome of Lower Egypt; today El-Bakalīyeh.

Khemenu (today Eshmunen) was the capital of the 15th nome of Upper Egypt and lay practically opposite Tel-el-Amarna.

Both towns were sacred to Thot; *Khemenu*, or Hermopolis Magna, the southern one, was an important centre for the teaching of theology.

HIERAKONPOLIS, or 'the town of the falcon' (today Kom-el-Ahmar), is the ancient Egyptian *Nekhen*, opposite *Nekhbet* (El-Kab), north of Edfu. Its *Neter* was *Horus*, in the shape of a mummified, or rather swaddled, falcon, symbolising as it were the embryonic stage.

In the legendary time of the *Shemsu-Hor*, 'the companions of Horus',[1] which came before Menes, *Nekhen* was the capital of the Southern Kingdom, while *Buto* was the capital of the North. *Menes* (Ist dynasty) is said to have unified Egypt by bringing the '*Two-Lands*' under his sceptre.

From that time it became usual to speak of the 'souls' of Nekhen and Buto'[2] as it had been to speak of the 'souls' of Heliopolis and Hermopolis. Nekhen and Buto symbolised, as it were, two phases in the history of *Horus*: at Nekhen, *Horus* was worshipped in the embryonic stage;

[1] See this Appendix, II, para. 3, p. 316, and *Her-Bak Disciple*, Comm. V, § 8.
[2] See above, page 308, *Buto*.

whereas Buto has remained, throughout the whole *Osiris-Horus* myth, the symbol for the place where *Horus* was born.[1]

The whole legend of Nekhen and Buto takes place in the prehistoric period attributed to the *Shemsu-hor*, the 'Companions of *Horus*', which were near him in his embryonic state.

It must be understood that these expressions—'souls' of Nekhen and Buto, Heliopolis and Hermopolis—signified the Principles behind the life of Egypt, and were, indeed, the 'archetypes' represented by the prehistoric divine dynasties, on the model of which historical Egypt was then built up and organised.[2]

KOM-OMBO, in ancient times *Ombos* and *Nubet*, in the nome *Qenset*, half-way between Edfu and Aswan, where a temple (built by Hatshepsut and Thutmosis III, and rebuilt under the Ptolemies) can still be seen. It was first sacred to *Sobek*,[3] but the latest rearrangement presents an interesting particularity.

The temple is governed by the characteristic feature of dualism: it is divided into two parallel parts, each having its own portico and sanctuary. The temple is sacred to a twofold symbol: the principles of *Seth* and *Horus*, who were frequently united under the name of *Neter-wy*, 'the two *Neters*'.

They are the two aspects of the Universal Light often compared to gold—*nub*—on the one hand the dark, material, fixed, contracted, satanic aspect—*Seth*; and on the other hand the radiant spiritual, penetrating, open aspect—*Horus*.

The ancient name of the *Neter* of Ombos was *Nubty*, which may mean both 'her from Ombos' and 'the golden one' (in the sense given above), and the ending *-ty*, although feminine, also means twofoldness.

MEMPHIS (ancient Egyptian name *mem-nefer*) lay at the southern point of the delta, on the site of the present-day Mit-Rahîneh. Menes, the first king of the Ist dynasty, diverted the Nile, according to Herodotus, by filling up the elbow it formed in the south and drying up the old bed of the river, to build Memphis there.

In Strabo's time the town was still impressive, although already in part demolished by Cambyses. The Christian emperors destroyed it, and its stones served to build Cairo. Today all that remains are the two colossi of Rameses II—one of them lying prone—one sphinx of alabaster and a little debris.

The tombs of the Apis-bulls were discovered near Memphis.

[1] *Buto* is assumed to be identical with *Shemnis*, the name of *Horus*' birthplace; see p. 335 (Fr. 6/7).

[2] See this Appendix, II, para. 2, p. 315.

[3] See *Her-Bak Disciple*, Comm. III, § 19.

The great temple of Memphis was that of *Ptah*, *Ha-Ka-Ptah*, a notable centre of teaching.[1]

PHILÆ, formerly *Pa-Lak*, is the island at the extreme south of Upper Egypt or Thebaida, on the frontier with Nubia or Ethiopia. About 440 feet (400 metres) long and 165 yards (150 metres) wide, it was never covered by the floods—until the dam at Aswan was built. On the map it looks not unlike a brooding bird, something like a swallow. The temple lies in the middle of the bird's body, as if the bird were hatching it.

Inscriptions found at Philæ contain the complete philosophy of the story of *Isis* and *Osiris* until their fulfilment by liberation of *Osiris'* Horian soul.

Furthermore there are found some traces of Amasis (XXVIth dynasty), a kiosk of Nectanebo, and the temple built by the Ptolemies and completed by the Roman emperors Augustus, Tiberius, Trajan, Hadrian, Antoninus and Lucius Virus successively until the fifth century A.D., when an altar was built to the Virgin in the chapel of *Isis*.

Isis' name at Philæ was 'Mistress of the Earth of the Bow', that is, of Nubia at whose frontier Philæ lay. Her temple is oriented towards the south, overlooking this 'land of the Bow'. And, in the wall of raw bricks which surrounds the temple of *Isis*, one part is built of stone in the exact shape of a bow.

The Bow; the 'Nine Bows'

There is here a pun and interplay of ideas based on the symbol of the *bow* and the nine *bows*. Nubia, 'the land of the bow' (*ta-seti*), is the country of gold (*nub*), the black country containing all 'odours' (*seti*) and seeds which go to fertilise the mud of Egypt. It is the earth of gestation.

The symbol of the 'nine bows', which is often quoted in Egyptian inscriptions, refers to the nine stages of gestation, the nine obstacles which threaten the embryo's growth. The nine 'bows'—or enemies (which are frequently represented on the base plinth and beneath the feet of the Pharaoh's statues)—are the nine 'enemies' whom the king must force to surrender 'under his sandals', in order to dominate the inferior forces and to manifest his royal mastery.

The Land of Cush, formerly *Kaushu*, was the old country south of the first cataract. According to the Bible, the *Cushites* inhabited Southern Egypt, Ethiopia, and even Southern Arabia.

"According to Genesis," says M. Lenormant, "Ham had four sons, *Cush*, *Mizraïm*, *Phut* and *Canaan*. The identity of the race of *Cush* with the Ethiopians is certain. Egyptian hieroglyphic inscriptions mention the peoples of the Upper Nile and South of Nubia always under the name of *Cush*. The usual name for Egypt in sacred literature is *Mizraïm*. . . ."[2]

---

[1] See this Appendix, V, para. 2, *Cosmogony of Memphis*, p. 337.
[2] cf. Menard et Sauvageot, *Vie privée des Anciens*, I, p. 12.

The 'Prince of Cush', the black prince—and he was supposed to be a 'black prince' even when the position, as often happened, was held by a son of the Pharaoh—played an important part in the symbolism of certain ritual ceremonies and processions.

SAïS—ancient name, *Saït*—on the Bolbitine arm of the Nile, near the centre of the delta, was the capital of the 5th nome of Lower Egypt.

The founding of the temple of Neith at Saïs is mentioned on tablets dating from the reign of Aha, a king of the Ist dynasty. Saïs gained great historical importance from the beginning of the XXth dynasty. The XXVIth dynasty was Saïtian.

The religious fame of Saïs was due to the worship of the cosmic Virgin *Neith*, the Virgin-mother of whom it is said in the inscriptions engraved on her temple: "I am that which is, that which will be, and that which has been. No one has lifted the veil which covers me. The fruit I have brought forth is the Sun."

A 'festival of the glowing lamps' (probably similar to the Christian Candlemas) was celebrated there to mark the triumph of light over darkness; all lamps were lit, "not only", as Herodotus says, "for Saïs, but for the whole of Egypt".

TANIS, ancient capital of the 14th nome of Lower Egypt, is the modern Sân-el-Haggar (from the Egyptian name Zânt), south of Lake Manzalieh. Mariette has discovered there remains of monuments built by the 'Shepherds' during the period of their intrusion, towards the end of the Middle Empire.

Recently the tombs of kings of the XXIst and XXIInd dynasties have also been found there, within the enclosure of the temple, conforming to the words of Herodotus (II, 169) that the Saïtian kings were buried "within the enclosure of Minerva" (= *Neith*) quite near the temple.

At Tanis also *Seth* was worshipped, and from Tanis originated the kings of the XIXth dynasty, Rameses I and Seti.

THEBAïD, the ancient name of Upper Egypt, which stretched beyond *Thebaica Phylakâ* (between Tel-el-Amarna and Aswut) to Asyan and Philæ, corresponds today to Saïd. Thebes was the capital of this Upper Egypt (see *Thebes*).

The name of *Thebaïd*, which has become synonymous with 'hermitage', referred then to the deserts around the Theban region, particularly to those west of the fertile valley. The arid mountains, the limestone rocks with their innumerable folds, contain deep cavities which served as hermitages to many Christian ascetics.

THEBES, formerly also named 'the town of the hundred gates', was called by the Egyptians *No-Amun* or *Nut-Amun*, which means 'the town of Amun'. In another aspect Thebes bore the name of its emblem: *Wast*.

This immense town stretched over both banks of the Nile. Its four quarters were covered with temples, palaces, and statues; on their site are now built:

1. On the east bank the modern villages of Karnak and Luxor, formerly connected by an avenue of sphinxes.

2. On the western bank the villages of Gurna and El-Baharat.

From the XIth to the XXIst and XXIInd dynasties, Thebes was the capital of Egypt; towards the end of this period a second capital was chosen in the delta. After various other incursions, Thebes was nearly destroyed by the Ptolemy Latyros, and shattered by an earthquake in the year A.D. 27.

In Thebes was fulfilled the initial mission of Egypt, with the XVIIIth, XIXth and XXth dynasties. The theological teaching given at Thebes summed up and brought to a *conclusion* all teachings that had gone before. As an old saying of the Sages runs: "The answer is given at Thebes."[1]

Later sages and kings merely 'repeated' the teaching received, giving it such outer forms as conformed to the symbolic character of their period.

The Valley of the Kings is indeed the tomb of Egypt's divine royalty.

THINIS or THIS must have been very near Abydos, but the exact place is not known at present.

Thinis was the capital of Menes, the first king of the Ist dynasty. Its fate was soon linked with that of Abydos, which became the sacred town of Osiris for the whole of Egypt.

II

THE HISTORY OF EGYPT

1. The History

HISTORY is the chronology of facts. These facts are results.

The sages of antiquity recorded exclusively the concatenation of the deeper causes and psychological reactions which produced these facts. An 'historical' inscription in an Egyptian temple is the outcome of a conscious interplay in which fact and cause tally, and now this fact and now that cause are shown, according to the aim which the inscription is intended to fulfil.

"It is obvious," says A. Varille, "that these inscriptions are analyses of the correspondences between a set Royal programme and the characteristic phases of a cosmic genesis contemporaneous with the dynastic structure. The votive inscriptions of a temple therefore convey not only an

[1] See *Her-Bak Disciple*, Chapter X.

historical meaning: they are equally intended to convey a certain teaching through their symbolism. . . . In his ceremonial and his cartouches, the Pharaoh synthesises the *Neters* of an epoch; and the whole dynastic history is nothing but a learned transcription of this Royal Idea through the ages."[1]

2. The Dynasties

The historic tradition has come down to us through Egyptian texts, through Greek authors such as Eratostenes and the Syncellus, and through Manetho, an Egyptian priest whose mother-tongue was Greek. Manetho, who lived under Ptolemy II, wrote a history of Egypt of which a shortened version was made containing the list of kings arranged into thirty-one dynasties. This epitome was taken up and 'rearranged' by the Christian apologists Julius the African (A.D. 217) and Eusebius (A.D. 327).

Eratostenes (Alexandria, third century B.C.) is supposed to be the author of a list of thirty-eight Theban kings in Greek transliteration. To this list Pseudo-Apollodorus is said to have added fifty-three further names, and the list was finally passed on by the Syncellus.

The royal lists given by the Egyptian inscriptions were engraved by order of the Pharaohs of the New Empire. They are:

1. *The Chamber of Ancestors at Karnak*, at present in the Louvre (cf. Lepsius, *Auswahl*, Pl. I; Prisse d'Avennes, *Mon. Egypt.*, Pl. I, and *Rev. Arch.*, II, 1845, Pl. XXIII; Sethe, *Urk*, IV (pp. 608-10).

2. *The Table of Abydos*, engraved by order of Seti I (cf. Dumichen A–Z, 2, 1864, pp. 81-3; de Rougé, *Recherche sur les Monuments*, Pl. II; Lepsius, *Auswahl*, Pl. II).

3. *The Table of Saqqara*, in the tomb of Tunro, a contemporary of Rameses II (cf. de Rougé, op. cit., Pl. I; Meyer, *Aeg. Chron.*, Pl. I).

4. *Papyrus of Turin* (damaged) (cf. Lepsius, op. cit., Pl. III; de Rougé, op. cit., Pl. III; Meyer, op. cit., Pl. II–V; Lanth, *Manetho, und der Turin pap.*; Farina, *Pap. de R.*).

These lists differ among themselves in number and order, and they do not give precise information which would permit us to give a date to the reigns or even the dynasties, particularly those previous to the XIIth or even to the XVIIIth. Events in those days were dated by the day of the current year, which was numbered as from the accession of the reigning Pharaoh, and with each reign began a new, independent era. It has not been possible to gain any certain date from the inscriptions, except some notions of the relation between certain historical events and the heliacal rising of the star Sothis; even in those cases doubts remain as to exactly which Sothiac period reference is made.

These uncertainties have given rise to several hypotheses about the length of known Egyptian history, and opinions are divided between the 'long' and the 'short' chronology. The former reckons the Ist dynasty

[1] A. Varille, *Mercure de France*, July 1st, 1951.

as beginning about 5500 B.C. and the XIIth about 3600; the latter places the Ist dynasty at 3200 and the XIIth at 2000 B.C.

The XVIIIth dynasty is established at 1580 B.C., as it has been possible to collate dates with contemporary events in the Middle East.

3. The Eight Periods of Egyptian History

The history of Egypt has been divided into eight great periods, each of which has a character peculiar to itself.

(A) *The prehistoric period,* comprising the dynasties of the Gods (7 or 9 *Neters*), the Half-gods, the *Shemsu* of *Horus.*[1] In these prehistoric dynasties, the Egyptologists thought they saw real kings fighting for the crowns of Upper and Lower Egypt. Actually the divine dynasties are symbolic expressions of cosmic Principles and their primordial operation, as factors and functions of a Universe which Egypt claimed to mirror as its living image.

In the divine dynasty the name *Horus* appears twice, but even the second of the two should still be taken as a 'principle'.

The *Shemsu* of *Horus* immediately preceding the first human dynasty must doubtless be regarded as the transition from the first of the 'divine' series, and as helpers in birth to the first Man-Kings, *Menes* (or *Aha-Menes*). That is no doubt the reason why Manetho calls them the 'Manes'.

The *Shemsu* of *Horus* are not his 'followers' or 'retinue', but his 'companions' (in the philosophical sense); they are sharers with him of the womb during his embryonic stage and from all of them together arises the human king Horus, i.e. Menes.

To prove this, the kings of the Ist dynasty claim to be descendants of *Horus*; but *their* Horus names are: *Hor aha* (the fighter), *Hor khent* (the one inside, i.e. in the womb). The Horus reigning in those times is he of Letopolis (*Sekhem*), a mummified falcon, and his name is *Hor khenti arti*, 'the two eyes inside', which means the two seeds, solar and lunar, male and female, whose union gives rise to gestation.

(B) *The Seven Historical Periods,* which are:

1. Thinian Epoch	I and II dynasties	Thinis (and Abydos)
2. Ancient Empire	III, IV, V	Memphis
3. End of Ancient Empire and intermediate period	VI–XI	Elephantina Memphis
4. Middle Empire	XI and XII	Herakleopolis Thebes
5. Second intermediary period	XIII–XVII	The Hyksos
6. New Empire	XVIII–XX	Thebes, later Tanis

[1] See *Her-Bak Disciple,* Comm. V, § 8.

7. Low Epoch
  —Priest-kings   XXI
  —Lybian kings   XXII and XXIII
  —Saïtian kings   XXIV
  —Ethiopian kings   XXV
  —Saïtian kings   XXVI
  —Persian domination and end
      of Egyptian dynasties
  —Alexander the Great, then
  —the Ptolemies, and finally
  —Roman domination.

III

CIVILISATION AND SOCIETY

1. The Pharaonic Civilisation

As early as the Ist dynasty we find the pharaonic civilisation already fully constituted:
  —the character of royalty is clearly defined;
  —religious ideas are fully established;
  —notions about life and death are settled;
  —almost all technical methods are known;
  —an exact calendar is in use;
  —finally, the art of writing is fully developed and practised.

2. The Pharaoh

Per âa, the Egyptian word from which 'Pharaoh' derives, is composed of hieroglyphs which literally mean 'twofold great house'. This symbol gives the Pharaoh the impersonal character of the 'Royal House', seat and embodiment of the royal *Presence*, a power considered to be in a state of continuous 'becoming' or 'unfolding' through successive dynasties. The class-name '*king*' is '*nesut-bit*'—literally: 'the one of the reed (*sut*, symbol of the South) and the bee (*bit*, symbol of the North)'. But it is the symbol of the South which has remained attached to the generic class-name of the 'king', *nesut*, and of the quality of royalty.

The Pharaoh's Names

The royal titles comprised several names and various epithets, according to the epoch; in the beginning they were simple, but little by little they grew more complex, right up to the extreme complexity of the Ptolemaic epoch.

In the middle periods, the title consisted first of two personal names, which distinguished each individual Pharaoh in history; thus, e.g., Amenophis III was actually called *Amenhotep Neb-Maât-Rê*. These personal names were preceded and followed by various other names and epithets: his Horus name (probably a kind of spiritual name, or name of his KA); his 'Golden Horus' name; his affiliation, e.g. 'son of Râ' or 'born of the Two-Mistresses' (that is *Wadjit* and *Nekhebit*, the Mistresses of the 'Two-Lands'); 'Horus master of births'; and finally the royal epithets specifying his sovereignty, like 'King of the South and the North', etc.

His two personal names were written inside two rectangles with rounded corners, which we call 'cartouches'. The cartouche is formed by the circuit of a cord fastened together at its base; from either side of the loop the ends of the cord protrude as if forming part of a continuous cord, the loop of which would determine the present existence of the Pharaoh.

In royal tombs, moreover, one can find frequent representations of the *cord* encircling the mummy of the defunct, or bearing his face (his surviving being as a type) in its circumvolutions, as by a conducting wire, through the successive phases of his life beyond the grave. The Egyptian name for the cartouche is *shenu*; the root of this word means 'circuit' and 'encirclement'.

The Pharaoh's names reveal on the one hand the nature of the Principle incarnated in him (e.g. *Râ-meses*, 'product of *Râ*'), and on the other hand his symbolic role within the genesis of his country.

The Pharaoh's Role

The Pharaoh's role is twofold: active and passive.

His *active* role comprises the passing on of the blood royal, the arbitrary decisions and interventions—in social, military or family affairs—which go to make up his personal destiny and the particular destiny of his people.

He is *passive* in several functions:

1. He becomes, for his people, the 'ferment' of the principle incarnated in him; that is why he is called 'son of *Râ*', 'son of *Amun*', 'magnet of *Ptah*' or 'of *Thot*', etc.

2. He accepts the character ordained by the astrological 'moment' represented by him; he *bears* the names assigned to him.

3. He *obeys* by carrying out the actions therefrom devolving; religious and warlike acts, symbolic decrees and writings, building or renovation of monuments in accordance with the times and the rules imposed by the sages of the 'House of Life'.

Evidence can be found in the texts: "Sesostris I convened the Grand Councils of the Companions of the Palace for the purpose of explaining to them his particular role in relation to the Heliopolitan *Neters*. . . . He then called his privy counsellor in order to tell him that the time had come to act" (A. Varille, *Mercure de France*, July 1951). The temple of Edfu, in the third century B.C., carried out its programme in accordance with the "Book of the Guiding Programme of the Temple of the *Neter*", the work of the Master of Rituals, Imhotep, who lived in the time of Zozer (IIIrd dynasty) (cf. *Journ. Egyptol. Assn.*, 1942, VI, 10, 10). And another text, at Dendera, mentions: "Great fundamental plan of *iun. t* [Dendera]. Erected afresh as a monument by the king of the North and South, *Menkheper Rê* [Thutmosis III], in accordance with the findings of ancient scriptures from the time of King Khufu [Cheops, IVth dynasty]" (cf. Mariette, *Dendera*, III, Pl. 78; Dumichen, *Bang.*, Pl. I).

3. The Caste System

In Egypt the 'caste' principle was not applied with the same rigour as in Brahmanic India, where it held each individual in lifelong imprisonment within the caste into which he was born.

As to the actual caste classification in Egypt, the classical authors disagree.

According to Diodorus the Egyptians had the same three classes as the Athenians: priests, peasants (from which class the soldiers were taken), and craftsmen. Elsewhere he quotes five: shepherds, peasants, craftsmen, soldiers, and priests.

According to Strabo the three classes were soldiers, peasants, and priests.

According to Plato (in *Timæus*) there were six: priests, craftsmen, shepherds, huntsmen, peasants, and soldiers.

The strange differences between these classifications and the fact that none of them mentions the scribes, goes to prove that here we have no tradition of permanently settled and rigidly closed castes, but a variable classification which could be adapted to the political and social needs of the epoch.

What is certain is that the social functions and the crafts were divided into professional guilds, and that most of them were transmitted from father to eldest son.

Records, documents, decrees, and legal deeds, however, show that occasionally men did change their professions, that they could marry outside their class, and that they could even transfer their function to individuals from other classes. In order to do this the approval of the competent authorities was required, and sometimes a ceremony of investiture in the presence of members of the priesthood.

This latter fact seems to indicate a link between the official order governing social life and a secret inner order filtering out and forming an *élite* without, however, doing any violence to the mediocre mass constituting the vast bulk of a society whose instincts were naturally selfish.

4. The Priests

The term '*priests*', which today describes men exclusively dedicated— by vows and a sacrament—to a sacerdotal ministry, can certainly not be applied to all servants of the temples, to the officials and craftsmen, teachers and masters of high sciences, all of whom exercised their functions within the framework of the Egyptian temple.

The hierarchy which emerges from the lists of dignitaries figuring in the processions does not tally with the indications given in the texts, as regards degrees of precedence, or the more secular or religious character of these dignitaries.

It is, by the way, probable that this strict division into 'secular' and 'religious' is quite contrary to Egyptian mentality and hence a misunderstanding. It is therefore preferable to quote without qualification:

1. The titles of priesthood (presumed): *wâb*, pure; *kher-heb*, reader (or perhaps Master of the Ritual?); *hem-Ka*, priest of the KA; *hem-Neter*, priest or prophet (?); first or second prophet of *Amun*; divine father; Grand Seer, etc.

2. Some of the parts played by the Officiants:

—service of the *Neter*, involving the care and cleansing of his statue with the rites involved. The service of each *Neter* was ensured by a college of priests under the leadership of a chief;[1]

—daily ritual, in which the king played a part, either in person or by proxy;

—ritual of festivals, individually for each day of every month;

—symbolic roles in various ceremonies (the *sed* festivals, the foundation of temples, funerals, etc.); *iun-mutef*; *sam*; (priest?) impersonation of a *Neter*;

—assistance at animal sacrifices;

—acceptance of offerings;

—lay priest service;

—astronomical and astrological observations.[2]

Some of these functions—such as the symbolic roles, *iun-mute₁*, sam-priest—were often carried out, at certain festivals, by princes, nobles, or court officers.

For the priests chastity was not compulsory: many had a home, wife, and children. But the priests in the service of certain *Neters* were bound to special observances, abstinences, and ways of life.

On the other hand, details gleaned from the texts concerning certain dignitaries of the temple serve rather to increase the uncertainty about how far they actually are of sacerdotal character. Some functions, such as that of Prophet of *Amun*, were hereditary and did not prevent their holder from administering estates or exercising other military or social functions. Some documents depict the members of *Amun's* clergy in a none too favourable light; and some records of legal proceedings accuse the servants of funerary temples of embezzlement.

But we also learn that anonymously—on the fringe of the official

[1] cf. Herodotus, Book II.
[2] cf. texts Diodorus, Herodotus, Jamblichus.

titles—the secrets of the crafts as well as the highest sciences were taught and applied by men who were part of the Temple.

The disparity of these various elements deprives the word 'priest' of any precise meaning, as it is applied in all too indiscriminate a manner to all members—the 'led' as well as the 'leading'—of the Temple. Herodotus and Diodorus speak sometimes of priests and sometimes of initiates. 'Sages of the House of Life' are also mentioned; 'those who know the secrets of the letters of *Thot*'; and those who keep the canonic 'books' of the temples, the laws, the traditional measurements and proportions. . . .

To bring clarity into a subject, two undeniable facts, at any rate, can be relied upon: the high opinion of critics like Diodorus of Sicily, Jamblichus, Herodotus, Clement of Alexandria of the Egyptian Temple as a fountain of Wisdom; the other fact is the continuity of the body of architecture that has been left in evidence. For when we read how the 'divine physicians' and architects, like Imhotep (IIIrd dynasty) and Amenhotep, son of Hapu (XVIIIth dynasty), describe their material works at the same time as their mystical role, we are obliged to conclude that 'The Temple' trained sages, scholars, and craftsmen who perhaps might more appropriately be called 'initiates' than 'priests'—unless the application of their science was considered by these men as a veritable priesthood—which might well have been the case to judge by the records.

IV

THE TEACHING OF EGYPT

To speak with knowledge of Egyptian teaching, we have first to ask ourselves several questions:
1. What material is available from which we may know this teaching?
2. *Who* taught?
3. *Who* was taught?
4. What were the bases and nature of the teaching?
5. Which methods of teaching were used?
6. What sciences were taught?
7. What were the various types of inscription?
8. The external (exoteric) teaching and the internal (esoteric) teaching.

1. Egyptological Material

Egyptological material consists of the following elements: the inscriptions engraved in the temples, on the steles and statues; the inscriptions in tombs and on sarcophagi; papyri and ostraca.

The subjects treated vary from the highest philosophy, which is usually veiled under myth and intricate artifice down to secular letters and schoolboy exercises: more or less cabbalistic inscriptions on pyramids and steles; cosmogonical myths, astronomical inscriptions, hymns and poems with initiatory meaning, philosophical narratives, historical records—almost always symbolic; royal decrees and enactments; lists of precepts called 'wisdom'. Scientific papers: mathematics, medicine and surgery, therapeutics, magical formulas. Countless descriptions of the life beyond the grave and the role of the Sun and his stellar retinue in the *Dwat*; on the transformations of being after its earthly existence; on the various aspects of the psycho-spiritual being. The majority of these texts have been compiled by the Egyptologists into various collections called *Book of the Dead, Book of Day and Night*, etc. Finally there exists a literature of personal and legal correspondence.

The available elements are:

—Some collections of precepts, counsels of wisdom such as the *Precepts of Kaqema*; those of Ptahotep; the *Instructions of the King Amenemhat to his son*; the inscriptions in the graves of nobles and high civil servants describing their duties and responsibilities (*Rekhmara, Ramosis*, etc.).

—Accounts of conquests and expeditions into foreign countries, indicating geographical knowledge of Africa, of adjacent countries around the Mediterranean, of the Grecian isles, and the countries which correspond to the modern Middle East.

—Tables of the dynasties which do not always tally with each other.

—Accounts of battles, military or athletic exploits, which are sometimes too puerile and sometimes too exaggerated to be taken literally.

—Lists of kings derived from historical 'annals' remote in time but unambiguous.

—Funereal texts grouped under various titles: *Book of the Dead, Book of Dwat* (which Maspero calls '*Livre des Portes*', *Book of the Gates*); the *Litanies of the Sun* (in the lower world); the *Book of the Passage through Eternity*; the *Lamentations of Isis and Nephtys*; the *Litanies of Sokaris*; the *Book of Apophis in Reverse*.

—Mystical texts, such as the *Book of Breathing* and the *Book of Amenhotep son of Hapu*.

And many more as yet unpublished.

—Various scientific papyri: on mathematics, astronomy (and astrology), medicine, both diagnostic and therapeutic; laboratory prescriptions, etc.

There are library catalogues (e.g. at Edfu and at Philæ) which reveal a wealth of manuscripts of which only a small part has come down to us.

The bulk of documents consists of the countless hieroglyphic inscriptions engraved upon steles, upon the walls of the great temples and of the votive monuments which nowadays are called 'funereal temples', and in the pyramids; the scenes and inscriptions engraved or painted on the walls of the tombs and on the sarcophagi.

Finally numerous papyri, ostraca, and some writings which are supposed to be schoolboys' exercises.

A number of texts have been translated in their ostensible meaning, sometimes correctly and sometimes not, owing to the imperfection of the copy, or to misinterpretation of the countless anomalies which much too readily have been attributed to the negligence of the scribes.

There are numerous texts, however, which have not been published or have remained incomprehensible to the present instruments of Egyptology.

2. Who Taught?

There is a large number of documents concerning social life: reports by scribe-accountants, legal enactments, disputes over wills and estates, complaints of extortion by priests or scribes, of embezzlements in funereal temples and of donations, etc.

The primary practical instruction needed for learning to deal with legal or business documents of this kind differed entirely—both in matter and quality—from the teaching implied in our answers to questions 1 and 6. Hence it is obvious that there were two classes of schools: a school of primary education which answered to social necessities, and on the other hand the higher teaching which seems to have been the prerogative of the *Temple*, distributed by it among the different places of learning, according to the opportunities of the epoch, to the sciences that were taught, and according to the character which devolved upon each temple.

This fact is confirmed by testimonies from princes and dignitaries who, recording the high responsibilities entrusted to them, add that they were educated and taught in the Temple from their early youth; some say: "when I was still a child . . .", or also that they were "instructed in the secrets of *Thot*", etc.

3. Who was Taught?

According to the documents known it does not seem that on the lowest level, that of the working or peasant class, much trouble was taken over matters of religion, the service or knowledge of the *Neters*. Traces only are found of traditional gestures or customs concerning certain rural festivals, interments, formulas and amulets with magic powers of protection or vulgar sorcery.

The class of petty employees, of small civil servants, scribe-surveyors and scribe-accountants—even of salaried priests—seems according to many testimonies to have ordered its way of life according to a utilitarian code of morals concerned with immediate results: reward or punishment. On the other hand, there are numerous examples of high civil servants or master craftsmen taught by the Temple, and even great sages who, on their own admission, have risen from the people and ascended the whole scale under the guidance of their Masters. Amen-hotep, son of Hapu, sage to King Amenophis III—architect of the Colossi of Memnon and Karnak (Xth pylon) and of the temple of Luxor—is a typical example. There seems to be no connecting bridge between the servile mentality of the middle class and that higher intellect which produced the leaders capable of directing and producing gigantic monumental works and perfect craftsmanship.

The logic of these established facts and the study of numerous documents (including popular records and stories) lead us to this explanation: the educational system of Ancient Egypt was limited and suited to individual ability; it gave to each what was necessary to whet his interest and his faculty for working, but reserved the teaching of the Temple for those who were willing to undergo complete adaptation to its mentality and a pitiless apprenticeship to responsibilities. We shall see the methods in the answer to the next question.

As regards the satisfaction of legitimate vital instincts, all known details of daily life, dress, and furniture show comfort and luxury confined to the strictly necessary. It seems that the sages kept the needs of the people at as low a level as possible in order to reduce the danger of acute covetousness and to concentrate all effort upon impersonal work; this, by the way, does not seem to have affected the Egyptians' humour, the happiness of their family life, their eagerness at work, nor their sense of *quality*.

4. Foundations and Character of Egyptian Teaching

The foundations: the tradition of the Ancients to which they refer on every occasion; a surprising factual knowledge of matter, which gave this tradition the poise of certitude and the character of an immutable and ample basis.

The consequence of this was that there was no groping individual research and no uncertainty.

Regarding the character of the teaching given in Ancient Egypt, our study must base itself on nothing but indisputable facts:

(*a*) The most ancient inscriptions known are *symbols* of *Neters* (*Osiris'* column, *Isis'* knot), clans or provinces, royal names, etc.

—the hieroglyphic script consists of *symbols*;

—the history of the 'prehistoric' divine dynasties is obviously to be understood *symbolically*;

—the religious Myth which developed from the earliest times up to the last days of known Egypt is *symbolic*;

—all pictures representing royal acts figure the Pharaoh accompanied by one or several *Neters*;

—it is written that *Thot*, the *Neter* of writing, himself teaches mankind the laws of geometry, land-surveying, music, and the various methods of notation for these laws, together with the science of the *symbol* and the secrets of the hieroglyphs.

It is therefore obvious that the Egyptological teaching is first of all characterised by the method of *symbolism*.

(*b*) Among the various categories of inscriptions listed in the first answer there are theories developed rationally by controversy or argument, according to the methods of today. Their absence, as well as the disproportion between the small number of scientific papers *written in clear language*, and the loftiness of the science implied in Egyptian works, all this bears witness to the existence of a teaching far more explicit and developed than that given in the documents mentioned.

On the other hand, the apparent triteness of the inscriptions covering the countless temples, the frequent anomalies found in the hieroglyphic writing, the improbability of numerous accounts, if taken in their ostensible meaning: all this makes certain beyond doubt that there exists an esoteric meaning which a more 'philosophical' interpretation will reveal. The opinion of classic authors like Clement of Alexandria, Herodotus, Plutarch, Jamblichus, etc., confirms this assertion:

Egyptian teaching comprised two aspects: one exoteric and the other esoteric.

5. The Methods of Teaching

The methods of teaching employed by the Egyptians are revealed in their own words and by certain anomalies in their inscriptions and pictures.

They transmitted their knowledge in several ways:

(*a*) By training man's senses and mind; by applying what they called 'the laws of *Maât*' (consciousness of the truth), which means the conformity of the name of each thing with its true nature; the conformity of the appearance given to manufactured things (shape, colour, decoration) with their purpose and function; the conformity of a building's measurements and proportions (whether temple, statue, or obelisk) with the laws it was meant to teach.

(*b*) By inducing people to "follow the lessons of *Thot* and *Seshat*", the *Neters* of writing, of the geometrical patterns and shapes occurring in Nature, and of all configurations and 'signatures', which in everything on earth reveal its character and properties.

All means were welcome to them for directing the attention of students; the accentuation of a characteristic in some species or individual; the association within one scene (hunting, fishing, or agriculture) of certain plants and animals which live in symbiosis; the giving to each being and each object a name composed in such a way that "everything that lives on the Earth, in the Heavens, and in the *Dwat*" should have its nature implied in its name; finally, they provided that through puns made on homonyms the attentive seeker should be led to look for analogies revealing common functions.

(c) By developing in the reader the unifying vision, by superimposition of the various aspects (physical, spiritual, historical) of a subject in one and the same text or picture. This was the spirit in which they taught various sciences; their application in detail may of course have been the object of specialised studies, but there can never have been complete specialisation, for in every phenomenon Ancient Egypt always saw the cause through the effect. Indeed, this was the essential characteristic of the Egyptian method: *observation of the concrete fact or the concrete symbol of a fact, for the purpose of rousing in the student the evocation of its abstract aspect.*

6. Which Sciences were Taught?

The Egyptological material which we have quoted in paragraph 1 already provides an answer to this question, if we consider, in addition to the inscriptions, the work that accompanies them: the architecture of temples as well as of pyramids, sculpture, statuary, the calculation and cutting of stones in quarries, the working of minerals, different alloys of metals, etc. A thorough knowledge of mathematics, geometry, statics, metallurgical chemistry, geology, etc., was required for all these labours without taking into account that certain work—such as the calculation of the cubits for the various nomes—needed precise geodetical knowledge.

Philo of Alexandria among other witnesses affirms (*Life of Moses*, I, 5) that Moses had learnt from the Egyptians the theory of rhythmics, harmony, and *metrics* (Lefebvre, *Chron. d'Eg.*, 49, p. 58).

What makes matters difficult, however, is the fact that in Egypt the different branches of teaching were not kept separate in water-tight compartments:

—Astronomy dealt with astrological influences.

—Medical prescriptions often contained astrological (favourable and unfavourable dates and hours) or magical constituents (words to be recited, etc.) or instructions—explicit or implicit—referring to the occult constitution of the human body, e.g. the enumeration of 'vessels' which often do not refer to blood-vessels, but to the invisible ducts of energy in the 'subtile body'.

—History is always mingled with mythology.

—The myth is an exoteric form of this unifying philosophy—cosmology, cosmogony, anthroposophy, anthropogony—extended to cover the various states of the being.

—Every text and every picture comprises several aspects of the subject treated, owing to the fact that in Egyptian thought these aspects were never isolated, and that studying them separately would leave out the vital connection, distort the global meaning of the composition, and in consequence also the particular meaning of the aspect under consideration.

It is therefore easier to sketch a general plan of the knowledge taught in the Egyptian Temple than to analyse its separate branches, since these continually become involved with one another. In spite of this, it is quite correct to speak of a general plan, for certain governing ideas constantly emerge from behind all sciences taught by the various modes of inscription, and seem to converge upon a definite goal.

A brief glance at these various branches will disclose to us the dominant note:

SCIENCE OF MAN

—*His physical body*: papyri on anatomy, surgery, medicine; therapeutic prescriptions and techniques; knowledge of embryology shown symbolically (e.g. in the temple of Luxor sacred to the 'microcosm').

—*His psychic being*: the forming of the 'double', modelled by *Khnum* at the same time as the physical body (and shown in the so-called 'birth-chambers' of several temples, among others Luxor and Deir el-Bahari). There are numerous texts concerning the (higher) KA and the lower KAS of man (that is his vital and animal forces, etc.); paintings and the accompanying inscriptions in royal tombs, etc.

—*The meaning of human life* and its consequences in the Beyond: texts of so-called counsels of wisdom. The negative confession; some symbolic stories (e.g. the *Story of the Two Brothers*).

—*Destiny beyond the grave*: Inscriptions of the Pyramids, numerous texts and pictures in tombs (particularly the royal tombs) and on sarcophagi. Texts compiled in the *Book of the Dead*, *Funerary Ritual*, etc.

SCIENCE OF NATURE within earthly life, but always held to be inseparable from the Universe; constitution and formation of matter; cosmogonic theories (cf. *Cosmogony*, p. 336).

—*Symbolism of the elements:*

—The *Earth*: its birth, its role, and its *Neter*, *Geb*.

—*Water*: the water of the celestial river, *Hapi*; the new water of *Osiris*; the water of the creative tears of *Râ*, the generative tears of *Isis* (tears = *rem*); the water of the earth, *mu*.

—*Air*: the life-giving air of *Amun*; air as divider between heaven and earth: *Shu*; earthly atmospheric air: *tau*.

—*Fire*: creative fire of *Râ*; the constructive fire of *Ptah*; the life-giving fire of *Amun-Râ*, later of *Horus*; the energetic fire, *sa*; the destructive fire of *Seth*, etc.

Countless texts and symbolic images—with both exoteric and esoteric meaning—give details of the manifold applications of these various themes.

—*Science of Matter*; geology taught symbolically through the nature of the stones employed for the various parts of a monument, in accordance with what they represented, each mineral being attributed to one specified *Neter* (lists given at Dendera, Edfu, etc.).

An utterly mysterious knowledge of the situation and orientation of the seams of an ore or metal in the quarries and mines. Work in various metals and alloys of extraordinary qualities (hardness). Work in stone and wood giving evidence of a subtle knowledge of their nature and their reactions.

Knowledge of the physical laws (lines of force, fall of bodies, statics, etc.) evidenced by the shape of the obelisks, by the solution of architectural problems such as the cutting of obelisks in the sheer rock, without errors of measurement or defects in their mass; their transport and erection in apparently impossible places and conditions; lifting and positioning of immense architraves and enormous blocks, without any sign of splintering in either joints or sculptures.

In addition, all the instructions needed for the various crafts, technical knowledge of which is evidenced by their works.

—*Knowledge of Seasons and of Nature*: continual teaching of the ritual of the festivals which refer to time and nature; processions and seasonal rejoicing; animals chosen as religious symbols because of their cry or their movements, which correspond to astronomical dates or hours (sunrise, lunar dates, etc.).

Interest given to the times and phases of gestation (list of the gestation periods of various animals, with their duration and their epochs within the year, found in the ramp of the tomb of Unas (VIth dynasty)).

SCIENCE OF THE UNIVERSE

—*Astronomical teaching*, spread over numerous texts; astronomical ceilings of Dendera, Esneh, Ramesseum, and royal tombs; stairs of Edfu and Dendera. Movement of the planets, journeys of the barques of the Sun, hours of the day and the night; constellations of the 'belly of *Nut*', etc.

Adaption of dynastic history to the great precessional periods of the Zodiac; passage of the Sun into the sign of Taurus, the bull (domination of *Montu* and symbol of the bull), into Aries, the ram (domination of *Amun* and symbol of the rams), then into Pisces, the fishes; end of Egypt and prelude to Christ announced in Philæ with the child *Horus* and *Horus* the redeemer.

—*Cosmogony*, the three aspects of which were developed by the major Temples as opportunity arose: primordial creation taught at Heliopolis (*Atum-Râ*); its realisation as manifestation taught at Memphis; the theory of its genesis[1] taught at Hermopolis; its achievement at Thebes.[2]

The study of the primary and secondary Causes follows naturally from this Cosmogony and constitutes the whole history of the *Neters*, which is the Egyptian theogony-theology.

[1] That is, the stages of its development [Translator's note].
[2] cf. *Her-Bak Disciple*, Chapter IX.

MACROCOSM AND MICROCOSM

Egyptian Wisdom thought of Heaven as the seat of the *Neters*, that is to say, the creative Causes or agents of continuous creation and the principles of Functions which through reflection into the earthly world maintained its existence.

Temples were conceived of as the seats of the *Neters*, each a dwelling-place of the particular Principle to which each of them was dedicated. The temple inscriptions are quite explicit on this point: it constitutes the fundamental theme of esoteric teaching. And in reality the situation of a temple, its plan, its dedication, and its emblem make it the *projection upon Earth of one aspect of the universal organism or 'macrocosm'*. The projection of the macrocosm into man (the microcosm) is the teaching given in the temple of Luxor; its projection, into the whole of Egypt has given rise to the 'organisation' of Egypt (disposition of its organs) in the nomes,[1] whose sanctuaries reveal their functions and character.

THE SCIENCE OF NUMBERS, MEASUREMENTS, AND PROPORTIONS

These are the factors of universal Harmony. As geometry was the indispensable basis of Pythagorean initiation, this science was likewise treated in Egypt as the operation of the forces and forms produced by the movement of *Number*: "I am one which becomes two, I am two which become four . . ."

And this number, the manifest power of the highest Power 'whose name is hidden', is the unknowable Absolute shown in action throughout the whole Genesis represented in the Myth.

It is at work in the first duplication, *Shu-Tefnut*, issuing from *Atum*, the primordial One. It is at work in all personifications of the various aspects of the four elements. It is at work in the generative action of the Ennead; it is at work in all the multiplying divisions of the first maternal *Neter, Apet*, who 'numbers' by producing the procreative functions, and multiplies them by the function of 'nourishing'. It is at work in the operation of the goddess *Sefekht* (seven), who personifies the power of the septenary in the manifestations of the Energy on earth (seven colours in light, seven musical tones, etc.).

It is at work in the numbering of the nomes and in the succession of dynasties, whose numerical order so strangely conforms to the evolutionary 'ages' or stages of Royal Man, whose symbolic history is represented by the Pharaohs.

Here is the point of junction between theological science and its projection into human life, between symbol and history.

The history of the Pharaohs is always conceived of as a genesis or succession of stages in the 'development' or 'becoming' of Man, for Egypt claims to represent the typical story of Man. Egypt says 'men' when she speaks of Egyptians; and she does so not out of arrogance, but

[1] cf. I, para. 4, of this Appendix.

because she 'sees' universally, because she speaks impersonally and in a preceptive spirit.

This same conception is applied to the Pharaoh, the 'Master of the whole Earth' and to the Myth in which the king plays the part of 'upholder' of a Principle, the part of agent 'subject to' the law of his Time, the part of a spokesman proclaiming the Will of the Ancients, the part of a semi-divine civil servant carrying out the work ordained for his epoch; he is the type of *King*, heir to the throne of *Geb*, master of the earthly domain, but including also the incarnated *Horus* whose name he bears. He is the model of Man as 'King of creation', for he has acquired mastery over his inferior KAS; thus he is able, after death, to 'lift himself on the ladder of *Nut*' and be 'regarded by the *Neters* as one of them'.[1] That is the reason why the description of the final triumph of the deified KA and its integration among the 'Masters of the Stars' is found only in the funeral texts of Pharaohs.

Such is the part of the Pharaoh within the Myth: he is the expression in history of the corresponding moment in the Myth.

This makes it possible to explain the gradual change in the attitude of the Pharaohs in the succession of dynasties. In the first dynasties we have the autocratic will within a limited group, which in turn seems to be a central cell which is closed to the masses. Later the Pharaoh progressively shares his powers and prerogatives (initiation and funeral rites) with a growing and extending circle, as if the royal ferment little by little transformed the value of the mass. This progress becomes ever more pronounced, until it produces dissensions which the liberties granted to some people make inevitable. But the guiding thread subsists without fail through troubles and invasions, thus proving the immutability of a 'presence' which abides independent of the person of the individual Pharaoh. Visibly or unseen in the shadows, the heirs of the Sages keep watch and under the name of each Pharaoh the will of the Ancients continues to direct the monumental work.

Now we can understand the eulogies and titles of '*Neter*' bestowed upon certain Pharaohs, however disorderly their private lives. The records of their reign, their acts and exploits, *once they are engraved upon stone 'for the duration of centuries'*, bear no other meaning than the description of the symbolic role assigned to the person concerned. They will tally with historical truth, or depart from it, as far as is needed *to bring the facts into line with the general Plan and the Myth*.

The Myth provides for the combination of history, ethics, and religion, which thus become the teaching of the law of cause and effect. The Myth welds into one the various branches of Knowledge; it brings them into play in one common action; it creates for them a concrete form with which their abstract structure may be clothed, and it enables the student to find their points of contact through the analogy of symbols.

[1] See *Her-Bak Disciple*, Chapters XIV, XVII, XVIII.

7. Various Modes of Inscription

Four means were employed and in a manner so co-ordinated that often one of them is needed in order fully to understand another, and certain subjects have been taught in their totality only through combination of all these four ways of recording them. They are the hieroglyphic and cursive *Scripts*, the drawn, painted, or sculptured representative *Image*, the *Statuary*, and *Architecture*.

(*a*) *The Hieroglyphic Script* consists of figures representing bodies or parts of bodies of human beings or animals, plants or sundry materials (wood, stone, water), man-made objects, parts of buildings, constructions, ships, etc., and some geometrical forms.

Some of these signs serve as alphabetical letters; a larger number represent a whole syllable by one image, or even a word, together with its sound. These are called phonograms. Others express an idea which gives the word its meaning, and these are called ideograms. A word can be written in several ways: with all the letters that go to make it up, or by writing one or several of these letters together with the phonogram, or by writing the phonogram alone. In the same way, the ideogram can be added to these combinations, or it can be left out.

For certain words or syllables there seem to have been fixed rules about writing or omitting letters and phonogram; but more often we find a great variety in the use and arrangement of the various elements of one and the same word. This variety is increased by frequent metatheses and ellipses of letters and words, abbreviations which deform the word-endings and countless exceptions from the grammatical rules adopted by Egyptology.

No blank spaces separate the words, no punctuation divides the sentences. Egyptian students had the pronunciation to guide them, but modern scholars cannot avail themselves of this aid, since vowels, properly speaking, did not exist in the Egyptian alphabet, and the pronunciation can therefore only be guessed by means of such words as still exist in the Coptic language.

Long experience and great practice in reading the manifold formulas known have permitted the establishment of the grammatical rules needed for the translation of the 'profane' meaning of the texts. But the pitfalls provided by the irregularities mentioned and the number of anomalies which have so far found no explanation have preserved the secret of the esoteric meaning, to which the Ancients were referring when they spoke of the "secrets of *Thot's* letters", i.e. the knowledge of the physical and metaphysical functions which were symbolised in the hieroglyphs.

The juxtaposition of signs, without separation or punctuation, made possible the cabbalistic method of writing, in which the sentence no longer depended on the laws of grammar, but on the total *meaning* of the hieroglyphs, by themselves or grouped according to their roots, and on their place within the inscription or the picture, and the play of homonyms, etc.

And it is the philosophical value of this script which has gained its characters the name of *medu-Neter* (words of the Gods), a name which the Greeks rendered as 'sacred writing'.

The hieroglyphic script was already complete with its characters fully formed at the beginning of the historic epoch, and it persisted without interruption up to the end of the Roman Empire.

The History of the Egyptian Language can be divided into five periods:
—*Ancient Egyptian* (Ist–IXth dynasties) is found in religious and funereal texts; the inscriptions of the pyramids built by the Vth–VIth dynasties are written in an archaic language.

—*Middle Egyptian* (IXth–XVIIIth dynasties up to the end of the reign of Amenophis III) is called 'classical' Egyptian because Egyptological grammars are mainly based on Middle Egyptian; it lives, moreover, in monumental inscriptions, and in the whole symbolic, religious, or philosophical literature, up to the Greco-Romans, admitting in later times an influx of foreign words.

Among the numerous documents in this language are monumental inscriptions, funereal steles, hymns, and philosophical, literary, and scientific (medical, etc.) works.

—*Neo-Egyptian* (XVIIIth–XXIVth dynasties) survives mainly in documents written in popular language (correspondence and contracts), but also in ostraca and monumental inscriptions. These inscriptions in neo-Egyptian began in El-Amarna (Akhenaton).

—*The Lower Epoch* (XXVth dynasty up to the end of the Roman empire): Monumental inscriptions in hieroglyphs once more revert to the archaising formulas of Ancient and Middle Egyptian. The Greco-Romans produced texts whose character is clearly inspired by ancient models but complicated by new monograms.

—*Coptic*, the last of the Egyptian languages, was probably based on Egyptian dialects and became the language of the Egyptian Christians, or Copts. This language made its appearance three centuries B.C. and incorporated many Greek words. It used the Greek alphabet with the addition of seven characters taken from Egyptian.

Other forms of Egyptian Script were:
—*Hieratic*, which appeared at the beginning of the IIIrd dynasty. It consists of simplified hieroglyphs drawn with the reed, and was used exclusively for religious, mystical, and philosophical inscriptions. It should not be confused with the *linear hieroglyphs* which served for the transcription of hieroglyphic texts on sarcophagi and the papyri of the *Book of the Dead* in coarser, less precise tracings.

—*Demotic* (popular) a cursive notation of the demotic language, appeared in the Lower Epoch: it was a simplification or difformation of the Hieratic. But this script served purely vernacular purposes; only the *sacred* characters, Hieroglyphic and Hieratic, were used for philosophic or religious inscriptions.

The Direction of Various Scripts:

—*Hieroglyphs*: These were written both in vertical columns and in horizontal lines. The older and more frequent direction was from right to left, but they were also written from left to right; sometimes different parts of one text were written in opposite directions. To ascertain the direction in which an inscription is to be read we must observe which way persons and animals represented by the signs face, and then read towards them.

—*Linear hieroglyphs* are written in either direction, like the other hieroglyphs.

—*Hieratic* is always written from right to left.

Writing Materials:

A scribe's tools comprised palette, water-cup, tablets, and papyrus-scroll. The palette was a long, narrow, rectangular wooden tablet, with a container for the reeds and two sockets for the cakes of black and red ink. The scribe wrote on papyrus, tablets of stuccoed wood, shards, pottery fragments, or limestone splinters (ostraca).

(b) Inscriptions by Picture

Ancient Egypt used images as a kind of mute language, and thus taught by form, colour, by the position of things and beings represented, by the grouping of the personages, their gestures, the position of their bodies, feet, hands, sceptres—each of these details having its own significance.

She was not shy of overstressing the character or function attributed to each personage, giving him, for example, two right or two left hands, thus to signify his active or passive role.

The images sculptured in the temples often indicate the symbolic relationship between various Pharaohs, by means of modified measurements or by the changes which each of them executed on the same image, all the while leaving visible traces of the previous drawings.

If one knows the symbolism of colours, gestures, and of the attributes given to the kings and the *Neters*, and also some of the keys which link every image to the context, one can find in each image the elements of those themes of which each particular scene represents one chapter. In this way one hall in a temple may explicitly develop a subject.

8. 'Outer' (Exoteric) and 'Inner' (Esoteric) Teaching

The sanctuary of an Egyptian temple, with its chambers, corridors, and various chapels surrounding it, was the secret part of the temple; its walls were covered with the most important texts, and it was separated from the 'open temple'—the peristyle—by the intermediate hall, or hypostyle.

In the present work the term 'peristyle' indicates that symbolic place which stands, in every initiatory teaching,[1] for the preliminary exterior that is exoteric instruction and observance. In cathedrals the only place to which catechumens had access was called the narthex. The Freemasons, on the other hand, when speaking of the disclosing or withholding of a secret teaching, used terms devoid of any reference to material facts or places (uncovered Temple or covered Temple, etc.).

There is evidence from several sources that in Ancient Egypt access to certain parts of the temples was granted only to a tested *élite*. "From the reports of Greek travellers it is seen that they are not allowed to enter certain parts of the temple. In Dendera this prohibition is stated quite explicitly as far as the crypts are concerned" (Mariette, *Dendera*, III, Pl. 26c, text pp. 226–7); ". . . Implicitly it applies also to the other parts of the temple which, with the exception of the courtyard—and for certain initiates perhaps also of the pronaos—were forbidden to all but the priests" (Chassinat, *Mammisi*, Edfu, p. ix).

Various standard formulas enable us to distinguish between these privileges connected with degrees of initiation: thus the expression *m khenu* ('to have access to the interior'), which doubtless refers both to the entrance of the palace and to the existence of a chosen group.

The *practical* teaching consists of set formulas and comprises no theory. The Temple is the seat of a fundamental Knowledge, which it does not divulge; it merely disseminates such positive elements of it as are necessary to train practitioners and craftsmen, from among whom it can choose individuals capable of receiving the Higher Teaching.

V

THE EGYPTIAN RELIGION

1. The Theological Myth

WHEN studying without any preconceived opinion the development of the theological Myth throughout all dynasties, and correlating it with all details of religious observance, language, and architecture that may have any bearing upon it, one cannot fail to note a series of periodically

---

[1] See *Her-Bak Disciple*, Comm. II, § 1.

occurring changes with similarities too marked to be ascribed to whim or chance.

In the following the main types of these changes are listed together with the best-known examples:

—At the beginning of each greater epoch modifications were made in respect to the grammatical forms, the use of syllable signs, both phonograms and ideograms, and the arrangement of these signs, etc.

—Some part of the myth was developed in connection with a certain place (e.g. *Osiris* has his grave at Abydos where he becomes the *Khent Amentiu*). *Horus*, the son of *Isis*, is born at Shemnis and is king of the Delta, whereas the myth of Edfu celebrated the struggles of *Horus* against *Seth*, and makes him king of the South.

—The cult of a particular *Neter* became dominant, or reappeared in connection with some principle which was exalted at the same moment. (Development of the worship of *Neith* in Saïs[1] in the XXVIth dynasty, when the sacred language returned to archaistic forms. *Neith* was a primordial goddess, a superior aspect of *Nut's* heaven, the 'Superior Heaven', the great weaver of the Universe. "I am that which is, which will be, which has been . . ." reads the inscription of *Neith* in the Temple of Saïs.)

—Emphasis was placed upon one or the other sanctuary at certain seasons of the year or of the precessional cycle. (*Abydos*: festival of the winter solstice and rebirth of the Sun. *Thebes*: temple of *Amun* and his rams, at the beginning of the sign Aries, the Ram, within the precessional cycle.)

—The temples on ancient sanctuaries were renovated or rebuilt, with modifications appropriate to the times; ancient sculptured stones were embedded in the foundations if their inscriptions and symbols bore relation to the principle taught in the new temple.

—The name of a *Neter* was modified, specifying for every epoch the character of his active function (*Andjet, Osiris; Amun, Amun-Râ*).

—The names for kings and civil servants were chosen in accordance with the character of the epoch.

—The measurements of the images of the Pharaoh in the sculptured scenes were periodically modified, leaving, however, visible traces of the previous measurements and thus accentuating the idea behind the modification.

—Themes were taken up again, or personages from other times were brought back to public memory, when their symbolic roles once more became opportune. Example: Imhotep (of the IIIrd dynasty), represented together with Amenhotep, the son of Hapu (XVIIIth dynasty) *as his brother*, under the reign of Ptolemy IX; a chapel was dedicated to them on the upper terrace of the temple of Hatshepsut (XVIIIth dynasty); as a matter of fact, their mystical roles found themselves in harmony with this temple at that last epoch. Note also that it is equally under the

[1] See this Appendix, I, para. 5, p. 31.

Ptolemies that the temples of Edfu (as a papyrus of that era says: "according to plans of Imhotep") and of Dendera were built.

All these facts are not the consequence of slow transformations such as give rise to a custom which then progressively establishes itself. These 'innovations' occurred in leaps and bounds, as if, at definite times, an act of will suddenly ordained them. And these times are seen to be precisely the most important epochs of Egyptian history: the epoch of the Pyramids, Vth–VIth dynasties, XIth–XIIth dynasties, XVIIIth–XIXth dynasties, XXVth–XXVIth dynasties, and the Ptolemies. In these moments of transition, between the last stage of one cosmic influence and the beginning of another, a modification was brought to bear on the outer form of Egyptian teaching; these modifications, though, *never modified the bases* of the teaching: they merely adapted its details to the characteristic needs of the new stage. And although each of these 'changes', studied by itself, does not immediately reveal its meaning, the study of all in conjunction with their astronomical dates and the concomitant circumstances reveals a well-defined system, a pattern which must have been planned beforehand, since its development shows a continuity that is not deflected even by crises of anarchy or foreign domination.

These considerations were indispensable for obtaining a sane view of Egyptian theology.

It is then clear that the cosmogonies as taught at Heliopolis, Memphis, Hermopolis, and Thebes *do not contradict* each other; the differences between them are of the same kind as the differences between the two records in the Genesis of Moses describing the creation of the first human couple. In Chapter I, verse 27, it is said that God created man: "in the image of God created he him; male and female created he them"; and later, in verses 18 and 20–22 of Chapter II, it is said that since Adam had no helpmeet like unto him, God took one of his ribs to make a woman of it. The difference between these two versions is a difference merely of stage within the same process, and, equally, the differences between the four versions of the Egyptian cosmogony have their reasons.[1] It is therefore impossible to study the various elements of the myth by themselves without seriously altering their meaning, for they were taught in conformity with the symbol reigning at the time and in the place. It is one comprehensive genesis, which has to be studied *through the totality of theogonic systems*; to study each system by itself would be a mistake.

2. The Four Cosmogonic Themes (according to the common tradition).

The Theme Taught at Heliopolis

In the beginning of beginnings there was:

—The primordial chaos, *Nun*.

[1] See *Her-Bak Disciple*, Comm. V, § 4: 'The Viewpoints of Egyptian Theology'.

—From this chaos, by his own power, rose the Sun, *Râ-Atum* (he who creates himself).

—*Atum*, masturbating and spitting, 'emitted' *Shu-Tefnut*.

—*Shu-Tefnut* produced *Geb* (Earth) and *Nut* (Sky).

—*Geb* and *Nut* gave birth to *Osiris, Isis, Seth, Nephtys.*

The Theme Taught at Memphis

Ptah and the Octad:

—*Ptah*, creator of everything that is on Earth.

—*Eight primordial Neters*:

Tatenen, the first Earth emerging from chaos;

Atum, whose divine intelligence is *Horus*, and whose will expressed by the tongue is *Thot*;

Four other Neters, whose names have not yet been ascertained.

The Theme Taught at Hermopolis

The Octad and the Sun:

—*Eight primordial Neters*, represented in the shape of frogs and snakes. Between them these four couples create an egg which they deposit on the 'hill' risen from the *Nun*.

—From this egg is born the *Sun* which organises the world.

The Theme Taught at Thebes

The original Octad of Thebes, and the Sun:

—*The eight primordial Neters* are carried by the waters from Thebes to Hermopolis (*Khemenu*); there they create the *Sun*, after which they return to die at Medinet-Habu near the Theban mountains.

The dominant principle of the Theban theme is *Amun*, who is presented in three forms:

1. *Kematef*,[1] "the one who has made his Time" (a snake God which is identified with the *Amun* of Karnak).

2. *Irta*, "who makes the Earth" (second snake God, identified with the *Amun* of Luxor), succeeds to his father *Kematef*; it is the *Amun Irta* who goes every ten days to carry funeral offerings to the eight primordials buried at Medinet-Habu.

3. *Amun*, the member of the Octad.

These cosmogonies here outlined belong to the Egyptian myth in their quality of themes presenting the first stages of a genesis (that is the three *creative* stages). The role of the creative cause is attributed differently in each theme, according to the stage to which this theme refers. The order of the principles which are active in each stage may vary according to

---

[1] Who is sometimes identified with *Amun Kamutef* of Luxor.

the 'product' of that stage; but the *way of expressnig it* depends upon the angle from which it is considered.

In this connection it should be noted that the dates at which these various cosmogonies were promulgated do not correspond to the sequence of the stages, but to symbolic correspondences between these dates and the character of the theme (and not to struggles for precedence among the clergy of the various temples).

—The theme of *Heliopolis* is that of the abstract character of the Beginning.[1] It begins with the creation in principle:[2] out of the inert original chaos (which has no movement nor differentiation structure) issues the universal *Râ* by his own power, his own creator; under the name *Atum*, and by his own movement he emits *Shu-Tefnut*, the first duality in principle, which in turn produces the second duality, *Geb-Nut* (Earth and Sky). Then, after their separation, *Nut* gives birth to the great *Neters* of Nature: *Osiris, Isis, Seth, Nephtys.*

—In the theme taught at *Memphis*, the creative Principle is the heavenly fire *Ptah*, which has descended into the primordial Earth, *Tatenen*, which *through Ptah* surges from the chaos. The *universal Atum*[3] is the power which manifests the divine properties—Intelligence and Will (*Horus* and *Thot*)—who 'speak' and 'organise' the 'ectypal' forms of Nature. *Ptah* is the author of this second creation (of the Powers); the other *Neters* of the Octad are its active and passive functions.

—The theme of *Hermopolis* is an entering into operation within concrete Nature:

The ectypal forms (in Ideas) of the theme of Memphis are projected into Nature. *Nun* is no longer the inert original chaos which precedes the Creation-in-principle: it is the primordial Ocean, the maternal water from which arises the first hillock.

Râ has become the Sun of Nature; he has been born from the cosmic egg created by the eight primordial *Neters*, the agents of the world of *Thot*; this is why the Greeks gave *Khemenu* the name Hermopolis (town of Hermes-*Thot*). For the head of the Octad of Hermopolis is Thot, the one who inscribes in *Thot's* characters the 'signatures' of the terrestrial beings.

Such are the three forms—much defaced—under which Ancient Egypt formulates the theme of the threefoldness of Creation; a sketch

[1] cf. 'Continuous Creation', *Her-Bak Disciple*, Comm. IV, §3.
[2] The 'Creative Principle' here involved is conceived as an abstraction and not, as in Judeo-Christian theology, as a creative act *of God* (Deism). The 'creation in principle' does not take place in Time, but provides, as it were, 'theoretically', the potentialities or possibilities of forms and types, that is their patterns or Ideas.
The realisation of these 'possibilities' takes place in the material creation—or creation in Time—of that which has been potentially created outside Time. (T.N.)
[3] *Atum* is here equivalent to the Adamic man before his fall, to the man who gives names to the forms which are going to populate Earth.

crude indeed if judged after *exoteric* interpretation of its texts, to which trustworthy authors ascribe an esoteric meaning of high philosophic significance. However, even read on the secular level they form a coherent whole if each aspect of the Principles quoted figures in its exact character in the hierarchy of *Neters*.

The teaching given at the Temple of Thebes facilitates this reading by placing in the centre of the puzzle the threefold aspect of the creative Principle:

"*Amun-Râ-Ptah, three in one.*"

Once this affirmation is established as essential, the Theban Wisdom can proceed to deal with the three functional aspects of primordial *Amun*: *Kematef* "who makes his Time", *Irta* "who makes the Earth", and the *Amun* of the Octad. At Karnak (which is *Aset-Apet*, the "place of the numbers") it can establish the seat of *Amun* as the king of the *Neters*; it can represent him as the condenser of Energy—ithyphallic *Min*—as quickener and fertiliser of maternal Nature, *Mut*, whose son *Khonsu* reveals the face of "him who has begotten him". And beyond all creation, the Wisdom can also religiously evoke the Unknowable *Amun* "with the hidden name". Into the centre of these extreme aspects, Thebes has placed the fixed, immutable point which sums up all themes in three names, which are actually, as it were, the common ground and guiding thread: "*Everything is Amun-Râ-Ptah, ONE IN THREE*".

Thebes sums up all *Neters* in this Trinity which is Cosmic Man, whose unknowable spirit (with the hidden name) is manifested in the functions of *Amun* whose "head is Râ", that is to say, the source and expression of all the forms of the Logos (in the three Worlds), and whose "body is *Ptah*" or the manifestation of the creative fire in all possibilities, functions and organs of Nature.

3. Theories Formulated in Ancient Egypt

If theology is taken to mean the *theory explaining* the various aspects of the Godhead, or manifestations of its Power, then there is no theology in Egypt, for theory formulated in rigid axioms and proved by argument does not exist there. Throughout the whole myth, however, there can be found a knowledge of the 'genesis' or successive appearance of the divine Powers or Properties, which have emerged from the original Unity where they are in a state of latency, then of the genesis in the continuous creation by which they manifest themselves through Nature.[1]

Seen in this light, these elements of a theogony establish a "Hierarchy of the *Neters*" similar to those found in other traditions—Hindu, Hebrew Cabbala—but unlike these, not 'dogmatised'; a hierarchy depending on the order of their appearance as primary or secondary causes, and on the nature of their functions: spiritual, subtle, or material.

But the Egyptian Sages have established no rigid system for this

[1] cf. *Her-Bak, Disciple*, Chapters IX, X, XIV, and Commentaries, IV, § 3.

hierarchy, perhaps because such a system would have revealed certain secrets about natural forces—secrets of dreadful danger, as recent developments of science have shown. As always, the Sages have scattered the elements of knowledge, and one has to fit them together if one wants to know the picture on the puzzle.

4. The Three Worlds: Heaven, Earth, and Dwat

The *Neters* are the causal Powers—primary causes and secondary causes —of everything that manifests itself in the Universe; they are the principles, agents, and functions of these manifestations.

The *worlds* or 'states' of the Universe in which the *Neters* act have been given different names by the Egyptian Sages. They have summed them up in one formula: "*That which is in Heaven, on Earth, and in the Dwat.*" With these words they postulated two extreme states—heavenly and earthly—and one intermediate state, the *Dwat*. To express ourselves more clearly we shall speak of the '*Celestial*', '*Intermediate*', and the '*Terrestrial*' world.

"*That which is in Heaven*" or the *celestial world*:

What the Egyptians here described as celestial did not refer to the absolute divine Principle, "The Father of the Essence", who could not be located anywhere, "immobile and unintelligible".[1]

Their *exoteric* teaching understood by 'celestial' the world of the principles, the causal powers, the spiritual Powers, the Properties-in-themselves, which act by the very fact that they *are*: the abstract, impersonal, impassive world, which contains *within itself* all Possibilities which might take shape and then manifest themselves physically in the successive geneses.

It is the world of the BA, the Universal divine soul, source of all BAS.

"*That which is in the Dwat*" or the *intermediate world*: which the Egyptians called *Dwat* (from *dwa*, the moment between night and day); it is the world of transition between the abstract world of the causal Powers and the concrete world of phenomena or world of Nature. It is the state of everything which moves towards a 'becoming' or towards a 'return'. Hence there are two Dwats: the first Dwat is the state of 'that which moves towards the terrestrial geneses'; the second Dwat is the state of that which has emerged from terrestrial existence, and now finds itself in a state of waiting, whether it be to return once more to earth, or to reascend, through the necessary transformations, towards its spiritual 'home'. It is the world of the KAS.

The first is the pre-natal Dwat, the world of the pre-formations. It is the world of the 'intelligible' *Neters* (in scholastic Latin: 'Natura

[1] Jamblichus, *Mysteries*, Part 8, 2.

naturans'), of the Form-Ideas which have emerged from the virtual Possibilities of the celestial world, and which will imprint their marks or 'signatures' upon all terrestrial creatures. It is the world of *Thot*, the *Neter* of 'specifications', which he determines in the *types* of Nature through the interplay of the numbers and the divine geometry.

The other Dwat is the state after death, where that which had taken body in the terrestrial world, now, after the loss of this body, still retains the consciousness acquired through experience of embodied life and undergoes the transformations corresponding to its new possibilities.

It is the world of *Osiris*, overseer and master of the Transformations in the Dwat.

"*That which is on Earth*", or the *concrete* and *terrestrial world*. (In scholastic Latin: 'Natura naturata')

In this world the 'types' preconceived in the intermediate world take form and materialise. It is the state of embodiment of the Form-Ideas in everything brought forth by Nature, from the four elementary constituents of matter up to their most complex combinations: stars, inorganic matter, and organic beings; it is the world of bodies (*khat*).

It is the world of *Ptah*—the innate fire of terrestrial matter—who created it, who is its secret motive force and the agent of its future development.

It is the world of *Osiris Un-Nefer*—the master and regenerator of vegetative life—of that Osiris who is master over all cycles of renewal in Nature.

5. The Neters and their Hierarchy

Since the *Neters* are the expression of the properties and functions of the divine Power, a hierarchy among them can be established only by trying to ascertain whether the function under consideration is more spiritual or more material, more universal or more particular, more absolute or more relative.

But as such an evaluation must necessarily be stultified by the inadequacy of human intelligence faced with such a task, the Egyptians have been careful not to fall into this error; instead, they have developed the various functions of each *Neter* through the multiple episodes of the myth, so that *it should be impossible to define a Neter by one exclusive formula*, while it should instead be possible to evoke his role in the geneses, his mode of action in terrestrial phenomena, and his relations with the three 'worlds'—Heavenly, Intermediate, and Terrestrial.

The Neters of the Heavenly World

To the higher (divine) heaven belong:
—*Amun*, the 'never born'.

—*Râ*, the Universal, who contains the function *Atum* as potentiality.

—*Horus*, heart and immanent Word of *Râ*.

—*Neith*, the cosmic Virgin of whom it is said: "I am that which is, that which will be, that which has been."

These *Neters* are the first intelligible aspects of the causal Power, which is the source of the inexhaustible life of the Universe.

Neters Acting in the Intermediate World

—*Amun*, descending towards the geneses and "bringing to light the sacred power of the secret language".[1]

—*Atum*, the author of the fall consisting in the first division into two, the solar *Neter* who stands between night and day.

—The *Neters* of the five intercalary days: *Osiris, Isis, Seth, Nephtys, Horus,* these five *Neters* "who are neither in Heaven, nor on Earth, and upon whom the Sun does not shine".[2]

—*Hathor* and *Nut*, in their character as *Neters* of lower Heaven (that is, the sky of stellar influences), and in their relations with the forces and beings of the *Dwat*.

—*Thot*, the real mediator between Heaven and Earth, 'messenger of Horus' and 'tongue of *Ptah*'; he formulates all the words (in the sense of the Logos) which have issued from 'the creative mouth'.

He is the Master over the forms begotten by the numbers, and the *Neter* of the 'signatures' which determine the terrestrial types (species).

As 'scribe of *Maât*', that is (of the impressions fixed in the consciousness of all things), he records them in the annals of the Dwat (universal memory, *akasha*, etc.).

—*Anubis*, the transforming power permitting the passage from the earth to the lower heavens. Under the name of *Up-uat*,[3] he is the 'opener of the ways' of the Dwat.

Neters Acting in the Terrestrial World

1. *Ptah*, who is its *continual* creator, agent, and motive-power.

—The triad of the Natural order: *Osiris, Isis, Horus,* "the last ring which brings the divine triads nearer to Earth, and of all triads the most intensely worshipped because it is the maintainer of the sublunar world".[4]

—All the *Neters* whose spiritual properties and abstract functions can be recognised in their concrete form in the properties or functions of the natural order, e.g.:

—*Amun-Min*, magnet and condenser of heavenly Energy.

[1] Jamblichus, *Mysteries*, Part 8, 3.

[2] *Harris Papyrus*, Pl. III, I, 5–6, ed. *Chabas*, p. 53.

[3] The scientific English transcription of this name is *Wep-wawet*; the French version has been retained as more readable (T.N.).

[4] Abbé Migne, *Dictionnaire Mythologique*: Osiris.

—*Seth*, principle of concreteness, fixation, and separation.

—*Anubis*, transformer of putrid matter into living substance.

—*Khnum*, power of attraction, who joins complementaries and fashions the new being.

—*Mut*, the *mother* principle, who decomposes the seeds in order to regenerate them (in this role she is called *Sekhmet*), and who then gestates them until the result has attained the required maturity.

—*Apet*, the principle of maternal fertility, and of the multiplication of substance.

2.—*The Neters of the elementary Properties* (dry, wet, warm, cold): *Shu, Tefnut, Geb, Nut*, whose principles have been evoked by *Atum* in the primordial creation, and are manifested by him again in the continuous creation in which they become fire, air, water, and earth.

3.—*The principal Neters of the fundamental functions*:

—*Sokar*: function of "*contraction-fixation*" (funerary *Neter*).

—*Serket* (scorpion goddess): function of contraction leading to dilatation (breathing in).

—*Neith*: function of dilatation leading to contraction (and breathing out).

—*Wadjit*: function of dilatation essential to vegetative life (opening out, blooming, unfolding).

—*Âmm*: function of absorption (*Ammit*, the 'devourer' of the dead, monster present at the weighing of the soul).

4.—*The four aspects of the feminine Principle in Nature*, whose images envelop sarcophagi and the chests containing the canopic vases with their wings: *Isis, Nephtys, Neith*, and *Selkis* (Sarket).

But, as Jamblichus explains and repeats, this multiplicity of names is merely an analysis of the various functions, which all refer to the *essential* Cause: ONE IN THREE.

MAÂT.—There is, however, one name deserving particular attention, since it is the most beautiful synthesis and highest philosophy of Egypt: *Maât*, who impersonates Justice and Truth. All feminine *Neters* are aspects of the great divine Mother, but *Maât* is at the same time her source and fulfilment. "Ceaselessly emanating from the divine *Râ* of whom she is at the same time herself the nourishment, she is the mediator and the vehicle of the essence of *Râ*".[1] She is the Presence of beginning and end, in all Times and all Worlds, "she is cosmic consciousness, Universal Ideation, and Essential Wisdom".[2]

[1] cf. *Her-Bak Disciple*, Chapter XVI.   [2] *Ibid.*

In the world of men she is the *consciousness of 'discerning'* and consequently the Maât of Judgment.

But there is something here which transcends the myth and all myths: since from her name to her effective reality, *Maât,* in this Cosmos, is the Truth in all things; *Maât* is the key to the reason for man's life, the key to the theological and mystical philosophy of Egypt.